*The Bride of Suleiman*

# The
# Bride of Suleiman

AILEEN CRAWLEY

ST. MARTIN'S PRESS
NEW YORK

Library of Congress Cataloging in Publication Data

Crawley, Aileen
    The bride of Suleiman.

    1. Suleiman I, Sultan of the Turks, 1495-1566—
Fiction.  I. Title
PR6053.R3758B7   1982        823'.914        81-14525
ISBN 0-312-09543-0                           AACR2

# The Bride of Suleiman

# Contents

# BOOK ONE
## *Novice*

# 1

'I hope you will be satisfied with the quality of the merchandise,' said Hakam smoothly.

His companion, who was looking down into the courtyard below, did not bother to answer, but a peremptory gesture indicated that Hakam should help himself from the tray of sherbet and sweetmeats on the table between them. Hakam sighed and took a porcelain cup. The Aga of the Girls was watching the newly purchased slaves clamber down from the wagons and cross the courtyard to the door, shepherded by impassive black eunuchs. If Mehmed saw anything he did not care for, he would stop the whole procedure, and was quite capable of having some unfortunate girl returned to the hands of the Istanbul dealers. When he had seen enough and had something to say, he would say it. As now.

'I hope you remembered that the Lady Hafise wants a competent embroideress?'

Hakam was careful not to sigh again. He had heard it said that the first quality of an administrator is an instinct for smelling out the shortcomings of lesser mortals. In which case old Mehmed was wasting his time in this provincial headquarters of Manissa, even if he did serve the crown prince and his awe-inspiring mother. He said shortly, 'I always remember the Sultana Hafise's needs and I have brought her needlewoman.'

Since he didn't seem inclined to elaborate, Mehmed looked at him in surprise and asked, 'Is she capable?'

Hakam was a master of the dramatic gesture. Now he produced from the folds of his girdle an embroidered handkerchief which he shook out and spread across the cushion beside him. Mehmed leaned forward to look and finally picked up the

9

square of silk and carefully examined the brilliant design which covered it.

'Most unusual,' he said at last, holding it close to his near-sighted eyes. 'Splendid colouring and bold design. I never saw anything like it before. Not Ottoman and not Persian. Where – '

Hakam had hoped to avoid any discussion of the girl at all, but obviously he had expected too much. He forced a smile. 'She came from a place called Galicia on the borders of Russia.'

'How very interesting! We have never had a Russian here before. Can you point her out to me?'

Hakam shrugged. What did it matter where they came from in this harsh world of the second decade of the sixteenth century? Once a slave entered the Sultan's service, he or she became an Ottoman and their origins were best forgotten. In the case of this girl in particular, the less said the better, on all counts. The last time he had seen her she had just bitten the thumb of one of his guards to the bone. A quick glance down into the courtyard showed him that he was lucky. She was not to be seen. The last of the girls, a blonde Circassian with exquisite hips, was swaying through the small door, which was then firmly shut behind her.

'Never mind. I shall see them all before long. I suppose she's clean and presentable?'

Hakam shut his eyes. Clean, certainly, and it depended what you meant by presentable. So far as he was concerned, at least, she was no beauty. What mattered was that by the time the Head Housekeeper, the eunuchs, and last but not least the other girls, had finished with her, her manners would have improved. He profoundly hoped so, because if not, he, Hakam, would be answerable. He said firmly, 'Yes.' Having committed himself, he temporized. 'One slight difficulty – '

Mehmed allowed a delicate frown to cloud his square, unexpressive face. Hakam hurried on. 'She's been very slow to learn Turkish. Of course, she's had less opportunity than most.'

Mehmed shrugged. 'Before the Sultana Hafise sees her, if indeed she ever does, she'll be well schooled. As you know.'

Hakam willed himself not to show relief in any way. It was his private opinion that the bitch understood a great deal more than she allowed to appear and was a great deal cleverer than the other girls. He was heartily relieved to have handed her over to the System which would turn her from an unbridled, screaming little hell-cat into a docile, useful cog in the great, big machine. The System had a place for everything and everything in its place. He heartily approved of the System, which disposed of everything, including, and in particular, women. This was good, because like all good sons of Islam, he was, at bottom, very much afraid of them. He presented, therefore, a courteously enquiring face, and Mehmed shook out the embroidered handkerchief and dropped it once again on a cushion. It seemed to fascinate him.

'How long did this take?'

'Sir?'

'How long did it take her to do this work?' Mehmed elaborated patiently.

'Ah!' Hakam raised his long eyes to the ceiling and made expansive gestures. A slightly pained expression crossed Mehmed's face. Hakam was nearly as old as himself, but he was still far too much of a Greek. Still, he supposed the poor fellow could not help it. His work took him among such strange people, and again, the business of barter . . . . He himself would not have cared for it. A small voice at the back of his mind whispered, 'No, and could not have done it, either.'

Hakam was saying, 'You will hardly credit this, Mehmed. She completed that handkerchief in one day.'

'Are you sure?'

'Absolutely.' And he was not lying now. He had seen her start it and stitch away as if her life depended on it. She had sat cross-legged on the carpet in the old merchant's tent, sulky at first, face set under the crown of fiery hair. Then gradually, she had become intent, and finally absorbed, even smiling a little and humming curious, and to his ears, discordant little tunes. He had sat part of the time with old Shems the merchant with his dyed beard, drinking sherbet and later, to tell the truth, a little wine. Then he had looked at two or three girls and bought one, and eventually Shems had brought him back to the big tent where this girl still sat, hair dishevelled and eyes heavy, busy on the elaborate medallion which filled the centre of the work. Then, suddenly, there was a flash of white teeth, the last thread was bitten through, and the square of satin, heavy now with coloured and gold thread, had sailed through the air and landed at his feet.

Shems had laughed and gestured to one of his men, who had

11

rather roughly shouldered the girl out of the tent. Hakam now understood why, but at the time he had merely thought the man inept or Shems perhaps trying to inflate her price by removing her from sight. Certainly the girl's handiwork was marvellous. Where had she been taught, he had asked, and Shems had shrugged and said, who knew? The girl was timid, did not understand their questions and they could not understand her when she did speak. What did it matter anyway? She came from a very distant place and Allah alone knew how roughly she had been treated before he, Shems, had bought her from a middleman, having realized her worth. And now, if he pleased, would he pay the price for her, or would the Sultana Hafise have to be disappointed? Because others were interested.

Of course, he had paid. Not that price, but one finally satisfactory to both. He had seen nothing to touch her skill and it was inconceivable that the Lady Hafise, a great and good lady in her own right − quite apart from the fact that she was the acknowledged wife of the Sultan Selim − should be disappointed. It was only after the girl had been formally assigned to him that he learned what a problem he had acquired.

It happened fairly gradually. The other girls did not like her. That was nothing. Girls frequently disliked each other and even more frequently the group took a concerted dislike to one of their number, who was usually downtrodden and pathetic. Not this one. They did not actually fight − it was a little while before he realized that the trouble was that she frightened them because she was so different. She laughed at them, mimicking them as they gossiped and tried on the clothes assigned to them. When they rounded on her, she stood, hands on hips, a stream of outlandish sounds, which he presumed represented a language, pouring from her mouth. Yet he was sure she understood a great deal of what was said. He had watched her, and seen the play of expression across her face as she listened to the talk around her. He could swear that she knew at least the general meaning of what she heard. Of course, when he sent for her and talked to her, or she was given instructions, her face was blank and she sat or stood motionless. No fool was ever more unresponsive.

Hakam had not known what to do. Good money had been paid for her. Not his, but the Sultan's. What a decision for a man to be faced with! She could be returned to Shems, who had certainly lied about her character – any girl less timid it would be hard to imagine – but not about her ability. And the Hanim Hafise was confidently sitting in Manissa expecting him to bring her an embroideress. Weighing one thing against another, he had decided to risk it. He believed in the power of the System, having seen it work all his life.

He had been relieved once he had made his decision, but she had still made the journey a nightmare; twice more she had tried to escape, and once nearly succeeded. The effect on the other girls had been disastrous, and he had kept discipline among them only by constant watchfulness. Finally, last night, she had bitten the guard. The man had beaten her, but fortunately she showed no marks and the earlier bruises had disappeared. He was heartily sick of her, but she had been delivered in good order and was, at last, somebody else's problem. If he got away with it.

He sipped from his cup, relishing the cool tartness of the fruit juice, and relaxed. Mehmed asked a question or two about the other slaves and Hakam answered him tranquilly. He did not have to lie or evade; the rest of them were of good quality in every way, and up to his usual high standard. He knew that Mehmed would wish to hear the talk from Istanbul, but equally would not want to have to ask for it directly. He therefore judged it time enough to give him the opportunity to extract it in the normal course of conversation, by asking formally after the Crown Prince's health.

'He is, as always, well, Allah be thanked. He works hard, too. Although he is young, I doubt if this province has ever been so well governed.'

Hakam murmured appreciatively. He had seen Suleiman Shahzade only once and found him disconcerting. A taciturn young man seemingly, with a straight eye and an excellent seat on a horse. But after all, Sarukhan was an easy province to govern, rich in vines and other crops, with a beautiful climate and a pleasant capital. The Shahzade was well served by his civil servants, too. Mehmed, for example.

He said, 'As you know, since the conquest of Egypt, the Sultan Selim has been in the capital – three years, a long time for him to be out of the field. Now it is being said confidently that he is planning a campaign in a new theatre of war – the Mediterranean, perhaps, who knows? But if this is true, we shall have more victories to celebrate before long.'

'Allah be praised,' said Mehmed, looking up at the ceiling. Hakam thought irritably, he manages to look pious at the very mention of Yavuz Selim. The sort of man he is must always be seen to pay the respect we all owe. I am a dutiful subject of the Sultan, too, but that does not prevent my realizing that he is, as well as a great conqueror, a grim, cruel and despotic man, with a devilish temper. Ill, of course, and often in pain. He had heard talk of this, too, in Istanbul, and decided to pass on what he had heard. It had worried him and he could not resist the temptation to disturb Mehmed, too.

'Also, it was being said in the bazaars that the Sultan's health is getting worse. Campaigning takes its toll on a man.'

'The war he fights is the Holy War, and Allah has always guarded him,' replied Mehmed. He went firmly on, 'He has built an empire, after all. And after Egypt, no one, not even Persia, wants to take Selim on. It will be the West next, Rhodes perhaps.' He raised his plump chin defiantly, 'Need I remind you, Hakam, what we were? A horde of tent-dwellers. And what have we become? An empire which stretches from the borders of Serbia to the Euphrates.'

He fixed his eyes meaningly on his old friend, who studied the carpet and murmured, 'And if he dies, what will become of us then?'

Excited movement disturbed the voluminous folds of Mehmed's caftan. He leaned forward and tapped the table authoritatively. 'If I understand you aright, you are asking a question best left unasked. Knowing what I know, I am for myself quite satisfied that the Sultan's death will leave our destiny unchanged.' He paused and repeated deliberately, 'Unchanged.'

'Well, you're in a better position than I am to know that,' said Hakam doubtfully, and added, 'You must understand that Istanbul is always full of rumours and I hear a lot I don't want to hear.'

'Don't listen then,' said Mehmed shortly.

'It's not as simple as that!' expostulated Hakam, wishing that he hadn't started the conversation; but he still went on obstinately, 'For instance, I had it on good authority that the Sultan collapsed and fell senseless at the Topkapi gate recently.'

'That's happened before,' said Mehmed robustly, 'even if the

14

story's true in the first place. Well, go on, man, what happened next?'

Hakam sighed and cursed his own ready tongue. All he'd meant to do was ruffle Mehmed's complacency a bit. He had forgotten the wider and more serious implications of what he'd said until he was well launched on his story, a failure in judgment for which he had had to pay before. He fingered his chin and went on more soberly.

'The fellow was an old soldier, part of the escort of some provincial beylerbey on a mission to the capital.' It all sounded hopelessly vague, he realized now, but he had spoken to the man himself. He said as much.

Mehmed looked at him shrewdly. 'I'm sure you did. What else did he see?'

'Well, he saw him carried inside the Third Court. And he watched the doctors arrive, and Piri Pasha.'

Mehmed pushed out his lips. 'So. But when you and I were younger, Hakam, and served closer to the Sultan than we do now, we both saw the same thing, more than once. The Grand Vizier always came, and the doctors. And always, they were sent off with a flea in their ears, or a present, according to how the Sultan happened to feel. And the next day he went hunting.'

'That's so,' agreed Hakam, and couldn't help murmuring, 'That was a few years ago, all the same.' He decided he didn't want to pursue the conversation any further, and added, 'I'm bound to say that Piri Pasha went home that evening. I suppose if the Sultan had been really ill he wouldn't have left him.'

'Just so,' agreed Mehmed, 'but now, my friend, you've brought me a problem. Is this merely a minor upset or a serious decline in Selim's health? Must I tell the Prince – to say nothing of his mother – or not?'

Hakam, now acutely uncomfortable, as he was meant to be, looked wildly round for a way out. He didn't want any rumours traced back to him, especially when they brought bad news. He said, 'If it were really serious, the Grand Vizier would surely inform his highness – '

'No, he wouldn't. You know it's not as simple as that,' Mehmed interrupted roundly. 'If the Sultan were at death's door it would be kept secret for reasons you understand as well as I do. However, I doubt if a man who feels himself failing would

15

be planning a new war. Moreover, all I've really gathered from what you've told me is that things haven't changed for the better. So I shall say nothing.'

Hakam glanced across the room to the balcony. The sun was low; soon, in minutes even, it would be dark. Mehmed's small eyes, which seldom missed anything, followed his glance. He pressed his fat hands on his knees in preparation for rising to his feet.

'I am grateful, Hakam, for all – ' He coughed, 'Everything, especially the needlewoman. The Sultana Hafise will be pleased.' The foot which had been resting on the divan slipped to the carpet. He stood.

Hakam also rose, 'Ah, yes,' he said a little sadly, for the subsequent talk had put her out of his mind, 'The girl. I trust she will prove satisfactory.' He bowed.

'I shall keep this to show to my mistress,' continued Mehmed, shaking out the handkerchief yet again. In the growing darkness, its jewel colours were dimmed. Also Hakam's expression of acute discomfort was invisible. He bowed himself out and when he was alone on the stone staircase pressed his own handkerchief to his suddenly damp forehead, and muttered to himself as he went down, 'I don't know what else I could have done. I only hope it turns out well.'

The girl was still in his thoughts when he emerged into the courtyard and climbed into the leading wagon to begin the long journey back to Istanbul. In the light of the torches flaming by the wall, he glanced back once more, quite instinctively, at the little door. It was of course firmly shut. The torches only illuminated the vulpine faces of the janissaries of the guard who stood motionless, looking rather like tents in their enormous leather cloaks, for the nights were still cold. Hakam did not like janissaries. He shivered a little and told his driver curtly to get on his way. As the heavy wooden door was opened to let them out he glanced back involuntarily, and only just prevented himself from speaking his thoughts aloud – I wonder what she's doing now.

# 2

If he could have seen her, Hakam would have been relieved but confirmed in his belief in her unpredictability. She was merely sitting, the little bundle which held all her possessions between her feet. She was alone in the tiny cubicle assigned to her by the Head Housekeeper. She had made no trouble for anyone and her state of mind would have bewildered Hakam very much indeed. It was one of profound gratitude and surprise.

She was surprised because no one had beaten her or said an unkind word or made an obvious threat. They had been brisk, certainly, issuing instructions in a manner which showed that no one questioned that they would be carried out, but not unkind. The black men – she had never seen one so close before – had scared her at first, but their impassivity had eventually reassured her. Finally, this impressive lady had appeared. She had sharp black eyes, and was clad in sombre, but to the girl's experienced eyes, rich silk. Was she the Crown Prince's mother, about whom she had already heard so much talk, she wondered. Apparently not, but a slave like themselves, she had heard one of the girls say. Of course, a very powerful and influential slave, the Head Housekeeper, no less, and in her obviously capable hands for the moment their fate rested. She had no standards by which to judge this place or these people. By now she understood enough of their language to get along when she chose to, and she listened freely to conversations not meant for her ears whenever she got the chance.

Ever since the appalling day when she had been snatched up, helpless but fighting, and flung across the saddle in front of an animal masquerading as a man, she had heard about these Ottomans, their power, their riches and their cruelty. Through

17

all the weary months of ill-treatment (but not enough to show, in case it reduced her price), rape and incessant journeying, she had had one idea constantly before her – to escape, get back somehow, she had no idea how, to her own people. Now it was too late. She had arrived, and a new life, good or bad, was about to begin for her. She knew only an immense wave of physical weariness; emotionally, she was numb.

The Head Housekeeper was very efficient, but not quietly so. She had a list from which she identified each girl, making personal comments, most of which were kindly in a rough sort of way.

'You there with the green veil – in here, bring your things.' She seized the girl's upper arm. 'H'm, plenty of fat here. Wherever you've come from they didn't make you work, to be sure. And you,' she made a sudden foray into the small group of waiting girls and seized the fair-haired girl from Circassia. 'In you go. Yes, you share a room. You're only novices, you know. We don't all get to the top of the tree at once, and some of us never do, even in Istanbul.'

The Circassian, who was beautiful, knew it, and had confidently expected to be purchased for some influential harem in Istanbul, stalked angrily across the threshold, muttering as she went. One word appeared to annoy the brisk lady with the list. A quick gesture, and one of the black eunuchs had swung the girl, now thoroughly frightened, back to face her.

'Yes, you're right, we are provincial.' The list crackled under the girl's nose. 'But never forget, this is a royal household. You can go up in the world from a provincial royal household. Or, if we do not find you satisfactory, we can send you away. In this case, your progress will be downward. Do you understand? Finally, I personally do not tolerate impertinence.' She addressed herself to the guard, 'Let her go. She will not be given supper.'

The door was shut behind the blonde girl, and presently they heard her whimpering. The Head Housekeeper ignored the sound, straightened her rather elegant turban of plum-coloured silk, and readdressed herself to her list. 'I can't see a thing,' she pronounced. 'Show me a light, Osman. It's cold here tonight. I must get you girls housed before we all shiver to death. Osman! The light.'

Osman, an elderly, moon-faced eunuch, came forward at a

18

slouching run and swung a lantern up to the redoubtable lady's shoulder. 'Not much better,' she grumbled. Her sharp eyes swept over the group again. 'Where's that Russian girl?'

She had not been listening, simply standing there, bundle hanging limply from one slender hand. One of the other girls giggled unkindly and pushed her forward.

'She doesn't understand a word, or else she's deaf, we've never found out which – '

The girl found herself being inspected by a pair of intelligent black eyes that took in everything. Equally intelligent brown eyes returned the scrutiny, and when she was asked her name she gave it promptly.

'Nothing wrong with your ears, or your understanding either,' commented the Head Housekeeper, 'But you'll have to say your name again, I didn't catch it.'

She repeated the name, but the other shook her head helplessly, while the girls tittered. 'Never mind, tomorrow we'll find you a new name, something less outlandish we can get our tongues round. This way, you get a room to yourself.'

'God be thanked, I wouldn't want to share with her,' muttered the girl who had spoken first, putting down her bundle and tucking her hands under her armpits to warm them.

As the girl turned to pass through the door and the light shone on her heavy plaits, the kiaya exclaimed, 'Look at that, her hair's as red as fire! Whoever saw the like?' If she heard, she made no sign, simply passed through the open door and pushed it shut behind her. She stood for a moment until her eyes adjusted to the light from the flickering lamp and the charcoal brazier. A tiny place, a cell really, with what appeared to be a wide bench along the wall on two sides and a lattice facing the door.

She sank on to one of the benches and dropped the bundle to the wooden floor. The bench was padded, soft and warm to her thin body. She sat with her eyes shut for a while, half-listening to the sound of feet and voices outside, but gradually becoming aware of unaccustomed well-being. She was not only intelligent, but articulate, and accustomed to understanding her own reactions. This sense of ease puzzled her, until she suddenly realized that for the first time for months she was alone. Not only alone, but alone in a place of her own. Had not the Housekeeper said, 'You have a room to yourself?' When the idea penetrated to her, she pressed one hand to her mouth and half-started to her feet. The thought was so momentous. Never in her life before had she had a place in which to be private, except of course the forest or the open fields.

The hope of escape back to her own people had kept her going up to now, but she had better accept that such hope was dead. She loved her father, she knew, and dutifully believed that she loved her mother and the large brood of children. Their life had been hard and dangerous, living apart in the borderlands of Russia because they were rebels. But these people — she got stiffly to her feet, tottering a little because she was so tired — obviously had different ideas about what was important. Look at this little table beside the brazier. It was — she ran a tentative finger across the top and sought for words — pretty, with its legs cut into patterns (that it was old and scratched, and obviously relegated from more important rooms did not occur to her).

She sat down again, easing her back against one of the cushions, and began to think, something she was remarkably good at.

She had no idea how much of the chatter she had heard from the other girls and the servants of the slave-dealers was to be believed, but she could believe the evidence of her own experience. And the thing that had impressed her most was the reason why the old man, Hakam, had bought her. When she had spent time at home, stitching away with blue thread round the sleeves of her loose white shift, her mother had scolded and told her not to waste time. 'People like us have no time for that sort of stuff. Sewing pretty patterns won't put bread into our mouths,' she had said.

When the Krim Tartars had carried her off she had thought — when she was able to formulate thought at all, for stark terror — that they had taken her for the usual reasons, well known and dreaded by all the girls of the borderlands, and she had been, up to a point, right, for she had been deprived of her virginity speedily, almost automatically.

She had not been their only captive — but it soon became plain that they were all destined for sale as slaves, somewhere a long way away, unspecified. At first she had only been relieved that she was not to end her days in the camps of the Krim, but as the days passed into long months and the journey went on and on, she began to know despair and even panic. The world was enormous and grew bigger with every passing hour. How could she ever find her way back to what was dear and familiar, and so far as anything in her life had been, safe? Looking back over that period she wondered how she could ever have been so simple, but since then she had seen and experienced so much. She had seen Kaffa on the Black Sea and sailed in a boat to Istanbul, which they said was the centre of the world. She knew what it was to be eyed impersonally and poked and prodded by strange men in strange clothes. Most of the experience had been humiliating and even shaming.

It had been sheer chance that had resulted in her sale to the high-class Ottoman merchant, Shems. Because her own clothes were reduced to tatters, she had been grudgingly issued with some drab cotton by the little rat-faced trader who had her from the Krim, and told to make herself decent. A skein or two of coarse thread in bright colours were thrown in. From these materials, sheer boredom and a certain resentment at some of the unflat-tering remarks made about her in her hearing, had led her to create a striking and becoming costume which caught the eye.

It had certainly caught Shem's. Her current owner obviously regarded this fat and prosperous-looking personage with rever-ence and paraded the whole of his stock-in-trade before him, while Shems appeared to look into the middle distance and obviously did not bother to listen to the poetic descriptions with which the man presented his wares. But he looked, all right, and when she appeared, he fixed a bright eye on her and raised a finger.

'That one,' he said.

She had been pushed under the old man's very nose, while the excitable little trader launched into a catalogue of her attrac-tions.

'Look at that hair — did you ever see anything like it? A virgin from Russia —' He was pushing his luck here. Shems, however, was not interested in her sexual attributes.

'Tell me, child, where did you get that — um — shawl?'

'I made it, reverend sir,' she stammered, when she had finally been made to understand the question.

'And where did the embroidery come from h'm?'

Scenting a sale at last, the trader pushes her behind him and launched into ecstatic explanation. Yes, the girl had made it and embroidered it herself. Very quickly. She was neat-handed and quick-witted. He knew this to be true, on the head of his mother.

Shems, who did not believe he even knew his mother, remained unimpressed and said two words. 'Show me.'

The bargain was struck over a period of several hours, during which Shems made it plain that if she had beauty he personally was blind to it, and that he doubted 'if we Ottomans would care for all that strange-coloured hair.' However, she would make somebody a useful embroidery hand and that was his last word which could be taken or left. He uttered several such last words, and eventually one of them was taken as he had known it would be.

In one way things had improved for her as soon as she came into the hands of Shems, who was a dealer of repute, whose slaves were purchased by the Sultan's agents and by other wealthy and influential harems. So the girl found herself better fed and housed. Unfortunately, she also, for the first time, found herself in the company of girls who had been bought for their beauty and accomplishments and were intended to adorn the harems of wealthy and important men as love objects rather than workers. They were not frightened nor downtrodden, but spoiled, capricious and vain. They were accustomed to make life difficult for those other slaves whose stock-in-trade was their usefulness in one way or another. The Russian girl, who found them unbelievably stupid and ignorant, not to say boring, was very soon at odds with them. She declined to fetch and carry, ignored threats, ignored insults, and laughed long and heartily when she saw one or other of them admiring herself in a polished metal mirror. Since she was quick to learn, she had soon contrived a working knowledge of the language, but when in the mood took refuge in her usual pretended failure to understand.

Another source of friction was her unwillingness to use her undoubted mastery of the art of embroidery for their benefit. They retaliated by making fun of her, commenting freely and unfavourably on her appearance, on her strangeness – for while they themselves came from all over the Middle East and Central Europe, girls from Russia were rare.

Most of this affected the girl very little. She was her own companion, singing to herself if she felt cheerful, eating alone, a little apart from the rest; sometimes when she felt low, she sat in brooding silence for hours on end, and then woe betide the girl who spoke to or laughed at her then. Her hard little right hand, nails curved, had a way of snaking out and leaving a bruise or an ugly scratch on the unwary recipient. This soon earned her the right to sulk all day if she so wished.

If she affected to ignore their talk she was not above listening to such of it as seemed useful to her. This city, Istanbul, she learned, was their great opportunity. Here the Sultan, the great ruler of all the world, had a splendid palace where he kept many girls, the most beautiful that could be found, as well as slaves of all kinds of lesser degree who looked after him and his family. As well as the Sultan there were court officials and wealthy men of all ranks, and they also had splendid harems and many slaves. From Istanbul boats sailed across the Black Sea to many places, but she was interested only in one place, Kaffa, the port from which she had been brought.

All these girls, especially the beauties, were convinced that Istanbul would bring them good fortune. They would all be bought for one or other of the great harems and live in luxury for the rest of their lives, while if they succeeded in bearing male children to their new owners they would be courted and made much of, becoming favourite concubines. The Russian girl sniffed at such pretensions. She did not see how all the slaves in the hands of all the merchants whose tents littered the Place of the Burnt Pillar could possibly be purchased as they hoped. There just couldn't be enough wealthy men to go round. But she did see that if Shems had bought her he must have hopes of selling her, for she had developed a very high opinion of his sagacity. So that, if she was bought in Istanbul, she would have one last chance of escape. Shems's girls were very well guarded, as she knew to her cost, but once let her get out into a house, an ordinary house, she would make an opportunity to escape and be on to a boat across the Black Sea before they, whoever 'they' might be, could turn round.

It was a preposterously naive plan, based on a complete ignorance of the highly organized society into which she had been thrust, but it gave her hope. Had she been more patient and had less contempt for her sisters in bondage she might have learnt a little more about the world she was up against, for many of them came from the slave 'farms' in Circassia and elsewhere and had been taught enough about the Ottoman system to understand their future part in it; but with her usual self-reliance she either did not listen to what did not interest her or dismissed their talk as highly coloured rubbish.

She had been ecstatic when told the news that one of the Sultan's agents had come to see Shems's girls, and impressed when she came face to face with Hakam. He had an air of authority and his clothes were richer even than Shems's. So, when he had asked to see her skill, she had surpassed herself and had had the satisfaction of hearing herself purchased for the household of the Sultana Hafise, wife of the great Sultan himself. Now everything was well, just as she had planned.

The blow, therefore, had been unbelievably cruel when Shems had told her to prepare herself for the long journey to Manissa.

'But I thought I was to go to the Sultan's palace!' she had stammered.

'So you are, child, he has many palaces. Sultana Hafise lives at Manissa, far south of here. It is a beautiful place and the capital of the Crown Prince's province, Sarukhan. Therefore, as is fitting, his mother lives with him and supervises his household. A girl like you may count herself fortunate.'

Too astounded to make a scene – and in any case there was something about Shems which discouraged scenes – she had stammered that she wanted to stay in Istanbul.

'Who does not?' Shems said simply. 'When you are a freewoman then you can decide to come back. In the meantime, go where you are sent. Go with God,' he added kindly on an afterthought.

Now, sitting over the brazier, she thought about all these things and admitted to herself that she had lost her head and behaved foolishly on the journey here. The point of no return had been passed and she must now accept it. In the meantime she had privacy and warmth, and supper had been mentioned. If she had learned anything over the past year, it had been to live one day at a time and to be thankful for small mercies.

She was dozing a little when a gentle clattering outside the door roused her. She sat up. Then there came a light but unmistakable scratching at the door. She rose hastily and opened to a small figure holding a wide brass tray. It was swathed in dark draperies and in the smoky light of the torches, only white teeth exposed in a smile were visible. The loaded tray was extended and a soft voice said, 'Take one cup, one bowl and an apple.'

The girl obeyed. The bowl contained some sort of pottage of chopped meat and vegetables. There was fresh water in the cup and the apple was firm and rosy. She put all these things on the table and looked questioningly at the figure in the doorway. Despite the dimness, the little creature – she could not even be sure of its sex, though she supposed it was female – brought such an atmosphere of simplicity and sweetness, that she could not forbear to smile.

The soft voice rippled on. 'You have a spoon and a platter on the shelf in the corner. When you are ready to sleep unroll your mattress. The guards will beat a drum when you should rise and make your room tidy. Then I will come again and take you where you should go.' The small head bobbed and the teeth flashed again in a smile, 'Sleep well.'

It was a long time since anyone had wished her a good night. The girl hoped it might be an omen for the future.

# 3

On a terrace at the rear of the palace of Manissa, a woman sat on a divan under the shade of tall trees. Not young, she was yet magnificent; pearl and garnet ornaments adorned her hair and flowered brocade from China fashioned her caftan, but her character triumphed over this superficial splendour. The way she sat, upright against the cushions, the directness of the look from her fierce grey eyes and the prominent nose were all evidence of firmness and determination. She also had kindness and the sort of simplicity which can perceive the fear behind the rage, and the despair behind the bluster. No one who knew her, like the two personal maids who were with her now, had any difficulty in understanding why Hafise, lawful wife of Selim, Sultan of all Turkey, had retained the love and devotion of that formidable man for over twenty years.

She also had her own way of being peremptory and a little tiresome and was being so now.

'I suppose that in the evening of my days, I must expect to be kept waiting.'

The maids exchanged glances, and the elder, who had been with her all her life, remarked tranquilly, 'That may well be, madam, but we can all see it's a long way off. Mehmed will come before long, I'm sure.'

Hafise glanced at her and Guzul dropped her eyes in tolerable imitation of a slave awaiting a stinging rebuke. It did not of course come. Instead, Hafise chuckled, an enchanting sound, and said, 'I want to know about the new slaves and whether I've got all I ordered! He knows this, but nothing can ever make him hurry –'

She stopped abruptly, because thought of the new slaves had

turned her mind to Istanbul, whence they had come, and in Istanbul was the husband from whom her thoughts were never far away. This separation, while she accompanied her precious son to his successive governorates in accordance with tradition and convention, was bitter to her, and sometimes, as at moments such as this, when she suddenly thought of it out of the blue, well-nigh intolerable. Eight long years, she thought, eight years, during which I have seen him so seldom that all the meetings have done is to emphasize how much we have become as strangers. The handsome face settled into such lines of sadness that the maids exchanged glances again. Because they had been with her so long and loved her so well, they did not need to be told what she was thinking about. They had heard echoes of the gossip brought by Hakam, too, and only hoped she had not.

Finally Guzul, the more intelligent of the two, thought of a way to distract her. 'That Mehmed wants the length of somebody's tongue. If he wasn't always mooning after the pretty girls, he'd have been here by now – '

'Silence!'

Wherever Hafise's thoughts might be ranging, impropriety and insubordination could always, as the shrewd Guzul very well understood, bring her back to the present and the claims of rank and good behaviour.

'Not another word! I wonder at you, Guzul, I do indeed, to speak in such a fashion of such a good man.'

'Well, I'm sure, madam, I meant no disrespect. But here you sit, waiting, and you did say – '

'What I say and what you may say are two different things. Bring me my book, and when you have done that, fetch the silks that came from Istanbul so that I can decide about their making up. And you, Sirhane, some sherbet and cakes and a bowl of rosewater.'

Pleased with their strategy, the women bustled away, but as soon as they had disappeared Hafise's thoughts turned back to her husband. Because of the devotion of her household, only the news of his victories reached her. But if she was not informed of the progress of his disease, she was not deceived. She knew that progress it must, and could only wonder how far or near was his end. His letters were brief; sometimes he sent a poem that told her he still loved her. This she knew, her only rivals had ever

27

been driving ambition and religious fervour. 'And those I could never fight. Nor want to,' she told herself sadly. 'He does what he must, and I do what I must. Only it is hard when he is so ill and I can do nothing – nothing!' She sniffed a little and passed her brocade sleeve over her eyes. 'I also need action,' she thought, 'scolding slaves and worrying about the cut of a caftan is hardly enough.'

Her mind turned to her childhood, as it often did. A Krim princess, she had known freedom and independence then, such as she had not known for many years. Yes, and if her reading of Muslim history was right (and it was, for she was an educated woman) their ladies in earlier times had not hesitated to go to war with their men. Her plump fist curled in her lap, 'Why could I not have done?' she demanded, not for the first time. She knew the answer to this very well, and all in all it was perhaps just as well that Guzul came hurrying back with the book at that moment, closely followed by Sirhane, without either cakes or rosewater, to make the simple announcement that Prince Suleiman wished to know whether his mother would receive him. He came every day, for he was loving as well as dutiful, sometimes more than once, but not always so early.

Hafise brightened at once, and Sirhane, who was prone to anticipate instructions in her anxiety to please, rushed to invite his highness to enter. She was stopped in her tracks by the organ note of her mistress's voice.

'Fool! A comb first, and my handkerchief. And bring me a mirror.'

Crown Prince Suleiman was never allowed to see his mother except at her most self-possessed and beautiful, and certainly today was to be no exception. Suleiman kissed her hand and held it while he seated himself beside her. Formality between them hardly existed. Indeed, so close were they that spoken communication between them was often minimal and yet they understood each other perfectly. If he knew about and sympathized with her incessant sick worry about his father it was only because he was sympathetic and sensitive enough to have divined it for himself. Now he turned and looked at her, smiling mischievously as he gently touched one of the necklaces that adorned her. Hafise's love of pretty hair ornaments and ropes of gaily coloured beads was a favourite mild joke between them. She smiled back, and allowed herself to relax against her cushions, asking, 'And what

28

does your highness plan to do with this perfect spring day?'

Suleiman shrugged and said contentedly, 'No Divan today, Mother, Ibrahim and I are going hawking. He has a new falcon for me to try.'

Hafise looked at him fondly.

'He is happy,' she thought, 'And safe. I should be grateful for that, it hasn't always been so,' and while she said idly, 'Ibrahim. Is that the Greek boy?' her thoughts turned briefly to the dangerous past, ten years before, when Selim, the youngest son of Sultan Bayezit II, realizing that his father was prepared to abdicate in favour of his favourite son, Ahmed, had been forced to attempt to seize the throne or suffer death himself according to the law of succession which prescribed death for all a new sultan's nearest male relatives. Even now she could not repress a shudder at the thought of this frightful Law of Fratricide which had cast its black shadow over the succession of the Ottoman sultans from the earliest times, and had at length been given the force of religious law by Mehmed II, the great conqueror of Istanbul, in words that were burned into her memory: 'And to whomsoever of my sons the Sultanate shall pass, it is fitting that for the order of the world he shall kill his brothers.' The source of all troubles, she thought. It's supposed to preserve the line and prevent civil war, but at what a cost! What does it do to a boy when he first realizes what he must eventually do, or die himself? Not for the first time she asked herself what it had done to Selim.

She remembered the day, ten years before, when the young Suleiman, just sixteen, had come to tell her delightedly that his grandfather had appointed him governor of Boli on the Black Sea. He had not understood anything except that his approaching manhood was at last recognized, but Hafise had. 'Oh, my son, we must be very careful!' she had said, realizing that her son and Selim's was now being moved into the area of danger nearest the throne, that his life could be at risk at the hands of any one of them, even his own father.

Thus it was that in the hard and hazardous years that succeeded his appointment to Boli, when his formidable father had staked everything, his own life and his family's, and had won, Suleiman had gone where he was told and done what he was told, conscious always of the power and protection of his father in the background, but seeing evidence every day of the anxious care and love of his mother. The bond between them

29

was absolute and he had learned in the hardest school that in the ultimate, she was the only person he could trust.

There had been times, when Selim was in the field, fighting for his life and sultanate, and they could do no more than wait, that Suleiman, unable to bear seeing his mother's distress, had cross-questioned her. Why was she so worried, what could they do, when would they know? She had never known the answer to these questions, and instead of helping either of them they had only accentuated the sharpness of the pain. Eventually they had learned not to talk about it. Allah was good, Allah was all-knowing and in his wisdom would deal with them. But her son had learned the lesson of resignation more easily than Hafise.

Certainly none of this was in his mind this morning. If he sometimes felt that a young man, and a prince at that, should have more power over his destiny than he had been allowed, he had to admit that since coming to Manissa, he had had more responsibility, and freedom to exercise it, than ever before. Today, certainly, he was happy at the prospect of a long day in the open air with his favourite companion. He laughed at his mother's question.

'Why is it,' he asked her, 'that every time I mention Ibrahim, you ask me who he is? I've had him for six years, Mother, and you recommended his purchase. In fact, he is the fellow who some-times comes to sing to you when you are low-spirited.' He looked at her quizzically.

Hafise roused. The question had been asked at random while she was busy with her memories. But what he said was true. It was her habit to ask innocently about members of his small entourage as if they were totally unknown to her. It was one of her ways of finding out, in this stratified community where even she could not come and go freely, if all was as it should be. 'But really,' she thought, 'I must stop asking questions, even about Ibrahim.' She remembered him perfectly, of course, a short, dark young man, cheerful, and a gifted linguist and musician. If she suspected that their relationship was more intimate than her son ever indicated to her, she made no sign. If his tastes ran in that direction in his youth, so be it. He had given ample evidence that they now took a more normal and useful course.

'So I do,' she agreed therefore, unwontedly meek, in answer to his question, and set herself to listen as enthusiastically as possible to a serious discourse on the merits and demerits of

Saker falcons, about which she knew nothing and cared less. She was perfectly happy to sit idly by his side, rousing occasionally to throw in a few words to show that she was listening. But when he wound up by saying, 'And if it's a good day, I'll have Ibrahim to supper for a bit of talk and perhaps some music,' she saw an opportunity, and said, deceptively tranquil, 'Speaking of music, I'm told that one of the new slaves from Circassia is a fine musician and can dance as well.'

'Oh, that.' He glanced at her again, half smiling, half reproachful. He saw very well what she was up to. He knew that she did not greatly care for his favourite girl, Rose of Spring, even though she had borne him a fine son. Hafise exercised remarkable self-restraint in the conduct of his harem, but still it was plain that she wished her son would interest himself in some of the other girls. Every now and again she would bring one or other of them to his notice. Quite unavailingly, because although Rose of Spring was certainly not very clever and totally unlettered, she was beautiful and biddable and suited him quite adequately. Girls were all very well in their way, and sometimes very necessary, but at the moment the worlds of sport and ideas were more exciting, and his friend Ibrahim was at home in both.

Not wanting to hurt his mother's feelings, he said, a little grandly, 'Well, I'll hear her sometime. Perhaps when I come to you tomorrow. Or the next day.'

Hafise, for her part, suppressed a smile at this assumption of superiority and looked affectionately at her son's profile. He sat now, cross-legged, back long and flat, and his head, well poised on an unusually long neck, erect. He looked as if he could spring up and fly into action at any moment, but was, in fact, capable of sitting so for hours if he was involved or his imagination was caught. She wondered what he and Ibrahim talked about after their supper and music. A crown prince could not afford to imbibe bad ideas or even only superficial or stupid ones. How difficult it all is, she thought wearily. They all tell me how wise and devout he is, and I can see that he is thoughtful and loving, but what can I do for him? He ought to supersede that vain and lazy girl, who will never be able to supervise a harem, but I cannot persuade him ever to look at another one! Even his own virtues work against me. And now she is the mother of a son and unless he has more sons by someone else, the mother of his heir. Mustafa is certainly a splendid little boy, but with Gulbehar for a mother what may he not become?

Suleiman, seeing her abstraction, said gently, 'If you don't tell me about some more of these splendid new girls and their dancing and singing and sherbet-making, I shall think you're losing interest in me, Mother. What else is on your mind today? New tulips for the garden, or the price of mohair?'

Hafise smiled. She supposed she'd asked for it, but she didn't care to be treated like a mere housewife. So she said loftily, 'The only girl I'm interested in is the one brought from Russia. I'm told she's a very skilled needlewoman.'

'Russia? Are you sure, Mother?'

'Certainly, I'm sure.'

'H'm, that's far afield – I've not spoken to a Russian since we were at Kaffa. I wonder how things are going on there?'

She relaxed. Sometimes he liked to play the statesman, and indeed he had picked up a remarkable body of knowledge of adjacent lands. He was sometimes shy and insecure with courtiers, but really enjoyed talking to simple people like soldiers and peasants, and the more outlandish they were, the better he enjoyed them. She wondered for a fleeting moment whether he might wish to talk to this girl, of whom she herself as yet knew nothing, but Suleiman continued tranquilly:

'A pity it's a girl. A boy, now, might have been worth talking to. Mother, I think I'd better go or we'll miss the best of the day.'

# 4

The bird had proved as gifted and fast as Ibrahim had promised and they had had a good day. At first Suleiman had been a little silent, oppressed by something, he could not decide what, a little forced in his mother's manner, but Ibrahim, who could respond instinctively to another's mood, had soon raised his spirits. Now they rode home through the quickly descending dusk, tired but happy, satisfied with the day's sport.

Suleiman's outings at this stage in his life were informal. There was no greater escort than was necessary to ensure his safety, and since he was in his own province the only company that rode with him today were the falconers, while a small body of Solaks, janissary archers, veterans of Selim's wars, ran before him, weapons ready for instant use. The two young men provided a notable contrast to these old soldiers and the falconers, swarthy little men whose villainous faces were hardly flattered by their flat, intricately draped turbans.

There was also an interesting difference in quality and type between the two young men themselves, and an onlooker, used to the conventional view of a prince, might have been forgiven, if, at first sight, he had singled out Ibrahim as the prince. Both were splendidly mounted, but Ibrahim, who had a taste for finery, was gaily dressed. He was excitable, too, enjoyed company, enjoyed hearing the men laugh at his jokes, and was forever turning round to see what was happening behind, reining in his Arab and then dashing up to his prince to be sure that he was happy and required nothing, and then wheeling off again, white teeth gleaming, to issue an order here, or examine a bird there.

Suleiman seemed almost taciturn by contrast. His clothes, as usual when at play, were negligible. And only the very observant onlooker, taking in the strength of the dark face with its hooked nose and unexpected grey eyes, would decide at last that here was the prince. He rode superbly, and kept his mind on the matter at hand. If he envied his friend's capacity for doing three or four things at once, he did not show it. Nevertheless, in his own way he enjoyed the day as much as Ibrahim, and perhaps one of the things he enjoyed most was Ibrahim's performance.

'We'll have supper together,' he said abruptly, as Ibrahim came flying up once again.

'Willingly, sir, your kitchen is better than mine,' laughed Ibrahim.

'In that case, you can pay your way with a song or two,' returned Suleiman, laughing in his turn. Not much given to witticism, he was pleased with his retort. He couldn't often score off Ibrahim. He decided finally that he wouldn't go to Rose of Spring tonight. He and his friend would talk instead, and perhaps in that talk he would find comfort for the doubts that disturbed him, or even better, so positive was Ibrahim, so full of hope for the future, gain from him some of that ebullient confidence.

So when they had eaten and Ibrahim had fulfilled his promise and sung to the music of his viol, they began to argue. Sometimes the exchange took the form of simple question and answer, the questioner always being Suleiman, for his friend's education, because of his European background, had been wider in some respects than his own. Ibrahim spoke Italian, as well as his native Greek and Turkish. Like his master he read Persian poetry, and he had from somewhere acquired a passionate interest in ancient history, and with it, an enormous admiration for the Romans as men of action. Tonight, however, Suleiman, so often silent, or at best questioning, was in a mood for discussion.

'I never denied the ancients their brilliance as soldiers. I merely said that that is not everything. War is not an end in itself,' he said, pouring a cup of sherbet and swallowing it at a gulp. He ate sparingly, never touched wine, but drank an inordinate amount of fruit juice or water.

'Your ancestors did not believe that,' rapped out Ibrahim with unusual directness.

'You're wrong. My ancestors were steppe folk. When they

34

found that life too hard, they fought for land and took it. And when they grew too numerous for that land, they took more and had to fight to keep it. When they found they preferred a gentler way of life they fought to preserve that, but that's all.'

Ibrahim grinned. 'Oh, come, Sir! Then answer me this – why did the great Mehmed conquer Istanbul?'

Suleiman was silent and his face stiffened into that curious non-expression which Ibrahim had never learned to interpret correctly. Sometimes, he knew, it meant anger, indeed, usually it meant anger, but as he was at last beginning to understand, anger against Suleiman himself, because he could not find words or was at a loss for an argument.

Ibrahim did not like silence, and as his master did not respond immediately and because he feared that he might be thought to have been presumptuous, he interjected gently, 'I remembered, Sir, that you once told me of a piece of advice your father gave you.'

Suleiman's face cleared and he smiled. 'It was not so much advice, as a general comment, of which I was to take notice. He said, "The Turk who descends from the saddle to sit on a carpet becomes nothing – nothing!" Is that what you mean?'

'Yes, Sir.'

'And that is to be accepted as support for your argument?'

It seemed self-evident to Ibrahim, and he said in evident surprise, 'Why, yes, Sir – and you haven't yet answered my question about Mehmed and Istanbul.'

Suleiman laughed with pure enjoyment, a rare sound, and Ibrahim looked at him sharply. He's going to defeat me, he thought. I'm a fool, I should let that happen more often.

'Of course it is true. We Turks like to fight, I'll never deny that, but – power, it's a chimera. Now you have it, now you haven't . . . and it has nothing to do with the will to fight. You know as well as I do, why the Conqueror took Istanbul, just as you know why my father fights in Persia and elsewhere. We Osmans have one purpose – to unite the world in Islam. So Mehmed and his predecessors had the conquest of Constantinople' – he used the ancient name deliberately – 'as a constant ambition before them and Allah was good and gave Mehmed victory at last. Just as He gave my father victory against these Sufi dogs of Persia.' His voice had risen as he spoke and shook with feeling on the last sentence.

Ibrahim nodding in instant and necessary agreement looked at him curiously, noting this phenomenon. Totally irreligious himself, and cheerfully willing to give lip-service to any belief that would serve his ambition, he recognized, respected and totally failed to understand his prince's own total devotion to his faith. He knew that Suleiman was always willing to discuss the nature of his belief, but it was a subject which he personally preferred to avoid. He said now, 'Sir, I think you feel more strongly against the Sufi than against the Christians.'

Suleiman said simply, 'To see the light and reject it is worse than never to have seen it. You know that Christians live in our midst, we allow them to pursue their faith, they have their own law-courts and go about their business unhindered. So, too, do Jews, but to be a Muslim, and yet not to be a Muslim – that is a grievous sin. For this the Persians have paid.'

Ibrahim fidgeted. They were, in his opinion, straying on to subjects which were not only beside the point, but worse, did not interest him very much. What on earth did it matter whether the Prophet's nephew was his true successor or not? The Shi-ite Sufi of Persia believed that he was; the Sunnite Turks believed that he was not. What a subject to make war about! The Romans were his men, they believed in war for power and power for its own sake. And so did he. When this prince of his was at last girded with the sword of Osman, would he waste his time in wars against what were, after all, his own kind? He supposed it did not matter. Selim's religious wars brought power and booty and opportunity for ambitious young men whatever their ostensible purpose, and so would Suleiman's.

He said slyly, 'Alexander had another kind of dream.'

Suleiman looked up. 'I often read the history of Alexander and I don't always understand the meaning of what I read.'

Ibrahim nodded. He knew that he did, which was why he had introduced the subject. 'Alexander would have conquered the world,' he pointed out.

'So he said, but his was a smaller world than ours. Could I – could we conquer this world? And if we did, what could we do with it? That was a problem that was beyond him.'

'Only because he didn't have time,' Ibrahim pointed out robustly.

To his surprise Suleiman roared with laughter and leaned forward to grasp his arm. 'Oh, my dear old fellow,' he gasped, 'how much good you do me! When I listen to you I am almost ready to believe that I have a contract with Allah for eternal life.'

'Not you alone, Sir, but the House of Osman. Just think of the achievement from the days of Osman himself. Its great sultans – Orkhan – Murad – Mehmed himself – and now your father. From Persia to Egypt the world trembles at his name.'

'And what part of it is to tremble before mine?'

Ibrahim chose to disregard the irony. 'Why, Sir, the inheritors of the Greek and Roman world we don't already possess or control. Hungary, Austria, Germany and France – why, they already quarrel among themselves like fractious children! While the Pope of Rome sits on his throne and shakes his finger. And they ignore him.' He leaned forward eagerly, 'Think of their Crusades which were meant to destroy us – pitiful! If they are the inheritors of the Roman world, then they've lost their way. I tell you, Sir, I love the Romans! They were truly great. Do you remember when we visited their splendid theatre at Epidaurus?'

'It lies in ruins,' Suleiman suggested gently.

'No, sir, it does *not*! It could be used tomorrow – but that is not all. Where is the serpent-headed column of Delphi, brought from the temple of Apollo himself? No longer in Greece, not in Rome, but here in Turkey, in our own Hippodrome at Istanbul.'

Suleiman smiled at the Greek boy's enthusiasm, but it warmed him nonetheless. He said, 'Very well, Ibrahim, there must be a point to all this. What is it?'

Ibrahim flushed but ploughed on, 'Nobody knows better than you, Sir. The Roman empire finally fell when Mehmed entered Istanbul, and we inherit it. Grass grew in the streets, and the last Roman emperor died defending it.' He chuckled, 'No grass grows there now except in the gardens we have made.'

Suleiman sighed. 'But all empires fall at last. Alexander and Genghis Khan are gone, and the time may come when the grass grows in our Hippodrome.'

'But not in our time, Sir! Empires rise before they fall. Yours is rising. Only remember your father's advice, and who can touch us?' He leaned forward and tapped Suleiman's knee in his excitement. 'You know this to be true, Sir, in your very blood. Have you survived the plots of your grandfather and your uncles for nothing? And you are the tenth of the line of Osman, which the learned men say is a mystic number. Remember that!'

He was a little wide of his mark here. Devout Suleiman

certainly was, but not much impressed by popular superstition. He smiled a little and grunted, but Ibrahim, by the association of ideas, had succeeded in turning his thoughts to something which did impress him and cheered him up. He said, 'I remember all that for what it's worth, and my father's advice as well. Also that when Mehmed took Constantinople, they found the tomb of the holy prophet and standard-bearer, Ebu Eyup, on the western side of the city. This was a veritable miracle and a sign for the future, and always makes me feel more hopeful for the future when I'm low-spirited.'

Ibrahim thought about this for a moment. He considered suggesting more music as an antidote to moodiness, but rightly concluded that this would be treating his master as a child. He had not served Suleiman for six years without becoming used to his withdrawn and introspective disposition, but accepted it as he accepted his own high spirits or Mehmed's carefulness. Men are as they are born, he concluded, to be made use of as they are. It was only lately that he had begun to wonder about the source of Suleiman's unrest. He knew him well, his personal courage, his skill as a sportsman, his devotion to duty. Everything about him bespoke the model prince and future distinguished ruler. But why must he question everything, especially if the questioning brought him apparently to no conclusions, and gave him no satisfaction?

He said softly, 'Well, then, Sir, what more is there? If conquest is not enough − '

Suleiman broke in immediately, 'Of course conquest is not enough! Did my father conquer the Mamelukes and the Persians and then leave them to go on as before?'

'No, Sir, of course not, or it would be all to do again.'

'Just so. What you've conquered you then have to rule. Do you know how peasants live in Rumelia, or holy men in Konya, or − or potters in Iznik?'

Ibrahim stared, wishing he wouldn't dart about so much. 'No, Sir, not yet. How should I, since I am not a peasant, nor a dervish, nor yet a potter.'

'Exactly. But I shall be their sultan and their ruler. When I ride through the streets of Manissa, poor men catch at my stirrup and ask me for justice. How can I give them justice if I don't know what it means to them? Later, when I ride through the streets of Istanbul, the same thing will happen, only this time before the eyes of the empire. I shall be grandly dressed and have an enormous following, but I shall be the same as I am now. What chance do I stand – what chance do they stand – unless I learn.' He got up and began to roam about the room, himself at last excited. 'That is implicit in conquest, and that is what troubles me. I am not much impressed by claptrap about everlastingly seeking new worlds to conquer. And I'll tell you something else, Ibrahim – Alexander said that, didn't he?'

Faced with such vigour, just when he was growing sleepy, Ibrahim said guardedly, 'So it says in the histories.'

'Well, if he did, it was a piece of stupidity, or at best self-indulgence. It is harder to rule than conquer. At worst, if you're beaten in the field, you die – like that!' He clapped his hands, and Ibrahim jumped involuntarily.

Suleiman went on, 'I'll wager that the Conqueror was never frightened until he rode through the streets of Istanbul and saw what he'd undertaken.'

Ibrahim's eyelids were beginning to droop in spite of himself. He jerked himself upright, and said, 'Well, if he was, he conquered the fear and rebuilt the city and ruled it, too. And you'll do the same, my lord, when the time comes.' Without thinking, he added, 'It is possible, too, that he only saw the challenge.'

There was a silence like a stone between them. Ibrahim came fully awake and cursed himself for a wide-mouthed fool. He knew better than to say anything.

Eventually Suleiman went on coldly, 'I doubt that. Only a fools sees one aspect of any problem and the Conqueror was not a fool.'

Ibrahim struggled to his feet, frightened and confused, and knowing he must correct the error somehow. He was rescued by telling the truth.

'Sir, Sir! I did not mean to imply that – that you see only the' – he swallowed, and ploughed on doggedly – 'problems. It is just that I have a bigger opinion of you than you have of yourself.'

Suleiman was silent again, but when eventually he answered his voice was gentle and he smiled a little. 'I have kept you awake too long. Go to sleep now, my old friend.'

Two sleeping-mats lay ready in an alcove. Ibrahim eyed them longingly, but waited. 'Whenever you're ready, Sir.'

Suleiman had reseated himself, this time on a divan by the

window, his head propped on his hand. His large eyes looked very heavy, but he said carelessly, 'Oh – no – I'm wakeful. You sleep.'

There was an unmistakable note of command in his voice on the last two words. Ibrahim wondered if he was really forgiven. On further thought he decided that he had been right to say what he did. It was not the first time he had presented his master with unpalatable truths, but he usually managed to wrap them up a bit better. Probably wants time to digest it, he thought drowsily, but I'd better learn to keep my tongue between my teeth. Sultans tend to be less amenable than princes . . . He threw himself on his bed, sighed, and was instantly asleep.

Suleiman sat on, his mood disturbed, but not entirely unhappy. Ibrahim, for all his nonsense, stimulated and comforted him, and he readily forgave the occasional plain speech or indiscretion. He had brought to the surface a great deal of disquiet in himself, and having examined it, knew that his worry was no more than legitimate and proper in his position. Enthusiasm was necessary but it was not enough and he hoped that Ibrahim did not really think it was. In the meantime the future was good, a clear pool, undisturbed by thrown pebbles or stirred-up mud.

On a low table beside the divan stood a gold ewer, set with jewels. The light from the torches blazing in the courtyard outlined the vessel and brought gleams of light from the stones. In the darkness Suleiman smiled towards the jug. It was an old favourite, he knew it well, for he had made it. Wise tradition decreed that all the heirs of the House of Osman must learn a trade, and Suleiman, like his father, had been trained as a goldsmith. He picked up the ewer and ran a finger over the surface, remembering the pleasure he had taken in its creation. Some of the purest I ever knew, he thought, like making a poem.

# 5

When she looked back on that first day, the girl always thought of it as one of the most memorable of her life; not simply because it was the start of a new life that was to live in other histories than her own, but because of two simple achievements. She acquired a name — and thereby a whole new identity — and she made a friend, the first of her life.

She was sleeping like the dead when the drum sounded, but deep as was this sleep she came awake at once, knew where she was and what she had to do now. Automatically, she made her toilet and combed her hair. There was still her room to tidy and she could hear the murmur of sandals on the wooden floor outside and the low-voiced commands from the guards. At last, she hurried out, just in time to see the backs of some of her fellows descending the stairs, and another girl advancing towards her. The girl glanced round and hurried after the others. She was stopped in her tracks by an anxious voice.

'Where's your veil? You can't go like that!'

The voice came from the slave approaching her. The girl took in the narrow face and the slender body. They were familiar. Of course! This little person had brought her supper. She ran on, saying, 'I can't stop now — I shall be late!' But a surprisingly firm hand grasped her wrist and compelled her to stop.

'There is plenty of time,' came the tranquil reply, 'but even if you do not eat, you cannot appear before the Aga of the Girls in that state. You will be beaten. Come.'

The girl allowed herself to be led back into her cubicle. It seemed to her that this little person was making a lot of fuss about nothing. On the other hand, she had no wish to get into any more trouble, so she allowed the other to worry a little more about her lack of a suitable head-covering and eventually to braid her heavy hair into a long thick plait.

'There,' she said. 'With luck you'll not be noticed and we are just in time. But we must hurry.'

Hurry they did, down the echoing stairs and through a narrow door, when the girl suddenly found herself jammed into a hall that seemed to be enormous and full of sunlight, girls and black men. She looked wide-eyed down at her companion, who slightly shook her head and put a finger to her lips. 'He has not yet come,' she whispered.

The girl nodded, not much concerned. She had not the remotest idea who or what the Aga of the Girls might be. She gathered that not to be present when he arrived would have been a grave sin, but since that had been avoided successfully she had lost interest and was much more intrigued by her surroundings and her companion. It had been a novel experience to receive kindness from anyone, especially another girl. And what a girl! She was such an odd — no, that was not the right word — such an interesting little creature with her gentle eyes and dowdy clothes. She had never seen anyone like her before. She's as out-of-place as I am, she decided, I wonder where she comes from. She determined to find out at the earliest opportunity, and turned her attention to her surroundings.

Such a big place, was her first thought, bigger than even the biggest caravanserai, and much, much grander. The walls were covered with beautiful flower designs in naturalistic colours against a background of white, rather as if, she thought, some of her own embroidery had been endowed with shimmering life. She had never seen or heard of ceramic tiles, she only knew that whatever this wall-covering was, it was beautiful. One end of the place was filled in with elaborate arched windows and the other by imposing carved wooden doors. The girl stared round, her mouth an O of admiring stupefaction. What was this soft woollen covering on the floor? More lovely designs, of birds and trees, she thought, and such vivid colours! She scuffed it experimentally with her foot and her new friend whispered urgently, 'Don't *do* that — it's very old and valuable. Be still, for the sake of Allah!'

She obeyed. She was not, she hoped, stupid. Obviously this was a good time to draw as little attention as possible to oneself, particularly as she had never felt so much out of her depth.

The purpose of this gathering was simple. Mehmed, as Aga of the Girls, needed to inspect the new slaves and in consultation with the senior women officials of the harem assign them to their duties. He enjoyed the experience every time it occurred, and was indeed inclined to make rather more of it than was strictly necessary. The girls were required to appear in their best finery, and Mirza, the blonde Circassian, was certainly a magnificent sight in a pale blue robe, the famous hips swathed in a pink and white gauze sash. The girl gazed at her admiringly, thinking, she looks as though she owns the place, which she probably will do if this Crown Prince has got eyes in his head. She was devoid of jealousy, but would have liked to have had something better to wear. And to have eaten. She really couldn't remember when she'd last had a square meal.

Mehmed kept them waiting a good half-hour. In largest and most spotless of turbans, he made his entrance in some state. This was not entirely because he was self-important; he also believed in what he would have called the Istanbul style. Sarukhan was a province, but was the premier province and its ruler was the Crown Prince; therefore he believed that this should be seen to be the case by the lowest as well as the highest. Shahzade Suleiman was young and tended to be impatient with this sort of thing. This was all right – he was young and would learn the importance of ceremony in time. Meanwhile those about him must show that they thoroughly understood what was due to a future sultan. Hence the guard of black eunuchs who entered before him, the eunuch clerks, who were not really needed but made an impressive show, the Head Housekeeper and her assistants who swept in in their finest attire (they were needed, because if any of the claims as to virginity or other attributes made for these girls had been exaggerated, it was these eagle-eyed and efficient ladies who would find it out), and finally there was himself, bearing his wand of office.

He swept a careful eye over them and was pleased with what he saw. Some of them were very pretty girls, very pretty indeed. He coughed. While others, he saw from their documents, were well trained in a variety of domestic and other arts. The Russian needlewoman, for instance.

He spoke personally to Mirza, eliciting that she had come from a famous slave farm where she had been carefully taught to dance, sing and play several musical instruments. But for the present, he decided to try her as a body-servant to the prince, looking after his clothes and dressing him. He thought this a happy arrangement which would please the Sultana Hafise. Then he made them his usual little speech of welcome and warning. Mehmed always found this the pleasantest part of the ceremony. It gave his on the whole gentle soul a pleasant sensation of power to see all these feminine eyes slide respectfully to his face. Large dark eyes, ringed with kohl, wide grey eyes fringed with dark lashes, sparkling blue eyes, all submissive and as he looked at them, suddenly downcast. Really, there were times and girls that . . . he coughed again and pulled himself together. A man might be a eunuch, but that did not mean he was impervious.

He began: 'You girls have been selected for service in the harem of the heir to the Sword of Osman. You rank as novices and must be obedient in all things to those in authority. In a moment, the kiayas will tell each of you where she is to work, and where necessary you will be taught what to do. Some of you will go to the harem school. You will be supplied with your food and slipper-money, and in certain cases, new clothes.' He noticed at this point an odd-looking girl at the back of the room whose bright, mahogany-brown eyes looked disconcertingly straight into his for a moment; he hurried on, 'You will never in any circumstances stray from the walls of the harem. In due course, where necessary, a mullah will undertake your religious education. That is all.'

He left after that, and the kiayas took over. The girl was soon dealt with when it came to her turn. The Head Housekeeper hardly looked at her, saying briefly, 'Off to the Silk Room with you, my girl – Meylisah, what are you dawdling about here for? Show this girl where to go.'

# 6

Her newfound friend said she was Jewish, then clapped her little hands to her mouth, giggled, and corrected herself. 'I mean I was of Jewish birth – in Egypt – but now of course I'm Turkish and a daughter of Islam.' She seemed to think more explanation was called for. 'You see, my parents were killed when I was a baby, travelling with a company of merchants to Cairo, but because I was wrapped in my mother's veil the robbers did not see me. And then a company of slave-traders found us.'

'Well, go on, did they bring you here?'

'No, they took me to Istanbul, and the Sultana Hafise said I was a poor little orphan and belonged to her, and so I have done ever since. Now I am eighteen and can bake and sew and serve a meal, and my name is Meylisah. What's yours?'

The girl laughed ruefully. 'The Head Housekeeper said it was outlandish and that she'd give me a new one that people could pronounce.'

Meylisah nodded wisely. 'Oh, that often happens. There are so many of us and we come from so many different places.' She giggled again, 'I know what I shall call you.'

'What's that?' asked the girl guardedly. She had been called a lot of things on the journey here by her companions and none of them had been complimentary.

'Why – Khurrem!' cried Meylisah triumphantly and then, seeing her new friend's blank expression, explained, 'It means the "laughing one". Do you like it?' she added anxiously.

'It's prettier than some of the things I've been called. But, laughing – me?'

'Well, I don't say you laugh a lot, but when you do, it's as if the whole of you is laughing. And you throw back your head and enjoy it. You don't see much of that here. I think the Turks are very grave people.'

'H'm, well, perhaps they've got good reason. Like my people. I'm a Kozak and we have to fight all the time or we'd be driven into the towns and made to change our religion.' She sighed involuntarily. Last night she had promised herself not to look back, but it was hard to do.

'Nobody makes the Turks fight. They enjoy it,' said Meylisah with simple conviction.

They were making their way along an upper corridor to the workrooms where Meylisah had been instructed to take the girl to start her new work. Their progress had never been noticeably fast, and now, with all these fascinating confidences to exchange, they were frankly dawdling.

While Khurrem lingered, gaping as usual, a child suddenly emerged from one of the doors and toddled towards them. He was about three years old, with liquid dark eyes and a puff of black hair. Not very sure of his footing, but quite certain of his welcome, he pattered towards them, a mischievous smile on his lips, while the two girls bent and extended their arms involuntarily to catch him, if, as seemed very likely, he should fall. Khurrem thought he was the handsomest little boy she had ever seen, though the thought crossed her mind that probably her own youngest brother would look very fine, too, if he were clad in as beautiful a little caftan of apple-green as this child. He had embroidered velvet shoes, too. Altogether a lovely and valued child, and her impulse to catch him in her arms and cuddle him must be shared by a lot of important people.

He had been taking faster and increasingly insecure steps towards them and it seemed obvious to the girl that he must fall over. She ran towards him, crying, 'Careful, now, darling – mind how you go!' and was bending to pick him up, when someone brushed past her and forestalled her. A tall fair woman she was, who bent, swept the child into her arms, and then turned and looked at Khurrem. Her expression of glacial enquiry and the way the child tucked his little black head under her chin made the girl feel as if she had intruded on something private and too fine for her eyes. The momentary sense of exclusion was so poignant that she reacted in her usual fashion with aggression. Turning to Meylisah, she said roughly, 'Well! Who does she think she is?'

Meylisah was looking anxious and slightly shook her head, mutely imploring her not to make a scene. Which, if it had any effect on Khurrem at all, made her rather worse.

'Next time, her brat can break his neck for all I care!'

The blonde woman's back was retreating along the corridor; so far as she was concerned it was obvious that Khurrem did not exist. It did not help at all that the girl even in her temper could not help noticing the extreme grace of her movements, or the richness of the robe that billowed out behind her. Even when she turned to go down the stairs she did not look at them, but looked down with what seemed like exaggerated care as she began to descend, one hand carefully guarding the baby's head. A slight flush on the exquisitely rounded cheeks might have indicated that she heard what had been said, but if it did, that was all.

'Oh, Khurrem, what have you done? You've made a dreadful enemy!'

'What, again? Who is she, anyway?'

'That is Gulbehar, the Rose of Spring.'

Meylisah spoke in such awe-stricken tones that Khurrem was impressed in spite of herself and even felt a twinge of fear mixed with shame. She had made up her mind to be good and settle down. She liked this place and most of the people she had met, and yet it hadn't taken her long apparently to make trouble for herself. She sighed and asked dully, 'Well, what of it?'

'Oh, Khurrem, she is Crown Prince Suleiman's favourite girl, his kadin, and that was his little son, Mustafa.'

'Well, Prince Suleiman's little son nearly got a nasty bump on his head because his mother wasn't watching him.'

Meylisah shook her head. 'She's always watching him! He probably ran away from her – but, Khurrem, don't ever speak like that in front of her again – in fact, it would be better to keep out of her way altogether if you can. She's proud and spiteful, that one, and would make trouble for any of us she didn't like.'

The girl always liked to get to the bottom of things. 'How would she make trouble – by telling the prince? After all, she's a slave, too, isn't she?'

Meylisah looked at her sadly. 'Khurrem, we're all slaves, but she is the mother of his son, his only son, you understand?'

Khurrem shook her head. 'Well, from what I hear, we could all be mothers of his sons, if he liked.' She chuckled at the outrageous idea, as she began to recover from her fright.

47

'It's no laughing matter! The fact remains that he has never looked at another girl, just as his father never looked at anyone else after he married the Lady Hafise.'

'There, you see, the prince isn't married to this proud-nosed – '

Meylisah put her hand over Khurrem's mouth, 'Be quiet, for very shame! This is no way to talk. Besides,' she added prudently, glancing quickly up and down the corridor, 'It's dangerous. Let us walk on. Not a word while I explain.'

Subdued, Khurrem fell into step beside her, and they went demurely on their way.

Meylisah had never heard of the Socratic method, but she was an orderly-minded girl and had already decided that the only way to keep control of any conversation with Khurrem was to involve her on one's own terms. She asked, 'Who do you think is the most important lady in this empire?'

'That bitch, I suppose.'

'Oh, hush, for my sake if not your own,' wailed Meylisah piteously.

Khurrem looked down on her, struck by the note of terror in her voice. So there was no respite even here, where she was prepared to be so happy and obedient, and display all those unexciting qualities connoted by the term 'good' as used by her mother. She sighed. 'I won't say another word, I promise,' she said.

'Very well, then. It's not her, but the Sultana Hafise, because she's the mother of the Crown Prince, you see,' Meylisah whispered rapidly; she had another quick glance around and her voice pattered on, 'And when Sultan Selim is taken to his fathers, she'll be the most powerful person in the land, except for the new Sultan himself. She'll be the Sultana Valideh,' she rolled out the title in a sonorous murmur which Khurrem found uncontrollably comic.

She kept a straight face, however, and because it was at last growing plain to her that things were not only not as simple as she'd thought, but not simple at all, asked, 'Well, what about *her*, then, Rose of whatever it is?' But she kept her voice down to a level which her friend found acceptable.

'If the Crown Prince does not have any sons by any other woman and make her his favourite, then *she* – ' Meylisah looked around yet again, and Khurrem noted that no names were being used, even in a whisper, 'Will be the mother of the next heir to the Sword of Osman, and become Sultana Valideh in her turn. Now do you see? She may be very powerful in the future, and even now, even in the harem of my own Hafise hanim, she can be very dangerous.'

Oddly enough, despite her totally different upbringing, background and religion, the girl did see. A world of women, she thought, that's what I've landed in; not a bit like home, where men and women work and fight side by side, and men are leaders, but only masters when everyone goes home at night. She thought it was significant that Meylisah hadn't bothered to answer when she asked if Gulbehar was dangerous because she might tell the prince about someone she disliked. It didn't work that way unless the someone was very important; a mere sewing-girl, newly acquired – there were plenty of people, ambitious and hopeful for the future, who would be very willing, just at the drop of a hint, to make life a hell on earth for such a humble creature. She shivered. And there was Meylisah, too, she was equally vulnerable. So were they all.

She said humbly, 'I'm very sorry, I didn't know. I'll be careful and guard my tongue.'

Meylisah still looked worried. 'Yes, you will – until the next time. You have a temper like the Lady Hafise. But she is a great and powerful lady and when she is unjust she will make it up to you.' She sighed, 'Well, here we are. This is the Silk Room, where you are to work.' She added in a low voice, 'And try to keep out of Gulbehar's way.'

# 7

The Silk Room was long and narrow and well supplied with windows. There rolls of silk and velvet and damask. Magnificent Bursa brocades were neatly disposed on cotton cloths on the floor, and embroidered robes, gauze chemises and veils in various stages of completion were piled on the long tables. Khurrem stood just inside the door and gasped at the rich display of colour and gold and silver thread.

The room at the moment had only one occupant, an energetic-looking middle-aged woman, clad in brown and gold cotton, who looked up enquiringly at the sound of the gasp. She had an array of sewing-silks of every colour of the rainbow piled on the table before her. 'Well, girl?' she demanded harshly. Like everyone else faced with Khurrem, she took a second, longer look. 'Well, well, what have we here?' she added, half to herself.

The girl, already troubled and uncertain, stared back mutely, and the older woman began to get impatient. 'Don't stand there like the idiot's child. Explain yourself. What do you want?'

Remembering her promise so recently made, Khurrem clenched her teeth and her fists and sought self-control. To the woman facing her, accustomed to every kind of demonstration from young slave-girls, her continued silence looked perilously like impertinence. She dropped a skein of silver thread back on the pile in front of her, folded her lips, and waited. Khurrem looked wildly round for Meylisah who had gone on her way, did not see her, and finally achieved a few words.

'I am to work here,' she stated baldly.

'Oh,' said Kiaya of the Silk Room, for that was her imposing title, and looked down her peg of a nose. 'Doing what, I wonder? Are you the silk-hand from Greece? Oh, do speak up, girl – what's the trouble, no Turkish yet?'

Khurrem swallowed, furious with herself. 'Please, ma'am, I make embroidery.' There, she'd got it out, humbly enough for anyone, even Meylisah. It seemed to please the kiaya, too.

'Well, at last! I thought we'd lost you. I've heard about you, yes, yes, now what did I do with it?' She rose and trundled, for she was remarkably fat, to the other end of the table, and began to grope through a pile of scraps of silk and gauze. She uttered a small crow of triumph and held up a square of rose-coloured silk. 'Know what that is, my girl? Here, feel it!'

Khurrem approached and obeyed. It was thick and smooth, and softer than anything else she had ever handled. She stroked it in awe.

'It's beautiful,' she said slowly, 'I can't say what it's like because I never touched anything like it before.'

The little woman nodded approvingly, 'Of course you didn't. Well, that's your first lesson here, soon learnt. That's diba, that is, the best satin in the world. From Istanbul, of course. Sit down, here on the other side of the table. That's right. Now, everyone tells me how good you are, and I've seen the famous handkerchief – '

She stopped, for Khurrem, pursuing her own train of thought, had interrupted. She had decided, an instant decision, made in response to atmosphere as much as to anything else, that she liked this vigorous little body and would be happy working for her. 'It seems as if everything good comes from Istanbul.'

The kiaya nodded; having herself made a decision, she was not annoyed at the interruption. 'The best *things* come from Istanbul because the best *people* go there. Eventually. But, of course, they don't always stay there. I didn't, for instance.'

She paused and glanced at her audience, but Khurrem nodded seriously, perfectly ready to believe whatever she might be told by this woman. Droll, even grotesque, she might appear, but her whole personality spoke of competence. Khurrem put it succinctly to herself: I don't know what she does, but I know she does it well, whatever it is.

'Why not?' she asked.

The kiaya was busy rummaging through her pile of thread. She pulled out a strand of pink, matched it against the satin which Khurrem still held, felt among the folds covering her

51

prominent bosom and produced a needle. This she threaded without apparently looking at it, and then she answered.

'Because I chose to stay in the Sultana's service, that's why. Don't think I wasn't a goodlooking girl, because I was. They could've made a marriage for me, easily enough. I liked my work, you see. The world's full of wives and mothers, but Kiaya of the Silk Room of Sultana Hafise that's something else again. I chose to stay with her and I've never regretted it. Nor will you if you're a sensible girl.'

Khurrem listened and watched attentively, as a narrow hem was expertly rolled all round the piece of satin and quickly hemmed.

'She seems much loved,' she suggested, as the other, engrossed in her handiwork, fell silent.

'Who, Sultana Hafise? So she is.'

Khurrem fidgeted. 'The girl who brought me here, Meylisah, says she belongs to her specially because she's an orphan.'

A gusty sigh rolled up from the kiaya's bosom. 'So she does, poor little lost one. Plain, into the bargain. Just as well she has Hanim Hafise to interest herself in her. There'll be difficulty in finding a husband for her, you'll see.'

They seemed to have strayed conclusively from the only two subjects which interested the girl at the moment, Istanbul and Sultana Hafise. Also, she thought that for someone who rejected marriage as a way of life the kiaya seemed to have it on her mind a great deal. Still, she had been given nothing to do, and it was pleasant and peaceful to sit in this sunny room and watch somebody else work. If only she could have something to eat! She sighed and folded her hands in her lap.

Two minutes later, however, the piece of satin, hemmed with almost invisible stitches, was placed on her knee, and the kiaya said firmly, 'Now, my girl, there's something for you to get your wits to work on. Embroider that for a handkerchief, so that I can see what you're made of. Spoil it, and I'll have you whipped.'

Startled, Khurrem looked up at her. By God, she means it, she thought, but decided that this did not frighten her. She had been beaten at home for faults, and at home she had never had the opportunity to do work she enjoyed as much as this, or such magnificent materials to work on.

'May I take what silks I wish from those on the table?' she asked cheerfully.

52

'Yes, but don't tangle them. And here's a good needle. Look after it. There's emery powder in this bag and a sharp knife beside you.'

The girl took the silk and settled herself at the table. She was for the first time anxious to succeed in a different way. Twice before she had stitched her way upwards, but now she actively wanted to please a formidable critic. She knew she would not spoil the silk; what she wanted to do was make this woman gasp in wonderment.

She spread the satin on the table in front of her, propped her head on her hands and stared at it. Pink, like poppies in the cornfields and roses in the hedges. Flowers, certainly, and where there are flowers, blue sky, green grass and trees. She sighed, for these thoughts brought her home fields vividly to her mind and that wouldn't do. She rose to her feet and went to the window; the other woman, who had returned to her silks, looked up enquiringly, watched her for a moment, and then went on with her work without comment.

Khurrem was looking at a different world. Never mind the forbidding stone wall, or the turreted gate where strangely dressed, cruel-looking guards stood watch. She had seen them yesterday when she arrived and today from the windows of the great hall of the harem. From here all she could see was a garden, where strange, stiff flowers with pointed petals grew in their hundreds behind narrow dark green hedges. In their midst under a strangely shaped canopy, a woman sat on a divan. Another sat on a stool nearby and a third knelt on the grass with a heap of coloured silk beside her. Even as Khurrem watched, the kneeling woman held up a piece of green brocade, and all of them began to talk earnestly, obviously discussing its merits. Khurrem turned back to the table excited. She had divined immediately who the woman on the divan must be and longed to see her better. It would be wonderful to paint her portrait in silk but she knew it to be beyond her skill. She sighed again, and the Keeper of the Silks looked up impatiently. 'What ails you, child? And when are you going to start work?'

Khurrem gestured out of the window. 'I would love to embroider that lady's portrait, but I can't do it, so it will have to be just the flowers.'

The older woman stared in horror, 'I should think not indeed! The holy Koran forbids such portraiture! In any case, what can be lovelier than the tulips? Just set to work and try not to be over-ambitious.'

The girl bit her lip and went back to the table to choose her colours, while the other, ever curious, took her place at the window and stared down into the garden.

'My God, she only wanted to portray the Sultana Hafise on a handkerchief! Whatever next, I wonder! I don't blame you, my girl, because you're an infidel still, but that would have got you into trouble, and what's more, me too, if they'd found out, which they wouldn't because I wouldn't have allowed it, but it would have meant waste. . . .' She ran out of words.

'It seems very easy to get into trouble here,' said Khurrem bleakly, threading her needle.

' 'Tis anywhere. But it was worse in Istanbul. Bigger the household, more the intrigue. That's my experience, anyhow. This is the most peaceful harem I was ever in. You're lucky to start here. Then, if you please Hafise Hanim, you'll go to Istanbul when Prince Suleiman becomes Sultan.'

'Oh.' Khurrem kept her eyes on her work. It was in her mind to tell this woman about her encounter with Gulbehar and ask for advice, but newly learned caution prevented her. Until she could be sure where everyone stood she had better keep her business to herself. Instead, she asked, 'When shall I see her?'

'That will depend on her wanting to see you, won't it? Why should you, unless you do something special to please her? Or displease her, if it comes to that.'

Khurrem was silent but her mind was busy. Naturally aggressive, she was anxious to impress her owner (it showed how far she had travelled that she was able to think in such terms without indignation). But it was true, the Sultana Hafise did own her. Gratitude hardly came into it, for she certainly hadn't wanted to be carried off and sold into slavery, but she knew she was lucky, and from all she heard, most of the good luck seemed to flow from the will of the beautiful lady in the garden. (How did she know she was beautiful? She couldn't see her very well, but strangely, she knew it to be so). Now she would have liked to see her close to, hear her talk, and most important of all, see her look at herself, a girl from Galicia, newly named Khurrem, and recognize her existence as a person.

Stitching away, she sighed again. She liked it here and she was tired of the struggle to keep alive, to get enough to eat, to prevent other girls bullying her. Now she had work to do that she liked, a place to sleep and enough to eat (that is to say, whenever another meal arrived, as she was sure it would). She had a friend – two friends possibly, if her relationship with this ebullient lady progressed as it had begun. She had a niche in a recognized scheme of things. It might not be exciting, but it was safe and a breathing-space. For the time being, she was content.

# 8

Khurrem's hope that she could lose herself, pass unnoticed in the harem, was a forlorn one. For one thing, she knew nothing of the boredom of the routines of the place where closely guarded, lonely women did dull and repetitive work and had no amusement except what they could make for themselves. The arrival of new slaves was an event; a girl's appearance and personality would be picked over and a decision for or against her arrived at before she'd been in the place a day. Khurrem certainly provided food for gossip. The girls who had been with her on the journey told sympathetic listeners of her attempts to escape and other escapades, while a girl who had been about to emerge on to the landing while Khurrem was screaming at Gulbehar had prudently remained behind the door, a fascinated witness, and later entertained her friends with the story, which lost nothing in the telling. Round-eyed, the slaves made the most of this and forecast a short and inglorious career for the Russian girl.

Meanwhile, Mehmed, reporting on the new acquisitions to Hafise, took with him the celebrated handkerchief. Hafise was delighted with it, kept it, and ordered that the girl must be given some of the new materials from Istanbul to work on. She was even more intrigued when Guzul, a talented gossip, returned from her midday meal with an account of everything that had happened to Khurrem to date. Hafise laughed aloud over the tussle with Gulbehar, remembered the presence of slaves and said:

'That sort of thing is deplorable, but we make allowances for newcomers and Meylisah will be a good influence.' She was diverted by another thought. 'What about that girl, Mirza – is she as beautiful as I have been told? If so, she could be useful.

Describe her, Guzul.' So Khurrem passed out of her mistress's mind for the time being.

Ironically, the only woman who showed no public interest in her was Gulbehar. This was certainly not because she had no feelings in the matter, but because she had been made to look ridiculous, knew it, and did not know what she should do about it. She had sent the little Mustafa out into the gardens with the nurse so that she could be alone in her room, where she paced moodily until she was tired and then sank down on her cushions to bite her thumb and stare at the wall. Meylisah had been partly right in her estimate of Rose of Spring's character; she was spiteful. The attribution of pride was simply hearsay. Her position as favourite was not easy and she felt herself out of her depth. She did not like the other women, was always afraid of them as potential rivals and had no sense of dignity or prestige – indeed, she was not even aware that such qualities were desirable. But she had enough sensitivity to realize that Hafise despised her.

A really beautiful fair girl, tall and graceful, a typical Circassian, she believed pathetically that her beauty should be enough. Prince Suleiman loved her and she loved him, devotedly. She ought not to be faced with problems, certainly not with impertinent strangers, because she did not know how to cope with them. What she would have liked to have done was to have scratched the girl's eyes out, but that, even if possible, would have been undignified, and Hafise had once told her, gently but firmly, that her position called for dignity above all; so she had, to the best of her ability, behaved with dignity. Now she was miserably uncertain. She knew, even if Khurrem did not, that the incident had had plenty of witnesses, she could even imagine some of the things that were being said. She supposed that Hafise would have quelled the girl with a glance – like she does me, she thought resentfully, totally unable to understand that Hafise would not have allowed the situation to arise in the first place.

So what should she do? Tell Mehmed, the logical person as Aga of the Girls, and have the beastly girl whipped? She sat up eagerly and then relapsed against the cushions. Mehmed did not like her. If she gave him instructions, he would receive them courteously, and either ignore them or consult Hafise. And Hafise? She would either laugh and dismiss the incident, or if she thought it important enough, send for Gulbehar and treat her to another lecture, as if she were at fault. She sat cross-legged on the floor, long graceful arms clasped round her knees, a picture of beautiful despair. Another idea presented itself. She would tell Suleiman; he wouldn't allow the mother of his child to be treated with disrespect. But she knew that it would not be as simple as that. Suleiman was her moon, her world, but he would cross-question her, making no comment either for or against, and then he would say that the harem was his mother's province and that she must decide what should be done. It was what he always did say, sometimes with a faint note of impatience in his voice, which of all things she could not stand.

So, as she had known all along she would do, she shrugged, and decided that at the moment there was nothing to be done. She sat inert for a moment or two, then reached up to a table for a hand-mirror. She carefully rearranged a curl with a moistened forefinger and then comforted her tender slovenly soul with a handful of sweetmeats.

During the weeks that followed, the girl learned that life in the Silk Room could be very hard. Sitting gossiping with Fatma over a handkerchief was one thing; it was quite another after Guzul and Sirhane descended upon them with the stuffs from Istanbul. Fatma thrust the tangled sewing-thread to one side, seized her cutting-knife and began shouting instructions, comments and condemnations at the top of her voice. Some cloth must go to the tailor, some she would cut herself because the man was not really to be trusted. Look at the quality of this *chatma* from Bursa and this *seraser* brocade from Istanbul itself — not really up to standard! Things were not what they used to be when she was in the capital. Where the devil had the sewing-girls got to? Was she expected to do everything herself with the aid of a novice from some outlandish place she couldn't give a name to? Her voice rose to a scream and Khurrem watched and listened, fascinated, wondering which she would injure first, herself, or the beautiful materials she was so wholesalely condemning.

Fortunately, while she was in full cry, six giggling girls were herded in by two of the black eunuchs. They apparently were the delinquent seamstresses and the irate kiaya turned her attention to them, grumbling about their lack of skill, their laziness, and in the case of one downtrodden girl, the fact that she was, so she said, half-blind (which was true). Despite her excitability, she soon had them organized. Within an hour the shouting and giggling had given place to a purposeful hum of activity, dominated by brief, crisply delivered instructions from Fatma.

'You, girl,' she grunted at Khurrem, who had managed to remain unemployed and in the background. 'Take this thread. Get it sorted into colours and ready for use. When you've done that, take any of these bits and pieces here and start devising a pattern for the blue mohair. It'll need to be done in three days, I judge, before her ladyship gets impatient for it. Sharp, now!'

So it went on. No sooner had the blue mohair been finished, than there was a tunic to be flowered for the Prince Suleiman.

'His highness takes no interest in what he wears, but I've noticed he favours pale-coloured devices, so no reds or sharp blues, Khurrem. I think we'd better work late tonight, girls. When supper comes, put your work aside carefully. Any grease spots and you'll be whipped.'

Khurrem went heavy-eyed to her cubicle night after night and could only muster enough energy to pull out her mattress and collapse upon it before sleep surged over her. Yet she remained happy. She saw Meylisah when that cheerful little creature served their meals, she liked and respected Fatma and got along well enough with the other girls, even making her own contributions to the gossip which was totally irrepressible unless Fatma screamed at them. Above all, she enjoyed her work. It went on from early morning to nightfall, but it challenged her. It was fun to work out patterns of flowers and castles and even tents, remembered from her brief stay among the Krim. Fatma did not praise her, but she did not slap her or pull her hair, either, as she did the sewing-girls when she disapproved of their work.

With a settled life, however, came a desire for simple things long denied. How lovely to walk out of the palace, she thought, glancing up at the blue sky beyond the window, along by the river which she could sometimes hear gushing and rippling outside the gate, or to play ball as she used to do at home with her brothers and sisters.

Meylisah sighed when she expressed these very natural wishes. 'We aren't allowed to go outside the harem, you know that, Khurrem. Only sometimes, some of the senior and very favoured slaves may be allowed to go into the town to buy something. But it is a great treat.'

'We might as well be nuns,' grumbled Khurrem, biting off a thread.

'What's a nun?' demanded Meylisah.

She listened wide-eyed while Khurrem explained and, as usual, giggled at the end. 'Shut up to worship God and see no man but the mullah — what a fate!' she cried.

'We're shut up and we don't see any men at all,' Khurrem pointed out.

'Oh, yes, but it's different for us. The eye of his highness could light on any girl here.'

'You don't believe it's going to light on you, and I don't believe it's going to light on me,' stated Khurrem baldly, and added, 'And anyway, I think it's immoral.'

'You say such dreadful things!' Meylisah wrung her hands. 'If they heard you — '

'I'd be whipped — I know. I can't help it. It's what I believe, but you needn't fuss, I'll keep my thoughts to myself.'

Meylisah put down her inevitable tray and looked at her, worrying. 'Anyway, when we're twenty-five we can leave here and get married,' she offered.

Khurrem carefully wiped her fingers and took up the velvet border she was flowering in gold. It was true. At twenty-five, girls were eligible to leave the Sultan's service and the Palace would make marriages for them. A pretty, gifted girl could do very well for herself in this way. But Khurrem, secure in a strict Christian upbringing, thought this immoral, too. She decided not to bother Meylisah by saying so.

'Anyway, we do get a chance to go into the open, only we're all so busy just now,' pleaded Meylisah, continuing to sit on her hunkers and stare at her friend with great earnest eyes. 'We do play ball,' she added.

It was impossible to resist such pathetic efforts. Khurrem dropped her work and hugged her.

'Get that tray out of this room, Meylisah!' yapped Fatma, suddenly spotting them. 'You, Khurrem! Watch that velvet, or you're done with laughing, my girl.'

So it went on, day after day, until instead of bales of silk and taffetas, woollens, velvets and brocades, there issued from the Silk Room a stream of elegant robes, caftans, tunics, trousers, handkerchiefs and even cushions and hangings. Now time began to hang heavy; some of the sewing-girls went to help the

Keeper of the Linen. The gossip among those left behind became bolder and was not hushed so often, and one afternoon Fatma suddenly nailed down Khurrem with a fierce little eye, where she sat mooning over a length of blue gauze over which she was supposed to be scattering silver stars, and barked:

'I believe I can spare you for a few hours of school every day, girl. For a little while, mind,' she added.

'Oh,' the girl put down her needle and thought over the idea. It appealed to her. 'What shall I be taught?' she asked.

'To keep house and sew — nobody need teach you embroidery, of course,' she conceded grudgingly, 'But the course in manners and deportment will certainly be of benefit. Also, I'm told, you're to be taught to read and write,' she added drily, for she had never perceived the need to teach the higher arts to women. *She* had always got along very well without them. The old ways were best, as any good Ottoman could tell you. But there were always those who wanted to change things, including apparently that wisest and greatest of ladies, Hafise. 'Ciphering, too,' she added gloomily.

'Well, I shall like that,' said her novice cheerfully. She refrained from stating that her father had taught her to read and write at home. She divined correctly that this would be construed as showing off. Anyway, it would be a blessed change to do something else for a while and have a change of surroundings.

Fatma's voice broke in on her busy thoughts. 'Sunrise tomorrow morning, to the schoolroom with you. Mind you work hard and do me credit. But you come here to me after the noon meal.'

If she thought it was going to be easy in the schoolroom, she was disappointed. She found herself a member of a class of ten girls who were learning to cook and clean house. Neither of these necessary arts appealed greatly to Khurrem, but the sharp-eyed and energetic kiaya who had charge of them allowed no slacking and no scamped work. Khurrem thought it strange how all these vigorous and efficient women seemed to have a strong family resemblence, as it were. (She would not have thought this had she known how carefully they were chosen and trained for their responsible work.) This one, despite her totally different appearance and personality, constantly reminded her of Fatma and the Head Housekeeper.

After what seemed a lifetime, but was in fact two hours, she was passed on to a similarly effective dragon, who instructed them in the apparently inexhaustible variations in the art of making obeisance, serving sherbet and other drinks and how to enter and leave a room. Khurrem, who was incapable of doing well what did not interest her, frequently came in for pinches, slaps and hard pokes from this lady. Eventually, taking the line of least resistance she achieved a curtsy which, while earning no praise, put an end to the violence.

It was with real relief, physically bruised and wounded in her self-esteem, that she finally made her way to a dusty little attic room where, a class of one, she humbly awaited the mullah who was to teach her to read. He proved to be very aged and very gentle, which was why he had been, not precisely relegated, but certainly judged to be 'only' suitable for work among the women of the harem. Expounding the Koran to them, so far as their limited minds and wandering attention could grasp it, and talking to them authoritatively about their mean status, was normally all that was required of him. It was not often that studious girls came forward, and faced with this sulky yet somehow eager creature he was not sure that he saw any future in the task. But Allah had willed that Sultana Hafise's wish should be carried out, and observing the girl's air of intelligence and determination, he judged that she would get further than most of them.

She did, too. In spite of his uninspiring methods of teaching, and the fact that in the first instance she regarded his lessons merely as a respite from the drudgery of kitchen and deportment, she began, despite herself, to be interested. For one thing, the old man's very real piety was impressive. She was privately determined to remain a Christian, but when he talked to her about the holy Koran, about the privilege that she might one day achieve of learning Arabic so that she might read it for herself, she could not fail to be moved. His calm certainty of the superiority of Islam and its destiny to conquer the world through the Ottomans, was instructive too. Any notion she might have nourished of conducting a one-girl holy war against it was just not possible; she had no gift and no taste for martyrdom. She would learn to keep her peace. In the meantime, she began to learn to read and write Turkish tolerably well, and became indeed a source of mild pride to her teacher.

Thus she cruised on, making a definite place for herself in the harem, even among the other girls, whom on the whole she continued to despise, and becoming a distinct asset to the Silk Room, where Fatma recognized in her a kindred energy and intelligence. Meylisah remained her best friend, though God knew she could sometimes be trying, with her eternal giggle and willingness to accept everything, even beating, as being for the best.

On the whole, then, she was approved of, and though some of the kiayas shook their heads over her, Fatma and others felt that here was another kiaya in the making.

# 9

A different fate was, however, in store for Khurrem and she took
her first steps towards it, indirectly at first, because of Hafise.
That great lady received a gift from her husband and a setback
from her son; these shattering experiences occurred within a day
of each other, and taken together were sufficient to cause her
normally invincible poise to waver. The gift came first. Ten
yellow diamonds, not particularly large but quite perfect, were
brought by a special envoy who had journeyed day and night to
place them at her feet. The letter that accompanied them was
brief but said all that Hafise wanted to know; she was constantly
in his thoughts and his health was good. These trinkets from the
Persian treasury seemed to him peculiarly fitting to adorn her.

Hafise behaved with becoming kindness and dignity towards
the messenger, saw to it that he and his escort were suitably
housed and fed, and retired to compose her letter of thanks and
greeting. Once alone, she cried like a lovelorn girl, clutching the
letter to her breast, the gift in its leather bag disregarded on the
carpet at her feet. Eventually, she collected herself, and with
much muttering and several false starts, the letter was prepared.
She spent the rest of the day dreamy with happiness. She kept
the diamonds in her sleeve, taking them out from time to time
and pouring them from one hand to the other, to see the light
reflecting in their depths. Selim's letter she kept inside her robe,
and did not take it out at all.

Early the following morning, she received her son, who,
having heard of his father's messenger, came to congratulate her
and hear the news. He quickly perceived that his mother in her
idyllic frame of mind would rather be left alone, but he had
something on his mind, and since she seemed so happy, felt that

there would be no harm in telling her about it. He had no wish to seem to make it an issue, and waited until he was taking his leave to broach the matter.

Rising and kissing her hand, he said, 'Mother, you have been kind enough to provide me with a female body-servant.'

Hafise roused and looked at him. He saw that she had not been listening, and patiently repeated himself.

Her eyes sharpened. 'So?' she said. Suleiman saw that, ecstatic or not, she was not prepared to have her arrangements questioned. 'I would prefer that she be given other duties,' he said quietly.

'Is she clumsy? Has she displeased you?'

'No, madam. It is merely that my needs are very simple. There is no work for her.'

He was being tactful. He regarded female body-servants as an unnecessary luxury, although he was aware that they were a commonplace in some households. Also, Gulbehar was jealous, and he felt her feeling was justified. After all, he was very well aware of the game his mother was playing. Sooner or later she would learn that he was not interested in other girls. Meanwhile he could afford to be patient. But he still did not wish to be bothered with a flouncing female who tacitly offered herself along with every garment. Besides, early in the morning, or before he slept alone at night, he liked to meditate. In short, the girl was an encumbrance and he simply would not have her. Gulbehar was gentle and loving and all he needed in a woman.

It will be perceived that Prince Suleiman, for all his experience, still knew very little about women. He had yet to learn that masculine and feminine logic have little in common. In his innocence, he thought that because his mother was happy, she would take his request in her stride. He had no notion of the fragility of her euphoric mood. The very gift itself served to underline the fact that what she had received was a very poor substitute for the husband she missed and needed. And now, here was his son – to whom she must be both father and mother – refusing to behave as any normal young man would. It was absolutely intolerable.

She said sharply, 'In the name of Allah, what is to be done to please you?'

Suleiman was astonished, and showed it. 'Why, Mother, I thought that today of all days – '

'What has the day to do with anything? I try to serve you, to assure the succession of this empire. You know you have a duty – and yet you will not look at any girl except – ' She broke off abruptly. What was she to do? How was she to make him understand what was required of him if he could not feel it himself?

Suleiman stared at her, concerned, but could not keep an edge of hauteur out of his voice. 'I don't understand you, madam. I have one healthy son and expect to have more. But I do not see it as my duty to beget children on every female slave who is put in my path.'

Hafise's hands flew to her mouth, and Suleiman went swiftly to her, where she sat on her divan, and gathered her into his arms.

'Oh, mother, why do you concern yourself so? Can I help it if I am like my father? This painted girl you gave me merely makes me laugh – when she doesn't annoy me.'

His mother said stonily, 'Then obviously she must be sent away.'

'Yes, she must.'

There was a long painful silence, each hoping that the other would break it. Hafise was now aware that she had been guilty of the sin she most depised – an error of judgement. But it by no means followed that she was prepared to admit it, at least not yet. Men, she felt, made use of women, went off to war, or to do other things that they wished to do, and left their wives with difficult and often impossible tasks, such as bringing up children who would grow into equally unreasonable and ungrateful men, who took light-headed and unsuitable girls into their beds, and yet could not be distracted by other equally light-headed (but beautiful) girls. She bore the weight of all this care and nobody helped her, could advise her. She longed for peace and a helping hand, and she was sent diamonds!

She said abruptly, 'I will see to it. Now please leave me.'

The prince rose immediately. It looked as if he was about to exercise his rather unfortunate capacity for taking her at her word, as he had sometimes done in the past. Instead, he hesitated, and sitting down again, placed his arm lightly around her shoulders. In a really bad mood she was capable of shaking it off, but today she did not move and they sat uncomfortably side by side, devoted, but unable to communicate.

66

Finally, Suleiman said gently, 'Mother, I am sorry to have made you unhappy, today of all days. I would not have mentioned this wretched girl, had I thought it would disturb you.'

She sniffed. 'It was a mistake, I confess it. I am bound also to say that I think female body-slaves a luxury more suitable for vulgar merchants in the big cities than in one of his majesty's households.' She sniffed again, a sound so desolate that her son grasped her hand and held it tightly in his own warm one. She turned to him and cried out, 'But what in Allah's name am I to do? I do not wish to upbraid you, or – or criticize the mother of your child, but your father will not live for ever. It will not be long now, I feel it even if I cannot explain how, and I am full of forebodings for the future – ' She stopped because she could not bring herself to be more precise.

Suleiman drew her closer and kissed her cheek. 'Who do you doubt, mother, your son or yourself?'

Whatever she had expected him to say, it was not this. She drew away, the better to look at him. 'Of course, I don't doubt you – you know that is not in my mind.'

He pressed her. 'And yourself, madam. When you become Sultana Valideh, will the burden be too much for you?'

'Sometimes I feel very old and tired, as if I were fighting a battle which will never end, but we are all doing that, I think,' she sighed, and added, 'but I can do as well as some and better than most. No, I don't doubt myself.'

He raised his hands, palms up, and spread them. 'Then you've answered yourself. It is quite simple.'

She persisted, 'No, it is not. We are only as good and as successful as those we love and who love us. You must think of *your* successor even now – '

He interrupted swiftly. 'My father has only one son,' and she countered promptly, 'Only but for Allah's grace, he might now be childless. Don't forget the hazards you've come through and don't tempt fate. This is too serious a matter to chop logic on!'

He got up and walked about. She could see that he was angry and did not care. She had said it at last, and however he took it she would rest more easily. She knew she was right, and, further, she had done her duty to her beloved Selim. That was all-important. So, no longer weeping, buoyed up by her own urgency that was almost anger, she sat, hands on knees, and watched him.

Finally he stopped pacing and faced her. 'I cannot do what you ask, mother. I am a simple man – I think. At least in that respect.'

She said harshly, 'It is easy to get a child. For a sultan it is needful. And the Koran allows it.'

He shook his head impatiently. 'No one need tell me what the Koran allows. It also recognizes that man is imperfect, but I do not believe that anywhere it makes it a virtue for a man to go against his nature.'

She shut her eyes and pressed her hands to her mouth. It looked as if she was about to burst into tears, violently. Her son stood by and watched, and when she had controlled herself again, as he knew she would, he added, 'You make problems where there are none. Gulbehar is young and strong, and so am I. There will be more sons. That is all I can say to comfort you. No one has the right to ask a man to betray himself for ambition. God knows,' he finished bitterly, 'only one of my illustrious ancestors did, and he suffered for it.' He added, more gently, 'Come, mother, do not always be looking on the dark side of things. You make difficulties where there are none.'

'You are begging the question,' she whispered at last. 'It isn't only more sons – '

'*That*, I won't discuss,' he cut in quickly, 'because it is equally useless and would make us bad friends. I could not bear that, and neither could you. So we will not discuss it. I love Gulbehar. I do not want anyone else. It is how things are, and nobody should regret it.' He looked at her expectantly, but she continued to sit staring at her hands, so he added, 'I will come to you tomorrow,' and turned and went swiftly and quietly away.

As for Hafise, the moment she could no longer hear his footsteps, she caught up the nearest breakable object – a beautiful and valuable Chinese vase – and hurled it at the wall, where it smashed most satisfactorily. Then she burst into tears. By supper-time she felt much better.

As for Suleiman, he went about his daily pursuits as usual, but Gulbehar found him abstracted and difficult to entertain that night, though he was as tender and loving as usual when they went to bed.

Although she could not claim to have influenced her son, Hafise's mind was greatly relieved. Now that she had broached the subject, she would return to it again and again. In the meantime her conscience was clear, and she felt happier than she had felt for a very long time. Also, there were the diamonds. She thought about them long and lovingly while Guzul and Sirhane dressed her and arranged her hair and headdress. It amused her also to consult her faithful slaves, if only for the pleasure of watching them react. She found something very satisfying in seeing people run true to type. Sirhane, for instance, in the intervals of dashing distractedly about the place in pursuit of mirror, cosmetics and combs, most of which proved to have been already provided by somebody else, readily voiced a number of suggestions, all of which were impracticable. When she could think of nothing more, she smiled innocently and said that her lady would be sure to know the right thing to do.

Guzul, practical and efficient, finished draping a turban of delicately embroidered purple silk and said, 'What this needs is an aigrette of yellow diamonds.'

Hafise examined her reflection in the mirror that Guzul held for her. 'I think it's very well as it is. No, no more jewellery. I would like to be able to wear them often, not just as a jewel whenever I wear something they will suit – oh, what am I talking about? I want to wear them all the time!'

'Then you'd best string them on a chain and put them round your neck,' grunted Guzul, who was capable of taking umbrage when her suggestions were rejected.

'Hold your tongue.'

'Yes, madam.'

Silence. Guzul began folding garments and stowing them away with emphasis. Hafise ignored her and sat in deep thought. Finally she clapped her hands and cried, 'Of course! Send me the kiaya of the Silk Room – what's her name? Fatma! Yes, send me Fatma.'

So Fatma came, made her reverence with becoming dignity, and listened while Hafise explained.

'Fatma, I want you to make me a robe.'

Fatma's unspoken comment was 'You usually do', but rightly concluding that this request was something out of the ordinary and not unconnected with yellow diamonds – of which the whole household had by now heard – she folded her hands across her stomach and listened in attentive silence.

'It is to be loose and sleeveless, so that it may be worn over all manner of underdresses, and it must be in some colour which will flatter me and blend well with other colours. I want it beautifully embroidered, and the centre of the embroidery is to be these diamonds. They will be the highlight. Do you understand me, Fatma?'

Allah, thought Fatma, only too well. Aloud, she said matter-of-factly, 'Yes, madam,' while her busy mind went to work on the problem.

'Well?' said Hafise, when she did not answer immediately. 'Have you no suggestions?'

Fatma took a deep breath, 'If I might examine the gems in the light, my lady — ' She took as long as possible over conveying the diamonds to the window under the watchful eye of Guzul, squinting at them against the light, but at the end of the time she was ready. She returned the stones to Hafise and crisply voiced her recommendations. Thick satin, the soft green of young vine leaves, bordered with gold-embroidered motifs in each of which a diamond formed the centre . . .

It was not, of course, to be as simple as that. Hafise did not think green was one of her colours. What about crimson?

Crimson, with yellow or dark blue, or even scarlet? cunningly interpolated Guzul, still smarting. Hafise quelled her with a glance, but dropped crimson. The argument raged back and forth throughout the morning. Tempers ran a little high at times and all the ladies present thoroughly enjoyed themselves. At the end of a couple of hours a final decision had been taken. The garment was to be of thick soft satin, the colour of young tulip leaves, the embroidery gold, with touches of crimson.

'What design will you devise for the gold work?' demanded Hafise, refreshing herself with a cup of sherbet.

Fatma looked wistfully at the cup as it was raised to the Sultana's lips, and spoke fateful words. 'For that, madam, we need the slave, Khurrem.'

'Ah,' Hafise put down the cup, and dabbed her lips with her handkerchief. 'The Russian girl. Is she up to such work?'

'We have had no one better, Hanim.'

'Well, I'm bound to say I have been very much pleased with the blue mohair. Of course, she will have to come and work here. You understand the diamonds cannot leave my charge. Also, I shall want to watch the progress of the work. Is she clean and presentable?'

Fatma bowed. 'She is also a good, intelligent girl and a quick worker, madam.'

'Very well, make the garment, Fatma, and let the girl make patterns to show me. When you are ready, bring her to me.'

# 10

Prince Suleiman found his mother's fears disturbing in a particularly personal way. He brushed aside her views on Gulbehar; hinted at as they had been, he still understood them, and considered them irrelevant. She wanted him to find himself a girl with qualities of character and intelligence comparable to her own. This he considered to be impossible. He valued his mother as a rare phenomenon; he had never met a woman who even approached her and did not expect to. Truth to tell, he was not even sure he wanted to. Irritating and ignorant as Gulbehar might be, she suited him. She was beautiful, she was warm and she looked up to him as a hero. What more could he want?

It would take an extraordinary man to extract hero-worship from Hafise, but then, Selim was an extraordinary man. Both his parents were larger than life-size; he, Suleiman, was content to admire them, but was not at all sure that he wanted, or indeed was able, to emulate them. What did now begin to prey upon his mind was the likelihood that Selim might not live much longer. His mother had seemed to feel that she must excuse her premonition, or what she regarded as a premonition. Suleiman's view was more matter-of-fact. As he saw it his father must die soon. A cruel disease, coupled with long years of incessant campaigning, must take their toll sooner rather than later. And then would come his own testing time. His anxiety was almost entirely on his own account. He hardly knew his father and therefore could not regret him, except impartially as a great ruler who had dared to do things that Suleiman believed he could never attempt. He knew already, if he knew anything, that his mind did not work on the same bold and decisive lines as Selim's.

How long had he? One or two years, or even only one or two months? He flinched from the unanswerable question, and could not avoid another, almost equally difficult. Was he ready? He remembered Hafise's answer to his challenge – 'I can do as well as the next and better than most.' He could say the same, but knew that in his case this would not be good enough – well, in her case it was not good enough, either. But she had been merely throwing away words, striking an attitude as it were. No one, knowing Hafise, could doubt for a moment her immense strength of character and ability, proved as they were over the dangers and difficulties of the last eight years. But when it came to her son, Suleiman – who knew him, or could trust to his powers?

He sat outside the selamlik – the men's quarters of the palace – alone on the terrace, looking out over the roofs and twinkling lights of the city. Like any young man of imagination, he knew this twilight mood of self-questioning and self-distrust, while not being able to break free of it. Indeed, he saw it as a form of self-indulgence. He despised himself for it, but deliberately exposed himself to it, because in some way not understood, it strengthened him. For the same reason he liked to lose himself in the unquestioning admiration of Gulbehar and the bracing optimism of Ibrahim, but he was not deceived; they were not good enough.

Tonight he knew that everything was different. Time was running out and his crisis was near. Ever since his sixteenth birthday they had been preparing him to govern. He had studied Persian and Arabic, he had read history and the law – what there was of it – and mathematics and the art of war. Above all, a labour of love, he had studied the Koran, and made several copies of it in his own elegant hand. He had prepared his body for the rigours of campaigning by enthusiastic attention to all forms of sport; he wrestled, shot with the bow and rode like the whirlwind – all these things he had learned to do with more than pleasure, because he enjoyed them, and not from a sense of duty. He actively longed to rule, while at the same time some part of his character drew back, sought refuge in contemplation and the making of poems and goldsmith work. He wanted power, but people were an enigma.

In the abstract, he wished his subjects well, would do his best for them, but always there was this sense of inadequacy when faced with them. He had governed his provinces conscientiously, was used to delivering judgement extempore in the Divan, or even from the saddle, when some poor devil threw himself beneath his horse's hooves. But this part of his duty was the hardest and brought him little pleasure – even when, as sometimes happened, he had broken through the invisible bonds that bound him and given good judgement, and had felt the warmth and approval of the officials around him.

Now he sat, austere, withdrawn, his serious expression at variance with the youthfulness of his face and slight body, and wrestled once again with an agony entirely his own and with which no one could help him. Indeed, those nearest to him contributed unconsciously to his distress, so superior in character were they, like his mother, so high-minded and efficient in the carrying out of their duties, like the many civil servants who surrounded him, that they underlined his sense of inferiority.

They were all so positive – even the carefree Ibrahim was sure he was right – while he, Suleiman, was sure of nothing. It was only when he thought of the power that was to be his that excitement rose. Not only would he rule the whole of Turkey in Asia and Anatolia, but there was this vast new empire his father had won for him – Egypt, Syria, Mesopotamia – and to the north, Jedistan and Bessarabia. When he thought on this scale, he was easier. He could forget the individual men, strangers, each one a world and a mystery to which he had not the key, and concentrate on the vast battlefield of the world.

This concept, which might have struck terror to the heart of another man, surprisingly gave him confidence. This is how my father thinks, he told himself. This must be so, otherwise how can he face some of the things he has done? Things which I, too, may have to face. He felt a sudden surge of contentment. On these terms I can meet it, he told himself. Let someone else win the hearts and give the popular judgements. I will decide the policy and the strategy and guard my inadequacies.

He did not like that thought and stirred, finally jumping to his feet and striding up and down the paved terrace. Come, he encouraged himself, it's not as bad as that. Guard them, yes, but fight them, too. Above all, don't ape the common touch. Mehmed the Great had it. Very well. God knows Selim does not, and he is as great as – history may say greater than – Mehmed. He is aloof and strikes terror to the heart even of his son.

He sank down again on the stones, now rapidly cooling in the night breeze, and clasped his hands around his bent knees. Oh Allah, he whispered, who am I, what am I? When I ride through the streets of Manissa the people stand still and smile at me. My own guards are my friends and would die for me, but Manissa is not Istanbul, and my guards are not the janissaries – and even Selim has reason to be afraid of them. I have honestly and gladly tried to prepare myself. Now, in your infinite wisdom, give me time to do the rest in my own way. And give me friends, for I cannot do it alone.

The luminous sky paled and then was dark. Suleiman sat on, looking at nothing, for there was nothing visible except the dark bulk of trees. A movement, and a pale hurrying figure roused him.

'Who is there?' he demanded sharply.

'I, my lord, Ibrahim.' The voice was cheerful, expectant, sure of its welcome.

'Ibrahim,' he repeated. 'I've missed you, where have you been?'

'To the bath, sir. Would you like lanterns to be brought, or shall we go inside?'

He sounded so confident, so pleased with life, and when they did in fact go into the men's lighted quarters, Suleiman could see that his friend was in fact in the best of spirits, full of physical well-being. The contrast with his own mood prompted him for once to make a confidence.

'I have been sitting in the dark, tormenting myself with the future.'

Ibrahim's merry dark eyes widened as he repeated Suleiman's last phrase, and added, 'Surely that is a contradiction in terms, your future lies in the sunshine.'

Suleiman's lips tightened. It had been a mistake. Even if Ibrahim could enter into his feelings, there was nothing he could say or do to help him. Indeed, he might come to feel contempt. Another lesson for the future, Suleiman thought wryly, a prince should keep his own counsel, except of course, when he feels confident. The little tussle with himself improved his mood, but he still had to answer Ibrahim, who was looking at him in a puzzled way, obviously wondering what was expected of him. There was one confidence he could make. He said abruptly:

'You know, Ibrahim, that my father cannot live much longer.

My mother is convinced of it, and so, oddly, am I.'

Ibrahim's expression became serious. 'So it is said, I have heard the talk,' then, remembering Suleiman's half made confidence, he looked at him sideways and added, 'He's been a great ruler.'

'To be sure,' said Suleiman eventually.

Ibrahim frowned. What the devil was he to say? What did his master's odd moods mean, except a very natural apprehension? He personally would revel in the opportunity . . . but the silence was lasting too long; something must be said. He brought out impulsively, 'He will be followed by a greater.'

He perceived immediately that whatever the point was, he had missed it. Suleiman merely looked at him levelly and went and sat down. After a moment he looked up, and smiling sweetly, said, 'Ibrahim, you should know better than to feed me with platitudes.'

Ibrahim knelt down beside his cushion. He was angry with himself for guessing wrong. Not a complex young man, he wanted to please his master and comfort him, but his self-confidence was a little shaken. It did not happen often, introspection not being his habit, but when it did, he judged it best to take refuge in truth. He said:

'Sir, I cannot enter into your feelings – how can I? Simply, I believe in your fate, and the fate of your house. You will build on what your father has created. I know I don't express myself very well, but that is what I feel.'

Suleiman's expression softened, and he spoke almost gaily, 'Oddly enough, that is how I feel – at the moment. But what I want is for someone to give me a guarantee, and that, unfortunately, cannot be done.' He clapped his slave on the shoulder, 'Come, prayers, and then supper.'

# *11*

Khurrem had progressed so far in adapting to the life of the harem that she received the news that she was at last to meet her mistress with something approaching dread. She had completely forgotten her early idyllic desire to impress that lady with her ability; now, all that bothered her was that she should produce a design that would please Hafise and keep out of trouble long enough to stitch it.

This was partly Fatma's doing. She stood over the girl, issuing a string of instructions and prohibitions as long as your arm, and complicated enough to confuse the sharpest and most ambitious of girls. They certainly confused Khurrem.

'How am I to approach on my knees and carry a basket of sewing materials at the same time?' she demanded practically.

Fatma looked at her suspiciously. She suspected a lack of reverence and up to a point she was justified, although her own training had done much to reduce the girl's natural levity. The very questions she was asking – and her own difficulty in answering them – indicated that Khurrem was making a real effort to make a success of the project. She had to think quite carefully and seriously about the answer to that question, a regard for decorum and ceremonial being a prime Ottoman characteristic. Eventually, she said, 'You will hand the basket and anything else you are carrying to one of her ladyship's maids outside the presence-chamber. Then you will be able to enter unencumbered. Make three reverences and keep your head *down* – no staring about, remember, don't look at the Sultana until she asks you a question. Look directly at her when you answer – '

'I hope I'll know the answer,' muttered Khurrem.

'Of course you'll know the answer. Hafise Hanim has no such

opinion of sewing-girls that she'd ask anything out of the way. She'll ask me anything important. Another thing. What else have you to wear?'

'Nothing,' responded Khurrem promptly.

'I knew it. You girls never have anything else to wear. You've only to get your eyes on my good clothes and you want them. But I'll have to rig you out, that gown's getting shabby and I've never thought that cap adequate.'

'Can I have pearls to plait in my hair?'

'Of course not! Most unsuitable − anyway, who'd pay for them? They wouldn't come out of *your* slipper-money, let me tell you! If you're so greedy as that, I'll have to choose your wardrobe. There's another thing. If the prince, or anyone else important, come to that, arrives to visit his mother while you're there, don't wait to be told − efface yourself. Make your reverences and go.'

'Will he?' demanded Khurrem, interested.

'Will he what? Come to visit his mother? Probably. He does so every day. That needn't concern you. You're there to work, not watch what goes on.'

Khurrem lowered her eyes demurely and muttered, 'Yes, ma'am.'

She now remembered that six months previously she had longed to see Hafise, to make an impression on her, and now all she was really worried about was getting through the difficult task she had been given without discredit and without being scolded or beaten. She was not at all sure that her present approach was better than the earlier one, but she was sure it was more realistic. And it would be nice to have some new clothes. Of the prince she thought not at all, except with empty curiosity, as an appendage to his powerful mother. Above all, she was a realist. She had heard, without listening to it, a great deal of nonsense about Prince Suleiman from the other slaves. In theory, his gaze could light upon any one of them, he could take her into his bed and make her his favourite and there was nothing to prevent him. Indeed, if some of the girls were to be believed, it was considered emimently desirable that he should take one of them into his bed, because, they said, Sultana Hafise did not like Gulbehar.

Since she did not herself like Gulbehar, Khurrem was perfectly prepared to believe this bit. She hardly knew what to make of the rest. The idea that a Muslim prince could have multiple concubines and that this was regarded as a perfectly honourable and legitimate situation she had gradually come to accept as true because she had heard it from so many sources that she could no longer discount it, but she found it confusing at least. The idea conflicted with everything she had ever been taught. However, she wisely concluded that she was unlikely ever to be put to the test and laughed heartily when she heard how his highness had sent Mirza away, not in disgrace, but what was worse, disregarded.

The sighing and whispering that went on among some of the girls struck her as merely silly. She had never been in love, there was no handsome young Kozak about whose fate she wondered now that she was so far from home. On the other hand, the endless sentimental adventures of handsome young men and beautiful girls with which some of the slaves whiled away their scanty leisure fascinated her. They were so beautifully high-flown and so totally divorced from life as she had known it anywhere. So far as she could see, life on the land back home was nothing but spoliation and backbreaking labour, and women got the worst of both. Here in Turkey, in the harem, the same held good, except that there was only one man and he was not, at the moment, bothering anyone. From that point of view, the harem had distinct advantages.

Her feet on the ground, and her head very far from the clouds, sturdily self-reliant and blissfully ignorant of most of the things that give meaning to life, Khurrem was prepared for her fateful encounter with Hafise. Fatma talked to her until she was dizzy, repeating instructions and sometimes contradicting herself, which added to the confusion. She drew her design, had it inspected by Fatma and returned for multiple corrections. She drew it again, and Fatma then decided she preferred the first one. The one part of the whole performance which she enjoyed was being given new clothes. Fatma selected them — a long gown of mauve print with a purple sleeveless tunic. As a great concession, following the tactless remark about pearls, she rummaged around in one of her numerous baskets and produced a net of gold links in which to confine Khurrem's heavy mass of hair. This she handed over with a grunted, 'Take care of that, it's gold. It came all the way from Venice and I must say it's very pretty work, for infidels, that is.'

Khurrem, who had never heard of Venice, received it with rapture and put it on straight away.

Fatma watched disapprovingly. 'It's better, but not enough. You must have some covering on that head.' She pounced on a short length of plum-coloured silk, left over from Khurrem's tunic and dexterously folded it into a small turban which she pinned securely to the back of the girl's head.

'Stop making faces at yourself in that mirror, and help me tidy up,' she said grumpily.

'But it looks lovely!' squealed her novice, ignoring her instructions and instead flinging her arms around her. 'Oh, Fatma, you have been kind to me! I will try hard – I promise. And, I'll be good and not speak until I'm spoken to and not stare around –'

Fatma straightened her own turban. 'Just see you do,' she directed, 'that's all.'

After all this preparation and anxiety it would not have been life if the first encounter with Hafise had not proved something of an anticlimax.

Unwontedly tidy, hair smoothed and confined, and her whole demeanour subdued, Khurrem followed Fatma into the presence the following morning. She did well; she remembered to hand over her basket to Guzul, she kept her eyes on the carpet and her curtsys were perfect. Above all, she remembered that she must not speak unless spoken to; the trouble was, she was not spoken to. Despite her common sense, she was in her own way both a romantic and an egotist. She behaved like a meek young slave whose one thought was to serve, but she did not feel like one and indeed was incapable of feeling like one. So she had been quite sure, despite every quelling warning from Fatma, that Hafise would talk to her, discuss her design with her and generally be aware of her. She was disappointed.

Hafise, that stickler for good manners and etiquette, bowed kindly when Khurrem was presented but otherwise ignored her. In the animated discussion that following the unfolding of the celebrated garment and laboriously prepared designs, she addressed herself to Fatma, of whom she approved as a servant of great efficiency and long service, and permitted an obbligato of comment from her own two maids because she was fond of them and they had served her faithfully and well. It never occurred to her to include a young novice in the conversation; she would not have considered it becoming.

Khurrem would have found all this less galling if she had not been so much impressed by the lady. It was the whole impact of her sweet yet formidable personality. Watching her closely from under demurely lowered lids, the girl decided that Hafise would never need to impose discipline as did the kiayas, by shouting or slapping or other punishments. She simply *was*; only a fool or another most remarkable person would ever attempt to face up to her. She sighed, deeply conscious again of the feeling of exclusion and inferiority which had attacked her at her first sight of Gulbehar. But that had been because Gulbehar was beautiful, had beautiful clothes and jewels, loved and was loved. She looked the part, even if her performance was not up to it. Hafise was the real thing. She looks like a queen, Khurrem thought, with unaccustomed humility, and she behaves like one, too. Oh, I wish she'd talk to me! If only so that I wouldn't feel so left out of everything. It was sheer childishness, as she realized as soon as the thought was formulated, but that didn't make the feeling any less poignant.

She spent the morning doing, literally, nothing, marooned in one corner of Hafise's salon, sewing basket beside her, hands folded in her lap, while the older slaves and the Sultana herself had an enjoyable time, first tearing the robe, the design and the colour scheme to pieces, and then putting the whole thing together again. Throughout, Fatma, deferring, and displaying an implacable dignity which made Khurrem wonder if this was the same woman who was wont to scream across the Silk Room, kept control of the situation by a word here, an expressive shrug there, until, by the time Hafise's midday meal was brought in, the whole project had been accepted as originally planned.

'That went very well, I shouldn't be surprised if you couldn't start to work this afternoon.' Fatma spoke rather thickly through a mouthful of rice and vegetables. They were eating a hurried meal in a corner of the terrace between the harem and Hafise's quarters, while her ladyship ate in state inside. Fatma was pleased. Their meal had been brought from Hafise's own kitchen. 'You did very well,' she added graciously.

'I didn't *do* anything,' replied Khurrem, stonily. She looked at the dish, copiously filled, between them on the carpet. She didn't want anything to eat. Another injustice.

Fatma's eyebrows went up. 'That will soon be remedied. You'll find you'll have enough to do once she lets you start. You'll be hard put to it to keep your work neat and your wits about you when madam comes looking over your shoulder every five minutes to see how you're getting on and then complains you're not working fast enough. Take it easy while you can.'

'She won't do that!' gasped Khurrem.

'Won't she, though! Oh, I saw you mooning over her out of the corner of your eye. All I say is, she's a great lady, and the greater they are, the more wilful they can be. You don't know the ways of the great, yet. You'll learn.'

Khurrem sighed, feeling again the sensation of being solitary and forlorn in the midst of superior beings. Fatma, slowly consuming an orange, watched her shrewdly. The girl was over-awed; possibly just as well, since she was normally more than a little forward, but she had backbone and Fatma judged that she would learn, as she had done herself, how to conduct the daily intercourse with those in authority. To appear to grovel, without doing so, to have faith in one's own ability, to develop a smooth and ready tongue — all these lessons she had learned over the years, until they were second nature. Now look where she had got to. A year or two, or even less, and the headship of that greater silk room in Istanbul would be vacant, and she, Fatma . . . She shook herself. It never did to lose herself in daydreams. If this girl who was looking so sulky and wasting her good food opposite to her, botched her work, or talked back to Hafise — which God forbid — then there would be no imperial silk room for Fatma.

She spoke sharply. 'Why aren't you eating? You girls are always complaining you don't get enough to eat and when you do — ! And another thing, watch yourself with Guzul and the other one. It won't do for you to get on the wrong side of them. Don't answer them back. Be civil to everybody. *Everybody*, you understand?'

Khurrem roused and sighed, 'Nobody speaks to me. I shan't have a chance to be rude or civil.'

'My God! The arrogance of it — stop feeling sorry for yourself and listen to me. In no time at all, they'll all be talking to you. Now, if her ladyship sees something to criticize, the other two will do the same. Mark my words, there's nobody more ready to kiss your arse when things are going well than a body-servant, or to kick it when they're going badly. So you have to see they go well — are you listening to me, girl? Because it isn't only your future at stake here, but mine as well. You have to do a good job and be nice to everybody in sight, even if you hate them and they seem to hate you. Right?'

She had Khurrem's attention now, all right. Eyes like saucers, cheeks glowing, she hung on Fatma's every word.

Fatma pointed to the cooling food. 'Eat!' she commanded. 'Whether you want to or not. She's capable of making you work all night if she feels like it.' She wiped her lips, sat upright, placed her hands on her thighs and glared meaningly at Khurrem.

As she watched, a slight change crept into the expression of the large red-brown eyes which were fixed on her face, a sharpness, a look of determination. A hand advanced to the dish and the long fingers began dexterously to roll rice and vegetables into a ball.

'That's better! Don't forget to wash your hands when you've finished.'

# *12*

On that prosaic note, a hurried dabbling of fingers in cool water and an equally hurried drying of them on Fatma's handkerchief – Khurrem hadn't one – they were swept back into the presence.

'Now we are ready to start,' intoned Hafise sweetly, the moment they appeared. She sounded, and appeared to be, in the best of moods. God grant she stays like it, thought Khurrem, suddenly conscious of trembling and sweating fingers. They seemed very thick and clumsy. It would be better if I could just start, she thought, if I could just go back to the corner over there where I sat this morning. After all, I don't want her personal attention, at least not yet. After all, if I'm on display, best to wait until there's something to display. Perhaps Fatma – she looked appealingly towards that lady, who did not look at her. Hafise did. Apparently for the first time.

'Now, child, show me what you can do,' she directed, and Sirhane thrust the basket of sewing implements and thread into her hands. Khurrem looked about her in dismay, but practicality would keep breaking in.

'There should be something to protect the carpet from loose threads, and the robe from the carpet, perhaps?' She spoke diffidently, remembering just in time not to address herself to Hafise, who had not, after all, asked a question, but to the maids. In the background she saw Fatma nod sharply in approval. Hafise merely seated herself on the low divan which served her for a throne, lifted her beautifully chiselled nose, and appeared to be waiting. Guzul and Sirhane looked at each other, apparently nonplussed.

'The girl has made a reasonable request. See to it,' came from Hafise.

Fatma rescued them, murmuring, 'A shawl, perhaps, anything of that sort,' and Guzul vanished into an inner room.

Hafise examined her delicate fingernails, rearranged the folds of her peacock-coloured tunic over the cushion of her divan, unmistakable signs of impatience. Fatma cleared her throat and was glanced at.

'Yes, Fatma?' The tone was cool, but still civil. Guzul had better be quick.

'If I may suggest, my lady, the girl should sit by the door to the terrace, to get the benefit of the light.'

Guzul reappeared, breathless, arms encumbered with cream-coloured damask, and her lady's large eyes swivelled momentarily in her direction.

'Over there, Guzul,' the forefinger flickered in the general direction of the terrace.

God bless you for ever and ever, Fatma, thought Khurrem, gratefully measuring the distance from the divan to the door. The fountain will be between us and she won't be able to see me directly at all.

Hafise's voice broke in on her rhapsody.

'Is there anything more you need, child? If not, get to work, get to work!'

Rattled, Khurrem gasped out, 'No, madam, yes, madam,' turned on her heel, remembered her curtsy, made it badly and fled away thankfully to her refuge by the terrace doors.

Fatma's eyes flashed, but the Sultana laughed, 'See, a good omen for the work! The girl's as anxious to start as I am. Work away, little one. Forget where you are.'

Small chance of that, thought Khurrem, as with shaking hands she laid out gold thread and implements. The thick damask cloth on which she sat, cross-legged, threw up the sunlight and Guzul, bringing the magnificent soft green satin garment, smiled at her encouragingly. She smiled back and drew a long, relieved breath. She had her own corner. Now the real test began.

She was already engrossed when Fatma padded across and threw her wide shadow across the work. She bent down without speaking and pulled the garment round to look at it. The pattern had been tacked neatly into place and the first few stiches in gold laid in.

Fatma grunted, 'Well, so far, so good. You've got that nice and straight. Any problems?'

'I don't think so. Oh, Fatma, you're not going to leave me?'

'Sh! Don't shout. Yes, there's nothing for me to do here, now. I'll come back from time to time to see how you're getting on. You've made a good impression, but don't forget all I've told you.' She nodded meaningfully, and turned abruptly.

Khurrem stopped work long enough to watch her superbly dignified leavetaking. She heard the distant ripple of Hafise's voice without understanding what she said. That it was something pleasant she could tell from the sudden change in Fatma's expression. She was actually smiling as she backed out of the room.

Left alone, Khurrem was once more a prey to nerves. She had forgotten to ask how long she would have to stay, she had forgotten to ask this, she had forgotten to ask that. Stupid, she admonished herself, you'll be told, and no mistake about it, when to come and when to go. But so far as the work goes, you're alone and nobody can or will help you. She withdrew her needle and looked at what she had so far accomplished. It looked good, just as her work always looked good. The design was the finest she'd ever done – Fatma had said so and she was inclined to agree herself. What was different were the circumstances. Something good must come out of this. What, she was not sure. Fatma was always on at her about her future as a kiaya, about their future when the Sultan died and the Crown Prince followed his father to the throne. According to Fatma, they would all be translated to the palace at Istanbul. None of this interested Khurrem very much. She was young, she lived in the present. But it would be exciting to see Istanbul again, especially as a member of the Sultan's household.

She started and looked guiltily around. Great God in Heaven! She'd only just started on this fateful piece of work and she was already daydreaming! This would never do. She gave her head a determined shake and took a careful stitch. Her work was good and would be good, wherever she did it and whatever the circumstances. So long as she remembered that she would keep her self-confidence and all would be well.

Above the pleasant sound of the fountain, she could hear the chatter of voices as Hafise and her two maids entertained themselves arranging flowers in enormous copper bowls. Or rather, Guzul and Sirhane arranged the masses of tulips and peonies and Hafise, head on one side and frowning in concentration, told them where they had gone wrong. None of the criticism was very serious and it seemed to be punctuated by outbursts of laughter from the lady and giggles from the maids. To Khurrem, frowning in concentration, it was a most relaxing and attractive sound, and the particularly elaborate medallion on which she was engaged grew effortlessly under her nimble fingers.

She took no notice of the passing of time. The sun grew hotter and then moved away. She stitched on, by now totally unaware of the activity on the other side of the large room. By the exercise of will and self-reliance she had created her own corner, just as she had done in the Silk Room; so that when an imperative voice broke her concentration, she looked up numbly, for the moment completely lost.

Hafise had most commendably continued with her usual avocations. She was, although her household would not have credited it, well aware of her faults of impatience and dominance. She was also aware that boredom was her chief enemy. Because she had nothing to do that extended her she harried the slaves. The creation of this garment as a setting for her magnificent gift was neither here nor there, simply a way of passing the time. If she could find nothing else to do, she would begin to worry this obviously promising yound maid who was doing the major part of the work and this would be wrong. At the same time, Hafise's principal interest was always in people, and Khurrem's appearance and personality, so far as she had been allowed to express it, was interesting. Hafise found her eyes straying in the direction of the terrace door more and more as the afternoon lengthened. The girl was reported, too, to have come from near her own part of the world. She had every intention of cross-questioning her pretty thoroughly, but supposed it would be unfair to unsettle her too soon.

The flowers had finally been disposed to satisfy her. Sirhane had been given precise instructions — it was an act of kindness to give the dear creature precise instructions and so save her the agony of taking a decision by herself — where to place the bowls. It surely was time to allow herself the luxury of doing what she really wanted to do. Hafise rose to her feet and crossed on silent slippers to the terrace doors. She noted with approval that her approach was not noticed. The girl was completely immersed in her work; indeed, the way she applied herself was almost feverish. Hafise allowed herself a moment to enjoy the unconscious picture the girl provided. Someone, presumably the girl herself, had done very well to select that precise shade of mauve for her gown, to blend with the richly coloured hair, and the green of her own magnificent robe was a pleasant contrast. What a lot of embroidery the child had achieved in one afternoon – obviously she had no lazybones here! She deserved a rest then, and Hafise who had controlled her natural curiosity far too long, deserved an outlet. She said gaily:

'Put away your needle, little one, and tell me about yourself!'

Naturally, Khurrem was both paralysed and stricken dumb. After a moment she began struggling to her feet and was told peremptorily to keep still 'and put away your needle or you will prick yourself and get blood on my beautiful gown.'

'Oh, no, my lady!'

Hafise noted approvingly that although her hands trembled, her movements were deft as the needle was carefully removed, stuck without fuss into its protective sheath and placed in the basket. The gown was folded over affectionately and the hands laid at rest in the nervous lap. The girl had large eyes, too intelligent to be doglike, and turned them on her attentively, but still she did not speak about herself.

'Come, come! Speak up. Where was your home?'

So began the inquisition, and although Khurrem had been obliged to tell her story so often that it was beginning to bore her, she told it well. With economy, too. She sensed that enchanting as this lady was, she would not have any scruples about making it plain if she found her a nuisance.

Hafise was far from bored. She approved of this direct young creature, basked in the admiration evident in her eyes and mentally tut-tutted in a motherly way at the slender figure and thin wrists. Perhaps the child was not getting enough to eat – sometimes she wondered if any of the younger slaves had enough to eat, but was always assured that they did. She exclaimed with pleasure when she elicited that Khurrem was being taught to read and write, but the intercourse cooled slightly when she enquired if the girl was being instructed in Islam.

After a brief silence – 'Yes, my lady.'

'That is good. And it gives you peace?'

A longer silence and then, 'No, my lady.'

The silence was even longer, while Hafise digested this and decided to take it in her stride. Khurrem sat silent, she looked worried, as well she might, and ever so slightly mulish. Fatma would have recognized the expression, and it was well for her peace of mind that she was not present.

Hafise was not used to a truthful answer when she questioned her servants as to their welfare; they told her what they divined that she wanted to hear. Since her household was one in which nobody practised cruelty for its own sake this attitude worked pretty well, though hardships there were a'plenty since hardship and suffering was the daily lot of everybody except those with rank and wealth. It said much for Hafise's greatness of mind that she instantly recognized that from time to time someone would give a truthful answer to what they regarded as a serious question. A lesser woman would have had the girl beaten for impertinence. Hafise said kindly:

'Why do you think this is?'

Khurrem looking miserable as well as obstinate, replied, 'I was brought up a Christian. I cannot change.'

'Oh, hush!' said Hafise involuntarily, shocked at this apparent determination to be a martyr. 'There is but one God and your Jesus is one of our prophets – '

'Yes, my lady.' Khurrem really did not know what had led her to speak so downrightly. She had kept her own counsel pretty successfully so far and had decided to go on doing so. She already regretted the impulse but knew she could not retract without ignominy. The Sultana's kindness and interest in her, her status, had all betrayed Khurrem into telling the truth without thinking, as if, like an all-powerful mother Hafise would be able to resolve her problem for her.

'Well, then,' Hafise looked at her expectantly. 'The problem is only a little one, surely, half way to solution,' and she smiled and waited for the girl to agree. With a little more adroitness, and experience, Khurrem could have seized this opportunity and escaped with her integrity and her doubts intact, but, conscious only of the enormity of what she had done and its possible effect on her future and Fatma's as well, she could only remain still, head downcast and obstinately silent.

'Come now,' Hafise spoke sharply. 'what is the difficulty? You must make an effort, you know. Have you told the mullah about your doubts?'

Khurrem shook her head and said desperately, 'I mean – no, my lady, I haven't.'

'Well,' Hafise looked up to the ceiling and spread out her hands as if calling on heaven to witness the unreasonableness of such a performance, 'If you won't discuss your position you can't hope to resolve it, you silly girl. Now, why have you not told him?'

Khurrem opened her mouth and then shut it again. Why, indeed? Except that she, like his principals, had soon perceived the old man's shortcomings. He was pious and gentle but not overburdened with brains. In no way, for instance, as clever or as courageous in defence of his faith as her own father. Thought of him steadied her. He would not have thought much of her present behaviour. She could almost hear his firm, unhurried voice delivering one of his favourite aphorisms: 'There is no situation from which a man may not extricate himself if he will only exercise his wits.' Well! By failing to use her wits she had certainly got herself into a very tight corner indeed. However –

'He is very old and gentle, madam, I am afraid to distress him.'

Hafise grunted, if so elegant a sound of disapprobation could be termed a grunt, but she was slightly mollified. The child was clearly a good, honest girl but with too much of a mind of her own. It was not entirely her fault if none of the senior officers of the household had failed to perceive this and deal with her before allowing her into the presence of her mistress. She looked kindly into the large tearful eyes raised to hers and decided to handle the situation herself. She asked, 'How old are you, girl?'

'Eighteen, madam.'

'Little better than a child,' Hafise nodded. 'And when you were at home did you do as your parents directed?'

Khurrem swallowed and nodded, remembered her manners and hastily said, 'Yes, madam.' This was as nearly true as it ever is.

'Very well. And now you are in my care and I stand in place of your parents, so you must do as I tell you and believe what I require you to believe.'

There was silence, and perhaps Hafise would have been wise

to terminate the interview there, rising, uttering some kindly platitude and leaving the girl to come to terms with the situation by herself. But the Sultana was too much of a human being, and too involved with any situation in which she found herself, to leave well alone. It is also conceivable that she found her final adjuration a little too much for anyone but a fool to take seriously. In her defence it should be pointed out that quite half of her time she had to deal with fools and succeeded admirably.

Certainly Khurrem looked thunderstruck and sat speechless, a flush rising gradually from her neck to her hair. Hafise, conscious of handling the situation badly, too self-possessed to flush, was also silent. Finally she said, 'Is it too much to ask − for your own good? Remember that is why I ask.'

Khurrem could not resist the appeal. At the same time she also felt that the Sultana little knew what she was asking. She said simply, 'My father is a priest of the Orthodox Church. As soon as I could understand he taught me that God is love. Ours is a religious home, my lady. How can I turn my back on that?'

How indeed? Hafise, not herself a particularly religious woman, nevertheless understood the gravity of the problem and contemplated her slave with fresh eyes. Everything she had learned about her was stimulating and interesting. Also, she was bound to admit, a lot of it carried the seeds of difficulty. Insulting Gulbehar, for instance. She had not lost sight of that incident, and really the girl's behaviour on that occasion sorted very ill with her present claims of a superior conscience. For a moment Hafise considered her with suspicion, but Khurrem looked − and was − so genuinely woe-begone that she dismissed the impulse.

What then should be done with her? She was obviously a good and valuable slave, and after all, still very young. It was totally unacceptable that she should be tortured or beaten or worse, and not to be thought of, executed, as the law required for heretics. One of the most learned imams, or even a judge, must be prevailed on to talk to her. Islam must bring its forces to bear and snatch this brand from the burning.

At this moment a shadow fell on them as someone walked unhurriedly along the terrace outside. Hafise looked up sharply, guessing who it must be. Khurrem, intent on preventing tears from spilling down her cheeks, did not notice.

Hafise exclaimed irritably under her breath. Her son was her joy and her delight, but this was not a moment at which she desired to see him. It would be most unbecoming if he should come face to face with a mere novice, especially a novice in such a state of distress, and quite unthinkable that she should not receive him immediately.

She said peremptorily, 'Dry your eyes, child, and go to Guzul in the inner chamber. I will think of some means to help you, and send for you when I am ready.'

Khurrem went thankfully; and Hafise noted that despite her agitation she gathered up her impedimenta neatly and remembered to make a reasonably good curtsy. A girl of character, she told herself, and I don't make mistakes about that, at least – I've seen too many slaves. She shan't be sacrificed if I can help it. She sank down on her divan, thoughtfully biting her thumb. It was possible, of course, that after a little reflection in the inner chamber, she might be more tractable, but Hafise thought not; indeed, such was the impression the girl had made on her that she would have been slightly disappointed if she proved so easily manageable.

Prince Suleiman, entering close on the heels of the fluttering Sirhane, was in time to see the baffled, worried look on his mother's face before it was replaced by her usual welcoming smile as she rose and made a deep reverence.

What now? he asked himself. He had had a pleasant and successful day in the Divan. He hoped selfishly that it was not to be marred by reproaches, as had happened too frequently of late. But then he reproached himself with lack of charity towards his mother. Poor lady, this time of waiting for they knew not what was harder on her than on him.

It seemed that whatever was disturbing her was not to be communicated. While they talked warmly and easily of the day's events, he watched without seeming to, the quick thoughtful glances she kept shooting at him, obviously trying to make up her mind whether to tell him or not. For a quarter of an hour this inner tussle went on until he could bear it no longer.

'Mother, would you rather that I left you? If not, will you in Allah's name tell me what is troubling you?'

She had been sitting, staring beyond him, biting her thumb. At this her eyes flew to his face and her fingers closed over the thumb, making a fist. For a moment she stared at him and then dropped the hand and gave a rueful sigh. She said abruptly:

'I am worried.'

'So I see.' He smiled and tried for a lighter note. 'Has some unfortunate slave displeased you?'

'You saw her?' demanded Hafise, incredulous. He shook his head, while she rose abruptly and began pacing, murmuring, 'Poor child, poor child.'

He murmured, 'I was only guessing,' and, perceiving her distress, stopped smiling, and asked, 'What has she done? If she it is, of course, and not he.'

Hafise stopped in her tracks and said abruptly, 'It is not fitting that I should discuss my novices with you. But' – the pacing began again – 'in this case perhaps you can advise me better than anyone.'

Suleiman spread his hands, 'I'm at your service, as always.'

She looked at him over her shoulder, 'You will be angry,' she warned him. 'And yet you should not be, for if the position was reversed you would behave in exactly the same way.'

Since his mother was talking in riddles, Suleiman said nothing and waited patiently for her to come to rest and be explicit.

'She's a Christian,' she said abruptly and turned round and faced him, frowning. She looked up into his face questioningly, obviously waiting for him to react with displeasure. But he said equably:

'Most of them are.'

She made a little clicking sound, tongue against teeth.

'No, no, you don't understand! I am concerned about this girl and therefore express myself badly. She is now – still – a devout Christian, a priest's child and intelligent, not one of these pliable little creatures who do as they're told and believe what they're told because they haven't the sense to do anything else.'

She sighed, relieved to have stated her problem in terms which she hoped would win sympathy for the girl and still very much aware that her own probing curiosity was largely to blame for bringing it into the open.

Suleiman looked grim. He found it difficult to sympathize with what he regarded as wilful heresy in anyone. In a mere girl he found it incredible. Women were subordinate, pliable creatures, to be protected for their own good. So the Koran and the traditions taught. Yet so much of what was taught was daily contradicted by his ordinary experience. When, for instance, had he ever believed his mother to be an inferior creature, or seen her need the protection of any man?

Nevertheless, a slave, and a young slave at that – and it was all very well for Hafise to affect to despise the majority. Where would she and he be if they were not pliable? He said as much, reasonably, and his mother turned round and looked at him.

'I am not devout,' she said accusingly. 'At least, not very, but you are and I honour you for it. And so, too, is this girl, and I honour her, too, and so should you – '

'She is a heretic, an infidel,' he pointed out. 'She has been shown the truth and will not change.'

'By a stupid old man who is relegated to teach stupid girls because he's not fit for anything else!' She was getting just a little heated.

Suleiman blinked at her vehemence. 'Mother, if he is not fit for his post he should not hold it.'

'As to that we shall see – certainly he has failed utterly to make any impression on this girl who says he is so old and gentle she did not wish to distress him!'

'She said that?' Suleiman could not restrain a smile.

'Exactly so.' Perceiving her advantage, she pressed it home. 'It seems to me that we cannot blame the girl if we fail to teach her right.'

'But, mother, do I understand that you also have failed to change her?'

'I am not a teacher of religion.' Eyebrows delicately raised and a half-smile, but he judged that she was getting impatient. He was well aware that she was as much an autocrat as his father and himself. She would, therefore, insist that her argument be taken seriously. She would not be fobbed off with half answers.

'Am I to look to everything in this household?' she continued. 'I must have advice – this child must have advice. Is there not some learned man in your circle – '

'Mother – a female slave, a novice?' His voice was gently incredulous.

'A member of your household, a valuable member of your household – or will be, when she is older,' she pointed out, chin in the air.

Suleiman became thoughtful. The idea of inviting his tutor, for instance, or the local mullah, to undertake the instruction of

94

a female novice certainly did not appeal to him. He could imagine the courteous incredulity with which it would be received. And such a precedent! At the same time, no truly devout Muslim could refuse such an appeal. Something must be done, both to save the girl, for even without a soul she was still valuable, and for his mother's peace of mind. At a lower level, he was conscious of a natural curiosity to see what kind of creature such a girl could be. He said stiltedly, 'If you wish, mother, I will speak to her myself.'

This was something she had not brought to the forefront of her mind. The idea might have occurred somewhere on the tempestuous wave of her thinking, but she had not examined it and certainly not adopted it. She said abruptly, 'That is not fitting. I told you, she is a novice.'

As she withdrew, he advanced. 'This seems to me unimportant. I believe I am well fitted to instruct an ignorant child – better than your mullah, for instance.'

She was silent, gazing at him with wide, troubled eyes.

'Today,' continued Suleiman, 'I have dispensed justice in the Divan and no one has dared to question what I did. I rule this province. Therefore it seems to me acceptable that I should try to resolve a small problem to please my mother.'

She was touched and smiled at him, but did not think it was as easy as that. 'This is your harem and we have rules for governing it. No girl below the rank of ikbal is ever presented to you. If we depart from them, there will be – talk. Some of the women here – '

He knew who and what she meant by that. 'No one questions what I do. And I have never heard that anyone was unwise enough to question you. Great heavens, mother, you break rules every day!'

She smiled a little at that but could not be cajoled again and became serious and silent for a moment before announcing her decision with a sharp little wag of her head. 'Very well, it shall be done. Now, if you are willing.'

He was surprised. 'You are very precipitate. Have you a reason?'

'Yes. The girl is here now. She is greatly troubled and will therefore, I hope, be more easily persuaded. No one else is here but Guzul, who would cut out her own tongue if I told her to – in this way the thing will not be underlined. It is too much to hope that it will not be gossiped about, but at least we can make it seem unimportant.'

He smiled a little but was compelled to admit that her reasoning was sound. Hafise clapped her hands to summon Guzul.

It is not usually held that the most direct way to a man's heart is through the intellect. Suleiman was certainly not predisposed to find Khurrem attractive. There were, he knew, a number of female Muslim saints noted for piety and learning and he did not feel any particular attraction to them, either. The character his mother had given her had certainly not prepared him for the actual physical girl. Moreover, Guzul, out of the kindness of her heart, had taken advantage of the sojourn in the inner chamber to get to work on her reddened eyes and nose with rose-water – in short, Khurrem appeared before him looking pale, defenceless and interesting.

Hafise said severely, 'Khurrem, do you know who this gentleman is?'

She performed her deep and graceful reverence, did not dare to look up, and murmured that she did.

'Very well. Now you will listen to what he tells you of the nature of Islam. He is much wiser than me or the mullah.'

'Yes, madam.' The girl gave a momentary, desperate glance upwards. Suleiman caught a quick flash of bright brown and found himself wondering if her eyes were really that colour or if he had imagined it. He decided quickly that it was beside the point anyway. He was not, he remembered, pleased with this girl, who had worried his mother and was giving him trouble at a time of day when he was tired and wished to relax. To his view, the opportunity to embrace Islam was God-given, to be accepted with joy, and unquestioningly, especially by girls. But charity is enjoined on all, and so he tried to understand and so to help her. Because he was insecure, he adopted a tone of grandeur.

'How does it happen that a girl like you questions the wisdom of the mullah?'

She came back at him, quick as a flash. 'My father is a priest of the Orthodox Church. He taught me, and what he taught me of God's all-embracing love bears little resemblance to what your priest tells, or indeed to what I have suffered at the hands of Muslims such as the Krim!'

For a moment the face of this wise courageous man with his ideas on religion and the place of women far ahead of his time was poignantly before her mind's eye. Above all, she was aware that she was shut up, and that the thing her father and her people prized above all was freedom.

Hafise watched her son blink and repressed a smile. Nobody had ever spoken to him with such conviction or such bluntness before. She waited anxiously, praying that he would not lose patience.

He was silent for a moment, and then said gently, 'So that recently you have not seen much evidence of the love of God, either with Muslims or if what I hear is true, among your own people. I mean,' he went on, seeing her questioning look, 'that the Kozaks have little enough reason to praise God since they are cast out of their own land and persecuted.'

'God does not do that to us, but man!'

'That is so.' He folded his hands on his thighs and smiled at her.

Khurrem, who was, after all, under considerable strain, for one did not lightly involve oneself in theological discussions with one's ruler, particularly when one was only a slave and a girl to boot, clasped her hands tightly. He was disconcerting in his good humour and also, she dared to think, a little self-satisfied. Common sense dictated that that would have to be accepted if he could not be punctured by reason.

'Well, but – ' she stammered and then remembered to insert, 'my lord.' She rushed on while she had the courage, 'Your priest says that the Holy Book allows you to make war, which we all know to be wrong, for we should love our fellow man; also it allows you to take slaves – '

Her objections were typical of the sort of thinking you got from Christians, thought Suleiman. Still, she was an honest and courageous girl and not to be demolished too roughly. He had to remember that his purpose was to persuade her, to bring her to Islam. He smiled at her again, therefore, and somewhat timorously, she smiled back. The young man lurking inside the theologian noted in passing that it was a surprisingly pretty smile, and he went on:

'Islam has regard to man in all his actions, it recognizes that he is imperfect and makes allowance for this. It knows that man is warlike and will not change his nature, therefore the Koran makes rules for the conduct of man. Christianity pretends that because war is wrong it does not exist. See how the rulers of the West make a mockery of their religion. And you – you complain of the position of slaves in Islam, but honestly now, are you worse off or better than when you were at home with your family?'

'I'm shut up!' she spat.

'So you are,' Suleiman blinked again at her vehemence, but continued to speak mildly. 'You are kept safe. You are a woman, and therefore sacred. How did you come here? Because your own people did not guard you. God knows they've lost plenty of young people to the Krim, but still they do not learn and so you were brutally treated and finally brought here, where we will keep you secure until you can earn your freedom in an honourable marriage. Surely that is worth something to you?'

He looked at her expectantly, and Khurrem looked long and earnestly back at him. She was settling down a little now, no longer terrified that she had botched everything, though pretty sure that she still had a very nervous path to walk and no room for manoeuvre. She had got into this situation through talking without thinking – she would have to think very quickly and surely indeed to get out of it. One thing was certain; neither now nor at any time would she underestimate Prince Suleiman. Glancing slyly up at him as he talked, she took in the controlled strength of the wide, narrow-lipped mouth, the dominating beak-like nose. She found his heavy grey eyes attractive, but very solemn, and wondered in passing what, if anything, would make him laugh. He was like no young man she had ever met, which, she supposed, was natural, since he was a prince and she had never met one before.

All this passed through her mind while Suleiman waited for a reply. He found this quaint little creature's intent gaze disconcerting but by no means unattractive. Her eyes were glorious, and it was impossible not to note the grace of the slender body, the small breasts rising and falling rather fast beneath her modest robe. He cleared his throat a little desperately.

Khurrem started, realizing that something had to be said.

'I – I hardly know what to say, Sir.' She swallowed hard. 'You have given me a great deal to think about, things I never heard before.'

Hafise nodded approvingly in the background, but Suleiman who had not entirely lost his grasp of the whole situation, said rather sharply, 'Did not the mullah say anything like this to you?'

She looked at him appealingly. 'No, sir. He teaches me to read the Koran, and asks me if I understand what I read.' She felt this was rather more than a fair statement. Of late, the old man had got into the habit of setting a passage for her to read and learn by heart and then falling asleep.

Suleiman made an impatient sound, and Khurrem, gaining courage, went on, 'I have been at fault — I should have asked him to explain more.'

'The teacher is in charge of the lesson, not the pupil.'

This downright statement disconcerted the girl utterly, although it was not meant unkindly. Suleiman had rather enjoyed the prospect of acting as mentor to an ignorant slave and here it had not turned out that way at all. Of course, he had defeated her in argument and it would have been a poor thing if he couldn't, but he did not feel that he had dominated the situation as he should. A girl, he felt, should not talk back; but on the other hand, when she did, how remarkably attractive she could be in a totally unusual and unexplained way! Now, of course, she was looking at him as if he had shouted at her, which he had not done, had not meant to do, but had simply stated an uncontrovertible fact.

Hafise, who had been a most interested witness of the whole interchange, decided that both parties needed a little help.

'I think it would be only kind to my novice to give her time to think over all the new things you have told her, my son. After a little while, I am sure she will be able to tell us both what we want to hear.' She spoke smoothly but with authority and looked meaningfully at Khurrem.

'Yes, madam. I am grateful to you, my lord.' The eyes swept up to his face again, were lowered, and Khurrem made two quiet curtsies and was gone.

Mother and son looked at each other. Hafise said, 'If I may say so, I think you managed that exceedingly well, my lord.' Privately, she thought her son look as if a small bird had flown into his face and pecked him, but that he had on the whole enjoyed the experience.

Suleiman said nothing for a moment, and then asked abruptly, 'What is that girl's name?'

BOOK TWO
# *Favoured*

# 13

Hafise's estimate of the effect of this encounter on the harem was just. First of all, the whisper spread round the place like wildfire: 'The girl Khurrem has caught the prince's eye!' Women gossiped in corners, behind doors, and stared after the girl as she went unhurried and apparently unconcerned about her business. Then, as the days passed, and she was not given better living quarters, finer clothes, or more important, was not (so far as they knew) summoned to the prince's bed, the whispered statement became a whispered question – 'Has the girl Khurrem caught the prince's eye?'

Presently, Hafise knew, if not given more to feed on, the gossip would cease altogether and things would continue as before. But, the question was, did she, and more important, did Suleiman, want things to go on as before? There was no doubt in her mind that he had found the girl interesting. She had watched the exchange of tremulous smiles, the effect of Khurrem's unusual personality on him – an effect which made itself felt in his unwontedly quiet, almost meek acceptance of her more vehement statements. There was no doubt about it, the girl had a way with her and Suleiman had responded. They had talked together in the kind of isolation which takes no account of surroundings or the presence of others. The thing could certainly go further, could be made to go further if she wanted it to. (Khurrem's possible feelings in the matter did not concern her. Any slave would jump at the chance, obviously.) But she hung back, why, she was not sure, except that possibly the role of matchmaker was distasteful to her, even if it was a recognized part of her duty as Sultana. It would be so easy to have the girl there in evidence, whenever Suleiman made his daily visit. She did not; indeed, she made very sure that she was out of the way, long before the sun showed the faintest sign of setting. She took herself to task; an opportunity to supplant Gulbehar was being missed. If she was not very careful her son would forget Khurrem, lose interest, and the chance, perhaps the only one, would be gone.

What was she waiting for? She approved of Khurrem; she had intelligence and dignity and probably stamina as well. What she was waiting for, Hafise decided suddenly, with the insight of love, was for Suleiman to show some greater sign of attraction to the girl than simply to ask her name. He had not even bothered to enquire if she had professed Islam. Sitting in her pavilion, hands twisting in her lap, Hafise glanced over her shoulder at the now familiar little figure occupying its usual corner by the window. She watched as the right hand holding the needle was vigorously extended and then drawn back, the red plaits quivering in the rhythm of the work. She sighed, propped her head on her hand, and went back to her worrying. Soon the famous garment would be finished and Khurrem dismissed with kind words and a present to the Silk Room. The thing would be over and done with, as if it had never happened. But it will be Suleiman's fault — she burst out to herself. I cannot make him follow his own inclinations!

At that moment a timid cough interrupted her. She looked up wildly to find that her novice was kneeling on the carpet in front of her and looking up expectantly.

'Yes, child?' Her voice was harsh and she cleared her throat.

'Please, madam, I'm ready to sew on your stones. The first part of the pattern is complete.'

'Of course.' This famous robe! Now she hardly cared what became of it. She sighed, and summoned Guzul. While the diamonds were being fetched, she looked down at Khurrem and instructed her to hold up the garment so that she could see it.

'It's lovely,' she said at last, and sighed, again.

Khurrem carefully eased the heavy silk back into her lap. Her lady was clearly not in very good spirits, but she was no longer frightened of her; like Guzul and Fatma she now had a pretty accurate appreciation of Hafise's temperament and was warmly devoted to her. She waited tranquilly therefore until Guzul returned with the jewelbox and presented it to her mistress.

'Come here, child,' directed Hafise. She opened the protective silken bag and shook a small drop of yellow fire into Khurrem's palm. She, who had never seen a diamond in her life, knew nothing of the reverence in which precious stones are held, looked at it with interest but certainly without awe and said, 'Oh, my lady, what a pretty thing!'

'Pretty, indeed,' interjected Guzul drily.

Meanwhile Khurrem, shaking the stone gently, had turned it over and noted the two holes drilled through it.

'Why,' she announced matter-of-factly, 'it's a button.'

Even Hafise was constrained to laugh at this down-to-earth statement, and presently Khurrem, for no other reason than that everyone else was laughing, joined in. They were in the midst of this cheerfulness when Sirhane preceded Suleiman into the room. Hafise was delighted. She swept to her feet and extended both hands, exclaiming, 'My lord, I am honoured by this early visit!'

Even as she greeted him it did not escape her eye that his eyes briefly followed Khurrem as she backed meekly away to her corner.

Suleiman visibly responded to the lighthearted atmosphere and his mother's warm welcome. Just lately he had not been sure of his welcome and this made a pleasant change. What was the joke, he asked, and could he share it?

Since it involved Khurrem and gave her the opportunity to bring the girl forward in the most natural way, Hafise was delighted to tell him.

'Ah, yes,' said Suleiman, 'Khurrem,' and it seemed to his mother that his voice lingered over the name.

'Come here, Khurrem, and tell us if you approve of my buttons,' said Hafise, beckoning. A silly remark, she thought, a little wildly, but I doubt if they're listening to me.

Khurrem, eyes downcast, cheeks becomingly pink, approached and curtsyed.

'They're very beautiful, madam,' she said demurely.

'In that case, you'd better give back the one you've got in your hand,' interjected the irrepressible Guzul, albeit in a low voice.

Khurrem's eyes flew wide open as she brought up the hand containing the stone and opened it. 'I had clean forgotten!' she gasped in her natural manner. The contrast between her previous remark and this one was so irrepressibly comic that everyone started laughing again.

Khurrem herself, however, was disconcerted. Her cheeks flamed and she extended her hand, the diamond winking on her palm, and bent back her fingers as if mutely appealing to someone to relieve her of it; which the practical Guzul promptly did and dropped it back into its silken bag.

'But, Guzul, give them all to Khurrem. She has now to sew them on to my robe.'

It seemed to Hafise that in the midst of the laughter and gentle confusion, her son and Khurrem seemed to stand aside. Both were smiling, both had actually laughed, but neither seemed involved. Khurrem's cheeks were pink — but then, hadn't she just made what might in other circumstances have been rather a serious blunder? On the other hand, she wouldn't have made the blunder if her mind had been wholly on her work.

As for Suleiman — well, what of Suleiman? He sat down, he continued to smile, his large eyes ranged round the room, but he did not look at Khurrem. Rather, he looked at anyone and anything but Khurrem. So that's it, thought Hafise. How foolish I am. I should have realized how difficult it is for a young man in his position. He simply doesn't know what to do next. She caught the eye of Guzul and indicated by the slightest movement of her head that she and Sirhane should leave, and as soon as they had reluctantly withdrawn, she looked at Suleiman expectantly. He looked helpless; and Khurrem, she saw to her exasperation, had put down her needle and was glancing anxiously at her, as if awaiting her dismissal as well.

Really, thought Hafise angrily, and not for the first time, is everything to be left to me? She controlled her temper however and spoke gently to her son.

'Since Khurrem is here, Sir, no doubt you will wish to hear from her own lips what progress she has made in her religious studies.'

Suleiman turned his eyes in the girl's direction with every appearance of discovering her for the first time. He smiled, and Khurrem's cheeks flamed again.

'Have you considered carefully what I said to you last time we met? Speak freely, now.'

Really, thought Hafise, has he no sense? Speak, freely, indeed!

Fortunately the girl had learned discretion. She bowed her head and murmured. Whatever it was that she said, Suleiman was satisfied, but he persisted.

'And you have realized the error of your thinking and are ready to profess Islam?'

For a moment Khurrem's soft jaw appeared to set mulishly, or perhaps Hafise imagined it, but she spoke without hesitation and more clearly this time:

'I'm ready to profess Islam, my lord.'

Suleiman laughed delightedly. 'This is splendid news! I am happy for you.'

Khurrem, who knew nothing of his piety, appeared somewhat taken aback, but thanked him demurely, and glanced at Hafise, obviously expecting to be dismissed.

That lady was drawing a sigh of relief on her own account. Suleiman would never know the hours of careful persuasion she had devoted to Khurrem during the past week or so; and while that young woman had listened carefully and agreed with all that had been said to her, one never knew. She, too, smiled with relief and added her congratulations, while wondering what Suleiman would do next. Now was the obvious moment to dismiss the girl, but if he wanted her he must now give some sign.

What he did was to ask 'You are a Kozak, I believe?'

Khurrem's face brightened as she gave him a hearty 'Yes!' and in a moment they had gone off again into another of their exclusive exchanges, but this time Suleiman asked question after question about the political misfortunes of that aggressive minority and Khurrem was apparently well enough informed to tell him all he wanted to know.

Hafise listened, half amused and clearly impressed. Presumably the girl had been her father's favourite child and consequently his confidante, but even so she was remarkable in the breadth of her understanding. Hafise could not think of any other woman of such lively intelligence.

She was recalled from her musings by a sudden lull in the conversation. Khurrem had grown self-conscious and lost the thread of her argument. Pink-cheeked again, she hesitated and fell silent. Hardly surprising, thought Hafise, noting Suleiman's ardent, concentrated expression, as he gazed at the girl.

The silence threatened to embarrass them all, but Suleiman rose quickly to his feet. His voice was gentle as he said to Khurrem. 'We will meet again. Please arrange this, mother.' He bowed to Hafise and was swiftly gone.

Left to themselves, slave and lady looked at each other. To Hafise, her son's meaning was plain. He wanted the girl, and her ambition to break Gulbehar's power over him had succeeded – so far. It was equally plain to her that Khurrem, while she might have a general understanding of Suleiman's feeling for her, had not grasped the exact meaning of his last few words. She was confused and a little shy, but no more.

Hafise chose her words carefully.

'It seems that you have aroused my son's interest. I shall talk to you more about this tomorrow. In the meantime, pack up your work and go to your quarters.'

# 14

The Sultan wished to go to Edirne for the hunting; and what Selim wished to do, he did. He sent for Piri Pasha, the Grand Vizier, and commanded him to make the arrangements. The old man came, observed the wasted body and the exhausted eyes, and had it in mind to expostulate. Instead, he paid attention to the note of fury giving an edge to the hoarse voice, and said calmly that everything should be done. The elder of the two foreign physicians, standing beside the bed, caught his eye and dared to shake his head. Piri Pasha ignored him and went outside the great royal tent to give his orders.

Preparations to strike camp were well advanced and Piri Pasha was writing in his own tent when the man came to see him.

'Bring him in,' he ordered the servant who announced him, and carefully covered what he had written. He was sitting quietly stroking his white beard when the doctor came in.

Elderly, and like the vizier devoted to his craft, he came straight to the point.

'He cannot do it — I doubt if he can sit a horse.'

Piri Pasha smiled gently. 'Have you told him this?'

The doctor became agitated and his command of Turkish deteriorated. Something of the sort had been suggested. He stopped.

'And?' prompted Piri Pasha.

The other old man sighed. 'He threw an enamel vase at me and swore to be my death. Instead, he will be his own.'

Piri Pasha shook his head. 'We cannot stop him going to Edirne and maybe the exertion will kill him, as you say. But if he goes there and finds that it is all beyond him, then I think it very likely that he will die of frustration. Neither you nor I can keep him alive. You know this as well as I do.'

'It is my business to save his life as long as I can.'

Piri Pasha became irritable. 'Don't be obstinate, my friend. Even I who am not a physician know that he is dying. He has been dying for months. Even Selim cannot stand it much longer. We must allow him to go about it in his own way.'

The doctor threw up his hands and was silent.

Piri Pasha looked down at the writing his hand concealed and changed the subject. 'You know that there are certain – conventions – to be observed at the death of a Sultan?'

The man did not altogether understand. Piri Pasha was patient. 'We have agreed that our master is near to death, have we not?'

'Alas, yes.'

'Very well. When you think the signs are unmistakable, send for me, but tell no one else – no one at all, not even his bodyservants – that he is dying. If death were to come suddenly so that you are taken by surprise, still send for me and still tell no one else. This is very important. Can I rely on you?'

'Can I ask if this is what he would wish himself?'

Piri Pasha smiled again, with approval. 'I can assure you that it is.'

The doctor bowed. 'Then you may rely on us.' And since there was no more to be said, he went, unhurriedly.

Piri Pasha did not lift his pen again. What he had written was brief, but he judged it enough. He rolled it small and carefully concealed it in his sleeve. Then he turned his orderly mind to what else must be done. Messengers, discreet, courageous, were the first essential. One to Istanbul to watch for any sign of a rising and, if necessary, act against it; the other to find Suleiman at Manissa and give him Piri Pasha's word that the Sword of Osman was his. Men of his own command, on whom he could rely implicitly, above all, to keep silent. Silence and discretion, these were the first essentials, and everything ready in advance, so that when the time came and the indomitable Selim came at last to his end his sword and his throne might pass without threat or bloodshed to his only son.

Eight days, Piri Pasha reckoned they would need, that was, of course, if the event happened at Edirne, as seemed very likely. Four days for the messenger to reach Manissa and deliver his message, four days for Prince Suleiman to reach Istanbul. Eight days' silence and concealment, in case the janissaries got wind of the Sultan's death, and rose in some kind of madness, or in case a revolt came out of Asia to threaten the new Sultan. The old man folded his arms on the table and began to consider the possibilities of trouble. Not high, he thought; praise be to Allah, Selim had no other sons to challenge the young Suleiman, and had long ago put to death his brothers so that they had left no offspring to challenge him, either. He did not question the harshness of these acts of the Sultan; they were prescribed by the law, and thus accepted by all dutiful Ottomans.

There still remained the janissaries; their behaviour could not be predicted. They were devoted to Selim, whose greatness as a leader and a soldier was unquestioned. His way of life – an annual campaign, constant warfare, and consequently constant booty – had been their ideal. They asked only that this should go on forever.

Violent revolt was the only serious worry Piri Pasha had in connection with the prospect of Selim's death. Whether such violence could be forestalled and prevented would depend on one thing: the personality and determination of Selim's son. The speed with which he responded to the summons, the face he presented to his ministers and commanders, and above all to the janissaries, when he appeared before them, was all-important. The plain fact was that Piri Pasha was unable to forecast what this would be. True, he had been the boy's early tutor, but he could have no way of knowing how the smooth-faced, biddable and quick-witted boy he remembered had developed. Reports had come regularly from his later tutors and had been a source of satisfaction and encouragement. He had progressed from governorate to governorate, always hard-working and meticulous, giving no one a moment's anxiety. And none of this, thought the old man, drawing a sudden sharp and tremulous breath, will be of the slightest use, if he has not the wit to grasp the meaning of a word or a situation without hesitating, or the courage and imagination to impress his own personality on those who had been Selim's men.

Piri Pasha sighed. He knew the young man, knew him as well as a tutor can know a favourite pupil, and still could not predict what he would do. Speculation was useless, certainly to a man of action like himself. He could do his duty as he had always done it and no more, and perhaps before he died Selim would give him

111

advice, though of this he was doubtful. His opinion, for what it was worth, was that all Selim's remaining energy and thought were concentrated on winning the battle to remain alive long enough to reach Edirne.

Therefore Piri Pasha, an old soldier, not a statesman, not wise in the ways of courts and supple men, must bear the whole burden. He smiled wryly to himself. The Bearer of the Burden, that was the meaning of his title of Grand Vizier, but never throughout his reign, brief and eventful as it had been, had Selim allowed any of his viziers a free hand. Until now, when he was beyond caring.

Piri Pasha switched to more immediate and practical matters. The messengers. He stroked his white moustache and cogitated, quickly discarding most of the promising men under his command, these as being too old and unable therefore to travel fast enough, those as too talkative to be trusted, others as too young for mature judgement. Eventually he was satisfied with two names, men he judged suitable in all respects. Then, without undue haste, he rose to his feet and went outside to see how the packing up was progressing. During the course of his perambulation about the camp, pausing to supervise the loading of a camel here, to advise on the stacking of weapons there, he found opportunity for short, earnest conversations with two men, one a divisional commander, the other a sword-bearer. Then, satisfied, he presented himself at Selim's tent. Within its green silk folds, he found the Sultan, remarkably restored, being dressed for the journey.

Such miraculous recoveries had happened too frequently for Piri Pasha to allow himself to be much influenced by them. Selim had never looked so ghastly, and the hand which waved away the body-servant who was winding his turban, trembled and was transparent.

'We'll have good sport at Edirne, eh, my old friend?'

'We will indeed, my lord.' Don't bother him with protestations. All he wants is support. He is near to death and must know it.

It soon became plain that he did. He was, to begin with, unwontedly affectionate. Speaking in an exhausted voice, he bade his faithful friend come closer so that he need not exert himself to speak louder. His voice was like dead leaves rustling and Piri Pasha was hard put to it to hear all he said.

'I shall not go beyond Edirne,' he managed and Piri Pasha bowed his head. 'But,' continued the threadlike voice, 'go there I will and hunt for the last time.'

'Sire,' agreed Piri Pasha.

'After that,' continued the Sultan, 'I do not greatly care.'

The Vizier waited for him to continue, although he was accustomed to the sparseness, not to say paucity, of Selim's directions at the best of times. Explicit he was, but never one to waste a word. Now he closed his eyes and was silent. Piri Pasha was frightened. Selim looked so ghastly that he might very well be dying at this very moment, and he had said nothing of the future of the empire, given no instructions. What were they to do without him, unless he told them what to do? He heard his own voice trembling as he leaned towards him.

'My lord, my lord, do you hear me?'

Selim's eyes opened, dull and black. They held no expression, then appeared to consider him and finally decided on recognition.

'Well, what now?'

Piri Pasha sought for words 'Sire, have you no instructions – the Prince Suleiman – ' he could get no further, realizing at last that he wanted a kind of reassurance that it was impossible for any man to give. Nevertheless, Selim apparently realized what was required, and in his own fashion, gave it.

He took a deep, slow breath and the tiny voice, weighing each word, came again: 'The empire – so far all is well. Prince Suleiman is my son and will therefore do what is required.' There was a long pause before he added, 'And you are my devoted servant and will help him to do it. What more?'

Emerging once more into the daylight, Piri Pasha took a deep breath and shook his head. It seemed to him that Selim's testament – if that was what it was – had been of such simplicity as to be valueless except perhaps as a declaration of faith; or, knowing the man, the expression of monstrous arrogance. Nevertheless, so complex are even the simplest and most direct of us, even as he thought these things, he was comforted by what Selim had said. In eight eventful years he had mastered an empire and had always been right, and behind his brief statements and commands had lain a world of thought. This was a matter of history. Therefore did he not deserve that what were probably his last words on these subjects should be taken not only at their face value, but as a summary of all his knowledge and philosophy?

Perhaps it was not arrogance to assume that those he had trained and bred and bullied should now be able to continue without him on the course he had set. His blood ran in Suleiman's veins and the prince's education and training in all things had been devised by his father. That he had not that father's ineffable presence and personality was to be expected, for when could the world expect to see the like of Selim again?

Meanwhile, the least he could expect would be to establish the young man as Sultan, advise and help him to the best of his ability until he was accustomed to his position and then, at last, ask for his freedom and return to his tulip garden. Nevertheless, the next eight, ten, fourteen days, he knew very well, could be the most taxing of his long and honourable career. On his unaccustomed and unwilling shoulders, the whole weight of Selim's empire would rest, and he did not want it.

He thought of these things painfully as the long, long cavalcade made its slow way to Edirne, that favoured and historic place beloved of the sultans for the good hawking when the rivers flooded in spring. He wondered at himself. He had never before shunned responsibility. Selim had issued orders and he had rejoiced to carry them out. There was no rejoicing now. It would be his fate and responsibility if anything went wrong. He watched Selim like a hawk. The worst that could happen would be for him to collapse and die before the eyes of his entourage. That was a fearful possibility which it would be impossible to retrieve.

But, miraculously, Selim contrived somehow an appearance of good spirits, if not of health. He insisted on riding for a while each day, but allowed himself to be carried in a litter for most of the time. He commanded the presence of favoured officials and soldiers as they journeyed and conversed briefly with each of them. Piri Pasha realized that after his own fashion Selim was taking leave of his friends but understood also that he was careful not to let them know this. Selim also knew the rules and was keeping them.

The old man rode on, face grim, heart heavy. He must be watchful of himself, too, and knew it. Useless to make his careful secret preparations, if he betrayed them by his own anxiety. So it was eyes front, too, and no more attention to Selim's condition and needs than he had been wont to give. Does he understand, he found himself wondering, does he know that my every thought is for him and his? And unbidden came the corollary: If he knows, does he care?

Selim never hunted at Edirne again; he did not get that far; less than halfway there, he collapsed. They had left the pleasant coast where the dolphins could be seen playing in the calm sea and plunged inland to the small town of Corlu. Fortunately Piri Pasha was riding beside the litter when it happened. His watchful eye saw the change in the ghastly face, saw the fleshless body slip sideways on the cushions. In an instant the cortège was halted and slaves flew to erect the great green tent, build fires, unpack vessels. The elder doctor appeared at Piri Pasha's stirrup. One pair of steady eyes was raised to meet another, equally steady.

'Very soon, I think,' he said calmly.

Piri Pasha nodded and dismounted. 'I will wait in the ante-chamber,' he said, restraining himself from harrying the scurrying slaves.

There was nothing they could do that they were not doing. A shelter had already been erected around the litter to protect the senseless man both from the late afternoon sun and the eyes of the curious.

In a very short time the tent was up and devoted hands carried the dying man inside. Once isolated from curious eyes, the doctor, an impressive figure, with hands tucked inside his flowing sleeves, appeared at the entrance of the inner chamber and said, 'Sir, it will be better if you wait by the bed. He may regain his senses briefly.'

Stricken, Piri Pasha hesitated. 'Is he – ?' The other old man frowned and made an impatient sound. 'If you wish to see him alive, don't wait. He may speak – I have known – ' He glanced toward the bed, beside which is younger colleague waited, and beckoned urgently.

On the floor beside the bed sat Selim's reader, young, beardless, anxious, a manuscript of sacred writings open before him. Piri Pasha frowned and looked at the physician who murmured, 'He sent for him.'

Piri Pasha's heart beat uncomfortably fast as he bent above

the body lying so flat in the wide bed. Control, control, he warned himself irritably, you've seen death before. This is not the end of the world.

Selim's eyelids quivered and suddenly the fierce eyes were wide open, lucid, looking directly at him. Piri Pasha bent down, but the voice was clear and strong and he heard with ease.

'Old friend, this is defeat at last – no hunting, eh?' He clutched at the Vizier's sleeve, a grasp as feeble as a child's. 'But' – and the hold tightened – 'for the rest, it will be as I say.'

The thin face was suddenly convulsed, and he was obviously speechless with pain. Then as it passed he raised the transparent hand peremptorily towards the youth whose voice began immediately.

'The promise of the All-powerful is salvation,' he intoned, and once again the hand moved – imperious or beseeching, they never knew, for at that moment recognition faded from the dark eyes, the stare became fixed, and immediately Piri Pasha knew he was looking at a dead man. The doctor came to his side and loosened the hand from his sleeve, laying it gently on the coverlet.

'I trust that at the end he told you what you wished?'

Startled, the Vizier stared at him, at a loss. Then he collected himself, said firmly, 'Yes – yes, indeed,' and gestured to the other old man to follow him into the outer chamber.

He was amazed that he felt nothing. The doctor showed more grief than he felt; his only sensation was intense weariness and, yes, relief. Relief that Selim had indeed given his final instructions and had been in control to the end and relief that the time for action had come.

He left the tent, went out into the sunlight and saw that a little knot of men taking their ease nearby were looking at him curiously. Piri Pasha stroked his beard and looked back at them, and apparently relieved at his normal appearance they turned back to what they had been doing, talking, lighting a fire and unpacking food for their evening meal.

Piri Pasha strolled away from them, casually acknowledging the salutations of the soldiers and slaves he passed, firmly ignoring any more curious glances, and apparently making his evening tour of the camp to make sure that all was in order, speaking casually in praise or reproof as seemed to him necessary.

116

Near the outskirts of the camp where the camels and horses were tethered, he came upon a couple of men seated on the ground idly throwing dice. To them too he spoke, whether in praise or blame no one bothered to notice. And when, at the sudden nightfall, they quietly mounted a pair of superb horses and vanished into the darkness, no one remarked that either.

# 15

Because Selim's path to the sultanate had been bloody with murder, anxiety attended his son's accession. To begin with, the brief personal message from Piri Pasha was a source of disquiet to his advisers. 'Do not trust it,' they had warned. 'It might be a trap to bring you to the city with only a small escort. Who ever knew what might be in Yavuz Selim's mind?'

Suleiman said briefly that the general tenor of the message was that Selim was dead, and while they argued he used his eyes. The messenger was exhausted, not pretending, falling asleep immediately, without bothering himself with the purse of gold which Suleiman had given him. And Ibrahim, speaking up for the first time in these august councils, had pointed out that for a message designed to lure a man into danger it was singularly indirect; it did not say that Selim was dead and that Piri Pasha urged him to come – only that the family sword awaited him.

'Which,' said Suleiman, 'is evidence of Piri Pasha's discretion and prudence. I will go.'

Go he did, on the fifth day, riding north along the coast road to Europe. The journey passed into legend: the small escort of trusted men including Ibrahim, his own unassuming appearance, riding a superb grey, but looking like a young monk in his unremarkable clothes. There was the mysterious dervish who stopped the little cortège, clutching at Suleiman's reins and chanting that he was fortunate beyond other men because he bore the name of Solomon and was the tenth of the House of Osman. There was the brief, sharp anxiety when the track ahead was suddenly seen to be blocked by an ox-cart which had jammed its wheels on a narrow bridge across a stream.

Suleiman, anxious only to get on, turned his horse into the

gully, ploughed through the stream and regained the road ahead of the block, where the outriders were still trying to help the peasant to free his cart. Momentarily he was alone and at the mercy of any ambush there might have been, before his companions came rushing up to surround him. Suleiman profited by the experience and after that was more circumspect.

Now the plains of Anatolia had been crossed on the old Roman road to Chamlija, the Place of Cypresses, a height overlooking the Bosphorus, and the Sea of Marmara. They were done with the quiet of the countryside: the red earth was warm in the September sun, where reapers and charcoal-burners greeted the little band courteously and looked after them wondering who they were and where they were going. There were more folk here. They thronged the road and stared, muttered and pointed. It was plain that the news was out and as they rode through Scutari towards the ferry, more people pressed forward and they heard the words 'Fortune attend the son of Selim', first as a murmur and then as an exultant shout.

Suleiman's escort exchanged looks of mingled relief and exultation. It was true, then. Yavuz Selim was dead. No one, and certainly not their young master, need ever again fear his terrible temper and bloody hand. The message had been true; and furthermore, across the gleaming lively waters they could see three galleys approaching to carry Sultan Suleiman to his city.

Suleiman himself showed no sign of relief, or indeed of any other emotion. He had decided about Piri Pasha's message on all available evidence at the outset, but his mind was racing ahead to the next step, the next possible hazard. He hoped, and since the news of his father's death was obviously known, expected, that Piri Pasha would be awaiting him on the other side of the Bosphorus. His support would be welcome, for prominent among those awaiting him would be the janissaries. Before he faced them, he would welcome a word of advice, or even simply of encouragement.

In the meantime, once embarked on the leading galley, where a priceless carpet was laid over the tiller seat, he looked about him with unmixed pleasure. This beautiful city, lying before him like a mirage shimmering beyond the water, was his favourite place, the one place of all that he counted as home. He gazed across, his eyes drawn as always to the great Mosque of

Aya Sophia and the white minarets rising like spars about it; he looked at the colourful houses, at the cypresses, at the grim walls and battlements and their twenty-four land and watergates. He listened to the voices of the boatmen as they pushed off and the excited cries of little boys who had been fishing along the bank. And suddenly he smiled and said simply to Ibrahim who had taken care never to be far from him, 'It's good to be home.'

The crossing of the Bosphorus was the only respite he knew that day. Ever since the arrival of Piri Pasha's message his mind had been in a turmoil. It was true that he could think clearly and sharply when presented with a practical problem, but his usual calm was gone. His father's death was a shock and surprisingly painful. He had not loved him, and had not understood or in one sense even trusted him, but he had relied on him. Selim represented power. He was a great conqueror and Suleiman knew that he would always measure himself against him and that others would do the same. Like Piri Pasha, he wanted quite simply to ask his dead father how to take the next step along the road. Sitting at the prow of the graceful boat, his eyes acknowledging one welcome landmark after the other, he tried to prepare himself for the next step. But when it came, he had to take it alone, for Piri Pasha was not there.

There were others. He saw them waiting at the quay. There were the palace officials and minor viziers, but of the horsetail standard of the Bearer of the Burden, his lean figure and white beard, there was no sign.

As soon as he was sure, Suleiman stood up. He made no comment, but those nearest him saw the grey eyes narrow and a tightening of the shapely mouth. If any of them understood the cause of this change, he did not care to comment. Already their attitude to him was altering. He was their Sultan; what thoughts and anxieties he had were his alone and he would – must – deal with them alone.

It was clear, even before the galley touched the dock, who would reach him first and what the first priority would be. From the palace gates, from all directions they came running, young lean bodies outlined in blue cotton, grey sleeve caps flying behind them. The bostanjis, that odd corps whose duties seem now so contradictory, for they were gardeners as well as palace guards (and on occasion, executioners) came to greet him silently and respectfully – not so these wild young men, the janissaries, the Young Troops, guardians of the city. They pressed on to the landing-stage, shoving each other aside in their eagerness, hands outstretched. Suleiman remained motionless, waiting for the vessel to be made fast.

He was surprised to find that he was calm, and a little angry. Dangerous they undoubtedly were if they got out of hand, but they were also soldiers, and this was a rabble! Moreover, there was a ceremony to be performed – and where was their commander?

Suleiman stood motionless until the galley was moored and looked down at his most formidable subjects. They in their turn looked up at him. There was a tiny pause in their yelling as he laid a hand on the prow and jumped down into their midst. The blue cotton bodies pressed against him. He smelt their sweat and felt the pressure of their muscles and the knives in their belts. As suddenly as it had stopped the shouting began again and resolved itself into an unmistakable chant:

'The gift – the gift – make the gift!'

Suleiman felt anger, but no fear, rise within him. They had called themselves Selim's children, had deserted his grandfather to serve him, had undoubtedly wept and cast dust on their clothes when they learned of his death, but now all they could think of was the money gift that must by right come to them at the accession of a sultan. He tightened his lips and forced himself to be silent. A show of anger in him would only provoke anger in them. Moreover, as they had been Selim's children, so they were now his, and like children they cried for what they wanted.

Then, and just in time, their commander, the Aga of the Janissaries, a scarred veteran, came pounding up, breathless from his run, grinning widely and proffering a red apple.

He took a long comprehensive stare at his new Sultan and striking him lightly on the shoulder, asked, 'Can you eat the apple, son of Selim?'

'In time,' answered Suleiman, taking it. The apple signified the ancient and most formidable of the janissary brotherhood's enemies – Rome, the home of Christian heresy.

The Aga nodded approvingly and began barking crisp orders. Suleiman noted with approval that they were obeyed. Instead of a blue cotton rabble there was now some semblance of blue cotton ranks, but the shouting did not cease, and would not until they got an answer.

'The gift – make the gift!'

'That also in its time,' said Suleiman, and pushed through them.

The Aga's eyes narrowed and he said nothing, but on the edge of the crowd there was comment.

'Don't talk much, does he?'

'Not much like his old man.'

Suleiman's little entourage heard it as they disembarked and looked at each other, but pushed on, relieved nonetheless. There had been a moment when he vanished into the press of bodies when they felt sure they had lost him, but if he had not been received with acclamation, at least he had not been rejected; had not made a fool of himself.

Under the great plane trees beside the fountain, a quiet man in undistinguished clothes had watched the little ceremony of the apple and the brief exchange of words carefully. Now he also expelled a sigh of relief and shook his head. He did not think there would be an uprising among the janissaries, but he felt a little disappointed. He'll have to learn to say more, he murmured as he turned away, unless he can prove himself in other ways. He wrapped his cloak about him and found somewhere more inconspicuous to sit and wait for Piri Pasha to come. He was the second messenger, a divisional commander sent to hold the city if by any chance Suleiman had failed.

Whatever others might think or say – and very little was said, for the discipline was iron hard – one man heartily condemned Suleiman's performance and that was the new Sultan himself. He knew that he had failed with them, yet could not think what else – or what more – he could have said. Yet once the words were out, he knew they were wrong. He saw it in their faces and felt it in the way they drew away from him. It did not occur to him that but for the force of his personality they might have found a very dangerous way of expressing their disapproval. He had merely walked through their ranks and made his way unhurriedly to the New Palace.

Now, alone, except for the slaves who served him food – which he ate without appetite, hardly noting what it was – he gave rein to anxiety. What should he do next? When would Piri

Pasha come – where in God's name was the old man? He forced his mind away from this dangerous subject. Piri Pasha was an old man and could not travel fast. Moreover, he would have to strike camp, arrange for the transportation of Selim's body – there were innumerable tasks to be performed. It was not reasonable to expect him so soon.

Suleiman swallowed a last mouthful of halva and nodded absently to the page who was kneeling to offer him iced sherbet. If only he had someone with whom to share this worry, someone with real knowledge who could give him advice! He thought of Ibrahim, but shook his head. To send for him would be a real mistake. He was only the Chief Falconer and there had been some surprise at Manissa when Suleiman had directed Ibrahim to accompany him. Besides, what advice could he offer? He was even greener than Suleiman himself in these matters.

It was plain that having eaten, it was now expected of him that he should sleep for a while. His mattress was unrolled in his old bedroom, but Suleiman was in no mood for sleep. These anxieties were pointless and exhausting and he must not dwell on them. If he must think, he would think to some point.

The Aga of the Janissaries had been slow to arrive, that was a point in his disfavour; but when he did arrive it was plain that he had control of his men, so the balance was even. Another point – had he not heard among the cries for 'the gift' the sum of five thousand aspers mentioned? They had demanded three thousand of Selim, so what was he to make of that? Suleiman licked his lips and set himself to think about his janissaries.

The backbone of his army they were, 15,000 dangerous young men, slave children selected for strength and stamina from the Christian peasant families of the whole Turkish empire. Forcibly taken from their families, they were sent to the principal provinces and Istanbul to be turned into soldiers and encouraged to forget homes, families, religion. Under the rigorous training, Christian country lads became single-minded Muslim soldiers, intent on conquest for their sultan and loot for themselves. They asked nothing more, and indeed the more intelligent, and those who seemed likely to ask more, had already been weeded out of their ranks and sent to the Pages School, there to be trained for higher things.

So there they were, a superb weapon or a killing final enemy.

Which would they be for Suleiman? Selim had usually held them in the hollow of his hand. They would expect at least as much of him.

He found that the prospect was less disquieting than he had expected. His whole life had been a preparation for this moment when he must take up where Selim had left off. He had expected nothing else. Today was but the beginning, and he would do better, especially when he had advice – and where was Piri Pasha whose business it was to give that advice? Anxiety began to give place to anger. The old man must know that until he brought the authority of his support and presence and experience, Suleiman would not even be Sultan in name.

He had succeeded in preparing, as is the wont of anxious young men, several cutting speeches indicative of extreme royal displeasure when the Vizier was announced. And, as is the wont of generous and relieved young men, he forgot them all as soon as he saw the weary, dusty figure that advanced and performed deep obeisance.

'Piri Pasha! My old friend!'

He got no immediate answer. The old man, he perceived, was concerned to do the thing properly, and so he allowed his hand to be taken and pressed to forehead and bosom, and while this was happening, noted with concern how aged and thin his old tutor had become.

'My sovereign lord.' Piri Pasha's voice was as deep and soldierly as ever and he made the acknowledgement sound more like a statement of defiance. 'I am concerned to come so late and' – here his eyes flashed angrily at the stewards who had preceded him to announce him – 'find you lodged so meanly. Why,' he demanded of the room at large, 'is the Sultan not given his proper apartments?'

Suleiman, who had himself elected to use the rooms that had been his as a boy, perceiving that there were even more pitfalls for an inexperienced sultan than he had anticipated, decided to maintain a prudent silence, at the centre of a short, sharp fracas.

Travel-stained and weary his vizier might be, but now that he had arrived he speedily made it plain that he had a very firm grasp of all essentials.

'The Sultan will sleep tonight in the royal bedchamber and occupy the royal apartments in the selamik. See to it. Also, send to the Sultan the slaves of his majesty's wardrobe. Immediately — if of course that is the august wish?' The red-rimmed eyes slid from the bowing steward to Suleiman's face.

'By all means,' murmured his majesty, who, relieved from immediate worry, was enjoying himself a little.

'Immediately,' echoed Piri Pasha, allowing his voice to die away on the last syllable and not even looking at the cringing man.

The men had hardly bowed themselves out before the old man began again.

'It is plain to me, sire, that this place is in need of a sovereign hand. Advantage has been taken of your father's long absences at war. These slaves are slack! I did not greatly like the appearance of the guard of janissaries — though their commander has been a good man, a good man, but growing old, I fear.'

'We will put these things right together, Piri Pasha,' said Suleiman simply, concealing his delight that the vizier's reactions were the same as his own. Honesty compelled him to add, 'I doubt if they feel to me as they did to my father.'

'How can they? You are not your father. Sir, sir, I will speak frankly. Your father was — ' he paused, seeking the right word, and hurried on, 'a desperado. Oh, I know he was much else besides, but that side of his character appealed to them, immediately. They felt it. Why? Because they are no more than violent children and so they felt they understood him. They did not, of course. You will find, once you have led them in the field, that you too will have a special relationship with them. What its nature will be, who can say? But it will exist. And they will forget Selim as if he had never existed. They can only think of one thing at a time.'

'Well,' said Suleiman, comforted, but not entirely convinced, 'the one thing they are thinking of at the moment is the accession money. And it seems that the price has gone up since my father's time.'

Piri Pasha's eyes twinkled. 'Sir, it always goes up.' He became serious again. 'It must be paid, by your leave.'

'Why?' demanded Suleiman baldly.

Piri Pasha perceived that Suleiman was not so much asking a plain question from ignorance as seeking an argument, a trick he remembered from his pupil in the past. He sighed, remembering how tired he was, and the ache behind his eyes and the other ache in the small of his back. He also remembered that despite the fact that here were an old man and a young man talking together amicably, it was a momentous occasion when a new Sultan and his First Vizier were consulting together on matters of high importance for the first time. He unconsciously straightened himself as he began to speak.

'Sir, in an unprecedentedly short time the Sultan Selim doubled the size of this empire. He came to power and was enabled to do all this because the janissaries elected to follow him rather than his father. The spearhead of his army is these same janissaries.' He paused and Suleiman nodded.

'So?'

'They are, as are we all, your slaves. They like to fight. They know nothing else.' He hesitated.

'Also, they like booty and there has been much booty over the past eight years,' Suleiman pointed out.

Piri Pasha produced a low growling sound in the back of his throat, and Suleiman almost laughed aloud in pure enjoyment. He remembered that sound from their past arguments. It meant that the old man was having to think hard. He proceeded to demonstrate that he still could do so. His voice was almost stridently military as he replied:

'True, sir, but it did not come from the Sultan; and sometimes, you know, he ordered that no booty should be taken.'

'But not very often,' said Suleiman gently. 'And even when he did, I think they did not go empty-handed from the field.'

Piri Pasha inclined his head in acknowledgement of that undoubted fact and they fell silent. Then Suleiman added:

'But you have made the point. The gift recognizes service. They have earned it. Only,' he added, 'I do not like to be held to ransom.'

Piri Pasha felt sufficiently relieved to stroke his beard. 'It is not necessary,' he offered, 'to pay it all at once. Indeed, soldiers being what they are, it would be to their advantage to pay it, perhaps, in two instalments.'

Suleiman considered this in silence.

'Or,' he amended, 'to give half now and the rest as an increase of pay.'

There was a pause while in his turn Piri Pasha considered. 'It would benefit the treasury. There has been much conquest, it is true, but the cost of war is high.'

126

The comfortable silence of complete accord fell between them. Suleiman felt a glow of satisfaction at the unexpressed but palpable approbation. It also occurred to him that Piri Pasha's intelligence service was both comprehensive and fast. How on earth had the old man learned already what he had said to the janissaries?

Any further pursuit of this intriguing question was interrupted by the arrival of his body-servants and a somewhat worried steward of the royal wardrobe, to whom Piri Pasha issued crisp instructions for a caftan of black and gold brocade, and a jewelled aigrette with a scarlet heron's feather. Suleiman listened to all this with a slight smile and delicately raised eyebrows.

When the slaves had gone, Piri Pasha glanced briefly at his master and explained. A king must be seen to be a king. To ordinary people who might not see him more than perhaps once in a lifetime, his grandeur was the king and the only thing by which they could recognize him. However trivial such a point might seem, he added, taking note of Suleiman's expression, it must be regarded. To have come to Istanbul dressed like a monk, in haste and with a mourning heart was one thing. Now that he was here the business of his life must begin and his first duty was to appear like a king.

Suleiman considered this silently, accepted the implied rebuke to levity and indicated as much by rising to his feet when the slaves returned and allowing his turban to be freshly wound, the aigrette and the heron's hackle affixed and splendid garments put upon him, but he was impatient with the efforts of the men and dismissed them as soon as he could. He had been enjoying the give and take of the conversation with Piri Pasha and regarded this nonsense about his appearance as a waste of time when there was so much to be done.

If the old man perceived this, he did not allow himself to be hurried, but walked slowly around the now splendid figure of the Sultan before pronouncing himself to be satisfied.

'By your leave, sir, tomorrow you will go to Eyup to see the body of your august father interred and there also assume the Sword of Osman.'

'Tomorrow, old friend, yes, all right, tomorrow, I shall be ready to do these things, but, now, today, I want to talk to you.'

Piri Pasha bowed, and inquired formally what it would please his majesty to discuss. Suleiman moved restlessly, irritated by this intrusion of formality. He wanted to get back to the cut and thrust of their earlier talk. And surely, God knew, there was enough to talk about. His own brain seethed. There was so much to be decided. Would he continue his father's policy, steadily consuming the world to the south and east? He thought not. He shrewdly suspected that the west, that did not know him, was ripe for an unexpected blow. The empire itself, was all well with it? He thought not. Yavuz Selim had not been interested in internal affairs – but the old man stood there, head bowed, waiting to be told what to talk about!

He stifled his impatience. Their earlier accord had grown naturally out of their immediate circumstances. He had mentioned a subject and Piri Pasha had responded. This was the way it must be from now on. He was the Sultan and must always take the lead, even from those older and wiser. He sat down on a low divan with the deliberate intention of introducing some relaxation into their talk.

'You have managed this transition with great skill, Piri Pasha. The city appears tranquil and the few people I saw greeted me courteously. Obviously the secret was well kept. My thanks to you.'

The old man placed his hand on his heart and bowed. 'Your majesty is well served by many besides myself.'

But if the gesture and the words were still formal, his face has softened. Suleiman thought the shadow of a smile was visible beneath the white moustache, but it was some moments before he spoke again and it was evident that he had, in his orderly way, been arranging his thoughts to give his new master a clear account of what would be expected of him next.

Tomorrow, he said, would be a great day. At dawn, Suleiman must receive the homage of high officers of state. At noon, there would be Selim's funeral at Eyup, to be followed by his own girding at that same holy place.

'Well,' said Suleiman simply, 'tomorrow I shall be ready.'

'I think,' said Piri Pasha with equal simplicity, 'your majesty has been ready for a long time.'

Heartening though he found this speech, Suleiman was too honest not to discern the generosity that prompted it. Later he learned to conceal and even to stifle his own ready response to enthusiasm, to turn the other man's motives inside out. But he had yet to learn that bitter lesson, and now stretched out his hand impulsively, once more thanking his old tutor.

One lesson he did learn at once. However anxious he might be for further discussion of policy, now was not the time. Piri Pasha, from the height of his experience, and perhaps also from the simplicity which allowed him to perceive the immediately essential, was continuing inexorably:

'By your leave, sir, I have one more duty to perform before I leave you. It will be my honour to instal your majesty in your own apartments. That done, I shall leave you to prepare yourself for tomorrow's ceremonies.'

Suleiman turned a long, considering gaze upon him. Piri Pasha met his eye blandly, fingering his beard.

Suleiman, who had been on the verge of stating in the firmest possible terms that he wished to talk further on matters of the first importance, met that implacably docile eye and took further thought. He remembered the anxiety bordering on panic with which he had awaited the Vizier's arrival, his uncertainty as to what he should do, how conduct himself, even whether he was or was not yet Sultan. Now Piri Pasha had come and was showing him what his first duties were. The fact that they were at once simpler, more superficial, even easier to carry out than he had expected, was neither here nor there. If he needed – and he did – Piri Pasha's advice, then he had better follow it. At least until he knew better. He smiled.

'Very well, old man, for the present we will do things your way.'

Nevertheless, once the little ceremony of leading him to the royal apartments (in a small procession, including the Chief White Eunuch and the Sarai Agasi and several lesser but still very serious minor dignitaries) had been gone through, he conceded, (thought not aloud), that there was wisdom in this arrangement. His old rooms had seemed friendly and familiar but were alive with memories of a young, on the whole happy, but insecure prince. These grander impersonal rooms held no memories at all – he did not remember ever visiting his father in them – but their stately dignity made no demands on him and he could even swear that, seated on the damask-covered divan, he began to feel like a sultan.

Piri Pasha took a kindly leave of him. 'I know it is unnecessary for me to recommend prayer or music to your majesty as preparation for a momentous day. But young men don't always think of the need for rest and your majesty has passed a taxing five days.' Abruptly he bowed low, and adding, 'I shall come at dawn,' went swiftly away.

Alone, but for two pages of the Inner Chamber – solemn-eyed boys who looked overwhelmed with their responsibility, Suleiman considered his surroundings and wondered what he should do next. He was conscious of a very slight sense of anti-climax, for which he castigated himself. A few short hours ago he had been approaching Istanbul filled with foreboding. Only two hours ago, he had been awaiting Piri Pasha in an agony of shame and, yes, fear. Now, here he was, installed in his proper place, looking like a sultan and even beginning to feel like one. Sufficiently like one at least to look about him with some curio-sity not unmixed with criticism. These rooms, stately as they were, lacked colour and elegance, and in his passage through this second palace built by Mehmed II, he had seen enough – not of neglect, whatever Piri Pasha might say, the Sultan's slave household would never forget their duty to that extent – but of a general air of perfunctoriness, as if the lord of the place seldom came to it and did not love it when he did. He drew in a deep breath and came to his feet so quickly that one of the attendant pages almost jumped.

Suleiman's probing eyes, which saw most things, noted this, as he walked swiftly to the window and looked out on the carefully raked gravel and shaven grass. Of course, any boy who had served Selim would be ready to jump. He vowed that *his* pages would learn differently in time, just as this palace would, in time, become beautiful and loved. He looked out at the empty court where no gardeners worked today, at the silent buildings, frozen tents of stone. He could almost swear he looked at the silence itself, it was so tangible. He had forgotten about the rule that beyond the second court there must be absolute quiet, no talking, no sound of urgent feet or bouncing balls or busy hands, all in honour of the presence of the all highest, the Shadow of God, the Sultan. In short, himself.

He smiled ruefully. He remembered resenting that rule as a young boy and was not sure that he altogether approved of it now, even though he was free to break it. Discipline, he supposed, was good for his household and certainly there would be more important decisions to be taken. But, in the meantime, everything else aside, how splendid it was to be here, once more, in his favourite place; to see the towering plane trees, and the sun glinting on the roof of Bayezit's glass pavilion where it would now be his pleasure to take his leisure and watch the roses and tulips bloom on the terrace outside. To know that beyond the three silent courts was the great, exciting world of Istanbul and the islands, the mosques and the bazaars, and above all, its people.

He drew a sudden deep breath and turned away. In the meantime, there was tonight. Presently the Kilerji-bashi would come to him and ask him if he would eat, and when he was ready he would dine – alone, this being the rule enunciated by the great Mehmed who had built this palace and conquered this city. It was a small price to pay for the privilege of being the mightiest prince in the world, but he felt bound to admit to himself that tonight, at least, he would have relished the company of old friends.

Here again, things were going to be different for him. A sultan had no intimates. The people he would see most of were his pages, his eunuchs and his women. Intimacy with the officers of his government was impossible. Selim had solved the problem by spending most of his time on campaign, and in any case Suleiman doubted if intimacy with his fellows had ever been very high in Selim's needs.

But for me – he had almost said it aloud. Whatever Selim had needed of the world, he had taken, and Selim's son proposed to himself to satisfy his own more modest needs, whatever the conventions of the past might say.

He allowed his eye to light on the nearest page and lifted a finger. The boy was instantly on one knee.

'Bring me,' said Suleiman, 'Ibrahim the Chief Falconer. Tell him to come after prayers and be prepared to make music.'

# 16

It surprised Suleiman that he not only slept, but slept well. Daybreak found him calm and rested. He had passed the previous evening in desultory but agreeable talk with Ibrahim and in listening to music. He had been able to think about the things that touched him closest, even if they were not the most important, and as a result had achieved a measure of peace. Now, after prayers and breakfast, clad in the sombre finery selected by Piri Pasha — black caftan and a gold tissue tunic — he was prepared to face the day's programme. Yesterday, in his state of eagerness and ferment, he regarded it merely as necessary but sterile, the mere fulfilment of convention. He had learnt something since then. He now perceived that this dawn ceremony of presentation was indeed no empty formality. The most influential of his slaves would be there to do him honour, and to weigh him up. Equally, this would be his first opportunity to inspect many of them, to look into faces and try to gauge from what he saw in them what he could expect from the men behind the faces, to read what he could from the unguarded gesture or the word spoken without thought. He found the idea stimulating, even exciting.

Piri Pasha, arriving exactly on the minute, was delighted with the impressive figure which swept out from the royal robing-room a second after he entered the reception room. This young man looked magnificent certainly — clad in such garments almost any man could become magnificent — but also formidable; cool, but with an air of controlled eagerness that he found both attractive and daunting.

Bowing low, he gave the customary greetings and if his eyes expressed his whole-hearted approval, Suleiman either did not notice or chose to disregard it. Instead, he said in a low voice:

'Piri Pasha, before we embark on this ceremony, I must thank you for your care of me yesterday, and your good advice. From which I believe I have profited.'

Piri Pasha placed his hand in the formal salutation on his heart. 'My duty and my pleasure, lord,' he replied gruffly. After the tiniest of pauses, he added: 'They wait, my Sultan.'

Gravely, Suleiman raised his hand in acknowledgement, and at the signal, the pages swept open the doors and he advanced to greet his court and his government.

But not immediately. Nothing in his training had prepared him for the scene that met his eyes in that blue and gold dawn. It was not the splendour of their custome, nor the beauty of the garden court which was their background alone which moved him, but their sheer solemnity and silence. There they stood, row upon row of them, massive snow-white turbans, bearded olive faces, flowing sleeves, hands – in particular the hands, some plump, some gnarled, some sensitive and slender, all clasped, motionless, in the attitude of respect. Hundreds of them had come and taken their places in the last hour and he had heard nothing.

Suleiman drew a deep breath and stopped. He would remember this moment all his life, and did not intend to be robbed of it. As still as they, he stood and regarded them, while imperceptibly the eastern sky lightened. Then, nodding gravely, he descended the shallow steps from the selamlik and began to move towards the Gate of Felicity where a throne had been prepared for him beneath a small tiled kiosk. He did not pace gravely as might have been expected of a more pompous or perhaps older man, but walked purposefully and lightly, the walk of a young man anxious to come to grips with the business before him.

Once he was seated on the low throne, he once more looked around him. On his right, the three viziers, led by Piri Pasha, and the two principal judges of the realm, the kaziaskers, white-bearded, magnificent in dignity as well as dress; on his left, the chief officers of his immediate entourage, the white eunuchs, who had charge of the five chambers of pages and the door-keepers and, indeed, all the inside service of the palace.

Directly facing the throne stood the military chiefs, including the Aga of the Janissaries, and the most important personages of the Ulema, the educational institution, or more simply, the Learned Men. There were the principal clergy, and jurists, headed by the Mufti of Istanbul, who, after the Sultan, might be regarded in some ways as the most powerful man in the kingdom, although he had no temporal power. Present in his group was Suleiman's own hoja, or tutor, who since he had presided over the Sultan's education, had earned enormous reverence, and the Head Physician of the Palace, who carried responsibilities on which most men would not care to dwell.

There were many more besides, the Grand Chamberlain bearing his staff of office, treasurers, judges of the army, each in his proper place, each wearing his appropriate robes, for to the Ottoman Turk a due regard for status and ceremony was almost a religious duty.

Suleiman regarded them gravely, still taking his time. Here and there he recognized a face; he recognized still more of the robes and characteristic folding of turbans, for each post had its characteristic uniform and he knew that before very long he would have to know them all, have an opinion as to the capacities and shortcomings of each man. He took a deep breath and signified his readiness. Piri Pasha advanced, prostrated himself and kissed the hem of his Sultan's robe in token of homage.

# *17*

It seemed to Suleiman that night that he had progressed in the brief space of one day into another world and another age.

He had just been served a carefully chosen, indeed exquisite, meal, designed to impress him with the artistry of the palace kitchen and had consumed absent-mindedly everything that was placed before him. The slaves who had worked so hard to give him pleasure would have been pained indeed had they known that he would not have been able to say what any dish placed before him had contained. He was young, he was hungry and had eaten copiously, but his mind was elsewhere. It was entirely occupied with a series of vivid pictures that came and went in no apparent order, and, try as he would, he found himself totally incapable of consecutive thought. That he was worn out, physically, mentally and even emotionally, did not occur to him. Until then, he literally did not know what it was to be exhausted.

So he sat, unmoving and expressionless, while the pages removed dishes and cups, each after his fashion deftly performing his duties and at the same time covertly examining this new, grave figure around whom their lives now revolved. They brought perfumed water and a gold-fringed napkin, and he roused sufficiently to dip his right hand in the bowl and allow it to be dried. Then he made an impatient gesture of dismissal and went back to his pictures. The cypress trees on the road to Eyup, slender and black, the old wooden houses, tumbledown, many of them, but their eaves exquisitely carved, the rapt face of the Mufti at the girding ceremony.

And how simple that ceremony had been, and how oddly unmoved he himself had seemed. It was as if he was split in two, one Suleiman standing, a lonely and, he hoped, impressive figure on the platform supported on marble pillars in the middle of the inner court, between the Mosque of Eyup and the tomb of the saint who gave his name and extraordinary sancity to the place, and the other, unidentified and unnoticed among those priviledged to witness the ceremony. They were very few – Piri Pasha, grave, yet somehow radiating support and approval, the Aga of the Janissaries, suitably grave today, and the two Kaziaskers, the chiefs of the judiciary, unknown quantities as yet. And himself? He had to admit he had felt surprisingly clear-headed and unemotional. Indeed, when the Mufti – old and clearly overcome with emotion of some sort (joy? fear?) – had approached with the Sword of Muhammed, Suleiman had noticed the trembling fingers and had quickly signalled to the Chief of the Emirs, who was supposed to assist the old man, to step forward and guide the frail hands. Without mishap, he had been girded with the heavy sword, and the simple ceremony had been over. He was Sultan.

Except for the vivid faces of the people pressing on all sides to see him, he barely recalled the journey back to Istanbul; but some things stood out – two cats, a black and a grey, gambolling in a deserted graveyard beside the road, the motionless figure of a woman, veiled, shapeless, standing beside a fountain, and dropping in curiously dignified obeisance as his cortège had passed. And more faces – always faces – one in particular . . . he frowned. Who was it? Something he particularly wished to remember about that extraordinary, that never-to-be-forgotten ceremony at dawn. Or rather someone. Now he had it. The Third Vizier, Ferhad Bey, swaggering, restless eyes in a sharp-featured face, the slight hesitation before falling into the required attitude of prostration and kissing the extended foot. Nothing to which Suleiman would point a finger and say 'This I do not like', but nevertheless a man to be watched. And there had been others . . . .

However, it would not do to cloud what he felt to have been, on the whole, a successful day – and God knew, a memorable one – by anticipating trouble. It would come in one form or another, as night succeeded day and when it came, he, Suleiman, now undoubted Sultan of the Ottoman empire, would deal with it.

He became aware of movement of the door, as a page entered

and dropped to one knee. Suleiman looked at him and nodded and the boy announced somewhat breathlessly that the Kapu Aga was waiting to pay his respects. Since this august personage had been much in evidence throughout the ceremonies of the day, Suleiman rightly concluded that his Chief White Eunuch now wished to draw his attention to some matter, perhaps of ceremony, which he had overlooked. Hastily suppressing (to his own amazement) a yawn, he signified that the man might enter.

The Chief White Eunuch, like most of those who had served Selim, had a military bearing, enhanced by his high white turban with its green plumes. He had also learned under Selim not to waste words. He trusted that majesty had eaten well, and that being so, the Chief Black Eunuch was available to provide whatever entertainment for the night majesty might require. Since the day had been a long one, he suggested that should majesty desire a girl, she could be brought to the palace, in order to spare majesty any further effort. If it was majesty's wish, the Chief Black Eunuch would now enter the presence and describe such beauties as were available at the Old Palace.

Suleiman stared at the man, suddenly appalled, and not knowing why. Training came to his aid and he managed to say gravely that he intended to retire immediately. The Kapu Aga bowed. Did Majesty require anything further? Possibly musicians?

Suleiman controlled himself. The man was doing his duty, but would he never go? He said curtly that he was tired and wished to be alone and the man bowed and went, leaving his Sultan to wonder at himself. Why had he felt this sudden anger – for such it had been – as soon as the man mentioned a girl? There was nothing wrong with the idea and in different circumstances . . . . What was wrong with him or this place? Nothing, and since he was accustomed to be honest with himself he could afford to be so now. The events of the past few days had driven her from his thoughts. A man does not waste time thinking about a woman in the face of such tremendous events, does he? Well, does he? He smiled ruefully. Whatever the truth of that might be, she had not been far from them, for as soon as the Kapu Aga had spoken, there she had been, in his mind's eye, as clearly as if it were only an hour ago that she had faced him in his mother's pavilion and murmured something, he hardly knew what, about professing Islam. And he had sat there and smiled and said what was required of him, while all the time wondering what it was about her that was causing this turmoil in his mind and body. Beauty hardly came into it; the world was full of beautiful girls and he had his choice of them. But no, here was this girl, with her laughing eyes and flushed cheeks (not to mention her passion for argument!), a peasant, no more, and he must want her to the exclusion of the rest!

The thing did not make sense — worse, it was witless — but he would have her, and maybe that would be the end of it. The desire would pass and he would regain his balance. After all, woman's place in life was well-defined, necessary, but limited. But, with the clear sight of extreme weariness, he asked himself whether he as Sultan, or any other man wealthy enough to own an extensive harem, might not be missing something that the poor man with his one or two wives might take for granted. Were there some feminine qualities of faithfulness or kindness never displayed nor sought in the mechanical love-play of harem beauties, for instance? He sighed. He knew perfectly well that there were, and feminine intuition and intelligence, too. He had only to think of his mother and her devotion to his father to see them in full array.

Suleiman shied away from this thought. He was not ready to contemplate sharing his life with a woman. He would have this girl Khurrem and see what came of it. Every aspect of his life was changing, this as all others. His mother had been right about Gulbehar, and he had known she was right, but loyalty and a natural masculine unwillingness to be pushed in any direction until he was ready to walk there for himself had prevented him from listening to her. There was Ibrahim, too, but he was an able and vigorous man on the threshold of his life's work. Given work that he would relish he would not miss a lover. And, thought Suleiman, I have work for you, Ibrahim, Allah knows.

He got up and went to his bedchamber, his thoughts turning back to Khurrem, wondering where she was, how soon he would see her, and whether he was making a fool of himself. Perhaps she would play her part and leave the scene as others had done. But that thought filled him with sadness.

The very next day he went to work. He soon found that the loyal officers of his court, with an eagerness that matched his own, all had their own ideas of what he should do first. Suleiman, who knew what his priorities were, listened courteously, kept his own counsel and went his own way. Outside his empire was a vast world waiting to see what manner of man he was and where he would move first. Without arrogance, he knew this. His father had struck terror to the heart of the Western world and he must prepare to do the same. When the spring came he must make war – against the West, since Persia was cowed and Egypt was his. In the meantime, he hoped his actions at home would teach them what to expect.

However, the Western powers, a prey to wishful thinking, noted only that Suleiman indemnified the Persian merchants of Istanbul whose goods his irascible father had confiscated, and set free six hundred Egyptian merchants Selim had imprisoned for no other apparent reason than that they were Egyptian, and decided that a peaceful and perhaps a timid prince had come to replace a tyrant. They ignored the fact that at the same time, he also hanged without ado a powerful admiral of his fleet whose cruelty and veniality had asked for it.

On the other hand, everyone in his household, indeed, in Istanbul, was relieved and delighted when he put down the first revolt against his authority with both a swift and a heavy hand. (Nobody in the West noticed particularly, with one exception, for Egypt was a long way away. Which was their mistake and their misfortune).

A certain Ghazali Bey was governor of Syria, promoted to that post by Selim as a reward for deserting his Mameluke masters when Selim conquered Egypt. When he learned of the Sultan's death and that he had been succeeded by a young, untried prince, treachery being, as it were, his way of life, he had promptly revolted against the Ottomans and made himself master of Damascus, Beirut and Tripoli and most of the adjacent seacoast.

Piri Pasha brought the news to Suleiman and waited, without comment but curious, for his reaction. It came swiftly, almost automatically:

'Then we will send an army and destroy him.'

'Who shall command? Shall I –' demanded the old man.

Suleiman smiled, 'Not you, Piri, I need you here.'

He relapsed into thought. They strolled – Suleiman was not much of a one for sitting when he could walk, but on the other hand Piri Pasha was no longer much of a walker – in the fourth courtyard of the Serai, a small area of pine and cypress forest right on Seraglio point, a favourite spot with Suleiman because there he could look across to Asia on his left and Europe on his right.

The silence lasted, so that Piri Pasha began to think Suleiman had forgotten. 'Who, then?' he pressed.

The Sultan turned his head and smiled. 'We will send Ferhad Pasha,' he said in his cool fashion. Ferhad Pasha was that Third Vizier whom Suleiman so much disliked. He had never said this to Piri, but the old man had sensed it, and was surprised.

'Ferhad, Sire?' he probed.

Suleiman nodded. 'Yes. It is true I do not like him. Ghazali Bey will not like him, either. He is a ruthless murderer and a good soldier.' He turned his head and explained, 'One of them will die, and I shall have one enemy the less. Probably it will be Ghazali,' he added encouragingly.

Piri mopped his forehead and murmured; not for the first time, his young master had disturbed him, reminding him of his outrageous father, but with an odd twist to his thinking which owed nothing to Selim.

He disturbed not only Piri Pasha; when Ferhad caught up with Ghazali, which he did at Aleppo, raising Ghazali's siege and chasing him back to Damascus, where he was killed, Ferhad cut off his head and sent it in triumph home to Suleiman, who received it with suitable plaudits and proposed to the Venetian ambassador that it should be sent to his government as a token of friendship. Or something. The ambassador, no doubt mopping his forehead in turn, had some difficulty in blocking this gesture.

After this, there was little excuse for the Venetians to fail to understand about this new Sultan. But Venice was waning and full of her own troubles, like the rest of the Western powers. Europe was dominated by young men who, unlike Suleiman, really were untried in the arts of government and war. That young man thought about them a great deal. They occupied a secret part of his mind, even while he sat in the Divan, which he did twice a week to dispense justice and promulgate laws, or visited the remoter parts of that enormous palace of his, which was more like a city than a palace. Sooner or later he would have to come to grips with them, and it would be a pleasure, but for the moment they showed no signs of wanting to come to grips

140

with him. Francis I of France was taken up with his bickering with that other golden boy on the edge of Europe, Henry VIII of England, while the Holy Roman Emperor, Charles V, and the Pope worried over the activities of an outspoken monk named Luther. In the meantime, there was Hungary.

A rather wolfish smile curved Suleiman's lips as he thought of Hungary. He sat, this particular day, in the Divan, and while his loyal dignitaries rambled on about foreign policy, giving him the benefit of their advice, he sat, gorgeously robed, apparently listening courteously, one hand absently caressing the ceremonial bow and arrows beside him on the cushion, and decided what he would do.

Hungary! Turkey's oldest and most persistent enemy in the West, now torn by civil war and social strife, and ruled by a king no more than fourteen years old. Ever since the unfortunate child had acceded to the throne, four years before, the conflict had grown worse.

Which, thought Suleiman, was only to be expected. If one thing exceeded the arrogance of these Christians, it was their stupidity. Who could expect to unite a ravaged kingdom under a child? Also, he would be interested to know how they were going to respond to his own demand for tribute, which had been justly despatched as soon as he became Sultan. And there was more to it than that, for even now, this Charles, the new Holy Roman Emperor, a man three years younger than himself, was preparing a marriage between his brother and the child king's sister, Anna, and another between the boy king himself and Charles's sister, Mary, this being their barbarous method of cementing alliances. This was a direct challenge to him, Suleiman, for presumably at some time in the future, even if not now, this alliance would be followed by military help. All the more reason, then, to attack Hungary now, at a time and in a place of his own choosing. That would be Belgrade, the White City, because it was the logical place, comparatively easy of access from Istanbul, a fortified city of great strategic importance, and one moreover which Mehmed the Conqueror and Murad I had both attacked and failed to take, which made it all the more attractive to him. He did not see himself as a tactical genius, God knew, but a gesture is a gesture, and a newly installed Sultan needed such things, especially if he had to follow Selim.

Suleiman allowed his eye and ear to return to the impressive scene before him, curious to learn whether he had missed anything of importance while he had been thinking. It seemed not. They still prosed on, endlessly debating the choice between Hungary and Rhodes as a venue for war. Well, he had decided – unless, of course, Hungary paid tribute, came to heel. He glanced at Piri Pasha who sat, silent in the white satin robes and tall hat of the Grand Vizier. He looked unhappy. Poor old man, thought Suleiman, the familiar enemy is lost to you now, you'll go no more to Africa or Persia, old familiar enemies who are almost old friends. It's the West for you, whether you like it or not. He fidgeted, wondering how much longer he would be able to spend two interminable days every week in this Divan, so much was there for him to do.

# 18

The ladies of Suleiman's household arrived at the Old Palace some little while after the Sultan himself was installed in Topkapi. Their removal had been a formidable undertaking, one demanding careful organization, a certain amount of ruthlessness and a great deal of hard work; in short the kind of enterprise at which the Ottomans excelled.

The principal ladies, of course, left first. That is to say, Hafise – withdrawn, grieving, unapproachable – and all the slaves and household property which she wished to take with her; Gulbehar and her son and her slaves and such property as Hafise was prepared to allow her to take; some of the more effective officers of the household whom Hafise had decided were worthy of the opportunity of serving her in the capital. (No one will be surprised that they included Fatma.) Finally Khurrem, taking with her her clothes, which was all she had, and Meylisah, because Mehmed, appraised at last of Khurrem's probable fate, decreed that it would be improper for a Sultan's kadin, however lowly, to arrive at the Sultan's principal dwelling without even a slave to her name. Clothes and jewels would no doubt be provided in due course, he had stated hurriedly, when, he coughed, Khurrem's exact status became clearer.

Mehmed himself was not making the journey to Istanbul, was torn between envy of those who were and relief that his ageing body and failing powers were not to be put to the test of the rigorous travelling and the even more rigorous infighting and jockeying for position which awaited the more successful at the end of it.

This girl, Khurrem, now. Whoever would have expected the young Sultan's eye to light on her, of all girls? She was not beautiful, and anything but submissive. Colourful, certainly, and as smart as a whip, but the type to comfort a man's bed? No, certainly not. At least, not if he were the man and had the choice. But, of course, the young are always different, and he must remember that he was growing old . . . . However, there it was. His lady had spoken. 'The girl Khurrem goes to Istanbul,' she had said, sitting bolt upright, and staring stonily ahead, and it was about all she had said, apart from such sweeping comments as 'make whatever arrangements seem to you to be suitable,' or, when he had brought her problems of protocol, of what to take and what to leave, which seemed to him insuperable, 'Whatever you decide to do, Mehmed, will be satisfactory to me.'

So, there it was. When he had asked what the girl's status was to be – for, after all, a man takes a pride in carrying out his duties with becoming decorum – she had grown impatient, and cried, 'All that will be arranged in Istanbul! Do but make sure that the girl is ready to travel and has a maid of some sort. Don't pester me, Mehmed!'

So, disappointed, he had made the necessary arrangements and sent for Khurrem to tell her what was to happen. If he had hoped to learn anything from her reception of the tremendous news, he was disappointed.

Understanding only that she was to go with Hafise's household to Istanbul, she had said sunnily, 'Oh, I shall like that!'

'Then you are thrice blessed,' Mehmed replied repressively. She had not even cast down her eyes and expressed gratitude. Sighing, he supposed that if he had had charge of her a little longer she would have learned better manners. What, he suddenly wondered, would the Sultan think of his training if she behaved like this before him? Mehmed shuddered, and added, 'No one cares whether you will like it or not. Remember this, you have been greatly honoured and should behave accordingly.'

Then she did understand. Her eyes widened and she blushed deeply and was unable to say anything. Mehmed, too, was taken aback. Was it conceivable that no one had told her what to expect? Had he been at fault? But he had not been asked to prepare the way with her. Of course, the Sultana Valideh was deeply distressed and might have overlooked this little detail with so much else on her mind. As for Khurrem, she was appalled. Because it had happened some time ago, and had all been so understated anyway, she had tended to dismiss the exchanges with the prince in Hafise's pavilion. He had certainly said they should meet again. Hafise had indeed said that she would talk to her the following day. But with that day had come the news of the old Sultan's death. (Thus did Khurrem distinguish between the great Selim and his son, 'the old Sultan' and the new). Everything had changed at once. Their great lady had been given over to grief and Prince Suleiman had ridden off to Istanbul. She and Meylisah and the other girls had watched him go from behind the barred shutters, wondering in their ignorance at the tiny entourage which followed him, at the speed with which they rode, and why he travelled with such little state. Told nothing, they had whispered among themselves, put two and two together, and, as was the harem's wont, arrived infallibly at the truth.

All that had been weeks ago. Nobody had said anything to her about any change in her status and she had really begun to forget the whole thing. Now this. With so much that she wanted to know, she still couldn't think of a thing to ask Mehmed. Perhaps it was his awful dignity that affected her. She stood, eyes downcast, and blushed. Mehmed found this entirely becoming and softened to her a little.

'When you get to Istanbul you will, of course, be provided with everything needful.'

What, Khurrem wondered, did that mean? Needful for what? Oh, why did these people never say quite what they meant? If the Sultan wished to take her to his bed, she supposed she was willing. She stopped dead at the thought. No, she was not willing! She was appalled. And yet she had not disliked him; and after all that had happened to her she could not feel, and certainly could not afford, gentle emotions, even if she knew what they felt like! So why did she feel such conflict within herself, why did she feel even that he had failed her in some way? She couldn't explain it and decided in the end that the only way to deal with this disturbing situation was not to think of it in connection with Suleiman at all. If she kept the image of the grave-eyed young man out of her mind, it was easier to accept.

Meylisah, representing the conventional harem view, was no help. As they gathered together their sparse collection of clothes and toilet articles, she prattled.

'Only think, if he likes you, he will send for you again and

145

again, and you might even bear him a son. And then, who knows? You might become his favourite kadin and take Gulbehar's place. . . .'

Khurrem was appalled, she was not quite sure why. Certainly, as they had walked from Mehmed's office back to their dormitory she had tried to think the thing over quietly and signally failed. All that had happened was that she had grown blindingly angry at this disposing of herself, this invasion of her most personal freedom, that had nothing to do with being a slave. She tried to tell herself that it was a compliment, it did not feel like one. Meylisah's thoughtless chatter was the last straw. Khurrem stopped folding her clothes and took refuge in one of her characteristic outbursts of violence. Picking up the old guitar with which they had sometimes whiled away their few hours of leisure, she flicked the strings savagely and burst out, 'Shall we take this, then, or shall I be given a new one, more in keeping with my exalted rank? Inlaid with pearls and diamonds no doubt!'

Meylisah stared at her, amazed. She had not the slightest idea what was troubling her. Of course, it would be a disturbing experience for any girl, but there was not one of them in the harem who would not sell her soul for the opportunity! Khurrem must be made to understand that, then perhaps she would be happy again and grateful for the splendid opportunity vouchsafed her. She tried, haltingly, to explain, and her efforts were brushed aside as she had feared they would be.

'The way these great people live is against nature,' burst out Khurrem as soon as she stopped. 'Picking a girl out for her looks one minute. . . .'

'I'm sure that happens everywhere,' interjected Meylisah wistfully.

'. . . and into bed with her the next, without even bothering to find out whether you actually like her, let alone whether she likes you!' Khurrem stormed on, cheeks scarlet. 'Now, among poor people like you and me, if a boy and a girl like each other they keep company for a little while — or at least mostly they do,' she interjected, with unwonted candour, for her thoughts had, as they always did, turned homewards again, and she had remembered certain little local irregularities, 'And *then* they get married. Or sometimes when there's a baby on the way they get married anyway. . . .'

To her amazement, Meylisah seized her shoulders and shook her hard. 'You mustn't say such things!' she cried, 'I won't listen, I won't. Such wickedness – if anyone heard you!'

'That's the way things happen,' insisted Khurrem, wrenching herself free.

'It's not the way things happen here! Turkish girls are virtuous. They have nothing to do with men until their marriages are arranged and the bride price agreed. Even among the very poorest it happens this way. What you say is dreadful, just don't let anyone else hear you, that's all.'

Cut off in mid-flight as it were, Khurrem gasped at her. Because she knew so little of the world, because she was so angry, she had assumed that peasant life must be the same the world over and that the enemy, her enemy, must be people with power, who could force a girl into a match whether she wanted it or not. She sat down in silence and finally said, 'I'm sorry, I didn't know.'

Unusually decisive, Meylisah said briefly, 'Well, you should. You're the one who can read and gets the Koran expounded to her.'

'Oh!' She thought about it. Of course she knew, just as she knew the teaching of the Bible. But she also knew that Christian peasant life had its wisdoms, too.

'I can't help it,' she said eventually. 'I still think it's unnatural. How do they ever get to know each other and like each other? Will I ever get to know this Sultan?'

'They manage, and so will you, I expect,' responded Meylisah stonily. 'And as to knowing the Sultan, that's as may be. Nobody will care whether you know him or like him or not – '

'I shall,' interpolated Khurrem obstinately.

'Well, I daresay,' said Meylisah. She began to tie up her bundle, 'But, Khurrem, it's time you forgot all about your home and your old beliefs. Remember you are a Muslim and a slave of the Sultan. And stop looking back.'

This was good advice and, indeed, exactly the advice she had given herself on numerous occasions. She could not quarrel with it now, but it did nothing to make her happier. Still, the outburst had cleared the air. She was calmer, she knew where she stood. She, too, began to collect her last bits of property and tie her bundle.

'I'll tell you one thing, though,' she said, 'I don't know how you'll take this, but it's true. I'd as lief stay here in the Silk Room with Fatma as go to Istanbul to the Sultan and that's a fact!'

Meylisah was totally silenced, and the rest of their packing was finished with unwonted speed because they wasted no time in talk. When they had finished, they drifted automatically to the window and looked down into the courtyard, which, usually so peaceful, was today choked with wagons being loaded with bales of silks and shawls and carpets and household impedimenta of every description. By the great gate waited an elegant carriage, like a great oblong box on wheels, and painted pleasantly with patterns of flowers and fruit, so that it looked a little like a travelling flower garden. Beyond it waited a troop of janissaries of the Sultan's guard, obviously an escort for the Sultana Valideh, whenever the great caravan should be ready to start its journey.

The two girls still had little to say to each other. Both were oppressed, Meylisah by the uncomfortable glimpse of reality as opposed to her own romantic imaginings which Khurrem had forced on her, Khurrem herself by the prospect of a change she could not evaluate and did not desire.

They had been told that they would be sent for when their transport was ready, and by mutual consent, unwilling to be alone any longer, they picked up their belongings and drifted out into the upper hall where again all was bustle.

Oppressed as they both were, they did not linger. Moreover, Khurrem found herself unnerved by the reactions of a couple of girls gossiping at the head of the stairs. They had obviously just stopped to exchange a few words as they went about their duties, one with a bundle of clothes on her head, the other cradling a heavy pot in her arms. As soon as they saw Khurrem, their eyes widened, talking stopped, and they drew back against the wall, ducking their heads uncertainly as slaves might when suddenly confronted with someone whom they knew to be important, but found themselves unsure of the degree of that importance.

Khurrem's own reaction displeased her intensely. Taken unaware, she stared at them, averted her eyes and positively scuttled downstairs. Embarrassed and angry with herself, she whispered to Meylisah, 'What did they have to behave like that for?' Meylisah was in many ways a fool, but she was sharp enough to interpret the remark truly to mean 'why did I have to behave like that?'

But perhaps it was as well for all concerned that the encounter took place where it did, with a couple of unimportant young slaves. For on the ground floor, in the presence of several of the more senior women, as well as some of the black eunuchs, they came face to face with Fatma, whom Khurrem had good reason to know was never embarrassed and always knew what was in the wind.

She stopped, bowed with the same dignity that she had shown before Hafise, but perhaps not quite so low, and remarked pleasantly, 'Greetings, lady, and good fortune!'

Khurrem managed a reasonable acknowledgement between a bow and a nod and thanked her in a cool little voice that hardly sounded like her own. Something more she felt was needful to someone she looked up to and who had treated her (on the whole) so kindly, and she added shyly, 'I hope we may meet in Istanbul.'

Fatma's smile seemed to express approval as she backed against the wall to allow them to pass, and Khurrem while maintaining a dignified pace murmured to her companion, 'Let's get outside.'

Into the courtyard accordingly they went, where there was too much coming and going and too much noise for anyone to notice them particularly. 'Did you hear, she called you "Haseke"? You see? I *told* you,' whispered Meylisah, and congenital worrier that she was, added, 'Now what should we do? Supposing we get left behind?'

Khurrem looked about her alertly. The exchange with Fatma had done her good, doing more to establish her new status in her own mind than anything else could have done in so short a time. She noted that the bustle, though extensive, was controlled, that the bundles, household objects and rolls of carpet were being stowed into the wagons with deftness and speed. She also noted, rather more to the point, that Mehmed and the head kiaya, both armed with lists, and a little retinue of clerks were stationed beside the great gate. Whatever her view of Mehmed's personality, she had faith in his efficiency.

'We sit here,' she said as serenely as she could, pointing to a great mounting block, a short distance from the door, 'and wait until they send for us.'

# 19

Khurrem was taken aback when she saw the Old Palace, but thought it was probably beneath her dignity to say so to anyone more exalted than Meylisah; which shows how far she had travelled since leaving Manissa, and not only in distance. She was also surprised to discover that the Sultan did not live there, but in another, newer and, she supposed, more splendid establishment on the other side of the city.

During the journey she thought long and not very happily about her situation. She would have to accept it, she saw very clearly, but was as far as ever from seeing it in the terms in which Meylisah saw it. It was not romantic, but degrading, and she didn't expect to be happy or even comfortable. Only one calming thought occurred to her: if all Turkish unions were made in this cold-blooded way, nobody could blame the Sultan if he went about things in the same way as everybody else. This somehow seemed important to her.

Physically, the journey had been without incident, and so far as she was concerned, comparing it with her original trip, the acme of comfort. Meylisah complained more than she did, and she was full of excitement when they arrived at Scutari and she could look across the Golden Horn to the city itself, exclaiming with delight when she spotted a familiar landmark, and digging her little friend in the ribs. But arrival at the Old Palace robbed her of all her gusto, if not her common sense. She remembered to behave with dignity, and said not a word when she saw the dark, even poky rooms which were assigned to them. She could see very well, as apparently the other senior women slaves could not, that they were all in the same boat. Nevertheless, she was treated as someone of importance, by Mehmed's Old Palace

150

equivalent, a stately and immensely dignified black man, younger than Mehmed, who received her with a bow and expressed a certain pained surprise that she had been allowed to make so long a journey with only one slave to look after her, and hardly any comforts. This, he said, would be rectified immediately. It was. Her rooms might be small and dark, but they were equipped with splendid carpets, damask cushions and carved tables, and there was an elegant stove which she thought would soon be very welcome, for there was already a nip in the air.

Meylisah, of course, ran from room to room exclaiming in delighted awe at all this luxury while Khurrem, sighing a little, established herself on a pile of cushions, and looked around with a decidedly muted enthusiasm. Still, she thought, I wanted to be important, I felt shut out when I saw how Hafise and Gulbehar looked and how they lived, and I've always been the same. This was a piece of truth about herself which she had never realized before, and she would have liked to think about it, weigh it up and get used to it. Unfortunately, a visitor arrived and put an end to the self-examination. This was Fatma, as fat and competent as ever, but looking slightly harassed.

Khurrem was delighted to see her. Here's a real friend, she thought, and to people in my position friends are very necessary. This, she felt, was another important truth.

Fatma had come, as she stated in her usual downright fashion, to fit her out with clothes. The warmth of her welcome delighted and touched her. Obviously her protegée was not going to give herself airs, and Fatma, who, after all, had her own problems of protocol and fighting for a place in the sun, put them all behind her and devoted the next couple of hours to equipping Khurrem with the obligatory wardrobe of muslin chemises, brocade and satin caftans, veils, slippers and furs. Since most of the selection was made by Fatma herself, the resulting outfit was elegant in the extreme. Fatma's shrewd little eyes quickly noted that Khurrem was not quite herself. She was docile and appreciative, but there was little sign of her usual zeal and liveliness. Worrying about it, concluded Fatma, which is natural, I suppose. With real kindness, she said gruffly:

'I expect you can have some pearls for your hair, if you like. The Keeper of the Jewels has orders to give you some, in reason, of course.'

'That will be nice,' responded Khurrem listlessly. She roused and smiled at Fatma and said much as she had once before, 'You have been so kind to me. I don't know how to thank you.'

Fatma thought there were tears in her eyes and became really worried. She did not know how to respond to emotion of any kind; it bothered her. The best she could do was to proffer some more advice about the matter in hand. 'If I were you,' she grunted, 'I wouldn't have too many of these pearls. I've said it before and I say it again, it's a vulgar fashion. Besides, if the Sultan likes your hair, he'll want to be able to see it and touch it.'

Khurrem flushed and shook her head. There was an uncomfortable silence, and then she burst out: 'What I want to know is what's supposed to happen to me now. Nobody's told me, you see.'

Fatma blew out her cheeks in combined relief and indignation. Practicalities were her meat.

'This place is disorganized. With so many people coming and going, nobody knows what's what at the moment. But I suppose, since you're her protégée, the Sultana Valideh will send for you and tell you that the Sultan's favour has lighted on you.'

'H'm,' interrupted Khurrem, with something of her usual spirit, 'what a way to put it!'

'No doubt,' responded Fatma quellingly. 'Shall I go on? Very well, then. You'll be taught how to conduct yourself before the Sultan, and *then*, if he wants to, he'll send for you some night, or come to you here.'

'I see,' said Khurrem tonelessly. 'Then what?'

'That will depend on you. If you please him — '

'Oh, I've heard all that! What I want to know is — if I don't please him, as everybody puts it, what then? Can I come back to you in the Silk Room?'

Fatma fidgeted on her cushion, amazed, but touched in spite of herself.

'Now, my dear girl! Why are you so sure you won't? You've come this far. Obviously he liked what he saw of you — whenever that was,' she paused, little eyes sharp with curiosity, but Khurrem was too anxious to think of enlightening her, and Fatma eventually went on: 'And you'll be well schooled in the art of pleasing, and really, you know, he's said to be a very amiable young man — where is the problem?'

This exercise in sweet reason, on a subject in which reason is

152

not normally involved, was all the preparation Khurrem got, for that night Suleiman sent for her.

He had been thinking about her when he woke that morning, and the final conclusion of that thinking was how delightful it would be to have her brought to this charming room where he slept (he had had his sleeping-room refurnished and rearranged in keeping with his own ideas, resulting mainly in the removal of articles of furniture and decoration rather than additions; but the result pleased him). Once there, he hoped she would talk to him in the beguiling fashion he remembered from Manissa; and that afterwards the exchange would take such course as it would. So Suleiman gave his orders to the General of the Girls and went about his daily routine.

Unfortunately, as the day wore on, his mood changed. He was irritated and eventually angered by the slow course of the Divan. He received a whining and almost truculent message from Gulbehar, detailing a list of complaints about her quarters in the Old Palace. He set himself to think about a million things that demanded his attention and found he could not concentrate. When he took up a pen and attempted to put his views on paper the result was worse. The upshot was that he felt gritty and restless and in no mood to set himself to please a girl. If he knew her better it would be less difficult, at least he thought it might be, though you never knew with girls, he concluded grumpily. He wished he hadn't arranged for her to come, wondered if he should countermand his order. But that would react against the girl, he realized. The harem would whisper. Even a Sultan must consider the niceties. His slaves were his family and not to be treated as disposable things.

Khurrem's own frame of mind was pitiable. It was bad enough that the blow should fall so soon, so that she was left without any of the preparation she had been promised, but, as she speedily learned, the harem had its own method of going about this business, with very definite rules which must be respected.

She was visited by the Keeper of the Girls, the same urbane gentleman who had received her on her arrival. He told her of her good fortune, congratulated her, smiling, and handed her over to a bevy of female slaves whose duty it would be to prepare her for the honour so dramatically and promptly bestowed upon her. These women led her away to bath and wardrobe, totally

153

ignoring the timidly expressed protests. In theory, the blushing maiden, trembling on the brink of her happy destiny, was ministered to by her fellow slaves who shared her happiness and delighted in making her as beautiful as possible. In fact, it was as cold-bloodedly impersonal as the preparation of a lamb for sacrifice, and nobody cared whether she was beautiful or not.

Khurrem was stripped, bathed, shampooed, perfumed, had her teeth and ears forcibly cleaned, and was then dressed. The first part of these activities took the major part of the afternoon, the dressing almost as long. She soon found that her protests were mostly ignored and if not, that dealing with them only prolonged the torment. She was moved to ask why she could not be allowed to wear some of the clothes selected for her by Fatma, but this was courteously defeated by the senior of the slaves who had charge of her.

'Your clothes have been selected for you,' she said briefly, 'together with the appropriate jewels. It would not be fitting for you to appear before the Sultan improperly dressed. This is the way it is always done,' she concluded chillingly, and extended a rose-coloured gauze chemise. There seem nothing to do but put it on, together with the long purple gown that followed it and the blinding silver brocade robe that went over everything. They were superb garments but they did nothing for Khurrem.

'I don't really think these colours suit me,' she suggested tentatively.

The two women looked at her and then at each other. 'Of course, you are difficult to suit,' said the older woman, looking down her nose. 'I suppose it's your colouring. Perhaps the jewels will improve things.'

She produced a casket, and handed Khurrem a hand-mirror. There was a diamond necklace, earrings which came down to her shoulders, rings, bracelets; and then they produced strings of pearls and began plaiting them into her hair. It was the last straw. Khurrem wrenched the first of them out of the braid of hair the woman had painstakingly plaited, and flung it on the floor.

'I won't have it!' she cried, and wished her voice sounded strong and resonant instead of merely tearful. All the same, there was a stricken silence.

Finally, the younger and more tactful of the women picked up the strand of pearls, and said, 'But every girl wants pearls for her hair, and see, they're the finest of stones!'

'I won't have them, they're vulgar,' said Khurrem desperately. Even now, she found time to wonder why she was making such a stand and realized that it had something to do with a blind and pathetic faith in Fatma, who now seemed like her only friend, and her own need to assert herself before she was completely overwhelmed.

'Don't you want to be beautiful for the Sultan?' asked the other girl, exchanging glances with her senior. They had had their instructions, which amounted to an article of faith. What were they to do?

'The Sultan won't want to see my hair tangled up with these things,' cried Khurrem, visited by inspiration. So definite was she that they were impressed, instructions or not. Besides, although they were slaves of the Old Palace and not members of Hafise's harem, they knew all about her, knew that she was raw, untrained in the arts by which the harem set so much store, that in some way not known to anyone, she had succeeded in fixing the Sultan's eye, and what was almost, but not quite, as important, had wormed herself into the good graces of the Sultana Valideh. All that made her important, but nothing about her made them either like her or understand her.

The senior of the two had had it in mind to utter a few hints on deportment in general and the art of sexual allurement in particular. She was certainly not going to do so now. A young woman so independent and ungrateful deserved nothing more. Dissatisfied, she ran a critical eye over her handiwork and tugged impatiently at Khurrem's skirt to make it hang better.

'Well, you're ready,' she stated briefly, and shook her head. The girl didn't pay for dressing, but still his majesty must know his own mind, and he must be impatient, too. After all, she'd only just arrived.

Apparently the departure for the New Palace must be private, not to say secret. She was taken to the rear of the building, led along ill-lit narrow corridors and conducted down a narrow stone staircase, holding up her heavy brocade skirt as best she could. The two women came too, helping to lift the train and the trailing sleeves, exclaiming with anxiety as frail silk and gauze caught on projecting ledges and splintered steps. Once when she missed her footing and almost fell, they got quite sharp in their worry. 'Be careful — you'll tear it!' cried the eldest.

'Do look where you're going.'

Khurrem stifled a sob and gathered the robe up almost to her knees. This furtive exodus seemed to her almost the most shameful experience of her life, but they were almost there, it seemed. She felt fresh, chill air on her forehead. There was a door, half open, the impassive figure of a black eunuch guard, and she was outside, in a little unimpressive courtyard where waited another of the boxlike carriages she had got used to on the journey from Manissa.

She was to have a companion on her journey, for one of the women remarked impatiently, as they stood beside Khurrem, holding up her train, smoothing down her veil and adjusting her skirt, 'Now where is she? She gets worse as she gets older – ' And the other said, 'I've never known her to be late, all the same.'

Nor was she late, for at this moment a small black figure materialized out of the shadows and grasped Khurrem's wrist with a clawlike hand. Khurrem gasped and shook it off and one of the maids, pitying her, said encouragingly, 'She's all right, really. Just old and a bit mad, but she's to take you where you're going. Get in the carriage now. You mustn't delay.'

Since there was no help for it, Khurrem allowed herself to be helped up into the vehicle and her spreading garments carefully disposed around her. The old woman followed, mumbling to herself, and they drove off.

# 20

There could not have been a greater contrast between this place and the one she had left. There it had been dark, shabby and ill-organized; here all was light, peace and order.

Khurrem felt rather than saw this, for she was given little time to see anything. The door of the carriage was opened, the old woman, batlike in her rusty draperies, appeared to fall rather than get out and then vanish in the shadows by a door, and a courteous male voice bade her come forward and descend. She was helped out with care and courtesy, had a glimpse of black faces and hands, was set on her feet and told to walk forward. She passed through a narrow doorway, saw another door indicated by a skinny finger.

'You'll find me waitin' for you when 'e's finished with you,' hissed the hateful voice of the old woman. 'In ye go.'

Khurrem shook her head against this final indignity, and stiff with fear but determined not to show it, tottered through into the presence of the Sultan.

She had not really had any idea what to expect, but certainly the room, its furnishings and the man it contained came as a complete, calming surprise. She had an impression of space, pale colour and soft light, of simplicity, and a man sitting upright in the midst of it all on cushions, writing on a tablet on his knee. He did not look up immediately, so Khurrem stood still and had a good look at him.

He was just as she remembered him, dignified, serious, withdrawn. She had not thought at all about how he would appear, except that the Sultan must be impressive, gorgeously robed perhaps, and seated on a throne. That he was not, but clad in a simple light-coloured garment and without even his turban, was a complication because, without any of the trappings she had expected, he still remained impressive, not a man to be trifled with, which was daunting enough.

She had other, practical, problems. They had reminded her that she must curtsy, make proper obeisance, not speak until she was spoken to; when he recognized her she must be docile, smiling and ready to oblige him in every way. But Khurrem in her simplicity had expected that since he had sent for her he would be waiting to welcome her with some semblance of pleasure.

In fact, his silence had continued, it seemed, for quite a long while now, was she perhaps supposed to make her presence known? But if so, how? If she curtsied and he did not acknowledge her, she would have to stay down there on the floor until he did, and she didn't think she could manage that. It was too much. And her heavy garments were becoming heavier; she longed to move. . . .

Suleiman looked up, and Khurrem sank into her curtsy.

Rising at last as best she could, she peeped at him and was dismayed by his expression of hauteur.

Suleiman for his part was simply taken aback. He had envisaged her as he had last seen her, clad in her simple cottons, laughing at the diamond in her hand, and crowned with the braids of her brilliant hair. This white-faced apparition, bejewelled and bedizened, was not the girl he remembered with such joy. He had forgotten that the harem would have to gild the lily and insert its crippling conventions between himself and her. He was angry with himself for forgetting, and quite unreasonably angry with her – he did not know why. For allowing it to happen to her, perhaps.

He pushed aside the writing-tablet with impatience.

'You look very grand,' he said stiffly.

No answer. An upward timid glance and a bob of a curtsy in acknowledgement. Fool of a girl! He felt inclined to send her away immediately, and would have done so, had it not occurred to him that she must be under considerable strain. The harem had not had time to prepare her for this assignation in any way except dressing her. She was not poised and smiling as the girls he'd had on previous occasions had been. Indeed, he knew misery when he saw it, but of course could not guess the reason for it. But if she did not talk and they could not communicate, what else could he do but send her back to the Old Palace? He sighed, and tried to think of the next thing to say. The small, impatient sound stimulated Khurrem to speech as nothing else could have done. She looked down at herself as if she had never seen her clothes before and said:

'I look preposterous — I think, Sire.'

The last three words were so clearly an afterthought, and the whole statement so unexpected that Suleiman nearly gave way to laughter. He now began to remember more about her, in particular her capacity for the outrageous, or rather the utterly truthful. He decided to encourage her a little. He must, though, remember she was after all a peasant girl, and not expose her naivety too much. He asked gently:

'What don't you like about your appearance?'

Khurrem expelled a very small sigh. 'Well — Sire — I don't think I'm cut out for these sort of clothes. You have to be beautiful like — like Mirza, for instance. Besides, it isn't fitting. *You're* not dressed up —'

She paused, clearly thinking she'd gone too far, but when he said nothing, went on 'And it must look very funny in your beautiful pale room —'

This so plainly paralleled his own thinking, that Suleiman sat up and decided to give her his full attention, which he remembered ruefully was something he never did with Gulbehar. He made love to her with his mind on other things; which in a way was restful. He was not sure how restful this girl was going to be, but was inclined to think she would be refreshing.

'And,' finished Khurrem, 'they're heavy.'

Suleiman did laught aloud at this, and Khurrem, relieved, ventured a small smile.

'I suggest you remove whatever you do not want of that — impedimenta, put them over there, and then come and sit beside me here and talk to me.'

Khurrem's eyes widened and she stood quite still for a moment. One of the attractive things about her, he decided, was that while you could never forecast what she was going to say, it was possible at times to read her mind quite clearly. Now she was wondering whether she ought to curtsy again, and obviously deciding against it. Probably, thought Suleiman, she'll do it when she's taken off whatever she decides to take off. He was quite intrigued to see what that might be.

159

All the jewellery, to begin with, which was a surprise. It was not his experience that women parted with jewellery. They were usually looking for more, and he was not going to deceive himself into thinking it was naiveté again. Then the brocade caftan, which he also was glad to see go. He watched with patient interest while she folded it carefully, showing, he noted, respect for its intrinsic value and beauty, whatever its use to herself might have been. Beneath the robe was another, in a purplish colour, which looked quite attractive in the dimly-lit room and seemed to accord quite well with what could be seen of her hair beneath an elaborate veil. She had her back to him now. Presumably her notions of modesty were at war with the convention that a slave does not turn her back on her soveriegn and modesty had won, for she appeared to be fastening a row of buttons down her front. Then off came the veil and the heavy lustrous hair tumbled down her back, but, no, she was not quite ready yet. She turned back to the jewels and appeared to be searching for something – a ring with a solitary ruby – which she shoved on the first finger that would accommodate it.

Now it appeared she was satisfied, faced him and sank into the magnificent reverence he had been expecting.

Suleiman inclined his head gravely. There was a slight edge of mischief about her mouth, not quite a smile, but enough to be noticed by an observant man, and by now Suleiman had become very observant. There she stood, quite delightful in the becoming simplicity she had contrived for herself, very much as he remembered her from Manissa. Now it remained to be seen if she would spoil it all. He had seen it happen. A nervous girl put at her ease by her master would then go too far in the other direction, and, in her relief, assume a most unbecoming familiarity. He hoped Khurrem was not going to disappoint him in this way, but women, even the best of them, were incalculable.

Khurrem, however, was not at all inclined to assume anything. So far she had reacted directly and readily because she had been frightened and keyed up and the Sultan had been kind – well, up to a point. Now that things had got this far, and she was beginning to think again, she was afflicted by overwhelming shyness. She had done nothing she had been told, she had not even carried out her resolve to be quiet and docile. And now he wanted her to talk to him! She remembered all too well what had happened when his mother had said much the same thing. Much better if he got on with what he'd brought her here for, but he showed no sign of that, unless the way he was sitting up and half-smiling at her was evidence of it. She had no idea, because she'd never met a man like him before. So she stood still, looked at the carpet, and ceased to smile.

Suleiman had no idea what was wrong but was by now much more inclined to be easy with her. So he extended his hand and said kindly but firmly, 'Come here.'

Cautiously, Khurrem advanced and settled herself on the cushion he indicated, then raised her eyes to his face. She was still apprehensive and was certainly not going to start talking to him with the freedom she had shown with his mother. She folded her hands in her lap and continued to look at him expectantly. Since for some reason she had again lost her tongue, he decided to help her on her way. His experience of Khurrem suggested that once her imagination was caught she would talk away happily and unselfconsciously until stopped. It was her lively mind, her originality and gusto which attracted him. He wanted to be able to lose himself and his preoccupations for a little while in the contemplation of her vivid little face and excited talk. Unfortunately, he knew so little about her he had no idea what subject would be likely to fix her attention. He was bound to admit also that drawing out intelligent young women, or indeed any young woman, was not a subject high on his list of accomplishments. He said kindly:

'Are you well-housed?'

Minimum response. 'Thank you, Sire, I have two rooms.'

Gulbehar, now, would have given him a complete account of the two rooms, with a list of complaints about their general unsuitability. It was plain that the harem had not yet put its mark on Khurrem. But he would have to try again.

'Did you have a comfortable journey from Manissa?'

'I thank you, Sire, yes.'

Silence. Suleiman began to be a little annoyed and Khurrem to fidget, and her attention to wander. Suleiman's lips tightened. He even began to wonder whether there was not something to be said for the harem system after all. At least properly trained harem damsels did not stare around the room, allowing their attention to wander from their duty. And what, in God's name, was she staring at? He followed her gaze and said impulsively:

'Do you like it? I made it.'

That certainly riveted her attention. The bright brown eyes fastened themselves on his face with a most satisfying expression of amazed admiration.

'You did, Sire? Really? But it's beautiful!'

It was that same small gold ewer he had made in the early days of his apprenticeship, plainer and less taxing to fashion than the more elaborate pieces he had made later, but one which pleased him because his master had praised its simplicity. It was one of his most valued possessions, a symbol of successful accomplishment.

Khurrem came impulsively to her feet. 'May I touch it, Sire?'

'Why not?' He took it from the low table beside him and handed it to her and she sank back on her cushion holding it in both hands.

He watched curiously as the thin fingers travelled over the surface of the gold, and then asked her what she liked about it. For once, although obviously full of attention and her eyes alight with enthusiasm, she was lost for words.

'Why, because – ' she began, and then stopped, deliberated, and finally said lamely, 'It's right as it is. There's nothing to distract your attention from it. I enjoy looking at it.'

Suleiman found himself disproportionately delighted at this praise. However, it was not, he thought, becoming for him to show his feelings, and so he said carelessly, taking the ewer from her, 'It gave me pleasure to make it. I was but fourteen.'

That set her off again. Why did he make it? And he had to tell her why Sultans and their heirs learned a trade, a circumstance which she considered gravely and was kind enough to approve. Suleiman began to wonder who was in charge of this encounter, or conversation or whatever it might be proving to be. But he supposed that if a Sultan selects a young woman for a reason other than the most conventional one, he must not be surprised if the relationship pursues an unusual course towards its inevitable end. She wanted to know next where it was made, so that he began to be a little restless and feel that he would be quite glad to get off the subject of the ewer, however admiringly she might be gazing at him. He told her briefly, 'Here, in Istanbul.'

Istanbul got them both out of difficulty. Khurrem said impulsively, 'Oh, I'm not surprised! Fatma says that all the best things are made here.'

162

Suleiman decided against opening up the subject of Fatma's identity, but was very well prepared to agree with her on the subject of Istanbul. At last they were able to talk without self-consciousness on a subject which roused them both to enthusiasm. Khurrem relaxed at last, mentioned her determination to get back to Istanbul and Suleiman, watching her flushed and now altogether charming face, asked:

'Why so?'

It had been in her mind to tell him the truth: she had believed that return to Istanbul would make eventual escape easier; but she had learned her lesson. She was at ease with him, she liked talking to him, but she was not going to forget that he was the Sultan and unlikely to be amused to learn that a slave whom he had singled out had cherished ideas of escape. She wondered in passing if she still did, and decided to reserve judgement. She said therefore truthfully, as far as she was prepared to tell the truth:

'Because it's exciting. It's the centre of things.'

This pleased him, she could see. He agreed with her gravely (it struck her again that he was not much of a one for laughing) and asked what she had seen of the city. Well, she had seen the Burnt Pillar and the great square where the slave market was held.

'Tell me about the slave market.'

She did so, with gusto, but with rather more sobriety than she had shown till then. It was plain that the place had left an impression upon her, but nevertheless her account of the dealers and her fellow slaves was acute and entertaining. Suleiman wondered about the slave market. When he thought of this delightful girl exposed to the eyes and hands of the rogues he knew to be about in the world, he was aghast. Nevertheless, the system seemed to have triumphed; she had been purchased by his agents, alert and efficient as they were, and here she was in his hands and dedicated to his pleasure. Nor did her mind or body seem to have been damaged by the experience. He suspected that perhaps the triumph was hers rather than the system's.

He took a deep breath, suddenly realizing that since he had first acknowledged her presence in his room he had continued to hold his pen. His right hand was painfully cramped and he was a little annoyed that he should, without knowing it of course, have been so much affected by her as not to be quite as much master of himself as usual.

On all counts it seemed that talk had gone on long enough and something more was called for. He put down the pen, furtively flexing his hand, and spoke authoritatively, cutting through what she was saying:

'Khurrem, come here.'

She looked up in surprise, but came with alacrity.

# 21

Suleiman's formidable anger shocked and delighted many and surprised himself. The occasion of this exhibition was the disgraceful return, without nose and ears, of the envoy sent to the Hungarian court to announce Suleiman's accession. The envoy had also been empowered to demand tribute in return for peace and it was undoubtedly this which had been the immediate reason for his being first thrown into prison, then disfigured, and finally allowed to return home in shame. No one at the Porte can have imagined for a moment that the demands he carried, couched in such high-flown and insolent language as they were, were likely to be received with anything but scorn, but Suleiman in particular had not expected this.

He paced his audience room, giving reign to such a flow of invective that even Piri Pasha, used to such behaviour from his father, was surprised, while the pages and attendants in the background glanced furtively at each other and attempted to slink out of sight.

At first Piri was not quite sure which aspect of the offence had elicited all this heat. Although he felt the insult himself he was not particularly angry or surprised. An envoy's was a dangerous trade and the Hungarians had fallen on evil times. Hence the mistaken violence of their reaction. An act of desperation you might say, and to be expected. Why then was Suleiman shaken by this monstrous wrath? Had he perhaps, contrary to every expectation . . .? He asked, very stiff and soldierly:

'Does this change your plan of campaign, then, Sire?'

Suleiman, after his first explosion, had taken to pacing the floor, something in his movements suggesting the lithe controlled swaying of some huge cat. Had he a tail, thought Piri, he'd swish it.

He stopped abruptly and looked at the old man as if at first he did not know him. Then he said abruptly,

'Change it? By God, no – except in one respect, to hasten it!'

His right hand was clenched against his chest. Piri saw it uncurl and the fingers tap his breast. 'One of my people, Piri, one of *my* people, done to death, as good as – '

The old man thought he understood. 'You have seen him, Sire?'

'Yes, I've seen him, brought to me by his people whom he feels he's disgraced as well as me! And he will not live long, he has that to bear as well. But there is another aspect to this, Piri, and you must know it as well as I. Had he been my father's envoy, do you think he would have been so treated?'

He faced the old man, and Piri whose thoughts had turned in their usual logical fashion to what must be done to bring the war machine into action, looked up, startled. Piri took a moment to marshal his thoughts in this new direction but when he had made up his mind he did not lie or placate.

'Possibly not, Sire,' he said calmly.

'Possibly not,' repeated Suleiman, accenting the first word. 'I *know* he would not. I have seen the intelligence reports. What do the Italians say of me, "a peaceful lamb"?'

'So I believe,' agreed Piri equably, 'That was not wise of them. So far, all they know of you, Sire, is that you are an unknown quantity. It is their own weakness that persuades them thus to make up their minds in advance. They hope you are a peaceful lamb.'

They smiled briefly at each other, with their usual agreement, and then Piri added:

'However, there is one European who sounds a note of warning. If they heed it, we may lose a certain advantage of surprise.'

Suleiman's expression of gratification was revealing to someone who knew him so well as Piri Pasha. He asked quickly:

'Who is he and what does he say?'

'The Venetian, Luigi Gritti.'

'The Doge? I thought he was dead.'

'The Doge *is* dead. This man is his son, an able fellow, but because he is a bastard precluded from service to his government. So he lives here, in Istanbul. He is a merchant and an agent and other things besides – we do not enquire – but a better friend to us than to his own people, I do believe. Briefly, Sire, he has written to the Signoria warning them of your possible intentions and your qualifications for carrying them out. His letter does not accord with the soothing pabulum which went from the Venetian ambassador here and they may discount it. They will certainly prefer to.'

'Well,' said Suleiman, 'Hungary is a long way from Venice, and even if the message is passed on it will not avail them, I think.'

He resumed his pacing and Piri thought that his mind had reverted to the stricken envoy. In fact, it was more complex than that. Suleiman was a subtle man and his reactions seldom direct, except in the heat of battle. At this moment, bitterness that his ambassador had been cruelly tortured, that his own youth and inexperience not only allowed but actively encouraged his enemies to flout him, and his own knowledge that he was facing his first major test before his own generals and army, all mingled to produce in his mind such an excitement that he hardly knew how to contain himself.

He whirled in his walk.

'Bring the standard from the treasury, sound the war drums –' He found his thoughts running so far ahead of his ability to speak, that he was forced to stop, gasping and glaring.

Piri watched sympathetically. If he could not now share a young man's urgency, he could at least sympathize with it. 'I will bring the Seraskiers together for a council of war. You will preside of course, Sire.'

'Aye, I will.'

Suleiman's rage seemed suddenly dissipated, or at least controlled. He looked Piri in the eye silently for a moment. He said, using his Grand Vizier's name as he seldom did,

'Piri Pasha, I am angry and excited and humbled at this moment as perhaps you cannot know. I stand on a precipice and I do not shrink from it. This is the moment for which I have been born and trained and prepared since I can remember. I find I need my friends as I had not expected, but I am not ashamed of this, either. I will not fail them and I look to you to see that they do not fail me, Piri –'

He suddenly held out his hand, his voice trembling on the last word with an emotion he could not diagnose. The old man, equally moved, took the hand and held it for a moment to his heart. Then, both slightly embarrassed, they drew apart, looked at each other and did not know how to go on. Suleiman was quick to realize that something more must be said to bring them past the awkwardness of the emotional interchange. He had not far to look to find it. It had been there at the back of both their minds since the bitter moment of the envoy's return.

'These Europeans sicken me. They cannot be honest friends to each other or honest enemies to ourselves. There will be no regret for a worthy foe when we defeat them.'

Piri smoothed his moustaches and bowed. He had no comment to make on this. Time would tell. He took leave and marched out.

As he went, he wondered. 'Like his father, but unlike,' he thought. 'I never knew Selim when he understood himself. This one does — if that is a good thing for a soldier. Act first and think about it afterwards, I say.'

The great bronze drum stood opposite the Great Gate of the Topkapi Saray. Too restless to settle to any minor task until the Council of War should meet, Suleiman decided to go in state to hear it sound, and accordingly ordered his household about him and went in procession. This act, a minor one which only he could do, led him to another. Beyond the gate, his splendid caftan billowing behind, his equally splendid officers grouped around him and his personal guard of halberdiers or peiks in the uniform that was unchanged from the last days of the Byzantine Empire, watchful about him, Suleiman waited in silence until the great drum under the plane-tree gave tongue.

It was a powerful and evocative sound, but because he had initiated its beating, or merely because his was not a simple imagination, it did not stir Suleiman as he had expected it would. Instead, he looked around him and observed its effect on others. Beneath the plane-tree, beside the drum, he observed that a detachment of janissaries had formed up to receive their pay. A very happy coincidence, he thought, since they would soon be marching, and noted with approval that despite their obvious excitement at hearing the summons for which they had been waiting since his accession, they neither spoke nor broke ranks. The excitement was to be seen in the changes in expression, the involuntary smiles. Inspiration came to him as he watched. He was their honorary commander as had been his forebears since the corps was founded. This was a moment to underline that link with a gesture that would please and be remembered. Now he remembered that he also held rank as a non-commissioned officer in the Corps. He caught the eye of the commander of his guard, said two words to him, and walked forward, alone.

He had perhaps one hundred feet to walk and the Aga of the Janissaries who had been standing idly by to see the pay parade without any particular motive, and had stayed because the beating of the drum heralded great doings, had the advantage of seeing his Sultan moving unhurriedly towards him without escort, before anyone else did. He also had the unenviable task of trying to guess that Sultan's purpose. When it became clear where Suleiman was heading, he saw out of the corner of his eye that the paymaster was rising to his feet.

The Aga thought quickly and took a gamble.

'Sit down. Continue the pay,' he hissed.

The officer obeyed. Suleiman was now in the midst of the men who fell back on either side of him silent and unheeded. They gaped at him and glanced wide-eyed at each other. An interested onlooker could have interpreted those glances – What does he want? Who does he think he is? – and noted the contrast between the drab uniform dress of the janissaries and the richness of Suleiman's robe and turban, but the only onlookers were the Aga of the Janissaries and Suleiman's guard, and neither of these parties could be called disinterested. The one was wondering whether he had wrecked an honourable career by one error of judgement; the others were asking themselves whether their Sultan had taken leave of his senses, and how soon they would have to spring to his rescue.

Meanwhile, Suleiman had reached the pay-table, where he stopped, drew himself erect and said simply, 'Suleiman, son of Selim.'

His face was expressionless and his grave eyes sought the paymaster's sharply. Already prepared by his commander's reaction, that gentleman was not going to risk another – almost – mistake. Also expressionless, or he hoped so, he pushed forward the next pile of silver aspers and the Sultan bowed his head in acknowledgement and scooped them up. He held them for a moment in the palm of his hand, looked at them, and then dropped them into the purse at his waist, where they mingled strangely with the gold pieces placed there that morning by his page. Then he went, quietly as he had come. He did not turn round when he reached the gate, but entered the First Court, the retinue which had waited, startled but disciplined, falling into their proper ranks behind him.

Suleiman, who, as he turned away from the pay table, had been wondering if he had committed the first imaginative act of his reign or merely made a complete fool of himself, was relieved as he passed through the gate, to hear the tremendous cheer that rose from a hundred vociferous young throats behind him. He did not hear, but would have been gratified by the comment of one of his shrewdest servants, the Gatekeeper-in-Chief:

'He's got them where he wants them, it'll be all through the army, by nightfall.'

# 22

The beating of the war drums did not make itself heard inside the Old Palace. The inhabitants had to wait for rumour to bring the momentous news, a little before the Sultana Valideh was officially informed that the armies of the empire were marching on Belgrade.

Not that Khurrem would have been much interested; she had her own weighty problems to deal with and news of war could affect her in one way only, she would have been desolated to hear that Suleiman was going into danger and that she would not see him for the best part of a year.

She had been awakened just before dawn by a stealthy scratching at the door. She knew what it was and what she must do, for she had taken in her instructions on that score at least. It was the old woman come to take her back to the Old Palace, and now she must rise without disturbing her master, collect her clothes and take herself off without any ceremony and without any leave-taking. It was not very easy to do. She was as naked as she was born, it was cold, and the clothes she had been wearing had been removed peremptorily and without much regard for where they landed. Carefully groping, she found them eventually, pulled on the purple robe anyhow, and bundled the chemise under her arm. The rest she could locate on the low table near the door. Involuntarily, she paused and turned back towards the bed. He was a warm, unmoving presence and she could barely hear him breathe. She sighed and began to feel her way, first to the table and then the door. There was the business of getting it open and shut again without dropping anything or making a noise, but she managed it and was then outside, where it was colder, not so dark, and contained the old woman.

Now that she had faithfully carried out the last of her instructions – and now she came to think of it, they were the only part of her instructions she *had* carried out – she had time to think and feel, and it came to her that she was totally unaffected by the presence of the old woman, dreadful as it might be.

Perhaps the cold livened up the old crone for she was more offensive than she had been the night before. Sunk in her black draperies, she wheezed out, 'Took yer time, you did. Come on, then,' and set off down the corridors at a smart pace without waiting for the girl.

Khurrem, for her part, was hard put to it to keep up with her without dropping anything from the jumbled bundle of clothes and gems which she carried. Even she could see the disadvantage of losing any of the splendid jewellery with which she had been equipped. It would be undignified in the extreme, she thought, but so is this undignified scrambling along in the dark with only this poor old wreck to look after me. If anything unforeseen should happen, I should have to look after her, more likely.

But it did not seem to take half so long to get out as it had to get in, and in the narrow courtyard she saw that dawn was streaking the sky and the colour and shape of the carriage was already visible. The old woman could also see her and was ready with a comment.

'You don't look too seemly. Better put that caftan back on and cover yer hair – no way for a kadin to go about the place.'

Still muttering, she stood back, ready to help Khurrem into the carriage, but Khurrem evaded her, placed her bundle inside, swung herself up through the door, and retreated to the rear before the old woman was ready. As soon as the door was shut and the carriage under way, the old crone started again:

'D'you hear what I say? Make yourself decent. I know what you girls are like – trying to make out 'e spent the night tumbling you, when like as not – '

'Be silent! Don't dare to speak of the Sultan in that way!' Khurrem was amazed at the power of her voice and its satisfactory effect. The old woman fell silent and was not heard from again.

It was not until she was safely shut into her own room that she had leisure or inclination to examine her feelings, but even at the Topkapi she had been aware that more had happened to her than the physical act of possession. That had happened before and she had hated it and striven to forget it and rise above it. But this time was quite different. Put at its lowest, no girl who had been treated as Khurrem had been treated could fail to respond to courtesy and imagination in lovemaking. She was too naive to question her feelings, but they affected her whole outlook and behaviour. She had dressed herself properly in the carriage, eschewing the caftan and the jewels, but plaiting her hair and covering it decently with the veil — all this without reference to the beldame's rough instructions — and when they arrived at the Old Palace she had clambered down from the carriage alone and walked with dignity to her room.

She found Meylisah there, sitting impatiently on the floor and coming to her feet full of questions as soon as she had entered. Khurrem had had no doubts about how she should deal with Meylisah, either. She had silenced her (something easy to do as a rule) with an imperiously raised hand and sent her to fetch the wardrobe maid who had helped to dress her the night before. Then she had dressed herself in her own clothes, made a neat pile of all the garments and jewellery, and sat down on a cushion to wait.

When the woman came, she pointed to the pile, bade her take them away and courteously thanked her for her help. She had not thought her very helpful at the time but knew this was the thing to do.

When the woman had gone, Meylisah, standing first on one foot and then on the other, and with eyes as large as saucers, looked at her doubtfully. Finally, unable to stand the tension any longer, she blurted out, 'Oh, Khurrem, did you — is he pleased with you?'

Khurrem said with dignity, 'I should like my breakfast, now, please, Meylisah.'

'Oh, yes, of course. I'll fetch it.' Deflated, she turned to the door. When she was gone, Khurrem took a deep, trembling breath and burrowed into her cushions. She found herself full of excitement without quite knowing why. She was sorry to have hurt poor little Meylisah although she also knew that she had done right. Not only would it have been unseemly but she did not want to confide anything to anyone. She was glad she had behaved with dignity and that she had begun to do so even before he had taken her to himself — it would have been unthinkable to have confided to him that nonsense about running away! If she was to be the Sultan's woman she must behave accordingly. And she could honestly say that from the moment that he had drawn her into his arms and fondled her, she had not thought for a moment of whether she was pleasing him or not, only that she was happy herself.

Perhaps she had not pleased him! It was a terrible thought but one to be reckoned with. After all, there was Rose of Spring, who was beautiful, and dozens of girls, all prettier than herself and all instructed in the arts of love, whatever they might be. She had known nothing about love until now, and for all she knew, might have bored him to death, though so far as she could tell he had not seemed bored. No, certainly not.

Khurrem sprang to her feet. Why couldn't Meylisah have been quiet instead of reminding her of the terribly narrow path she'd been walking! She would have liked to daydream a little longer, to deceive herself, if that was what she was doing, until somebody came and told her that the Sultan had not liked her – but no, they would not do that, would they? All she would be left to do, was wait.

From the first moment she had been told of it Khurrem had disliked and condemned this system, which, while it protected women, set them apart as playthings and instruments by which it assured its own continuance. Now she hated it on her own account. It cut her off from the one person in all the world she wanted to be with. It did not even allow her to know whether he felt the same towards her. It was cruel, it was unnatural, and there was nothing she could do to fight it.

When Meylisah returned with her breakfast, she found Khurrem precisely where she had left her, wearing such an expression of baffled misery on her face that Meylisah was frightened. What could have gone wrong? she wondered, but dared not ask again. She could have sworn when her friend had come through the door that she was as happy as a girl could be, but her unnatural reticence, and now this apparently settled melancholy, were more than she knew how to cope with. She put down the loaded tray before Khurrem, and set about rearranging it temptingly, but even that small act of service, it seemed, did not please.

'Don't fidget,' said Khurrem listlessly.

Meylisah sighed and sat back on her heels. There must be

something she could do, but what? She knew her own tendency to fuss, knew that it could annoy. Resolutely she controlled herself, though her instinct was to put her arms around her friend and comfort her. Presently, unable to endure the silence any longer, she said timidly, 'If you were to eat something, perhaps you'd feel better.'

There was no reply, but presently Khurrem heaved a sigh of her own, looked unenthusiastically at the bountifully spread tray between them, and finally took an apple and began to munch. This was less helpful than it was intended to be for presently tears began to flow.

The old Khurrem would have dashed them away, wiped her sleeve across her eyes and continued to eat. The new kadin put down her apple, looked into space and clicked her fingers until Meylisah put a handkerchief into them. The eyes were carefully wiped, a mighty sniff controlled just in time, and the old Khurrem said in a small voice:

'There's nothing wrong – at least not so far as I know. It's just that I *don't* know.'

If Meylisah did not understand this, she was at least relieved by it. She said mendaciously, 'Oh, I see,' and waited, but nothing further came, and presently Khurrem took up the apple and started on it again, but there seemed to be some mysterious connection between the act of eating and the flow of tears, and after she had been compelled to dry her eyes again, she put the apple down impatiently.

'You might as well take it all back to the kitchen, I don't seem to want it,' she said.

So Meylisah got to her feet and pattered off with the rejected breakfast and Khurrem made use of her absence to let fly several racking sobs and blow her nose properly. She felt better for all this, but still had no inclination to talk, or indulge in any of the making of outrageous plans for her future which had always been her solace in time to trouble. Meylisah came back to find her sitting cross-legged, her arms folded on her knees, as if she were trying to make herself as small as possible, and staring into space. Since she had nothing else to do, and in any case did not want to leave Khurrem, Meylisah knelt down in the corner and sat on her heels. So they continued, still and silent, while the sun rose higher, grew hot, and shone through the lattice on them and the dust motes on the floor.

Fortunately for both of them, the system, though rigid, had room for everything, and in its own stiff way could take care of even Khurrem's dilemma.

At about mid-morning, when Suleiman in the New Palace was issuing his instructions to Piri, the Aga of the Girls at the Old Palace ascended the stairs to Khurrem's rooms. He was attended in his stately fashion by his secretary, by a slave carrying a small box with exaggerated care, and followed at a respectful distance by a plainly dressed female slave, whose brisk walk behind all this masculine dignity was very noticeable.

Arrived at Khurrem's door, the Aga turned to the black guard on duty on that corridor and nodded to him. The guard beat on the door with his halberd, and inside, Khurrem and Meylisah jumped convulsively. Meylisah ran to open, and Khurrem struggled to her feet. The Aga of the Girls entered and bowed, his broad black face spread with a conventional smile, his eyes bright and watchful. As he bowed in the small room, his high yellow turban almost brushed Khurrem's chin. She bowed back, startled. She was not going to curtsy, she was not in a curtsying mood. At the rear of the little procession, the small intelligent eyes of the woman slave narrowed in approval.

'From his majesty,' intoned the Aga. He recited a string of Suleiman's titles and finished, mellifluously, 'Greetings, and,' he added, 'a gift.' He half-turned and gestured the slave with the box forward.

Khurrem, suddenly alert, stepped forward, but the Aga forestalled her. He approved of success — he was a success himself — and he was glad that this odd child had been such a pleasure to his majesty that, so he was given to understand by his friends in the New Palace, he had himself selected the jewel with which to honour her. But the jewel had arrived from the treasury already wrapped in gold tissue and packed into this choice cedar box, and the Aga, who was an inquisitive man and liked to know what went on in his own establishment, wanted to see that jewel. Its comparable value would provide him with a useful clue as to his own future behaviour towards her. With matchless dignity, he bowed again, dipped fat black fingers into the box and extracted the small, gold-wrapped object. At that moment Khurrem stepped forward and scooped it out of his hands. There succeeded a brief, stricken pause. Khurrem faced him steadily, eyes narrowed and blazing, but she spoke, he found, courteously, even gently.

'The gift is mine, I believe, sir,' she said.

The Aga's eyes narrowed. To be sure, it was not perhaps the wisest thing Khurrem had ever done, among so many things that had been unwise. Her justification was that she believed passionately that whatever the gift that Suleiman had sent, it was for her eyes alone. In this, of course, she was wrong. Understanding the system as she did not, he wished the value he put upon her to be seen and understood. But less harm was done than perhaps she deserved. The Aga was observant and quick-witted. He was also unsure of her importance in the Sultan's eyes. He had handled the tissue-wrapped package and knew that it contained a ring; he also knew that to many people in many places a ring is more than a token, it is a pledge. He decided against being offended despite the rebuff to his dignity. He also reasoned that the girl must be very sure of herself to treat himself with such discourtesy. He raised a placating hand and bowed low for the second time.

'Madam — ' He looked sideways at her and discovered her to be smiling at him. Actually smiling! Truly, he would never understand women!

'Madam,' he repeated, 'it is my pleasant duty to inform you that henceforth you will bear the title of Ikbal, or fortunate, that you are entitled to the services of a second slave and the use of such jewellery and garments as you desire. Together with slipper-money to the value of so many aspers' — he mentioned a sum that meant nothing at all to Khurrem, but caused Meylisah's eyes to widen. He paused, in case she might wish to thank him.

Thus prompted, she did thank him, proving once again that she had learned something since leaving Manissa.

Mollified by this softness, but still wary, he enquired if she had any further wishes which it would be his pleasure to fulfil.

There was another pause. The Aga of the Girls had thought before that she was a little absent-minded, overcome, no doubt, by the signal honour shown her. Now, it was plain that she simply had ceased to listen. Patiently, he repeated his question and Meylisah coughed, a sound so palpably false that it recalled Khurrem from her daydream in time to hear the end of the question. She roused herself, made an effort to please and conciliate. She bowed again. She had no further wishes, so well was she looked after, and she was grateful for his courtesy

The Aga began to looked pleased. This wench, then, was not going to be spoiled by success, at least not yet. Unlike some with whom he had had to deal, and still had to deal. But he had a further message to deliver.

He raised his hand for attention, and then stated solemnly that the Sultana Valideh required the Ikbal Khurrem to appear before her at the mid-hour of the afternoon. A summons to the Sultana Valideh, it was his experience, was usually sufficient to quell the most forward of slaves. He himself found her formidable in the extreme. It was with some amazement therefore that he heard this unpredictable young woman remark joyfully.

'Oh! My dear madam – I shall be so glad to see her again.'

The Aga just avoided shaking his head in reproof and wonderment. He made his stately adieu, to which Khurrem at last responded with a curtsy, and withdrew, glad on the whole that so far as he knew he had refrained from making an enemy of a young woman who positively rejoiced at meeting the alarming Sultana Valideh face to face. He left behind him the new slave.

When at last he took himself away, Khurrem was still not free to examine her gift. There was this woman, a plain, down-to-earth, rather tough-looking person, standing there with folded hands, looking expectantly at her, and obviously waiting to be told what to do. Khurrem looked at her helplessly, though even at that moment, full of impatience to be rid of her as she was, she sensed in the woman's somewhat independent stance a kindred spirit. The new slave solved the problem for her. She walked from one room to the other, surveying them with a critical eye, and returning said crisply that flowers, bowls and other ornaments were needed and that she personally would get them. She then bowed perfunctorily and departed, leaving Khurrem and Meylisah to stare at each other.

'Well!' said Meylisah, who was nettled.

'Oh, never mind her!' cried Khurrem. She sank down on her cushions, holding her precious gold-wrapped parcel at arm's length. She wanted to open it, but even more she wanted to savour the moment. She looked up, caught Meylisah's wistful gaze and smiled uncertainly. She was, once more, she was surprised to find, near tears.

'Shall I go away?' asked Meylisah humbly.

'Oh! I'm sorry, sorry! I don't mean to hurt you and I don't want you to go – you're my person, but that man, he was just trying to find out — find out I don't know what. But I do know he had no right.'

Meylisah nodded as if she fully understood, but kept her eyes on the fingers now slowly removing the tissue. Inside was a small bag of white silk, which Khurrem upended a little clumsily into her palm. Out tumbled a ring set with one splendid ruby. A ruby, moreover, not so large as the pigeon's-egg rubies from India, which were too large for anything but ceremonial use, but large enough, yet small enough, for a woman to wear at all times if she so wished.

'Oh!' Two sighs were expelled at the same moment, and Khurrem followed hers with, 'He remembered!'

'Remembered what?' asked Meylisah, and naturally got no reply.

BOOK THREE

*Fortunate*

# 23

Khurrem was naturally roused to a state of rapture by Suleiman's gift and all that it implied, and was therefore unable to settle down to do anything, or contemplate anything, except of course her ring, which she wore, Western fashion, on the fourth finger of her left hand. As she had been unable to eat any breakfast from misery, so happiness and excitement robbed her of any appetite for the midday meal. Meylisah was exasperated almost to tears as she prepared to remove yet another succulent meal untouched.

The new slave, who had returned laden with a satisfactory collection of vases and other odds and ends, was engaged in rearranging the furnishings of Khurrem's sitting-room to her own satisfaction, while the familiar process of timid persuasion and downright rejection was going on. She now added a crisply decisive voice to the discussion.

'If your stomach starts rumbling while the Sultana Valideh is talking to you, you'll look silly.'

This statement silenced both the Ikbal and the slave, and both looked at her, startled, and Meylisah, certainly, indignant.

'Mind your own business,' snapped Khurrem automatically, and then added in a different tone, 'All the same — '; she giggled and added, 'it wouldn't sound very well, would it? Put the tray down again, Meylisah, I'll try the kebabs and pine kernels.'

She lifted a silver skewer, nibbled experimentally and then took a larger mouthful. When she was able, she looked thoughtfully at the newcomer and asked, 'What's your name?'

'Hulefa,' responded the woman equably, standing back, apparently to examine critically a sparse arrangement of coloured leaves in a narrow-necked vase.

Doesn't even bother to say 'madam' thought Meylisah indignantly. And she's older than we are. I don't think I'm going to like her.

Hulefa was, from her appearance, in her early thirties, but might have been younger, for her lined face and dogged expression suggested a life of work and worry behind her. Khurrem, examining her while she ate, wondered, couldn't make up her mind, and finally asked, 'Where are you from?'

Hulefa looked at her briefly and replied, 'Rumelia.'

She did not enlarge on this and Khurrem after another thoughtful look at her, decided against more questions at the moment. It occurred to her that if she was to make a proper appearance before Hafise she had better begin to think about it. She had had no opportunity to think about her until now and she realized with something like shock that whatever relationship she had had with the Queen Mother in the past, it was destined to be very different in the future.

For one thing, she was now a widow mourning a beloved husband, and Khurrem, for the first time, dimly realized what that could mean to a lady of such strong feelings as the Queen Mother. Too, her own position was different. She was no longer a humble sewing-maid, favoured because she worked hard, was gifted at her work, even because she was different and good for a laugh. More was going to be expected of her and she only wished she knew what pitfalls lay before her. Once again, she must be on her guard and on her dignity. There must be no more silly talk or unwary confidences, and it would be more difficult than last night. It had been one thing to put on a show, to flirt with a young man who was already disposed to like her; his mother was going to be a much more formidable problem than Suleiman; she was likely to be more critical than he had ever been, both because she was a woman and because she was his mother. Also, at the moment she was very unhappy, and with the great and powerful, who knew what form that unhappiness would take?

Khurrem took a deep breath, and decided that she wanted no more to eat. She wiped her fingers carefully on a napkin and looked around for Meylisah, who, always watchful, was on her knees by her side in a moment.

'I've finished. You can take it away. Thank you,' she added as an afterthought.

Meylisah nodded, lifted the heavy tray, and was forestalled at

184

the door by Hulefa, who took it from her bodily, saying as she did so, 'That's too heavy for you, sweetheart,' and swung out of the room without another word.

'Well, really!' said Meylisah, but she found it difficult to be really resentful. The woman's tone had been kindly.

Khurrem glanced round. 'She's taken us over, and I'll tell you something else — I'd prefer to have her for a friend rather than an enemy.'

'Well, I don't know — ' began Meylisah.

'Well, I do,' said the new Ikbal firmly. 'Please go and find Fatma. I need advice.'

Khurrem set off from her own quarters that afternoon in something like state. That is to say she had dressed with extreme care and largely according to Fatma's advice, in some of the elegant garments selected by that lady, and was accompanied by Hulefa, also on Fatma's advice.

'From what I hear, the Sultana Valideh's a very busy lady at the moment. You may have difficulty getting into her presence-chamber.'

'But she sent for me!' cried Khurrem, who had constructed for herself an interesting mental picture of Hafise suffering in proud seclusion and was reluctant to part with it.

'Did she, now.' Fatma nodded approvingly. 'All the same, if I were you, I'd take that girl, Hulefa, with you. If she sent for you, she wants to see you, but it isn't fitting for you to have to push your way through the crowd in the ante-chamber. Hulefa can do that for you. You've got to remember your dignity.'

'Yes, of course,' the new Ikbal hastily agreed, 'but why should there be a crowd in the ante-chamber?'

'You'll see,' responded Fatma in her usual downright fashion.

The Sultana Valideh's apartments, being the most extensive in the Eski Saray or Old Palace, were comparatively easy of access, which, thought Khurrem, as she walked demurely behind Hulefa that afternoon, was just as well, for she found herself very nearly as nervous as she had been the previous night on the journey to the New Palace. Moreover, nothing was turning out as she had expect. Hulefa led her briskly along gloomy corridors until they reached impressive double doors guarded by the usual black eunuchs. She was intrigued by the buzz of female voices from inside which could be clearly heard even before the door was opened, but hardly had time to wonder about it before a worried-looking man whom she recognized as the secretary to the Aga of the Girls opened one leaf of the door sufficiently to peer out. He was sweating profusely. He made no bones about admitting Khurrem and even seemed relieved to see her.

The room she entered, some kind of ante-chamber, was not very large, and was jam-packed with women, all of whom turned to look at the newcomers, and stopped talking in order to do so. They parted ranks in order to allow her to pass, and as she went through them Khurrem had such an impression of disorder and sorrow that she was swamped by apprehension. They were not very young women and she recognized none of them. What could it all mean? She had no time to wonder further. Another set of double doors was flung open. She saw a high narrow room, magnificently appointed, Hafise seated on a throne and looking superb in the middle of it.

If the Sultana Valideh was, as Khurrem had expected, given over to grief, she gave no sign of it. Anger, yes, certainly, for the Aga of the Girls was present, looking as unhappy and harassed as his secretary had appeared in the ante-chamber, and it was fairly plain that the emotion that was causing Hafise's lip to curl and her eyes to flash, was directed at him. Momentarily however, all this – whatever it might be – was apparently to be suspended, incredibly, on Khurrem's account.

Hafise extended both hands and cried, 'My dear child! You are doubly welcome – come here and let me look at you.'

She approached the throne, had her hand seized between Hafise's two warm ones, and was bidden to stand still 'while I look at you!'

And look she did, from the girl's head to her feet, with a quick glance at the ruby on Khurrem's finger. 'Yes, yes,' she said warmly at the end of this examination, 'you have learned – I knew you would. Your appearance does you credit, dignity without display. It does my heart good that I can rely on you in small things and in large as well, I don't doubt. But we cannot talk as I had hoped yet awhile. We have here a problem,' the large eyes turned with devastating effect towards the Aga of the Girls, who appeared to shrink. She indicated a cushion at the foot of her low throne. 'Sit there, Khurrem, and pay attention. Learn, if you will, that one in my position has bitter tasks as well as pleasant ones. And that apparently, no one, *no one*, however highly placed, can be relied on totally.'

Khurrem hastened to do as she was told. She thought she was used to Hafise's moods and tempers, but in Manissa laughter had never been very far away. Today, she was deeply serious and, more, deeply troubled, as if the problem before her might be beyond solution. Today, as if they were a reliable index to their mistress's mood, Sirhane and Guzul stood, one on each side of her throne, subdued and grave.

'Khurrem, did you see the slaves in the ante-chamber?'

Startled, Khurrem half-turned on her cushion and attempted to get to her feet in order to reply with becoming courtesy. Hafise's hand descended on to her shoulder, 'Never mind that, we have no time for the niceties, did you see them, I say?'

'Oh, yes, madam!'

'You do not, I am sure, know who or what they are, so I must tell you, Khurrem. Briefly, then, they are slaves of the Sultan Selim's harem for whom there is no place in the harem of my son. Some of them are too old to work any more, for some there is no longer work to do, for naturally I have brought many of my own women here from Manissa. Some, of course, have reached the age of twenty-five and will be given in marriage — for them there is little in the way of a problem.' She shook her head, 'But others — and it is of no help that officials on whom we depend have, it seems, neither common sense nor imagination!'

She raised her head and glared at the Aga of the Girls, who looked at his feet. Even Khurrem, who knew no more of the situation than she had just been told, felt that he should make some effort to defend himself.

Hafise leaned forward and extended an accusing forefinger.

'Why did I have to learn of the misery you have created from my own kiaya?' She glanced briefly at an imposing, middle-aged woman who stood self-effacingly, as far as she was capable of self-effacement, against the wall.

'Why,' continued Hafise, 'if you found the problem beyond you, did you not come to me for advice? Is it becoming that women who have served this house well over the years, no matter how lowly their tasks, should suddenly find themselves without a home or support? Not to mention those for whom you have made provision which they find intolerable?'

She spat the last word at the unhappy man and was compelled to stop for breath.

The Kizlar Agasi goaded at last into self-defence, cried, 'Madam, madam, I have done my best — these women torment me — and there are so many of them! Had there been more time I could have done better for some of them, but for others, I defy anyone — ' he shook his head and was silent.

'Well, we shall see,' Hafise was suddenly herself subdued, imagining, perhaps for the first time, the impact of so much unhappy femininity on a man so self-important. 'We must go on; bring me the twins.'

The Aga motioned faintly to his secretary, who vanished into the ante-room and returned shepherding two small women, who took one desperate look at the magnificence confronting them and reached convulsively for each other's hands. Clinging together, they faced the throne and were apparently incapable of further effort.

'Down on your knees!' hissed the secretary. They looked at him and did not move. Hafise forestalled his next effort with a sudden, savage gesture.

'Never mind that!' To the women she said with as much gentleness as the magnificent voice could express: 'Tell me, how old are you?'

They turned to each other and consulted silently, and then finally one, said in a grating voice which seemed as if it was not used very much, 'Twenty-seven, ma'am.'

Hafise glanced at the Aga, 'Why were they not married two years ago?'

He looked helpless, then consulted a list his secretary thrust at him.

'We tried, madam,' his voice grew firmer as he read, and possibly remembered. 'Several men, decent, honest fellows in an appropriate way of life, but, as your majesty sees, they are not,' he swallowed, 'handsome, and worst of all, there are two of them. They refuse to be separated.'

There was a little silence. Khurrem, wide-eyed, wished suddenly that she hadn't to see this. The twins reminded her of Meylisah, she didn't know why, perhaps it was something about their rusty cotton gowns, for Meylisah was, at least, gay and alert most of the time.

Hafise said, with assumed briskness, 'As to that, if we could find a husband for each, then they would have to be parted, painful though it would be.' She was obviously not prepared to

188

pursue that line of thought for the moment and changed the subject. 'What is your work?' she asked.

Again the mute consultation, and the same twin replied for both, 'We – we are cleaners, ma'am.' She gestured downwards, 'Carpets and cushions, we do, and curtains. And the brasswork, and we clean pipes and prepare the braziers and light the charcoal,' a note of innocent pride came into the ugly little voice, and her sister nodded as if mentally ticking off each item.

'Can you cook?'

Yes, they could cook.

'Really,' said Hafise to the Aga, 'Here are two girls who are totally competent housekeepers. Each would make a good wife. It does not seem beyond the power of man to find in Istanbul two artisans or shopkeepers, say, who would be glad of such reliable wives as they would be.'

The Aga shook his head. 'Madam, they are no longer young and they have never been pretty.'

Hafise's lip tightened. 'They are not old, either. I am not satisfied that enough has been done. Clearly, if husbands can be found, they must be parted.' She shook her head. 'That is sad, I know it, but as against that they would be looked after and even cherished, perhaps. You must try again,' she told him firmly; 'and when you have succeeded, I will talk to them and make them understand.'

She turned back to the twins. 'Go back to your quarters now. And do not despair. I will see to it that you have a better life.'

Still clasping hands, the twins looked doubtfully up at her. Clearly, they did not want a better life or any other sort of life. The secretary led them away.

There was another silence while this was done. The Aga of the Girls looked expectantly at his mistress's face. You see? his expression seemed to say, it isn't so easy as you thought. That Hafise understood what he had not dared to say was made plain by her next words.

'Well, you cannot have many such twins.'

He sighed deeply. 'No, madam, but many kinds of problem.'

She suddenly smiled at him. 'Very well. Bring me another.'

He looked easier, but hesitated before plunging in. Eventually he said, 'This woman, majesty, is a troublemaker. The originator, I think. I made the marriage for her myself. A good man, and well enough off. I took trouble, madam, she would

189

want for nothing,' his voice rose in genuine indignation, 'and then — '

Hafise's voice cut in. 'Let me understand you. You made a marriage. Was the bride-price agreed?'

'Oh, yes, madam. We would have taken less even. But no matter. He is not a young man and needs a strong woman to keep his house and help with his shop. A splendid opportunity! And she would have none of it!' He almost spat the last words, and rushed on in bubbling indignation, 'And, now, because of this, *he* wishes to back out, while she sets the harem by its ears and encourages others to complain!'

Hafise looked serious. 'A virago indeed,' she murmured. 'And have you done nothing to persuade her? Have you talked to her?'

'Repeatedly, majesty,' the rich, Negro voice boomed. 'She has been beaten, also, but nothing avails.' Distraught, he produced his handkerchief and mopped his forehead.

Khurrem, breathless with indignation, half-turned on her cushion and looked up into Hafise's face, but if the Sultana glimpsed the movement, she ignored it.

'Why does she refuse?'

'She says she does not wish to marry an old man.'

'I see.' Hafise's voice was small and cool. 'How difficult things are made for us, between men who do not wish to marry old women and women who do not wish to marry old men. However,' she sighed and made a small aimless gesture, 'let her be brought in. No doubt there is more to it than that, there usually is.'

She was not brought in. It is true she did not actively push the little secretary aside. She merely gave the impression that she did. A tall, strapping woman, bulky of figure, she strode to the carpet before the throne, delivered a magnificent curtsy as if it were a challenge, and looked Hafise in the eye. Her own were black and fierce, under straight black brows. Khurrem thought she was perhaps thirty-five, or even younger. Grey eyes met black thoughtfully. If a challenge had been offered it was not taken up. Hafise had no time for such things. She came straight to the point.

'Why will you not marry this man?'

The woman gave a hoot of laughter. 'Lady, if you had seen him! Old, rheumy-eyed — I have no need of such as he.'

Hafise's brow wrinkled. 'But you would be free and a married woman,' she said reasonably.

'A married woman is not free, except when she chooses for herself. She is not free then, but does not mind so much,' proclaimed the apostate offhandedly. She said seriously, 'Lady, you have not asked me what I do want, so I shall tell you. I want to go home.'

Against the wall, Hafise's kiaya, expressionless, examined her fingernails, but the Aga of the Girls raised his eyes to the ceiling as if he expected it to fall on the slave, who, except for Hafise and the kiaya, seemed the most composed person present. As for Khurrem, she found she was clenching her fists and had to make a conscious effort to fold her hands demurely in her lap. Quite desperately she willed Hafise to make some move, some gesture, towards this splendid person. She held her breath, and Hafise said matter-of-factly.

'And where is your home?'

'Macedonia, madam.'

The Sultana Valideh had not learned enough yet. 'What do you do here – what is your work?'

The woman's face became fixed in expression. She paused, and then said, it seemed unwillingly, 'I was gösde, lady.'

'Ah,' said Hafise, and she, too, paused. Khurrem could sympathize with her hesitation, for she knew this word and what it meant. She, too, had been gösde, chosen, a girl on whom the Sultan's eye had lighted with interest. But now Hafise went smoothly on with her question, her voice unchanged.

'When was this?'

'Eight, no, nine years ago, madam. Before the uprising, before your husband took the throne.'

'I see.' Warmth crept back into the splendid voice. 'And so nothing came of it?'

'No, madam.' The voice in reply was so low as to be almost inaudible.

Hafise's voice pealed, in indignation, this time. 'Then why have you been kept here all these years?'

Khurrem pressed her fist against her mouth. This woman's fate would have been hers, had not Suleiman remembered her and kept faith. She would have been disregarded, and worse, scorned by her fellows. She took a trembling breath and listened for the answer, as if her life depended on it. But there was none, only a despairing shrug.

191

The Kislar Agasi stepped forward. She inclined towards him as he spoke confidentially close to her ear. In the disorder following Selim's seizure of the throne, the harem of his father had been left to its own devices. There was no Sultana Valideh in charge, it was some time before order had been restored to the harem, in short, there had been a backlog of women to be disposed of, and this Greek woman had been difficult, a trouble-maker even then, he implied.

'But nine years!' expostulated Hafise.

He spread his hands. His conscience, he implied, was clear since his appointment was a recent one. Also, he pointed out, she had been very young and comely. There had been no reason then to consider her career necessarily ended.

Hafise sighed and her eyes sought the unhappy woman. 'I cannot do as you ask. A woman alone – it is impossible, you must see that!' Her hand went out in appeal, but the Greek woman shrugged again.

'I'm as strong as a man. I can work,' she stated briefly. 'It's only a question of getting back to my village. My family is large. If the old are gone, I can work with the young.'

'Only!' repeated Hafise softly. She sat silent in thought and said to the Aga of the Girls, 'And there is the man to consider also. Can he be brought here, say, tomorrow?'

In what he understood, the Aga was efficient. He bowed. 'He waits in the First Court, madam.'

'He is here, in the Old Palace?' demanded Hafise. 'Well, bring him, bring him!' She turned to the Greek slave: 'It is not fitting you should meet face to face. Go to your quarters, but when I have discovered what to do, I will send for you again.' She bent and tapped Khurrem's shoulder, 'And when he comes, my dear, remember to veil yourself.' She looked authoritatively round the room and raised her voice. 'All women who have no immediate business here should now leave.'

They went, reluctantly, led by the Sultana's kiaya, who swept a superb curtsy and went quite briskly. If she was as curious as the rest she concealed it admirably.

It took a quarter of an hour to get him there. The Sultana Valideh passed the time biting her thumb and staring into space. Once or twice she grunted. Khurrem sat silent on her cushion, full of comment and questions but rightly concluding that Hafise required quiet.

The Greek woman had been right. He was old, he was not pre-possessing and his eyes were red. He was not without dignity, however, and though obviously deeply impressed by his surroundings, not to be stampeded. He fell to the ground as prescribed when Hafise addressed him, and then stood, attentive on his sturdy old legs, cautiously watching her face. His clothes expressed a quiet prosperity.

Hafise began warily also. 'I believe you have now repudiated the woman with whom a match was arranged?' she suggested.

He bowed again and spread his hands. 'Having encountered her, your majesty. In a word, yes.'

'Encountered her?' said Hafise, 'How splendidly you put it! How did that come about, pray tell me?'

The old man's eyes slid to the face of the Aga of the Girls, who looked worried and took a moment to think before coming to his rescue.

'You will understand, majesty, in the case of these women whose beauty we cannot guarantee, an opportunity is sometimes made, when negotiations have reached a certain stage, for seeing and,' he coughed, 'being seen.' In case she was going to be annoyed about what shouldn't happen but did, he hurried on, 'Otherwise there would be difficulty in arranging some of these matches. More difficulty than we have already.' He finished unhappily.

'I understand that, but surely – she is not young, but still comely. You are much older than she,' Hafise addressed the reluctant bridegroom with a certain severity.

He spoke up robustly in self-defence. 'I wouldn't care if she were plain, even to a harelip. I am not a doting old fool, majesty, at least I don't think so. My dear Amina has been dead these ten years and I'm not seeking to replace her, but I grow older and I'm tired of looking after myself. All I want is some decent, quiet body who will keep my house and look after me. I would be good to her,' he continued, 'but, majesty, a man of my years seeks a draught of cool water, not a raging torrent!'

There was a pause, and then Hafise said gently, 'She must have been very rude to you, I gather.'

Both gentlemen hastened to assure her that she had. The Aga of the Girls, because his voice was louder and he had not been personally involved, was most vociferous. She had not been there, he said indignantly, to speak at all. It had been most improper. All she was required to do was show herself briefly at a certain window while the bridegroom-to-be walked past below. And as soon as she looked at him . . . which she should not have done . . . she had screamed out the most vulgar abuse. It had been disgraceful; it had also created a scene in the courtyard.

'Most regrettable,' said Hafise blankly. She looked down at her hands, and then said gently to the old fellow: 'And now you have had a most humiliating experience and have no bride into the bargain. I am truly sorry. I feel that we should make it up to you in some way.'

He raised his hands and let them fall, and then feeling that such graciousness needed further acknowledgement, assured her of his devotion to her and her son the Sultan.

Her raised hand silenced him and she spoke to the Aga of the Girls, 'What was the bride-price for the Greek?'

He told her, with the help of his secretary and one of their lists, and Hafise with her sweetest smile turned back to the old man, who was now looking a little wary.

'We have in this harem two women for whom we are seeking a husband,' she raised her hand again as he broke into voluble speech, and went calmly on when he was silenced. 'They are younger than the Greek, only twenty-seven, and they are twins and do not wish to be parted. They have been carefully taught to keep house, and they only speak when spoken to.'

She paused to let that sink in, and possibly it did, but he was not going to be caught again. He did not want two wives, that would mean another woman to clothe, an extra mouth to fill, and there was the bride-price! He was not made of money!

'The bride-price will naturally be what you would have paid for the Greek, no more, but no less. Also, I understand you required a wife who could help you with your shop. Tell me, I have not asked before, what do you sell?'

'I am a tailor, madam.' There was the same note of pride in his voice which she had detected in the spokesman twin.

Hafise smiled on him delightedly. 'But, there, you see! And I suppose you need a woman to do a certain amount of sewing for you, and other such jobs. But in this way, you would have two.' She let that sink in, too, and then added seriously; 'It is not my wish to over-persuade you, or force you to do anything you do not wish to. You shall have time to make up your mind, and see them, by all means. That is only fair after your previous expe-

194

rience.' She glanced at the Aga of the Girls, and said, 'Take our friend to your office and make such arrangements as he requires.'

She bowed to them with all her usual grace and watched them make their farewells. The old man looked a little bewildered, but thoughtful too.

When they had gone, she bent sideways to Khurrem and said, 'He is a nice old man. I hope he takes them.'

# 24

'Oh, madam,' began Khurrem, and stopped because she had so much she wanted to say that she couldn't organize her thoughts properly. Hafise either did not, or chose not to hear her. She stretched unashamedly and with simple enjoyment.

'How hard I have worked, and how much talking I have done! And how I have enjoyed it,' she finished in a lower voice. She clapped her hands peremptorily to summon her maids, and added: 'It cannot be wrong, Khurrem, to enjoy one's work, even if it involves pain for others. Though I can honestly say I do not enjoy it when I am less successful than I may have been this afternoon.'

Guzul appeared, eyes bright with curiosity, and Hafise said briefly: 'Sherbet, Guzul, I am parched. And, Guzul, we may have married the twins! Remember to pray for this.'

'Oh, madam!' said Guzul and went.

Khurrem found her voice. 'But what will become of the Greek woman?' she asked timidly.

'What, indeed?' said Hafise.

At that moment Guzul returned with a pitcher and goblet of Iznik glass, and Hafise said no more until she had emptied a full goblet, and then said: 'I saw that she impressed you and indeed, you were right. She is a most forceful and courageous woman and independent, too. She must go, of course,' she finished matter-of-factly.

Khurrem looked anxiously into her face. 'Do you mean you will let her go home?'

'Yes.' Hafise was pouring more fruit-juice. When she had done, she said, 'Do not be too happy for her, Khurrem. She will almost certainly die before she gets there. The world is not kind to women alone. I shall give her her freedom and enough money, but I cannot protect her. She faces robbery, rape perhaps. It gives me no pleasure to think of this. Also, splendid as she is, I wish she were less of a fool, for in her nine years, Khurrem, she has learned less than you have in one.'

Khurrem had certainly not thought of this. She was overcome with bitterness. 'Why is the world so cruel to us?' she cried. 'Women are ill-treated everywhere! Look what happened to her, neglected and scorned –'

'Yes,' broke in the Sultana Valideh decisively, 'she has been. But, Khurrem, before you become too tender-hearted on her account, remember this. The world did not do all this to her, by which I suppose you mean men. You must learn to know who your enemy is, otherwise you are in danger of growing old and bitter before your time. Women are at the mercy of their nature. It is no one's fault that they bear children. And, Khurrem, for every man ill-treating a woman, there is a woman ill-treating a man. What do you think would have been the fate of that little man if he had married your Greek? She would have eaten him alive! Oh –' she stretched her arms over her head, 'I do so hope he takes the twins! They all have a chance of being happy. And, you know, she, your Greek, will be happy when she leaves here and sets off on her journey –' she stopped uncertainly and looked down at the girl. 'Khurrem,' she said, 'are you listening?'

She was. She turned on her cushion, and said in a small voice, 'Yes, madam. You are saying, I think, that I must be happy, too.'

'Indeed I am! And aren't you?'

Khurrem thought about it. Last night seemed a very long way away. She said eventually, 'Yes, madam, oh yes, I am.'

Hafise considered her carefully: 'Such occasions as you have just seen are very disturbing, and if you are not disturbed by them, then you will be no use to the harem. But they are not the whole of life, certainly not of your life. So now, put these people to the back of your mind and talk to me about yourself. First of all, let me tell you I am very, very pleased with you.'

This, of course, cheered her immensely. She suddenly thought of herself preparing for this afternoon's visit. Hafise was right, nothing was changed so far as she was concerned.

Hafise continued: 'Without any preparation, you succeeded

brilliantly and have pleased my son. Positively. And as I look at you now, I can hardly believe you are the same girl who came to sew my yellow diamonds – ' she stopped, sighed, and changed the subject.

'Ah, yes, the woman, Hulefa. I have to tell you about her. She is not perhaps very polished in her manners, but she is knowledgeable and sensible in the extreme, one of my own people. I selected her especially for you. Do you like her?'

Khurrem considered, and said truthfully, 'I'm not sure if I like her, but she is my sort of person, I think.'

Hafise nodded sharply. 'That is good. If you let her, she will serve you well. Now,' she looked closely at the girl again, 'is that ring my son's gift?'

'Yes, majesty.'

'An unusual choice,' Hafise mused. 'Perhaps it has special significance for you – for both of you?'

Khurrem felt her cheeks growing warm. She hoped Hafise would not probe further.

'Yes, madam,' she whispered.

Suleiman's mother nodded sharply again.

'That too is good,' she stated with her usual decision. 'Guzul, bring me my jewel casket. But do not hurry.'

Guzul chose to take this somewhat amiss. She tossed her head as she went. It savoured so much of Manissa that Khurrem could have laughed aloud.

When she had gone, the Sultana Valideh said simply, 'What you have told me lightens my load indeed. I have not yet seen my son today.' And Khurrem thought she sighed. 'But,' she continued, 'I will tell you the reason for that in a moment. Now *you* are to tell me: have you given thought to yourself, your new status and establishment?'

'Yes,' said Khurrem eagerly. 'Yes, indeed, madam, I have.'

The Sultana Valideh smiled a little at this enthusiasm and asked, 'And what have you thought?'

Khurrem said simply, 'That I must be more discreet and not talk so much, and also be more dignified. And also, my lady, pay attention to people's feelings more.'

'And what does that mean?'

Khurrem hung her head. 'I am afraid, madam, I hurt the feelings of the Aga of the Girls this morning. I truly did not mean to, but I don't yet always understand the reasons why people do things here.'

Hafise sighed and her attention seemed, for a moment, to wander.

'With such good intentions you cannot go far wrong, and do not worry about the Aga, his self-esteem will support him, no doubt. You have forgotten your enemies.'

Khurrem stared again. 'I am too unimportant to have any, except perhaps one of the sewing-maids I once slapped.' She thought further, 'Oh, and Mirza, I bit her — but that was a long time ago.'

Hafise stared at her impatiently. 'Spare me these trivia. You disappoint me, Khurrem, you do indeed. You are no longer unimportant, and you are simple indeed if you imagine that Gulbehar has not known of you and your probable position almost as long as I have.'

Khurrem hung her head. Gentle as was the tone in which the reproof was delivered, it hurt. And she had thought herself so clever and had congratulated herself on her goodwill and dignity!

'Moreover, you are my protégée. If you lose status, or worse, are injured or even disgraced, to that extent, so am I. Remember this.'

Khurrem looked up, appalled at the thought. 'But what could she do? I have not even seen her, and I'm sure I don't intend to.'

Hafise smiled a little sadly. 'Well, that could be a cause for complaint in itself. Remember, her status in this harem is second only to my own. But, seriously, child, she will find cause to blacken you to my son. There she will not succeed, I know him too well. But, be warned, he is impatient of squabbling women, as I am. Neither of us will look with favour on a girl who screams her wrongs from the rooftops. Do not let it be you who does this. Is this much clear?'

'Yes, my lady.'

The Sultana Valideh looked at her in silence for a moment, thinking, she will take everything I tell her away and digest it and then go to work in her own way, but what that way will be, now that she is deprived of the use of her fingernails and her tongue, God knows. I hope I have chosen wisely. She said:

'And Khurrem, it is not only Gulbehar.'

199

'No, madam, I see that all her slaves will also be my enemies.'
She sighed and added, 'And even her little son. As he grows up
he will hate me, too.'

Hafise nodded. 'There is more,' she added. 'If my son were to
come to love you, if you have sons, your power will grow, particularly if you conduct yourself wisely. But if these things do not
happen, then you will have even more enemies, until eventually
your failure destroys you.' She stopped and looked at Khurrem
with such a sad expression that the girl cried out.

'Oh, my dear, dear madam, what is it?'

Hafise shook her head. 'I am distressing you and myself to no
good purpose,' she said at last, with an assumption of briskness
and cheerfulness. 'Gulbehar is a fool and you are not. That is
really what it all comes down to in the end. Also,' she added
sharply, 'neither am I! One final word, Khurrem. You have been
provided with two good maids, but do not let them involve you in
quarrels with Gulbehar over,' – she shrugged – 'I do not
know – whatever slaves do quarrel over – precedence, jewels,
the best food, the quickest service. You understand me?'

She did not wait for a reply, but went on, more tranquilly,
now that she saw the end of her harangue in sight. 'There! I have
done with warning and lecturing.' She raised her hands to her
shoulders and let them fall with a slap on her knees. 'Here comes
Guzul with the trinkets. Let me see what I have for you.'

The casket of cedarwood was placed on the cushion beside
her. It was so large and heavy that it was all Guzul could manage
to dispose of it without upsetting it. Khurrem, chastened and
subdued, looked at it without much interest, and the Sultana
Valideh, disturbed by the distasteful task she had just carried
out, had to sit in thought for a moment before she could remember what she wanted from it. Probably, no two women had ever
been so little moved by the presence of a fortune in precious
stones and metals.

Finally, Hafise said, 'Ah, yes, of course. I wonder if I still have
it?' She lifted the lid and opened several compartments experimentally. At last she was lucky and brought out of the box a
delicate crescent of rubies and diamonds set in gold.

'You see, it is also set with rubies. Take it, child, in recognition
of this happy day. And happy it is, despite the warnings I have
showered on you. I do not believe you are in great danger
because you are a wise and courageous girl and you will have the

Sultan and myself to support you. So, wear this with joy.'

She placed the brooch in Khurrem's palm, where they both looked at it in silence for a moment. Eventually the girl gathered her wits together sufficiently to voice her thanks in a few halting phrases.

Hafise heard her out and then raised her hand for silence. 'One last word, my dear girl. You can no longer afford to be heedless or simple. Dignity and kindness have their place but guile is never very far away in a place like this. It is to be regretted but it is so. Now, there is something else.'

She paused and Khurrem looked at her mournfully, sure that the 'something else' must be as frightening or painful as what had gone before.

Hafise glanced towards the marble-framed lattice. 'We hear nothing of it here, but the war drums are sounding all over the city. In a few days my son marches against the Hungarians.' She paused and looked hard at Khurrem who could only stare, wide-eyed.

Hafise looked away, swallowed, and went on.

'You will get used to this. It is the pattern and cannot be changed. The Turk is a warlike creature who, if he does not attack first always, will be destroyed. Or he believes this, which is the same thing,' she finished wearily. 'So, almost every spring he goes to war and every autumn he returns, victorious, to gather the harvest. Now, tomorrow the armies will converge on Istanbul and there will be a great mustering. I shall be present to watch this and you and Gulbehar will attend me. After what I have said to you it is not necessary for me to warn you further as to your conduct. And now, my child,' she took a deep breath, 'I have much work to do and you have much to think about. The audience is ended.'

Khurrem left Hafise's presence-chamber with her head in a whirl. She would have liked to have gone somewhere where she could be alone with her tumultuous thoughts, but with Hulefa padding inexorably behind her, there seemed nowhere to go but her own rooms. There would be no privacy there, for she knew she had not reached the stage when she could comfortably bring herself to tell them to go away and leave her alone; anyway not Meylisah, who was her oldest friend. However, when she got there it seemed that her quarters welcomed her like an old home. She also found that she had underrated the kindness, or perhaps the tact of her maids, as she realized she must now learn to call them.

Hulefa said, with her usual brevity: 'You look tired, mistress, why not take a nap? I'll unroll your mattress,' while Meylisah, not to be outdone, volunteered to fetch rosewater to bathe her temples. These things done, they went off to get their supper.

Squatting on her mattress, hands clasped between her knees, she found that they were right. She was tired, but not particularly unhappy, simply bewildered by the richness of experience of the past twenty-four hours.

Despite everything else that had happened and been said to her during the couple of hours she had spent with Hafise – and how wonderful it had been to see her so splendidly herself, instead of aloof and grieving as she had expected – her mind constantly returned to the night with Suleiman. Hafise had said, 'If my son should come to love you', implying that there was a doubt that he did or might. Khurrem thought long and earnestly about this. Innocent as she was, it had not yet occurred to her that love-making could be anything other than the expression of love. For the first time she asked herself why Suleiman should ever have wanted her in the first place, graceless as she was, and at first could find no answer that would give her comfort. Now perhaps, she thought despairingly, he has finished with me, now that his lust, or curiosity, or whatever it was, is satisfied. She was appalled by this dreadful thought until she remembered that she knew what lust was like, having been its victim.

She was ashamed of herself when she thought of the warmth and happiness of their hours together, of how easily they had talked, and how patient he had been with her. She refused to believe that all this delight had meant nothing more to him than a pleasant evening's pastime. There was comfort, too, when her thoughts turned again to Hafise. There was no doubting the Sultana Valideh's affection; it showed in the way she spoke and looked, in the gift of the ruby crescent. Would she have lavished so much care and attention on a girl who was no more than her son's passing fancy? She must reject all these doubts; they were unworthy, both of the kind of man she knew Suleiman to be, and of herself. Instead, she turned her mind to Hafise's warnings against her possible enemies. Here was food for thought indeed!

The Sultana Valideh had spoken as if it was impossible for her or Suleiman to protect her if she was attacked by Gulbehar or anyone else. They were all-powerful, and yet. . . . Biting her thumb, she worried away at the problem, just as Hafise had known she would, and gradually came to realize that her view of things was over-simple. Even a fool like Gulbehar would not attack her openly; this would not be the exchange of slaps and hair-pullings in which she had so readily played her part and so often come off the victor. All Gulbehar would have to do would be to accuse her of something, impertinence, theft, no matter what, and she would have to defend herself. Hafise would be in the position of judge, not advocate, and if Khurrem did not defend herself, she would be condemned by default. The very virtues of mother and son would prevent their defending her.

Khurrem shivered; she was, she decided, losing her taste for warfare, at least warfare of the sort she had been used to. Still, even while she shivered, she was conscious of a certain thrill of excitement, of a challenge, unspecified but accepted. She would be good, she would be watchful and she would make friends, she decided. How glad she was, for instance, that she had been courteous and gracious to the Aga of the Girls!

She roused and looked at the sky outside her lattice. It was clear and dark and the stars were very bright. She sighed. Last night at this time she had already begun to talk to Suleiman. She remembered how he had smiled, as it were involuntarily, when she admired his gold ewer. She sighed again. Tonight there would be no summons. He would be busy with his generals, with a thousand and one duties more important, or at least more pressing, than herself. She must learn to accept this, to be patient, but above all, not to be jealous. That way madness lay. In the meantime, she felt a more homely and pressing discomfort. She hoped those girls would hurry back from their supper. She was hungry.

# 25

From its earliest days the city of Istanbul was accustomed to seeing preparations for war, and since it had become the capital city of the Turks such manifestations had become more frequent, more urgent and certainly more aggressive. The spring of most years saw the armies come together and set out against the enemy of the day. Certainly the first spring of a new reign was watched by the citizens with eager interest. It was not so much a question of 'whether' as of 'when'. Suleiman in common with his great ancestors did not disappoint them. In the February of 1521 he set out on his first campaign.

This was to be a war with a difference, serious as all wars are, but carried forward with youthful lightheartedness and panache, a demonstration of the power of the Ottoman, warning his enemies that they had a new Sultan as watchful and warlike as any they had had in the past.

So the war drums had sounded and the horsetail standards had been brought out. These were the ancient and visible signs that 'God Almighty's army' was on the move, but more to the point hard and devoted work on the part of the whole state made sure that seven days from the first sounding of the drum at the gate of the New Palace, the army was ready. The whole machinery of the state was involved, for the army incorporated the state, and wherever the army went so too went the courts, the chancery and the seat of government. Not to mention the Church, for there was no war at this time that was not holy, an expedition against the forces of the infidel Christians.

Suleiman, sitting a magnificent Cappadocian horse, watched a sea of men flood through the great Hippodrome Square, his face beneath the huge turban, grave, expressionless, certainly showing none of the exultation that flowed through him at the sight of such warlike splendour. Behind him, on a platform erected for the occasion, stood Hafise, unveiled, white-robed and bejewelled as befitted her state, and flanked on each side by the ladies Gulbehar and Khurrem, both veiled, both staring straight ahead. And around and about, wherever they could insert themselves without danger of being trampled underfoot by the cavalry or crushed to death by the thundering wagons and siege engines, were the ordinary people of Istanbul, come to see, to point and shout and generally approve.

Not that all those fighting men who would converge on the White City were present, or even represented; some, such as the dreaded Tartar horsemen would only link up with the main army when they were well on their way towards the Danube. But there were assuredly enough and more than enough to strike dismay into the hearts of such Western observers as might have been courteously and no doubt sardonically invited to witness the spectacle.

First the light horse, the Akinji, irregular troops of disorderly ruffians who could never stand up to the attack of the disciplined Christian cavalry, but who attached themselves to the army for the sake of the plunder they might take if they were lucky. Also their effect could be devastating enough when they swept around the flanks of an enemy already disorganized by the attacks of the more formidable regular cavalry, murdering, pillaging, and swooping away again.

There were in all perhaps 40,000 of their infantry counterparts, the Azabs. Many of these were in peacetime criminals and ruffians who got their living as best they could. In time of siege such as the present war promised to be, they were particularly valuable, for they would be sent forward to break the enemy's charge, or fill the ditches and moats with their bodies. They were expendable in the fullest sense of the word. Nor did they care. Their philosophy was simple: if they lived there would be booty; if they died, martyrdom, and immediate translation to paradise.

After them rode the Delis or Madcaps, the 'crazy' company of scouts, their horses oddly festooned with fur and feathers, themselves equally outlandlishly clad in capes of bear or lion skin, the whole crowned with leopardskin caps beneath which long hair flowed over their shoulders. These were religious fanatics who had mastered the art of the forlorn hope and carried out raids no one else would have attempted. Behind them came steadily on the cavalry themselves, following their red banner. Each man was heavily armed with knife and pistol, scimitar and mace, and each bore at his back his buckler and his bow and arrows, those short, long-flighted Turkish bows which could sometimes hit their target at over 600 feet. All were splendidly mounted, some on Arabs, some on Turkomans or Persians. These were perhaps the most colourful corps of the whole army, with their lofty white turbans, and the chain mail glinting beneath their purple, blue and scarlet robes. Precious stones studded their weapons and the trappings of their splendid horses.

Suleiman gave special attention to the auxiliary corps who followed the cavalry, for with his grasp of essentials he had already learned the importance of supply. He watched with a sharp eye as the commissariat wagons, laden with grain, trundled by, and cast an appreciative glance over the hundreds of swaying camels laden with powder and lead.

No one, however, had eyes for anything or anyone else once the guns had rumbled by, for they were followed by the janissaries, the corps d'élite of Suleiman's army, then at the height of their efficiency as a war machine and, perhaps, of their loyalty to their Sultan. They marched on inexorably, rank upon rank of them, following their white banner, embroidered in gold with a text from the Koran and a two-edged flaming sword, and the three-horsetail standard of their Aga, who ranked as the third greatest man in the empire and was as much a minister of war for them as a general.

As jealously guarded as their banner and the standard were the great copper cauldrons which they carried into war with them, symbols of the food which came to them by right from the Sultan, and which, scanty as it might be, together with love of fighting and lust for booty, made up the only pleasure and ambition of their harsh lives. Indeed, the importance that food represented in their simple régime was pointed by the fact that the very officers took their titles from the kitchens: a colonel was the Chief Maker of Soup, a captain a Chief Supplier of Water. Their cooks marched in stations of honour, wearing black leather aprons. The horses of the water-carriers were wreathed with flowers. Plumes and dark blue cloaks swinging with their stride, their appearance was exotic indeed in the midst of that

Asiatic horde, for young, beardless, as most of them were, they were also unmistakably European, recruited as they were from the sons of conquered Christians. Forcibly circumcised, taught the arts of war, forbidden to marry, they knew no home but a barracks and no pleasures but those of war. No wonder that their periodic outbursts of rage against authority were feared and dreaded by everyone from the Sultan down.

Suleiman watched them swing past him with a smile which might well have held a touch of irony. Today they were happy at the prospect of action and loot. He would have no trouble with them while the war went well and there were plenty of pickings. But there had been times in Egypt and Persia when they had refused to follow even Selim. This had better be a short and glorious war, he thought, until I get to know them better, or they get to know me.

He turned his attention to the hordes of dervishes who ran beside the ranks in their tall Persian hats of brown camel's hair, naked except for green aprons fringed with ebony beads. As they ran they yelled martial texts from the Koran or blew raucous blasts on horns. The din they made was supposed to inflame the troops to greater warlike activity, but as he very well knew, would also inflame the janissaries, if not his feudal troops and cavalry, to disorder and unrest if things did not go their way.

Nevertheless, he was happy and approving of practically everything he saw. The noise, enthusiasm, the steady movement of colourful uniform and steel chainlink armour delighted him. It would be a splendid adventure from which he promised himself he would learn much and return home triumphant.

Behind him, the ladies closest to him reacted each in her own way. Hafise, the daughter of a soldier, and the wife of another, with all that that implied, had seen it all before, but still could not resist its spell. Gulbehar, insecure and miserable behind her veil, was conscious only that the noise was making her head ache and the dust drying her throat.

Khurrem alone was in her element. She had never seen anything like it. If it came to that, she had seen very little during the past few months, except the faces of women and the tops of turbans glimpsed from high up through lattices. All these fierce, swaggering men in their gorgeous or preposterous clothes amazed and fascinated her, the dervishes made her want to laugh but she restrained the impulse, sensing that they must mean something special to the soldiers and the watching crowds. Even the noise, and especially the military bands with their shrill, wild music, delighted her. She stood motionless, eyes wide, unconscious of the passage of time. Now and again, she glanced down at the erect figure on the splendid horse at whose command this whole magnificent display had been set in motion, and wished that he might just once turn his head and look at her. She understood that this was a foolish whim that could not be gratified, but supposed there was no harm in wishing. She had another reason for pleasure, and was very well aware of it. For the first time she was one of the chosen few; she was no longer excluded and quite frankly gloried in the fact. She intended to remain in that élite, accepting all the advantages and the responsibilities and drawbacks as well.

Now the army had at last passed by, but the endless-seeming procession still showed no sign of flagging. Indeed, there now began to pass a considerable body of very important men, and Hafise, allowing herself a quick glance to her left, was amused and heartened to see (for Khurrem's veil was of the flimsiest silk) that her protégée was bending slightly forward and looking very thoughtful indeed as she watched.

Now passing by were the judges of Istanbul and the army, impassive and dignified in their huge white turbans and fur-edged robes. Khurrem watched them carefully, wondering who they were and which was which. The army's procession had been a spectacle which frankly delighted her as a spectacle. These distinguished men were a different matter. They were Suleiman's men and as such she felt they must be of interest to her. She wanted to be able to distinguish them, one from the other, to be able to form, however inadequately, an assessment of each man's character, at least to know what he looked like. That it was not her business, a mere woman, to stare frankly at men, particularly men of such outstanding importance and dare to weigh them up, never began to occur to her. Everything about her Sultan concerned and interested her and therefore his other slaves were her business. It did not cross her mind even that the time might ever come that he should discuss matters of state or men of consequence with her. It was instinctive in her to make herself acquainted with as many of his people and as many of his affairs as she could, and that was all.

She made rather heavy weather of it. She had gathered from the gossip she heard from Fatma, from Hulefa and from a middle-aged woman who had helped to dress her (and she would get to know her name for she seemed to have her wits about her) something of the order in which these distinguished men would march, so that she knew at least that these gentlemen in fur-trimmed robes were judges and that those in green turbans were the dignitaries of the priesthood and descendants of the Prophet. These haughty personages, whose weapons and clothes were covered with precious stones — even the caparisons of their horses glittered with gems — were, she supposed the viziers of the Divan, but she had no means of knowing which was which, or even which was the most important. She shook her head and sighed with frustration. Then, remembering her own troubles, took herself to task. She had enough to worry about, while this campaign lasted. Just let her dear Suleiman come back safely at the end of it. Then if she still lasted, she would learn more and perhaps even make herself useful to him.

She did notice one man more than the others around Suleiman. He stood out because he seemed superlatively plain, with his underhung jaw, but she was disposed to like him because he was, unlike practically all these Turks with their solemn faces and stately movements, merry. Something in the procession amused him and he laughed heartily, gesticulating and drawing the attention of the man beside him to what he had seen, so that that dignitary laughed too, or at least smiled. Khurrem remembered him and his ugly jaw and laughing eyes, and later that day Hulefa told her briefly that he was Ibrahim, the Sultan's new Captain of the Inner Household, a coming man, not yet of any importance.

At last, with the sacred camels bearing the Koran and a piece of the Kaaba stone, that relic most sacred to all Muslims before which the crowds fell suddenly silent, the great mustering came to its end. Suleiman and his entourage rode away, and the Sultana Valideh caught the eyes of her two attendant ladies, and stiffly descended to her carriage.

# 26

Suleiman visited the Old Palace that night to say his farewells to the ladies of his family before leaving at dawn for Belgrade. His mother received him in state. He thought he had never seen her so splendid, though he recognized a measure of feverishness in her behaviour. This he rightly attributed to weariness, for he was well aware of the incessant hard work in which she had engaged ever since her arrival in the capital, and her concern for him on this fateful departure on his first major campaign. But she positively glittered with gaiety and tenderness and he knew that he need have no major worry for her well-being in his absence, so long as she did not wear herself out.

Gulbehar was a different matter. Duty compelled him to visit her, even to spend the night with her if circumstances led to that conclusion. They did not. Forbearing, he listened with such patience as he could command to a reiteration of all the complaints to which he had already been subjected. He attempted to reason with her, although he knew it to be useless, and saw it as a weakness in himself which he despised. Finally her language became so unbridled that he rose and left her weeping.

He felt that he could stand no more tears and was tempted to return to Topkapi, there to send for music and conversation in the form of Ibrahim. Rather to his surprise, he hesitated. An autocrat of autocrats, he was accustomed to deciding what he wished to do and doing it without reference to the feelings or whims of others. Gulbehar's performance had annoyed and ruffled him and was, he decided, typical of the way women behaved when taking leave of the men they loved. Even his mother had evoked by the very things she refrained from saying and doing, a similar disturbing emotion in himself and he wanted no more of it on his last night. Nevertheless, although he was sure that she would distress and unsettle him, he still wished to see Khurrem. He could not escape it, and what he regarded as further evidence of weakness in himself surprised and annoyed him. He would, he decided, see her briefly and take a formal leavetaking of her. So thoroughly charming and satisfying a girl deserved that of him.

Satisfied, he had himself conducted to the suite of rooms provided for his use in the harem, and sent for her. She came quickly, and her gift for surprising him did not fail. This dignified girl was more like a princess than the timid little peasant who had so delighted him before. Nevertheless she was exciting in her plain dark gown, and he detected tenderness and concern for himself in her attitude without any disposition to tears or any attempt to make him feel guilty because he was going away.

He felt relaxation begin to steal over him. He was tired and he was taut, and all he wanted at the moment was something delightful to look at and something to listen to which would not extend or stimulate him too much. Khurrem, it seemed, could supply both these requirements. He sighed with contentment and leaned back, while she, who had a great deal to say about what she had seen during the day, chattered on, eyes bright, hands busily illustrating her talk. Moreover, what she had to say tonight did not involve the answering of too many questions.

It was only when she characterized one of the more respected members of the Divan as 'a weary old bull looking for a field to lie down in' that he stopped her. She had been describing with considerable enjoyment and gusto the appearance of many of the distinguished men she had noted in the procession, and Suleiman, watching her with increasing pleasure and listening with only half an ear, had suddenly recognized the man from the description alone. He laughed with rich enjoyment, and Khurrem stopped talking to look at him with surprise.

'Where have you seen this man before?' he demanded when he was able.

Her eyes wide, she replied, 'Never,' adding with truth, 'I never see any men, except the eunuchs and you. Until today, of course.'

'Well,' said Suleiman, 'and when the old bull finds his field, what will he do?'

'Lie down and eat and sleep in the sun,' she replied cheerfully.

211

'And will he get up again?'

'I think he has got up again and again. Now he's too tired.'

This so exactly coincided with his own thinking about this particular commander, an old and valued servant of Selim, that Suleiman was impressed. He continued to look at her in silence, and Khurrem, sitting upright on her cushion, rested her chin on her hand and looked at him doubtfully.

'Have I been impertinent?' she asked eventually.

This was indeed a new Khurrem; he had hardly thought she knew the meaning of the word. Though even now she did not look as if she was prepared to take it very seriously. He assured her she had not, and she expelled a small sigh and remained silent.

'Do you remember this man?' he asked, and described as best he could Piri Pasha and his position in the procession.

She said she did and added, 'But I can't be funny about all of them.'

Suleiman sighed in his turn, and said patiently, 'Don't try. What is he like?'

Khurrem looked at him doubtfully, obviously expecting a trap or an inquisition. Finally she fixed her eyes on his face, pursed her lips and said, 'I wouldn't want to make trouble for that one.'

'You are not going to make trouble for anyone,' he told her repressively.

But she was adamant. Piri had struck her as an impressive elderly man, but she had nothing more to say about him. She had not particularly noticed him, and that was a fact.

Suleiman was inclined to be annoyed. It seemed, at first, like wilful neglect on her part to have failed to remark so impressive and distinguished a man, and one about whom it would have comforted him to hear a fresh opinion. He repressed his irritation, attributing it to over-anxiety and weariness, and indeed, it soon struck him that a lesser girl, one more supple and awake to her own advantage, might have tried to cobble up some word picture of Piri for him, leading him, perhaps, to tell her unconsciously what he wanted to hear, so that she could astound him with the brilliance of her insight. Whatever Khurrem's faults, duplicity was not one of them, it was plain. At the moment she was watching his face, again slightly puzzled perhaps by his own quick changes of mood.

Impulsively, he leaned forward and took her hand. It was, he noted, a remarkably firm, not to say hard, little paw, and that seemed right too, in a girl who had worked so hard for survival in so many ways. There was plenty of evidence of feminine softness about Khurrem as he had reason to know; she was entitled to her sign of competence. He held on to the hand, therefore, while he asked himself, with some surprise, what he had intended to say to her. He was not given to such tender impulses, nothing in his way of life and certainly nothing in his station encouraged them. He searched his mind a little desperately, wondering again if he was making a fool of himself, while Khurrem looked up at him, intent, serious and questioning.

The thought came, momentous in its simplicity: this girl is to be trusted; this girl loves you. Nothing like this had ever happened to him before. He needed time to get used to the idea. So he found something to say.

'Khurrem, my mother works very hard.'

She looked surprised, as if that was not what she had expected to hear, and indeed, he had spoken somewhat abruptly. She collected herself quite quickly and agreed. She had, she said, been with Hafise the previous afternoon and heard her giving what amounted to judgement in the case of the harem of his father. It had been, she said quietly, distressing and wearing even for a lady as buoyant as his mother.

'Apart from her senior servants she has no one to watch over her welfare except you.'

To his surprise he discovered that this bold statement was true. Apart from himself, he had heard Hafise speak with tenderness and affection only of this girl, and could understand why. Had he himself not very nearly betrayed himself into – he cleared his throat.

'Watch over her, Khurrem, for my sake. Do not let her weary herself too much.'

She promised readily, and if she thought a little ruefully that between attempting to prevent so autocratic a lady as Hafise from overworking, and guarding herself from the machinations of Gulbehar and such other enemies as she might make, her life was opening out most wonderfully, she did not show it. At least, she told herself, I shan't have time to worry.

Suleiman did not, after all, confine himself to a brief or formal leavetaking. Indeed, just before dawn, when she

# 27

There was no sound, Suleiman believed, more exciting than the jingle of harness and the click of iron-shod hooves heard in the last darkness before dawn at the beginning of a campaign. As he rode out in the midst of his guard that February morning, his spirits were as high as they were ever to be. All the weariness and worry of the previous days were forgotten – even Khurrem and his mother were put out of his mind – and he pressed forward, full of keen enjoyment for the moment and confidence in his and his Turks' ability to conquer.

It was a notable undertaking. Sixty-six years before, the great Mehmed the Conqueror had set out to capture Belgrade and with it the road to Vienna and the West. He had been defeated, with the loss of 25,000 of his best troops, all his military supplies and 300 cannon. Now his great-grandson was attempting the same thing.

Suleiman, essentially pragmatic in outlook, hardly saw it either as impudent or dramatic. If he had had little hand in his father's great victories, he had been reared in his father's tradition. He might wonder at his ability to continue that tradition or enlarge on it, but it was too much part of him for him to dream of attempting to escape it. Moreover, he was never so much part of it as when actually in the field. Action stimulated him as nothing else. He might doubt himself in the night watches but not in the thick of the battle, or on the road to it. In this noisy dawn, surrounded by devoted servants and familiar friends, whose faces became every minute clearer as the sun rose, he was at his happiest, and would have changed places with no man.

'It is a good omen,' he observed to Ibrahim cheerfully, 'that we take the road to Edirne. That place is lucky for me. I have known many a good hunt there.'

Their way was a much-travelled road over the Ergene River at the point where Murad II had built his great stone bridge, with its hostel for travellers, its mosque and its school. Here had grown up a town of nearly 500 families and they all turned out to see the armies pass.

Ibrahim agreed with equal gaiety. Had Piri been there he might have thought, but not said, that the place had been less than lucky for Selim. But Piri was not there, having already set out with his force of janissaries, cavalry and Arabs for Nish in Serbia.

The whole undertaking had been most meticulously planned. Suleiman, with Ibrahim as senior aide-de-camp, in addition to his new post as Captain of the Inner Household, had scrupulously attended each Council of War and both had learned much, and in his own way. Suleiman, listening intently to the speeches of Selim's generals, quickly realized the value of their ability and experience; most of all he appreciated their forbearance with himself, the unlicked cub in their midst. Not by so much of a flicker of an eyelid did any one of them betray surprise or impatience at what he was sure must strike them as gross inexperience and ignorance. Indeed, with a little leading from Piri, they had made it appear that the major features of the plan came from himself. For this he was grateful, but he was not deceived.

Three armies were to converge on Belgrade. Suleiman, with most of his household troops, moved steadily towards Nish by way of Sofia. Ahmed Pasha, the governor of Rumelia and an outstanding general of cavalry, moved against Sabacz, an important system of forts on the south bank of the river Sava, sixty miles west of Belgrade. Piri's destination was Belgrade, via Semlin on the Danube. Suleiman himself was making direct for Belgrade. At the same time, the Akinji, those wild irregulars, would ride out in two columns, all 30,000 of them, one to effect a diversion against Transylvania, the other to carry out their traditional role of devastation, this time against the land between the Drave and Sava rivers, south of Belgrade. This was an undertaking large enough to satisfy even their appetite for personal annihilation or glory.

Much depended on the orderly linking up at Sofia with Ferhad Pasha's enormous camelborne force coming from Asia laden with ammunition and grain. As they rode, Suleiman's mind, incessantly busy with every detail of the day's business, turned frequently to this first major event in the sequence so necessary to their success. He worried at it incessantly, but as the days passed, drew comfort from seeing, almost hour by hour, the steady arrival of groups of feudal knights with their followers. These would appear suddenly on the skyline, horseborne figures in all manner of motley armour and helmets, stand silhouetted motionless while presumably their leader identified the army, and then come hurtling down, white teeth very much in evidence as broad smiles split tanned faces, to mingle with their fellows. If the force was large enough, and their leader important enough, he was brought to Suleiman to do homage and exchange such military chat as might occur to them.

Suleiman enjoyed these interchanges with outlandish and sometimes extravagant personalities, and took great trouble to draw these men out, to discover what they were thinking, how they lived and what their ambitions. Although he was unaware of it, he was at his best with them, the stiffness and solemnity which sometimes marred his appearances on formal and courtly occasions in Istanbul was never in evidence, and men on whose loyalty to himself he must depend in the ultimate gave it gladly and thought him a very worthy successor to his father.

Almost before he knew it, it seemed, they were well past Edirne, set in its ring of hills, and making good time for their first great rendezvous at Sofia. The further they travelled, the more Suleiman felt his spirits rise. He had had some experience in the past of the movement of an army, but never on this scale, and its orderliness and the ease with which it appeared to be controlled delighted him. He took every opportunity given him, and made many himself, to mingle with the men and to talk with them. The relaxation of his own strict rules of conduct which made it possible for him to eat his meals with Ibrahim or some other companion, chosen for his knowledge, or even merely because he liked the look of him or what he had heard about him, delighted him; so too did the fact that they were now in country which, while still part of his empire, was unknown to him.

He looked about him with delighted interest, especially as they were now passing through the curious and historic environs of the ancient city of Philippopolis. There it stood on its high granite crags rising abruptly from the wide, fertile valley in which they stood. Suleiman and his party reined in, admiring the dramatic setting, and wondering at the curious mounds of earth with which the plain was covered. The Sanjak Bey of the district rode up in great importance to tell his Sultan of the local belief that they marked the sites of ancient battles, and that beneath them lay the bodies of those who died in the fighting.

'Who were they?' demanded Suleiman. 'Were they here before Philip?'

The man had no idea; he had just about heard of Philip of Macedon and no more. He shrugged, 'No man knows, Sire.'

'Well, what did they fight for?'

The Bey shook his head. No one knew that either. Suleiman looked at him quizzically. If no one knew, he was wasting his time. The unknown past stretched out behind him. Men had fought and fallen and been forgotten, and that might be his fate. But as long as he believed in what he did and enjoyed the doing of it, he would be content.

Suleiman, despite his impatience to be in Sofia, had time to spend in this city which also had a special interest for one of his race and family. What had been a frontier post to Philip of Macedon had been an important conquest also to Murad I, for after his decisive conquest of Edirne he had marched on Philippopolis and taken it, cutting off Constantinople from the rest of Christendom and menacing Bulgaria and Serbia at a stroke. So Suleiman saw all that was to be seen of crumbling walls and eyeless buildings with delight, but was equally impressed to see the rice growing healthily in the marshland below. To him, the sight of today's crop growing on yesterday's battlefield was as impressive as the past itself. But having gained an idea of the place he was very ready to press on, for once they had crossed the plain before Philippopolis the army had to cross the Rhodope mountains by the pass known to them as the Narrow Gate, and he was eager to see how this would be accomplished. They made camp for the night therefore and prepared for the crossing at first light of morning.

They were now, he knew, on the old Roman road to Sofia, but there was, he saw, little evidence of it at this point. He stored the memory for a purpose: his armies and his merchants would come this way increasingly, he hoped. The road should be restored. In the meantime the guns must be manhandled, horses and mules and men driven, and where needful flogged, through this unfriendly country.

When he himself achieved the summit, which was, he saw, rendered difficult to such a horde more by reason of its narrowness than its steepness, he paused to look at the summit of Mount Rhodope, rising clear and beautiful under its snow mantle, to follow with his eye the course of the River Hebrus, and then, without a word, signalled to his entourage to ride on across the plain to the foothills and finally to the pleasant valleys and fields surrounding Sofia.

They were in no doubt as they approached that considerable city that Ferhad Pasha was either already there with his combined force, or just arriving. The din was appalling; so was the smell. Also the press of civilians, either fleeing from something unspecified or come to see the arrival of the Sultan and his army, made the road almost impassable.

The inexperienced Ibrahim's eyes suddenly started from his head. 'In God's name,' he demanded, 'what is that?'

Suleiman's lips were parted already in his most wolfish grin and his eyes were bright.

'Camels!' he answered succinctly. 'Ferhad is here.'

He turned in the saddle and demanded imperiously of the commander of his guard, 'Why am I delayed? Clear the road!'

That worthy was already asking himself the same question and giving himself and his men the same instruction without much success, until a detachment of janissaries succeeded in slashing their way through the mass of humanity. A detachment of Sipahis was seen to be approaching from the other direction. They appeared as dusty and travel-worn as their own men and Ibrahim, eyeing them doubtfully, asked 'Ferhad's men?'

'They had better be,' replied Suleiman shortly.

They were. Their message was brief. A camping ground to the north of the town was prepared for his imperial majesty. Ferhad's own army and baggage-trains had taken up their station on the lower land to the east. As for the Sultan's army, his scouts had already selected suitable camp sites.

'Well, and better. You will lead me to the camping ground and bring me your commander,' said Suleiman, pleased.

He had neatly placed the onus of getting himself and his guard out of this intolerable press on the shoulders of the officer commanding this troop and sat back in the saddle, interested to see how it would be managed. His lips tightened, however, when he saw that the man combined maximum efficiency with maximum brutality, and when he had seen an elderly woman beaten into the ditch beside the road, her face a mass of crimson jelly, he reined in his horse and roared at the man, who came spurring back to see what was wrong.

'It is not necessary to destroy the entire population of this town to get me where I am going. Nor will the conduct of this war suffer if I am delayed five minutes. If you have judgement, exercise it!'

The man's face suffused with colour and rage, but he curbed the violence and within a quarter of an hour, Suleiman found himself dismounted on the edge of a glade outside the city and watching the orderly preparations to make camp.

To him there now came Ferhad Pasha, quick, brisk, and well satisfied with his achievement as, thought Suleiman, watching the man warily, he had every reason to be. It was simply that he could not trust him. However, he was to be congratulated and consulted, for his war experience was exemplary, as this lastest exploit of bringing 3,000 camels laden with ammunition across the Bosphorus out of Asia, and from as far away as Arabia, and a further 30,000 more, laden with grain and heavy baggage, demonstrated. Ferhad was happy to be consulted and equally ready to give his opinion. They would need time now, he explained, to integrate their two armies. Perhaps two weeks, perhaps a month, he could not tell.

'Make it two weeks,' suggested Suleiman gently.

Ferhad nodded seriously, and pointed out that the collection of barley and flour, 10,000 wagon loads, as they had computed in Istanbul would be needed, from the inhibitants of this whole Danube basin, was proceeding apace, but could not be hurried.

'No?' asked Suleiman, 'But we are paying for it, it is not a levy. There is no reason for delay. The sooner it is delivered, the sooner the farmers will be paid.'

Ferhad sighed, and conceded that this was so, but pointed out as to a child that there were difficulties of administration to be overcome. He was a humourless man and could never perceive when he was being cajoled or mocked.

'Well,' said his Sultan, 'if there are difficulties, you are undoubtedly the man to overcome them, considering what you have overcome already. Every assistance I can give you is at your disposal, but make it two weeks.'

He gave his hand to be kissed, bowed, and went to supper, which he ate with Ibrahim and two grizzled Sanjak Beys of no importance whatsoever.

# 28

Ferhad Pasha made it fifteen days, and on a fair day in April the enormous armies set out along the old military road on the last leg of their journey for Nish on the borders of Servia.

Suleiman now found himself not in the best of spirits, perhaps because of the necessity of working in close proximity with a man he both disliked and distrusted. He did not understand Ferhad's temperament, at once capable of grasping the broad essentials of transporting large numbers of men and animals – and what animals! Ferhad's devotion to the objectionable camel was something else he found incalculable – it was also fussy enough to concern itself with the details of payment for fodder and grain. Moreover, he disliked the rough and ready attitude of Ferhad's officers and men. Training of men seemed to have been scamped in favour of the movement of animals and things.

Suleiman knew his attitude to be unreasonable; he should be grateful for a general of such unusual abilities and so he learned to control his impatience, particularly as he knew, none better, that this careful provision for more than adequate ammunition and food had been his own individual contribution to the planning of the campaign. But still, he wished Ferhad other than what he was. He wished he himself knew more of the conduct of war. He was irked by the fact that everywhere he went a human barrier of solaks – the 150 veteran janissaries whose sole duty was to guard his life – formed around him. As if that was not enough, another detachment ran beside his horse. They were trained runners, who carried his messages and ran his errands. These necessary guards, whose presence he had taken for granted in Istanbul and on the earlier stages of the march, now began to seem to him an unbearable restriction. He wanted to live still closer to the war and his men, for, except that he slept in a tent of luxurious green silk, guarded at night by archers whose bows were always ready strung, and travelled onwards and northwards every day, the business of government travelled with him and he must, however irksome it might now seem, bear his part in its routine.

But still, inexorably, the miles fell away and some three weeks after leaving Sofia, he saw at last through the dust the outskirts of Nish, that not inconsiderable town where the final councils of war would be held, where all his veteran generals would come together to exchange ideas and make their final dispositions before the general onslaught on Belgrade. Suleiman was divided in his mind about this. He dreaded dashing his inexperience once again against the stone wall of their devotion and their inexhaustible courtesy, and this time in the presence of Ferhad. On the other hand, he must accept the fact of that inexperience and seek to replace it with knowledge, however hard won. So he came to the councils with his head and courage high and fared better than he expected.

For one thing, the proceedings were formal. For another, the plan had already been made and there were no decisions to be taken. He knew as well as they what was to be done. Here they would divide once again, Ahmed Pasha with his cavalry moving on Sabacz, and Piri rapidly against Semlin on the Danube a little north of the city. The purpose of these two movements was to cut off Belgrade from all assistance and isolate her for the final blow. Suleiman himself with the main body and the cream of the standing army, the core of the janissaries and the heavy artillery which had never given ground before any enemy, was to make his way directly to Belgrade itself.

So, at last, Suleiman was facing enemy territory and with a definite task before him. With his huge army he was to advance into Hungary and as soon as he heard of the success of Ahmed Pasha to the south of Belgrade he was to advance to meet him and show himself at Sabacz, the victorious Sultan coming to lead his army to its final destination. And, he told himself, he would have a hand in this, or die in the attempt.

Despite his gloomy view of his own place in the campaign, he could not fail to feel a thrill of exultation when he saw the first signs of his army's activity. It was nothing much, for such peasants as the land would support elected to be out of the way whenever they heard of the advance of a Turkish army in their direction: a village destroyed and deserted, dead animals, scorched fields and the bodies of two or three men beside the track, one an akinji, but as the long days progressed and they passed more and similar signs of desolation, he noticed a change in his guard as well as in himself, a new alertness, quick glances and sly smiles of satisfaction. The commander of the solaks without a word to him, increased his guard both by night and day. Watchfires burned by night, and there was more activity by day, scouts rode in and spies materialized and disappeared again; the pirs, those strange holy men who accompanied the army, exhorting, prophesying, cursing the enemy and praying aloud to Allah, became a perfect nuisance with their shrill cries and lamentations, demands for food, which they always got even if others starved, and their habit of getting in the way of legitimate military business.

It was now high summer, their way leading them along the course of the river Morava, with its fields and pastures which would have been pleasant but for the increasing evidence of devastation. Intelligence brought satisfactory news of progress on all sides. Piri had taken Semlin. Ahmed Pasha sent to say that he was before Sabacz, forty Turkish vessels had been seen on the Danube within easy reach of Belgrade. All that was wanting was sight of the enemy, who were conspicuous by their absence.

Hungary was, in fact, in a bad way, and Suleiman might congratulate himself that he had chosen the optimum time to attack this onetime bulwark against Turkish power in Europe, against which two of his most distinguished forebears had flung themselves in vain. She was at her lowest ebb. A child king had succeeded a weak and vacillating father. A disunited nobility had just succeeded with difficulty in quelling a peasant revolt. There was no money in the treasury to pay a bewildered army. Final blow: there were no allies willing to give help from outside. Even while Suleiman advanced on Belgrade, the country was given over to the celebration of the marriage of King Louis and the Princess Maria, sister of the emperor, who, greatest irony of all, proclaimed his readiness to help in the future and his inability to do so now.

It was not that responsible Hungarians were blind to their danger. They were not, but Suleiman's army had been on the march for over two months before envoys solicited help from all over Christendom and received the same dusty answer from all sides. It was perhaps not surprising therefore that, disunited and disorganized as they were, the Hungarian government received no intelligence of the Turk's intention until he was already at Sofia.

When finally their Council of State was convened on 24 April it was plain that the defence of the two border fortresses of Sabacz and Belgrade was the first problem to be faced. But both were under the command of fiercely proud Hungarian noblemen who stoutly maintained their ability to defend their posts to the end, so long as they were provided with the necessary money, food and ammunition. What they would not do was hand over to any soldier appointed by the Crown. When the Council insisted, both took umbrage and retired to their estates. Further, the crews of the defence vessels on the Danube, unpaid for three years, took the opportunity to go off to Buda Pesth to complain of their neglect. When they were fobbed off with promises, they refused to return to their posts.

All this was bad, as bad as could be, but if it could be made worse by anything, it was the feverish atmosphere of unreality and unwillingness to face ugly facts that made it possible for the Hungarian court and society generally to turn their backs on the approaching whirlwind and betake themselves to Pressburg, on the border with Austria, there to celebrate their child King's marriage with the Princess Maria and take part in the glittering festivities designed to mark this occasion. This was in June, and at the end of that month Piri in his businesslike and orderly fashion took the fortress of Semlin and opened the way to Belgrade.

Belgrade, the White City, the ancient capital of the Serbians and Hungarians, lies on the southern side of the Danube where it joins the Sava coming from the west and turning at this point nearly north. Thus Belgrade lies on a tongue of high land, with its citadel at its highest point at the tip and is protected on two sides by water. Immediately below it in the Danube lies a large island, thickly covered with trees, and opposite, to the north above the confluence with the Sava, is the crucial town and fortress of Semlin. Few places have been besieged and captured so often as Belgrade. In the fourteenth century it had been a constant bone of contention between the Serbians and Hungarians. In the next century the Turks twice laid siege to it without success. After that there was constant irregular warfare on the borders between Hungary and the Ottoman Empire. As late as 1516 John Zapolya, the governor of Transylvania, had led an extensive raid into Turkish territory, taking with him the guns of Belgrade. He was defeated with the loss of the cannon, so that in addition to its other defects of defence, it was now short of artillery.

Thus Suleiman, surveying the unfortunate city at the beginning of July, had every reason for satisfaction. Sabacz, defending itself with desperate heroism, fell to Ahmed Pasha and the news was brought to the Sultan on 7 July, together with the heads of the hundred men who survived the assault. These, mounted on pikes, were placed along Suleiman's line of march, but this was but a grim anticipation of final victory.

Now, to his own immense satisfaction, Suleiman was to take a hand in the business. But first, the victorious Ahmed Pasha and his Sanjak beys must be received and congratulated. This done with customary grace, Suleiman went to see the fort for himself and ordered the building of a bastion and a moat. Then, noting that the Sava was in flood, he ordered a bridge to be built so that his armies could cross to the northern bank. Feeling all the responsibility of command, he quartered himself in a hut so that he could supervise the job and stand no nonsense. The labouring pioneers worked under the eyes of grim-faced pashas armed with canes, well aware of that other stern young face watching them.

The bridge was finished in ten days. Such devotion deserved better fortune; but the Sava continued to rise, and by 19 July Suleiman was compelled to admit that the bridge was no longer usable. There was nothing for it but to send the heavy baggage, cannon and provisions overland to Belgrade, while the men took to the boats. It took another ten days for everything and everybody to be embarked; on 29 July Suleiman himself set out and arrived before Belgrade two days later. It had not been the most dramatic incident in the campaign, far from it, but Suleiman enjoyed it immensely and learned from it, too. If he was present, he was responsible.

Now, around Suleiman's tent rose the enormous Turkish encampment, orderly, clean and quiet, the despair and envy of visiting European envoys used to the dirt, disorder and disease of their own camps.

Now the plight of Belgrade was desperate indeed, its south side completely blocked from the west, and menaced from the Danube itself by the enemy's boats, but still the defenders of the city were not prepared to throw their hands in. What they knew of their enemy's short way with survivors no doubt stimulated them to hold out.

Once before the city Suleiman took a day to survey the scene and consult with his commanders, and on 2 August the first general attack was launched. The watchful Suleiman was there at first light to see the start of it. He noted the work of the engineers as they built the great movable wooden towers to be pushed against the battlements, the battering rams and the enormous catapults to hurl the firebombs. Others built zig-zagging trenches in the glacis and laid mines against the foundations of the walls.

Then, to the sound of the janissary music – camel drums, elephant drums, mule drums, cymbals and hautboys and all – the attack began.

Under the first light of the sun came the Azabs, the rabble, expendable and undisciplined. After them came the janissaries, rank upon rank of them in their red tunics and white sleeve-caps, marching inexorably. The cavalry flanked them, led by the 'Mad' Delis, the most ferocious of that whole ferocious corps, wearing the wings of black eagles in their spiked helmets, and armed with maces. Soon the pleasant water-meadows awoke to hideous sound as the bronze cannon added their voices to the din of music and the screams of men and horses. Smoke drifted across from the burning towers and fireballs and hid the scene. All day the battle raged, and at nightfall the Turks fell back, repulsed, and with 600 men lost. Such a beginning showed plainly that the besieged could defend themselves effectively, and because of a rumour that reinforcements had been promised them by way of the river, it was decided to send a party of 500 janissaries up the Danube by boats on the following day. Some of the heaviest cannon were planted on the island opposite the town, and Suleiman watched this operation, too, with breathless interest. Only when he heard the bombardment begin from that quarter, could he be persuaded to go to supper. This day, 3 August, was a bad day for Bali Aga, Aga of the janissaries, who was wounded as he led yet another attack against the walls.

The beginning of the end came a week later when those serious, not to say experienced, students of siege methods, Ahmed and Piri, judged the city had been sufficiently softened up, and proposed a triple attack. Once again the Azabs rushed into the ditches, and the janissaries poured after them. The merciless week-long pounding had had its effect: the defenders abandoned the town, set it on fire and retired into the citadel. When the first flames were seen to rise from behind the unhappy walls, a great rolling roar of satisfaction rose from the throats of the army, but, 'The end will not come yet,' said Piri sternly. 'These are determined men, they have nothing to lose. Something more is needed.'

'What, then?' demanded Suleiman, shielding his eyes from the pall of smoke. To his mind, it seemed impossible that anyone could live in the place, let alone fight. 'The towers of the citadel must be mined, and the guns moved up closer.'

'All that,' agreed Piri approvingly. He thought privately that his pupil had come on amazingly through this long summer, and it had not escaped his notice, though it seemed to have missed Suleiman's, that wherever the Sultan went he was greeted with the same approval and even affection by his soldiers, especially those spoiled darlings, the janissaries. 'But we have not much longer to sit down in front of this place while these Christian dogs make up their minds. The summer is ending. A little treachery would help us now.' He smoothed his moustaches thoughtfully.

Suleiman studied the terrible scene before him and digested this latest lesson. He would have thought the end had come already, and of course it was possible he was right, but the probability was that he was not. The thing was, then, never to rest, never to be satisfied with what was achieved, until the ultimate was accomplished. There must be always at least one more thing to try. He asked, with as much humility as he ever attained:

'How is that to be arranged?'

'It may arrange itself,' explained Piri, 'but we will not wait for that to happen, by your leave. In there' – he jerked a thumb forward into the smoke behind which Belgrade crackled and burned – 'are Hungarians who may, for all I know, be patriots. There are also Serbians who are mercenaries and are certainly *not* patriots. They should soon begin to quarrel. When that happens it will be to our advantage. Among our numbers there are fellows who can hasten things along with a word here and a word there. Among their other accomplishments are the arts of swimming rivers and cutting throats in the dark. They are always at work.' His eyes met Suleiman's limpidly.

'Do you know them?' asked Suleiman unexpectedly.

Piri's eyes widened. 'I, Sire? Do you mean personally? No, to be sure. It is impossible to know every man who serves, no matter how valuable his activities.' He looked at his Sultan sternly, 'There is nothing to be gained, Sire, in getting too close to the fray and impossible, however much one may wish, to know everything or see everything. For a commander the broad view is best.'

He coughed violently from the smoke and apologized. Suleiman, staring straight ahead, acknowledged him absently, and then suddenly rousing himself, awarded him his sweet smile and with 'Thank you, Piri,' wheeled and vanished into the murk, his watchful guard about him.

During the next three weeks, Suleiman had the pleasure of watching Piri's prophecies and organization work themselves out. The Hungarian defenders, reduced by the constant attacks by the janissaries and the incessant bombardment, began quarrelling with the Serbians as to what must be done next.

The Hungarian artillerymen were the first to desert, but by the end of the month the citadel was attacked from within when two deserters showed the janissaries where the walls were at their weakest at the Sava–Danube confluence. The great guns thundered against the point and opened a breach. One of the great towers was successfully mined and blown up.

So, on 29 August, another dawn rose on the end of yet another siege of Belgrade, as the last Turkish attack was mounted against it. Once again such inhabitants as remained within the walls heard the dreaded military music and the equally dreaded janissary war-cry 'God is most great!' They looked out and saw the Turkish barges on the Danube and the steady approach of the Turkish infantry. Then when all were in position, the music ceased, and the janissaries, a blue and red mass packed against and on the walls, surged into the breaches and over the walls and wherever else they could gain a foothold. In silence they entered the citadel and in silence cut the throats of such Christian defenders as they could catch.

Among his aides and his commanders, Sultan Suleiman rode to survey the scene. As became the occasion he was splendid in steel chain mail damascened with gold and set with diamonds. Before he crossed the river, he assumed with his own hands the splendid ceremonial helmet made for such occasions. It carried a plume of black and grey heron's feathers and a phoenix plume of gold and enamel, attached by a diamond and emerald chain. When eventually he entered the castle, he was preceded by the Standard Bearer in full panoply, carrying the Horsetail Standard with its gold staff and seven crossbars, and attended by Ibrahim and his senior commanders. They rode between a line of pickets topped with the severed heads of Serbian noblemen.

The commander of the garrison, coming to surrender, kissed Suleiman's hand and was given a robe of honour. Then the Sultan inspected the castle and commanded that his engineers should repair the walls and convert a church into a mosque, where he went the next day to say his Friday prayers. Bali Aga, his wounds on the mend, was presented with 3,000 aspers and made the new governor of Belgrade.

Hungarian captives were allowed to cross the river and depart. As for the Serbian mercenaries, who had impressed him with their bravery, all 400 of them were transplanted to a district south of Istanbul which they renamed Belgrade. Now Suleiman had Sabacz, Semlin and Belgrade, he turned the captured batteries north across the river and cut down the forest that screened the shore. Once more he rode through the city to inspect it, and then reasonably satisfied with his achievement, went hunting.

Thus, before he set out for Istanbul, the Sultan did all things needful and did them with dignity, patience and panache as he had by now learned.

As the first frosts of September made themselves felt, the Turkish army turned for home, laden with the spoil which had made it, for most of them, thoroughly worthwhile. On the march back, the feudal levies scattered, to be home in time to get in the last of the harvest. Some, of course, did not bother to go home; there were always more attractive lands to find and cultivate, and stronger and better-looking women to master. But for those who did, the campaign had been well managed. The grass would last until the horses got home; the camels would be away to the warm south before the first autumn cold attacked the north.

As for Suleiman, free at last to allow his mind to range where it would, he looked back over the past six months with satisfaction and a good deal of pride. He had won a victory, by no means alone, to be sure, and he had learned much and not, he felt, disgraced himself. The relationship he had forged with his commanders and his army was warm and genuine. He watched the departure of the feudal armies with regret, and rode on with the regular forces in warmer and deeper understanding.

Now he could reread and dwell on the letters from Istanbul, particularly from his mother, with pleasure and affection. The one he reread most often was among the briefest. It had been written to announce that the Ikbal, Khurrem, was pregnant, and contained no other news, as, she wrote, she hastened to send it as soon as possible, thinking the news would give him pleasure. It did. He was moved and delighted beyond anything he had felt before. Thinking of that last night, when he had taken her hand in his, and tried and failed, to say something to her, he was ashamed of his uncertainty and hesitation. Besides, he knew now what he should have said, a simple statement of emotional fact, and determined that it should be the first thing he said to her when next they met.

# 29

In the meantime, back in Istanbul, the summer was long and hot, and nowhere, it seemed, longer or hotter than in the imperial harem. It should have been a very happy one and so it was at first, for Khurrem's pregnancy was a source of satisfaction and joy to all concerned, but, as soon became apparent, nothing is ever as simple as it seems. The first indication that something was not quite as it should be came to Hafise's attention towards the end of July. It was not that there was anything wrong with Khurrem's health so far as she could tell from looking at her and questioning her. It was just that she was a bit too quiet.

She could not put a finger on what was wrong. Tactful questioning of Hulefa, who happened to come face to face with the Queen Mother one day as she passed through the Great Hall, elicited that Khurrem ate and slept well; also that she had twice sent for the mullah. This last was unexpected and disquieting. Hulefa did not know why he had come, though both she and Meylisah had done their best to find out. Hafise went on her way thoughtfully and promptly sent for the mullah herself, only to learn that the reverend gentleman who had attended on Khurrem had now undertaken a pilgrimage and was not available. Then there's nothing for it, I'll have to ask her, thought Hafise, and wondered why she shrank from doing so. Still, never one to neglect her duty, she decided to ask the question the very next time she saw the girl.

In the meantime, she sensed, with the sixth sense which is the uncomfortable possession of all those who have responsibility for large organizations, that all was very far from well with the atmosphere of the harem. She said as much to her own housekeeper, when that formidable lady reported to her that two young slaves had had to be whipped for pulling each other's hair. The kiaya, hands folded in the position of respect, agreed.

'But, of course, madam, it is August and very hot in the city. I'm not one to complain, but this palace lacks the amenities even of Manissa, and there, of course, we were near the sea.'

Hafise raised her eyebrows. 'We are near the sea here,' she pointed out irritably, and suddenly realized that the woman was right. The Old Palace was hot in summer, draughty and cold in winter.

'But it isn't that,' she said, and realized that she had spoken her thoughts aloud. She said no more, but she had said more than enough. The other said meaningfully:

'No, madam, indeed it is not.' She hesitated, and added, 'When I was a young slave I would have laughed at anyone who tried to tell me that one lady's ill-temper can upset a whole harem, but it's true.' She shook her head and went on: 'And it isn't as if she means to. I doubt if she's aware what effect she has on others.'

'Which of course she should be,' said Hafise, a trifle grimly, and ended the conversation there. Her kiaya was an old and valued friend as well as a slave, but she did not discuss the senior ladies of her son's harem with anyone, however discreet. Gulbehar, she thought sadly, and sighed. I should have foreseen this, but I didn't. Entirely my own doing: I gave him Khurrem to distract him from a vain and lazy girl and succeeded very well. It never occurred to me to wonder as I should have done how Gulbehar would take it. Though what I would have done differently I do not know. Exasperating as she is, she cannot help her feelings. It's not in question that she loves Suleiman, just that she's not suitable to be the mother of his heir. Only, I thought she'd accept this situation, and she hasn't.

She sat on, alone in her summer pavilion, its long windows shaded from the late summer heat, and rested her chin on her hand, and wondered what she could do about Gulbehar. Ever since he had gone off on the spring campaign, leaving unmistakable evidence of his preference for Khurrem, Gulbehar had been impossible. But that isn't the right word, thought Hafise, angry at her own helplessness. If she were really impossible, abused her slaves more than she usually does, or was impertinent to me, I should know what to do, but she does nothing but sulk in her rooms. She doesn't neglect the child – indeed no, she's a

233

devoted mother. Nor does she neglect herself. Far from it. Anger seems to suit her, for I've never seen her look more lovely, and Allah knows her demands for clothes and jewels are more insolent than ever.

She shook her head. If Gulbehar had had the brain of a female Solomon she could not have upset the social life of the harem more effectively. She simply refused to take part in anything. She would not join their games or their music-making, she would not talk, not even about clothes, and she only came near Hafise if summoned to the presence-chamber. On the rare occasions when Hafise brought herself to send for her son's favourite kadin (officially she was still that and must continue so unless Suleiman repudiated her), she came, she stood or sat as directed and spoke when spoken to. And that was all.

It was an old rule of the harem that the favourite kadin welcomed her sister when her master took a new love, and even prepared her for the first night with the Sultan. As for many of the harem's old rules, Hafise had little time for this one, opining that it asked too much of human nature. But there is measure in all things, and Gulbehar was now asking too much of everybody's patience.

Khurrem was a different matter. It was possible to talk to her, to get her to communicate what was wrong. And if, in the past, some of the things Khurrem had communicated had been like bombshells, it was still as well to know the worst. Hafise shook her head and bit off a sharp exclamation. There were women, she believed, who envied her her power and position.

'Just let them have my worries,' she found herself saying aloud, 'they'd soon learn.'

While the Sultana Valideh sat and pondered the problem of Gulbehar, Gulbehar, several corridors away, in a less splendid but still very elegant apartment, lay back on her cushions and thought about Khurrem. She did not wonder what to do about her, since she had by now convinced herself that she knew what was going to happen to her. Like many another person of limited mental ability she had an infinite capacity for self-deception, and found it very easy to convince herself that what she wanted to happen, would indeed happen. It was impossible, she day-dreamed, that Suleiman could really prefer that redheaded peasant bitch to herself. What had happened had indubitably happened, but probably only because the Russian girl had bewitched him. (She passed over hurriedly her own behaviour back in February when she had screamed abuse at him when he had come to take leave of her. She hadn't meant it, Suleiman should have known she hadn't meant it.)

Now, when Suleiman came back in October or November, or whenever his campaign ended, he would see the difference. His redhaired doxy was enormous and her face was pale now, and by then would probably be drawn as well, whereas she, Gulbehar, would be as lovely as ever she had been. She genuinely did not remember that when she had been big with little Mustafa, she too had been enormous and pale and drawn, and evilly bad-tempered into the bargain. But none of that had prevented Suleiman from visiting her as often as he could, sitting with her and attempting to amuse her and soothe her fears. She understood nothing of deep emotion or loving kindness, her emotional life being lived in the realm of make-believe, and superficial make-believe at that. She was also cushioned by other day-dreams. The child might be a girl, or deformed or stillborn — anything could happen. Khurrem might die in childbirth. This was her favourite theme and she dwelt on it with pleasure and at length.

This state of euphoria was, of course, sometimes displaced by a glimpse of reality, and then her temper, always imperious, became intolerable to any but those who had no choice but to put up with her. Her own slaves kept their distance as far as they could, while others, hearing the hectoring voice, or the sound of slaps or of things thrown, hastened past her door, averting their gaze. Guzul and Sirhane naturally brought Hafise news of these outbursts whenever they happened, but all agreed that her behaviour at its present level was not bad enough to be noticed officially.

'That is to say, not *yet*,' said Hafise darkly, 'but it doesn't make for a happy harem.'

# 30

The principal cause of Hafise's unease remained to all intents and purposes quiet; docile and apparently as happy as a girl in her position could be. But now, as Khurrem's pregnancy advanced, she seemed positively to withdraw into herself. Nobody, with the exceptions of Hafise and Meylisah, found anything to wonder at in this. The midwives pronounced her health to be almost indecently excellent, while uncritical old friends, such as Fatma, said that it was a nice change to see her so much at ease. Meylisah, to whom this remark had been addressed, agreed hesitantly, and got away from her as soon as possible because she was afraid of saying something indiscreet. But, like Hafise, she sensed that something was wrong. It's not like her to sit around thinking all the time, I don't care if she's having twenty babies, Meylisah told herself.

Back in their quarters, she found her mistress and old friend sitting tranquilly by the window, a book on her knee, her size hidden by a voluminous garment of yellow gauze. She looked so peaceful and so pretty that Meylisah was immediately shaken by doubts. She knelt down beside her and asked anxiously, 'Is there anything you want? Some sherbet? Isn't it too hot by the window?'

'No, thank you. I like the sun,' replied Khurrem in the new, patient voice that worried her little friend so much, and since Khurrem showed no inclination to say any more, Meylisah got to her feet, sighed, and went off to find some completely futile occupation in the next room.

It happened that both she and Hafise were right. Khurrem was very seriously disturbed. In the past, any disturbance to Khurrem's peace of mind had always been followed immediately by outcry or action, often violent. Now she found herself existing as it were on two levels and was quite fascinated by her ability to sustain all this mental and emotional activity and not show it. She supposed it might be because this was the first time in all her life when she was able, indeed compelled, to be physically still. Everyone told her, implored her even, not to exert herself and Khurrem thanked them prettily and did not exert herself, channelling all her available energy into the consideration of the overwhelming problem that faced her. This was at one level. At the other, in which she longed to be able to lose herself but could not, was the orderly, inexorable preparation of her body to bear her child. Nothing could interfere with this, she wanted nothing to interfere with it, and at some time every day, and increasingly as the weeks progressed, it took over her mind as well as her body, and she would sit back and dream about the little boy — she was sure it would be a boy, and nothing could shake this certainty — who would look and be like Suleiman.

The rest of the time she gave to the problem. It was quite a simple one, and a kindly, visiting kiaya had crystallized part of it for her. 'How pleased your mother would be to hear about the baby,' she had said, after exchanging the gossip of the day. Khurrem was only just in time to prevent herself from saying what came immediately and unbidden into her mind: 'She wouldn't. She would call it a bastard.'

At first she was surprised to find that this consideration troubled her. She had never been very close to her mother, a busy, hard-working and necessarily domineering woman who kept a tight rein on her children. Khurrem, her eldest daughter, had always felt that her mother was particularly hard on her, who was too young to understand that eternal vigilance was necessary against poverty and the dangers of the borderland where they lived. She had not missed her particularly at any time in the course of her captivity, so why should she think of her and fear her disapproval now?

That, however, was the minor part of it; ever since her pregnancy had become apparent, the more senior women in the harem had begun, indoctrinating her tactfully and carefully about her own and the baby's status. Her future importance, they said, depended on the baby's sex. If it was a boy, splendid! She then became Khurrem Hasseki, the third most important woman in the harem. If, on the other hand, the child was a girl, well, that was a pity and could not be helped, and her own status would hardly be affected. Of course, the Sultan would make her a freewoman as soon as the baby was born, whatever its sex.

Khurrem brushed all this aside. As she saw it, her own importance resided in Suleiman's love for her and nothing else, but she found herself desperately concerned for the baby. She had accepted, because there was no choice, what she still regarded as the outlandish way in which these people conducted their family life, and she was prepared to embrace it with fervour if it meant that her child would be safe and secure, if nothing more. At this stage she received a shock. She had assumed that little Mustafa must be, as Suleiman's eldest son, his heir, but this, she learned, was not so.

'When the time comes,' she was told, 'the Sultan will select as his successor that son who seems to him the most suitable to rule. The choice has nothing to do with being first or second or even third born, but everything to do with the young man's character.' Her informant looked pityingly at Khurrem, and added: 'And when the time comes that he is Sultan, he will dispose of his brothers. It is the law.'

'Dispose?' asked Khurrem, 'What does that mean? Are they sent to govern provinces?'

'Perhaps you should ask someone wiser than me about that,' said the other woman uncomfortably, and shortly afterwards found an excuse to take her leave.

Khurrem thought about this with increasing disquiet for the best part of a day and it was then that she sent for the mullah the first time. He was a wise man as well as a kindly one. He did not beat about the bush. It was incumbent upon a new sultan to have any surviving brothers executed when he acceded. This, he explained, protected the House of Osman from civil war and internal disorder arising from rivalry between brothers. The state must come before everything. He went on to explain that this was a sacred law enacted by the great Mehmed the Second and could not be set aside or disregarded.

He watched while she took a deep breath, but she said nothing, and after a moment he asked compassionately whether he could tell her anything more, but she only shook her head and looked at the floor. He waited until she raised her head and thanked him formally, and added:

'If I have any more questions, will you come again?'

'To be sure, my child,' he told her and took leave.

It took her rather longer than a day to come to terms with this dreadful news. At first she sat in her usual place under the window, sunk into cushions, and stared at nothing. Nobody seemed to notice anything wrong with her and in a way this helped, for it seemed important to her that she should seem as usual. After a while she began to be angry – with Suleiman, who allowed such a dreadful state of affairs to exist, who begot children and did nothing to protect them, with Hafise and her friends in the harem who must have known about this appalling law and had not told her, and eventually with the wise, crafty man who had been responsible for the thing in the first place. Rage surged through her, but still she sat and showed nothing, and eventually the great blinding waves of anger subsided. Useless, she thought, to waste time blaming a man dead these forty years, and as for Suleiman and Hafise and the rest of us, we're just his victims. Worn out, she went to bed and slept, as usual, like the dead, a sleep filled with fragments of ugly dreams which left her in the morning with a sense of foreboding. But during the course of the day, her orderly mind took over, and she began to think what she could do to protect the little boy who was not yet born.

At first nothing very much suggested itself. She supposed she could try to persuade Suleiman to change the law; after all, he had had no surviving brothers. How would he have felt if he had had to. . . . She shivered. But she knew that even to attempt it would take time, perhaps more time than there was. And how would Suleiman react to interference from a mere girl, a slave, in what she supposed must be described as an affair of state? And men, she suspected, are never more implacable than when they are dealing with imponderables with high-sounding names like 'the good of the state'. It was then that, as so often happens, the thoughts of the back of her mind, which seemingly had nothing to do with the present case, pushed their way to her consciousness and seemed to offer a partial solution.

She was sitting by the window again, and it was evidence of her returning normality that the thought crossed her mind, I ought to go for a walk in the garden. This sitting about can't be good for the baby. Almost simultaneously, she remembered a little sadly what she had almost said to her visitor about her mother's likely reaction to the baby. A bastard, she thought sadly, that's the least of his problems, poor little soul. And then the great thought struck her. She was so excited she could hardly contain herself. As was usual with Khurrem after distress, regained equilibrium meant action, and if it was only a walk round the close and rather dusty garden of the Old Palace, it was at least a sign that she was fighting back. When she returned to her rooms afterwards, sweating and panting a little, attended by a concerned and equally panting Meylisah, her eyes were bright with excitement and she sent immediately for the mullah.

As August progressed, the weather grew hotter. The sky was white with heat and the leaves hung limp and dusty on the trees. The atmosphere everywhere was tense and in the harem it was well-nigh intolerable. Hafise, eyes aching with the sun's glare, found herself imagining all kinds of disasters, from plague in the city to mayhem in the Palace. 'And that seems a distinct possibility and not the product of an overheated imagination,' she told herself grimly, and decided that the time had come for another visit to Khurrem.

When she entered the girl's room, followed by Sirhane, who carried her carefully selected gifts of a phial of precious scent from India and a plant flowering in a porcelain pot, she was, like Meylisah, relieved to see how well and charming Khurrem looked. She inspected the girl with loving, careful eyes, noting with approval that a book lay open on the cushion beside her.

'I am all for keeping an active mind at a time like this, but you must not overdo it. What are you reading?'

Khurrem handed over an Arabic grammar for inspection. 'I thought I would like to learn Arabic so that I can read the Koran, but it's too hot to make much progress and the sun makes my head ache.'

There was an air of intensity about her which the Sultana Valideh found disturbing. She said carefully, 'No doubt discussion of the Book-that-is-to-be-read with the mullah is a joy to you, but religion and philosophy are tiring, especially in this heat.' She raised her eyes and looked the girl full in the face. It disconcerted her to see Khurrem flush darkly and say nothing at all.

'That is the reason he came, is it not?' she asked. Her voice was sharper than she had intended, and the girl dropped her eyes and still said nothing.

Seriously worried, Hafise leaned forward and took Khurrem's

hot little hand which closed convulsively round her own. 'Khurrem,' she said soberly, 'you have no reason to try to deceive me or keep anything from me. So, tell me now, why have you had these discussions with the mullah?'

The book dropped unheeded by either of them to the floor, and Khurrem said simply: 'I suppose I wanted to know my position.'

Hafise did not understand her. She said blankly, 'Your position? Well, yes, I suppose we all want to know that. Did he tell you?'

Khurrem hung her head. She had known that an interview of this kind with the Queen Mother must come. Had indeed wanted it, but it was not going at all as she had planned. She had overlooked in her worry that Hafise, while kind and loving to those she approved, was also formidable, with a very shrewd eye, and deceiving her, when it involved acting out of character oneself, almost impossible. She was further hampered by the fact that she was, herself, without knowing it, almost hysterical with shock and worry. She determined to continue with her chosen plan, however, and said at last, in a tone of assumed tranquillity:

'He told me that when the baby is born, the Sultan will free me.'

Hafise frowned, and said, 'Yes, that is so.'

'Well,' said Khurrem, swallowing hard, 'when I am free, I cannot stay here.'

There was a silence. It went on so long that both, perhaps, became afraid to break it. Hafise stared at Khurrem, eyes wide with amazement, a small frown marking the centre of her forehead, but Khurrem looked only at the carpet and her throat worked convulsively. At last the Queen Mother said coldly, 'You had better tell me the rest of your thinking.'

A small sound that might have been the clearing of her throat, or even a sniff, came from the girl, but her voice was fairly steady when she said at last:

'While I was a slave I had no choice, but when I become free it will be — will be — adultery.' She stopped and looked desperately at Hafise, adding, 'I will not do it!'

That lady for the moment had nothing to say. She was being presented with a totally new idea, one certainly that had never occurred to the concubines of any previous sultan, but one which was certainly true. A freewoman must sleep with no man but her husband, otherwise it was adultery. The Law was definite on the point. At the same time, there was something in the girl's demeanour that did not ring true. She is not a good liar, thought Hafise, and it is true that she has not yet told me a lie, but I think she intends to. She said steadily:

'Go on.'

Khurrem raised her eyes, still full of desperate appeal, but said calmly: 'I wish to be married. The Sultan loves me, I am sure of it. And I love him, but I will not belong to him again until I am married to him.' She folded her hands in her lap, and Hafise saw how they trembled and how tightly they were clasped.

She said blankly. 'But this is impossible! Why should he marry you, a slave, a girl of no importance? Moreover, many sultans do not marry, but those that have have married women of some status in the world in order to cement alliances. I myself am a Krim princess—' she stopped, and then added wearily, 'but from what I know of you, Khurrem, I could not have believed you to care one atom about your status, I really could not. You disappoint me bitterly. I cannot stay and hear any more of this—' and she began to rise to her feet.

It took her rather a long time, much longer than usual for so active a lady. Long before she had got the tail of her gown out of the way and turned to the door, Khurrem had flung herself at her feet and burst into a passion of weeping, in the course of which Hafise distinguished broken words which included, 'I don't—' and 'it's not like that', and eventually, 'my baby!'

Hafise reseated herself with care, and drew the dishevelled and distraught little body into her arms. The sobbing redoubled and Khurrem clung. The Sultana Valideh suffered this for a few minutes, but when after this period there seemed no sign of cessation, and indeed a new rather ugly note of hysteria obtruded itself, she said sharply:

'Stop this noise at once! You will make yourself ill. I shall go away unless you stop!'

To her secret relief, this worked. The storm began to abate somewhat and the sobs became drier. Khurrem slithered from her knees to sit on the floor, one arm across her eyes.

'Get up!' said Hafise crisply. 'Get up and sit beside me. Now, let me look at you.' She looked, and added, producing her own handkerchief (splendidly embroidered, of course, but not by

242

Khurrem), 'Take this and dry your eyes. When you have done so, oblige me with the truth, and if you really think my son should marry you, tell me the real reason. Which so far you have not done.'

Khurrem climbed laboriously to her feet, so laboriously indeed, that Hafise found it necessary to help her. When this pushing and pulling had been accomplished and the girl was seated on one cushion and propped up on two more, her shift tidily disposed around her, she said simply.

'I'm sorry, Madam, I shouldn't have tried to deceive you.'

Hafise said, 'I can't think why you should have wanted to,' and raised her chin. She was amazed how bitterly hurt she felt.

Khurrem went on, 'I was afraid because you are Sultana Valideh you – you might not understand how I feel about my baby. You may think this dreadful law is right.'

'What dreadful law?'

Khurrem told her. She told her everything in a great spate of words which poured out of her, as previously the tears had. 'You were quite right,' she concluded, 'I don't really care about myself. I suppose it would be sinful but I don't seem to care about that. All I want to do is protect my little son. It will be a boy. I know it,' Khurrem stated with quiet conviction.

'But,' began the Queen Mother, and then stopped and shrugged her shoulders, and said quietly, 'go on.'

'Well, if I were married to Suleiman, it must make a difference, surely? I shall be able to watch over him always if I am – what is it?'

'Hasseki Sultana,' supplied Hafise.

'And surely, surely the Sultan will care more for his son born in wedlock. That must be so, mustn't it?'

'Perhaps,' said the Queen Mother gently.

'And you will help me, now that you understand?' Khurrem rushed on: 'Oh, dear madam, I have been half mad with worry! If I had been myself I wouldn't have tried to deceive you, but sometimes I don't believe I quite knew what I was thinking or doing. It's all been like some terrible, terrible dream – ' she broke off abruptly and blew her nose.

Hafise drew her against her breast. 'You must now stop thinking about all this. I am very concerned that you should have heard about this thing as you did. But so it is, you have. Now you have told me and relieved your feelings and I hope you will be at peace. I will help you, that is a promise. But now I think you should eat and then go to bed.'

She kissed the girl tenderly and rose to her feet to summon Sirhane.

Hafise returned to her quarters shattered by what she had heard. She sent her people away and sat down to think. Distant memories stirred of what she had learned of Christianity in the past. These people, she thought, profess a religion based and centred in love, but administered by the harshest and cruellest of laws. With us, if a man begets a child, he gladly accepts responsibility for it. All children are equal. With them, one child is treasured because born in wedlock, another is scorned as a bastard. It is pointless to tell Khurrem her belief is wrong, especially now. What must I do?

Obviously, she thought, my first concern is with the status of my son. I will do nothing to injure that. But how would marriage with Khurrem injure him? She is a warm and splendid girl, born to share greatness, and I believe Suleiman will be great. But he is strong and autocratic and if things pursue the course Khurrem is set on now, I can only foresee disaster, for he will certainly not allow himself to be forced into marriage. That is what it will amount to, and he will see this. She pushed back the heavy hair from her face and found a new position among her cushions.

Her thoughts seemed to race away from her in all directions, examining every aspect of the problem, probing for a solution, any solution, and finding none. She wondered if she herself should consult a mullah – and in her case she could command the wisdom of the Grand Mufti himself – but she shrank from involving him. If it ever came to that, it would be Suleiman's prerogative and not hers. She wondered what her son's attitude to marriage might be, and found to her amazement that she had no idea. He had never mentioned it, certainly never sought it, and apart from her own marriage to Selim, it had tended to be disregarded by the House of Osman now that they had grown so powerful in their own right as to need no longer the support that marriage alliances might bring. So what would Suleiman think and do? She found that she simply did not know. Her own son, and she could not predict how he would feel! The thing was simple, she thought, smiling wryly, but he is unlikely to see it in such terms. Men never see things in the same terms as women do, especially when the women are attempting to conceal something from them.

She rose unsteadily, for she was by now very tired, and went to stand by the lattice, looking out at the hot, dark city. Its myriad lights looked back at her and brought no help. One thing is plain, she told herself dully, we must temporize. There must be no haste. She pressed her forefinger to her lips and considered carefully. Khurrem must be induced to be quiet about her fears and desires until the baby was born. Suleiman would surely be more receptive to the idea of marriage if it were presented when he was rejoicing over the birth of a child, than when he was anxiously awaiting its arrival. At the same time, she herself might begin, if his mood on return was propitious, to implant the germ of an idea.

Her eyes grew sharp and intent as she considered ways and means. This she understood, this she was good at. She even found herself wondering if it was too late to go to the girl's quarters and impress on her the need for quiet and caution. She decided that it was, and instead despatched a slave to find out how Khurrem was. The answer came back that after eating a tolerable supper she was now sleeping peacefully. Well, thought Hafise, on receiving this welcome news, and now perhaps I will, too. And so she did, eventually.

# 31

Sultan Suleiman, returning from the first military victory of his reign, made a triumphant entry into Istanbul at mid-October. His capital city received him with acclamation, and so, in their different fashion, did the ladies of his household, when he went on the following evening, and in state, to visit his mother at the Old Palace. As soon as Hafise had received the news of her son's imminent return she had decreed a magnificent welcome for him. She had much to do, and was herself at her most alert, overseeing everything, issuing meticulous instructions and making sure that they were carried out.

Nothing must go wrong on this momentous day. Her victorious son must be received as he deserved, and made to feel the value put upon him by his family. In particular Khurrem must be prevented from breathing a single word of her marriage plan, while Gulbehar must be allowed to show herself in her true colours as far as possible, while at the same time being discouraged from making a scene, or doing anything else to mar the festivities. Finally, and, she sometimes felt, most difficult of all, she Hafise, must receive him with every appearance of whole-hearted carefree welcome, conveying no hint of the racking anxiety that consumed her. All this, of course, in addition to overseeing the activities of the harem officials, all of whom knew their duty, and driving them half-mad with her interference.

For the past six weeks or so, the harem had been broodingly quiet, and as the dusty, golden days of September gave way to a damp and almost spring-like October, the atmosphere had perceptibly lightened. For one thing, as the slaves murmured to each other whenever they had time to gossip, the Sultan would be home soon, Khurrem's baby would be born soon, and things must come to a head one way or another, mustn't they? By which, of course, they only meant, knowing nothing of any other threat to the collective peace and *status quo*, that Gulbehar would win him back or get her come-uppance.

As the Sultana Valideh dressed for the ceremony, she gave a lot of thought to Gulbehar. She had, of necessity, been bidden to present herself, together with little Mustafa, in Hafise's throne-room at the appointed time, and had signified her obedient intention of coming, but once there she might do anything. She had continued through the late summer as she had behaved throughout the earlier months, sulky, arrogant and silent. And the harem had got used to it.

Suleiman won't, though, Hafise told herself, thoughtfully holding an emerald aigrette against her splendid headdress, 'Not this, but the rubies,' she said in parenthesis to the maid who had proffered it, 'I'm too pale today for emeralds.'

Suleiman won't, she continued, picking up her train of thought again, but what he will do I can't be sure. On the other hand, she may mend her ways now he's returned. One thing is certain, things won't stay as they are, which is probably just as well. But she shivered a little as she formulated the thought. Her sense of humour came to her aid, too. My poor son, she thought, he probably thinks he's returning to well deserved peace in the bosom of his family! Another reason why I must be sure that he receives no unexpected jolts: everything must be gradual, imperceptible.

When she was ready she went to see Khurrem. Ostensibly this was an act of kindness to the poor little invalid too far gone in pregnancy to be present at the reception. 'I want her to see how we all look,' she gaily told her kiaya and her maids as they traversed the corridors. In fact, she wanted to reassure herself as to the girl's state of mind. Ever since Khurrem had unburdened herself to her in August, she had seemed calm and happy, glad to leave her problems in Hafise's hands. But one couldn't be sure, and if Suleiman came to see her this evening, as he probably would, for he had written to her almost as soon as he reached the New Palace, who knew what the girl might say to him in the first joy of meeting? One can't be sure of anything, Hafise told herself. Only prepared.

Khurrem, however, appeared exactly as she should. Pale, and a little tremulous as was to be expected, but also radiant, particularly when she mentioned her letter.

'How wonderful, madam, that he should think of me so soon!' she said when, the ritual display of jewels and finery over, the Queen Mother had dismissed her women in order to have a few words with the girl alone.

'Why not?' demanded Hafise bracingly, 'especially at this time. My son is no fair-weather lover. But, remember, Khurrem, he will certainly come to greet you. If he does, or I should rather say, *when* he does, remember what I have told you. Do not speak to him of marriage or – or freedom or anything we have discussed. Leave it all to me. It has been a gruelling campaign, the first where he has been in command, after all – '

'Oh, madam, as if I would!' exclaimed her willing pupil a shade indignantly. 'I will gladly do as you say, for I must confess that I do not seem to want to think of anything very much except the baby. Only,' she added wistfully, picking up a handmirror, 'I wish I looked better. He'll have a shock when he sees my shape.'

'You look just as you should,' Hafise told her. 'And as for your shape, he has seen a pregnant woman before. I must go now, for I hear shouting in the streets. Rest easy, child.' With that she departed.

If Suleiman would have preferred to meet his mother alone and then hurry away to Khurrem, he gave no sign of it. By now he had learned that things must be done in the appropriate way and with due ceremony. So he came escorted by his Life Guards and attended by cloth-of-gold clad pages. Once the preliminaries were over, it did not take him long to divine that something was, not precisely amiss, but certainly different in his mother's demeanour. She looked splendid as always and her greeting was touchingly affectionate; despite the presence of slaves and officials, she clung to his hand, but there was an excitement about her, a tension that he could not place and found disturbing.

For her part, Hafise was taken aback by the physical changes in his appearance, his brown face, and soldierly manner. It was only when she met his eyes, cool and quizzical as ever, that she was reassured. Meanwhile, the simple ceremony of greeting the women of the family and the senior harem officials began. Gulbehar, naturally, with Mustafa by the hand, was the first he turned to. Resplendent in silver tissue and rose brocade, she swept him a splendid curtsy and looked confidently into his face. Suleiman returned the look gravely, bowed to her, murmured an enquiry as to her health, and turned aside to sweep the little boy into his arms and kiss him. Still carrying him, he turned to the next in line, his young sister, and greeted her affectionately. He did not look at Gulbehar again. His mother drew a deep breath, almost expelled it in a sigh of relief but did not, and turned a quelling eye in the general direction of a slight murmur of comment, no louder than the ripple of a breeze, which she had detected somewhere at the back of the room.

Later, mother and son sat together beside the superb white marble fountain and exchanged a few private words while they drank a little sherbet and nibbled choice sweetmeats. The inexorable gentle splashing of the fountain effectively drowned what they said, as it was intended it should. Suleiman's first words were of Khurrem.

'Is she well and happy?'

Hafise smiled. She felt she could afford to relax a little, everything had so far gone more easily than she had dared to hope.

'As well and better than you can expect a girl in her state to be.'

He smiled involuntarily, and Hafise, examining his face with more care than she had yet been able to do, saw with approval a sharpening of his features, a new expression of confidence, as if the rigour of war had etched away everything insecure in his thinking. This will not make my task easier, she thought, but I am glad to see him so.

He talked generally for a few moments of the campaign and his pleasure in returning to Istanbul, and then he said abruptly: 'And you, Mother, you too have had a hard summer I think.'

It was not clear to her whether this was a question or a comment, and if it were a comment, how could he possibly know how hard a time she had had. Who could have told him? She drew a sharp breath, and then saw that he was looking across the wide, beautiful room at Gulbehar where she stood, rigid-faced, alone by the double doors.

'Yes,' she said calmly, 'it has been difficult.' She was glad, she found, that she was able to tell him part of the truth, at least.

'Very well. Sometime tomorrow, I cannot say when, but sometime during the day, I will visit you privately and we will talk about what is to be done. But in the meantime, I suppose we must continue with this ceremonial, and I have brought you gifts – but, you know, Mother, I must see Khurrem.'

She smiled radiantly in her relief, a circumstance which he noted, and which caused him to think privately that Gulbehar must have been very trying indeed. Poor Mother, he thought, I must remember that she is no longer young. Had Khurrem not been pregnant, she would have been her support. I must learn to time these things better in future. And he smiled again, a little fatuously, and then ceased to smile as the thought drifted into his mind, I wonder what else she is worrying about?

He did not find out. The ceremony of greeting came quickly to its end. It had been pleasant and not too stiff. Suleiman had found himself enjoying it. He was delighted to see his family and faithful officials again. Even the hard-eyed presence of Gulbehar did not mar it. Above all, and trust his tactful mother for that, it was soon over, and he was free to hasten to Khurrem.

He found her as enchanting as ever and strangely, touchingly docile. Seeing her so, heavy with his child, moved him in a way he had never previously experienced. He wished their lives were differently arranged, so that he need not leave her, he feared for her, however healthy they might say she was, wished he could find some way of expressing all this without frightening her. It was better when he induced her to laugh, which she did as wholeheartedly and uproariously as ever. He had brought her a giant ruby, as big as her fist. Her eyes widened when she saw it.

'Whatever is it?' she demanded, gazing at it as it lay on the cushion between them.

'A ruby, like the one in your ring,' he told her.

'How splendid,' said Khurrem, and added: 'What shall I do with it?'

He had not thought of that, and after a moment they began to laugh again, she so heartily that he involuntarily extended his hand to prevent her toppling over.

'Don't worry, I'm too heavy to fall,' she told him, and dissolved into another paroxysm.

It occurred to Suleiman that he had not laughed so much or so heartily since he had left Istanbul eight months before. Clearly, he thought, riding back to the New Palace, except for one small matter, all was well with his harem, and that he would deal with at the earliest opportunity.

# 32

Hafise, too, was pleased with the way things had progressed. So that, the next afternoon, when Suleiman came to her as he had promised, she was disproportionately disappointed when he made it plain that Gulbehar was not to be sent away from the harem.

'It is impossible to live with her. She mistreats her slaves, insults my officials and ignores Khurrem!' she flung at him angrily.

His eyes widened at this catalogue of sins but he refused to be shaken. 'Mother, it is not becoming that disagreements in the Sultan's harem should become public property,' he told her gently. 'Also, in a very few years Mustafa will go to his first governorate and she will go with him.'

'A few years! He is only four now! Must we all suffer from her outrageous behaviour for more than ten years?'

'Of course not. She will be induced to conduct herself more discreetly. She must already be aware that her position is no longer what it was. That is one reason why I treated her so coldly last night.'

She shook her head in something that was nearly exasperation and he looked at her with a touch of hauteur. She was not to be subdued, however.

'Have you thought of Khurrem,' she demanded, 'in all this? If her child is a boy, she too will be Hasseki and she is your favourite girl. To allow Gulbehar to continue as she is is not fair to her!'

He looked at her steadily.

'Khurrem is my only girl. She understands this, I think, but if she does not, I will make it plain to her. Nevertheless, I will not banish Gulbehar because she is the mother of my son and

251

because she is totally helpless – '

'Helpless!' Hafise heard her own voice rising to an unbecoming squeal and made a supreme effort at self-control. She swallowed and said carefully, 'I don't understand you.'

Suleiman got up and began to pace the room. 'Since I found Khurrem she has satisfied me in a way I never believed possible. When I am with her I am happier than I have ever been before and I cannot believe that I shall ever feel differently. As companion and lover she delights me, but that does not mean that I can abandon Gulbehar entirely. She has lost my favour. To take away her status would be too cruel and I cannot do it. After all, she has not your strength or Khurrem's. Say no more about this, Mother, I will not do it.'

She was silenced. Then it was on the tip of her tongue to say, 'If you feel like this about Khurrem, why do you not marry her?' and afterwards she wondered why she did not, but on the whole she was glad she had not spoken. A man who could be so adamant about a woman he had discarded could be equally so against an idea he did not favour. So she contented herself with saying:

'She can still do a great deal of harm.'

Her son sat down again. He took his time about making himself comfortable against the cushions, as though in the past few months he had learned the value of an occasional moment of comfort, and said, 'Can she? Do you think she has friends in the harem?'

Hafise shook her head. 'No,' she said honestly, 'she is isolated and unpopular. But,' she went on urgently, 'she must be stopped from hounding the slaves and creating a bad atmosphere generally. It is useless for me to talk to her any more and as for the Khizlar Agasi and the other officials they are powerless!' She thought for a moment and added, 'She seems to live in a world of dreams and no one can approach her.'

Suleiman nodded. 'She will listen to me,' he said grimly. 'I will talk to her.' The prospect seemed not to daunt him so much as it would have done before be went away. He rose to his feet. 'I will make her understand that if she remains here, she must conform. But I will not send her away, and in your heart, you know that I am right. Now, if there is nothing more, I will go to Khurrem.'

When he had gone, Hafise sat down again and stared blankly

at her hands. She was inclined to be angry, very angry indeed. She had not got her own way, and when that happened, as a rule she could work herself up into a very satisfying rage. Today, however, she realized the matter was too serious for temper. Besides, Suleiman had achieved for her something very important. Ever since Khurrem had confided in her, she had been aware that despite her promise to help bring about a marriage between Khurrem and her son, she had been less than enthusiastic for the match, and that her reasons for attempting it were not Khurrem's. Now, because of his desire to see justice more than tempered with mercy towards a woman she despised and instinctively feared, he had caused her to range herself wholeheartedly, and for the first time in his life, against him. Gulbehar may be powerless now, she thought, but she will not remain so unless her position is finally destroyed. I do not accept Khurrem's pathetic belief that marriage will protect her child, but it will protect her, and that is enough for me. How to go about achieving it is a different matter.

In the meantime, Suleiman was as good as his word. In a few days the whole household knew that he had sent for Gulbehar and reprimanded her. A slave with an over-developed sense of the dramatic talked of seeing her wandering the corridors with tears streaming down her cheeks. This was not true, but the girl enjoyed telling it, and her hearers were rapturous on hearing it. Gulbehar's own maids had nothing to say on the subject at all, which tended to confirm the story rather than disprove it as everybody knew. The harem, as it were, cleared its collective throat and looked around for the next item for comment.

# 33

They had not far to seek. Khurrem's baby was due in the middle of November. Then there would be something to talk about! Whether boy or girl, they would make the most of it, but in the meantime the tension departed from the atmosphere. It was too much to hope that Gulbehar would turn overnight into an angel of light, but at least she ceased to torment her slaves quite so much and was civil to the Keeper of the Jewels when he had occasion to tell her that she could not have a certain magnificent pearl collar which she had set her heart on.

Autumn began to close in with heavy rain and icy winds from the steppes. The charcoal braziers were brought into the sitting-rooms now, and gauze shifts were covered with velvet caftans deeply edged with fur against the draughts that sneaked along corridors and through lattices.

Despite the weather, the temper of the place was sweeter than it had been all the year. The only person who worried was Hafise, who could not make up her mind what to do, an unusual state with her. Although she had determined at the outset to say nothing to Suleiman about marriage, she found it difficult to keep her resolve as the weeks crawled by. Fortunately, events tended to dominate her, for Suleiman, after eight months in the field, was very busy with government affairs and spent such free time as he had with Khurrem, to whom, she was glad to see, he seemed increasingly devoted. Opportunity to talk to him seriously was therefore lacking. This was just as well, for while other tempers began to mend, Hafise found hers growing shorter. Action was essential to her temperament, and to be compelled to conceal her feelings, to appear amiable and comparatively carefree, when all she wanted to do was join battle, was maddening. Her maids found her snappish to a degree and her officials agreed that she was absent-minded and inattentive. Fortunately these shortcomings were imputed to a concern for Khurrem, to whom everyone knew her to be devoted. 'We shall all be relieved when the baby is born,' the harem gossip went, and there was no one who did not agree.

Hafise's plan of action was simple and direct. That is to say, as direct as any such feminine plan can be. Once the child was born, Khurrem must remain inviolate for a month, the period of purification, during which no woman might have sexual relations. Consequently the question of her refusing herself to Suleiman, with all the attendant possibilities of hurting, offending and angering him, could not arise, and during that month Hafise must do her work of persuasion, so that no direct collision between the two need occur. It won't be easy, she fretted, I know it won't be easy, for Suleiman is even more formidable now than he was. Oh, if only something would happen to help me!

In the event things were even more difficult than she anticipated.

All the preparations for the birth had been completed, the birth chair carried into Khurrem's apartments, the swaddling bandages, the amulet and the blue beads against the evil eye provided, and the most competent of the harem's midwives summoned. All the signs were propitious. Khurrem, the pink glow receding from her cheeks as she watched the activity around her, was at her meekest and most willing to oblige. Only, she said, when questioned, she did not feel any different. There were no pangs, no contractions, nothing. Gradually, as the hours passed, a feverish note made itself felt in the proceedings. Hafise, unable to go on as usual any longer, arrived and sat beside the girl, holding her hand. Messengers from Suleiman, obediently marooned in the New Palace, arrived almost hourly and were sent empty away. Khurrem's particular friends in the harem came to enquire after her and hung about outside her room. Everyone, it seemed, who had any right to be there, and many who had not, found their way to Khurrem's apartment and stayed; but the one person in whose honour all these activities had been set in motion, remained obstinately locked up and gave no sign of life.

The midwife took it in her stride for three days. These things often happened. She had known, she said, many similar occur-

255

rences, and proceeded to bore her captive audience with chapter and verse, until the Sultana Valideh, seeing the sweat break out afresh on Khurrem's forehead, brusquely bade her be quiet unless she was prepared to try the effect of another recitation of the Declaration of Faith, which was held to help matters along at such times. They tried it. They tried everything they could think of, but nothing had any effect and they began to be frightened. Women in Khurrem's outer room wondered aloud if a wise woman, by whom they meant a witch, should be sent for to see what she could do. Rumours of the evil eye and impending death sped through the harem, and of course, reached Gulbehar as she sat in her dim and softly scented room. She smiled to herself and said nothing.

Only Khurrem remained comparatively unmoved. No one in her position could entirely escape the effect of the everlasting whispering and the covert, pitying glances, but she managed somehow to keep her head and her courage.

'He's going to be a big boy,' she said firmly, 'like my brother, so he's taking longer to get into the world. It'll be all right, you'll see.'

'Of course, dear,' said the midwife, whose own forehead was sweating freely by now. 'Now, repeat after me, "Allah Akbar, God is great —" '

'If you insist,' said Khurrem courteously, and repeated the Declaration through twice with no noticeable effect.

Then, without any drama, in the middle of the sixth night, Khurrem, who like everybody else, had been drowsing quietly, sat up in her bed, squeezed Hafise's hand, and said urgently, 'Oh dear, I do feel odd —'

They hoisted her into the birth chair without any ceremony, which was as well, because within the hour a healthy prince of the House of Osman made his entrance into the world weighing over nine pounds.

They could all have done without this prolongation of the agony. Suleiman had grown silent and haggard, unable to attend to even the most routine affairs of state; Hafise, already overstretched, felt at times that she was going mad; certainly it was a long time before her judgement return to normal. But the effect on Gulbehar was disastrous.

At the first meeting of mother and son after the birth of little prince Mehmed, Hafise came to the point. Her attack did not go very well, possibly because she was peremptory and he was abstracted. She said, without any preliminaries:

'My son, have you ever considered the possibility of marriage?'

Suleiman, who was sitting opposite to her, quietly looking into space, did not hear her at first. He had just spent a short time with Khurrem and his new son, and would have preferred to sit in companionable silence, relishing his restored peace of mind. So he raised his eyes, cloudy with thought, to hers, and asked her to repeat herself.

'I said, have you ever considered the possibility of marriage?' said Hafise, a little stridently.

He looked at her, incredulous. 'Certainly not. Who would you have me marry?' He laughed shortly, 'Some Western princess, perhaps? Whatever can have put such an idea into your head at such a time?'

'I am serious, and I am suggesting that you marry Khurrem.'

There was a long silence, and then Suleiman said, coldly courteous:

'I perceive that you are adverting to our talk about Gulbehar. I thought I had made my position on that subject clear, but if I have not, why, no, Mother. Khurrem and I could not be closer or happier if we were married. There is no necessity for such a thing.'

Hafise took a deep breath and said with care, 'You must allow me to make my position clear also, something which I had not done when last we talked. Now I have thought deeply about the subject. So, will you listen to me?'

He extended his hand, but looked displeased. 'I will always, I hope, listen to argument, but please understand that I will not banish Gulbehar.'

His mother took a deep breath. 'You know the ways of the harem as well as I —'

He smiled coldly and interpolated, 'I think not,' but she ignored this and went on:

'Gulbehar is isolated and powerless now, as we have said, but things change. The people here are always changing, and there will be those who do not know her. You think that you and I will always be here to support Khurrem, but you will be away at war at least half the time, while I — well, I shall not last for ever.'

'Oh, come, Mother, you are not in your dotage! And even when I am away, I trust my word counts with my household.

Moreover, you forget that Khurrem herself is no cipher, and everyone knows her worth to me.'

'Then why not marry her and make sure of her position?'

'Her status is secure in my word. Why, Mother, are you so anxious to have me marry? Why has this suddenly come into your head? Have you perhaps reasons you have not told me? If so, I would be happy to hear them.'

She was greatly tempted to tell him the whole story, but so vivid a picture of his formidable anger rose in her mind as to paralyse her. Therefore she said reasonably, 'I want you to make it plain to the world that Khurrem is supreme in your life.'

'And I believe that it is already plain.' He rose and said with finality, 'I have heard enough on this subject, madam.'

So, impasse. Yet Hafise was not despairing. She still had twenty-five days left out of the thirty. When she visited Khurrem that evening she found her sufficiently recovered to feel herself able to give the girl a discreetly edited version of what had been said.

'But you did not tell him that I will not sleep with him until we are married?' demanded Khurrem, a feverish flush creeping into her cheeks.

'No! My child, whatever next? No man who is a man will allow himself to be dictated to in that way!' She looked at the girl incredulously. 'Has that never occurred to you?' she demanded.

Khurrem hung her head and confessed that she did not know very much about men, except Suleiman, who, she said, loved her devotedly. She began to look mulish and added, 'When he knows how I feel, he'll understand.'

'He will not,' said Hafise crisply. She was really beginning to feel at the end of her tether. 'Every man believes he and he alone knows best how to guard the welfare of his family. Especially when he is a sultan,' she finished a little bitterly. 'He would be outraged if he heard what you have told me. I agree with you,' she hurried on, 'that goes without saying, but it does not do to deal directly with men, they do not expect it from women.' With that she left, and returned to her own rooms to ponder her next move.

The following day, Khurrem found herself thinking longingly of the pleasures of hot water, scents and gentle massage, and felt herself in fact sufficiently recovered to visit the bath. Never one for pomp or standing on her dignity, to her to think was to act. Attended only by Meylisah, she betook herself to the splendid bath which was a redeeming feature of the Old Palace. After Meylisah had administered the customary three washes at the white marble fountain, Khurrem entered the Warm Room wrapped in towels and was greeted with such kindness and rejoicing as the new mother of a Sultan's son by the women already taking their ease there, that she was deeply moved. They could not do enough for her, chattering excitedly, sending for sweetmeats and fruit and sherbet.

At mid-afternoon, greatly refreshed in mind and body, she emerged, Meylisah leading the way, carrying her toilet articles, and sauntered back towards her own apartments. She did not walk very fast, a Turkish bath is notoriously relaxing, and Khurrem, although a strong and wiry girl, was, after all, not long out of childbed. Rounding a dark bend in the maze of corridors, she found her way suddenly barred by a veiled and menacing figure which she instantly recognized as Gulbehar.

The fracas that ensued has echoed down the centuries. Precisely what happened has been hotly debated, but three facts seem to be agreed: that Gulbehar was the aggressor, that she advanced on Khurrem screaming that she was butcher's meat that had been left to rot on the slab, or some such pleasantry, and finally that she was the victor. Certainly she was heavier and taller and had the advantage of surprise. The contest, however, was hardly allowed to go to a decision. Meylisah, although well ahead of her mistress, heard the outcry, ran back, plucked ineffectually at Gulbehar's flailing arms and then decided to find help. She ran screaming back the way she had come until she found two black eunuchs, and her screams, as well as the noise of the fight itself brought slaves, officials and finally the Khizlar Agasi himself. The panting Gulbehar was dragged off her victim and carried, kicking, to her rooms, where she was locked in. Khurrem, a forlorn heap, sat on the floor with her hair over her face.

Meylisah flung herself down beside her and clasped her in her arms. 'Oh, are you all right?' she panted, 'It took so *long* to find anyone – they're never there when you need them – '

'I ache,' said Khurrem, and added sharply, 'Let my hair alone!' She was lifted tenderly and carried, her hair still unplaited and covering her face and neck, to her room by the third largest of the black guards. It had taken the two largest to dispose of Gulbehar.

By now, of course, the whole household was in the corridors. Those who elected to seek the neighbourhood of Gulbehar were enthralled to hear her still screaming within; those who had made for Khurrem's quarters were less lucky. Not only was there no screaming, but all the doors were shut. Further, Hafise, looking like a figure of doom, arrived as soon as they did, and crisply commanded the guards who accompanied her to clear the corridors and whip the last to get away.

'I have sent for the Sultan,' she said abruptly as soon as she was admitted to Khurrem's room. She advanced to the bed, saying anxiously, 'How are you, my child? What did she do to you?'

Khurrem rolled over stiffly. She was not crying, but her voice was unsteady as she answered, 'Well, she hit me rather hard, her arms are longer than mine – did you say you had sent for the Sultan?'

Hafise seated herself on the bed, and attempted to brush aside the long red hair, while Hulefa, who had risen from the bedside on the Sultana Valideh's approach, said in parenthesis, 'She doesn't seem to want to show her face, Madam, and I'm sure it's bruised.'

'Outrageous!' breathed Hafise, trying to gather the little figure into her arms. She was resisted, and finally said commandingly, 'Let me look, child, if there are bruises or scratches they must be tended –'

There was silence as all eyes focused on Khurrem who had now somewhat tentatively emerged from behind the screen of hair.

Hafise said blankly, 'Oh, my dear girl!'

Khurrem sniffed, turned a sob into a gulp, and said miserably, 'Not very dignified, is it? I don't think he ought to see me like this, I don't really!' She accepted the handmirror silently proffered by Hulefa and studied her reflection.

Gulbehar in her frenzy had undoubtedly made for her adversary's eyes, and had very nearly found them, as a series of ugly scratches from temple to chin testified. At some time in the fray, and probably more by luck than intent, she had found Khurrem's right eye with her fist, and closed it. A plum-coloured bruise was already spreading to eyebrow and cheek.

260

There was silence while they all contemplated the catastrophe, and finally Hafise said thoughtfully, 'No, certainly not, he shan't see you.'

Then she looked at the girl again sharply, noticing how awkwardly she was lying.

'What else?' she asked quietly.

Khurrem began to cry and winced with pain. 'It hurts me to breathe and it's dreadful here,' she laid a trembling hand on her stomach.

They took off the remains of her clothes at once, but there was nothing to see.

'Tell him,' said Khurrem, sniffing, 'that I am unworthy to receive him. I'm not fit for him to see. I'm not bitter, truly I'm not, but I'm so afraid – '

What she feared was choked by her tears. Presently she found her voice and said:

You'd better leave that last bit out,' and cast herself into Hafise's arms.

When Suleiman, full of anger and tender concern, hurried into Khurrem's outer room, he found the door to the bedroom shut and his mother, hands clasped before her, standing in front of it.

She did not adopt the stance of an avenging fury, nor did she say 'I told you so', but she did not mince matters. Khurrem, she said, had been badly battered and bruised in her own home, going about her own concerns and injuring no one. A girl just out of childbed, she added, looking him firmly in the eye and watching him wince. She went on.

'In your care for the helpless,' she paused on the word, 'perhaps you should spare a thought for the innocent. Khurrem is strong, it is true, but she will not long stand up to such treatment as she has received today.'

'Everything you say is true!' he cried impatiently. 'But do not harry me any more. Only let me see her!'

She delivered Khurrem's message, and he tried to push it aside.

'No,' she told him firmly, 'she does not wish to see you. Can you not understand? She has been cruelly beaten and cruelly humiliated, and she does not want you to see her in that condition. You must wait. After all, it was all on your account.'

Watching his white face, she hesitated for a moment, and

then added a comment. 'You must proceed very carefully, and above all, be very patient and kind. After all, she is now a free-woman, and need never see you again.'

Her face convulsed and cleared as she fought back her tears and repeated, 'Surely, surely you understand? She is afraid for the future, she is afraid she will be useless to you.'

It was clear that he did, for his face darkened with rage or some other emotion, but he spoke calmly.

'I am not an animal. Take me to her at once.'

But in the meantime all the stresses had at last taken their toll and delirium supervened. When Suleiman sat down by the mattress and took her hand and spoke her name, Khurrem did not know him. She did not know anyone. Her mind wandering, she imagined herself home in Russia with her mother, trying to make her understand what had happened to her.

In the world from which she had taken refuge, those who loved her did what they could, nursing her devotedly. A woman learned in herbal remedies was brought from the hospital of the New Palace and dressed the dreadful bruises. An experienced nurse, she cheered them by suggesting broken ribs to account for the painful stomach and tortured breathing and contrived a rudimentary bandage. But she could do nothing about the dis-jointed and seemingly meaningless babble which came from Khurrem's lips.

It terrified her maids and the friends who came to help look after her, but they did not panic, that not being the Ottoman way. They went about their duties quietly and thoroughly. Only as time passed and she grew no more coherent and still looked at them with unseeing eyes, they lost heart in what they did, and Meylisah, who cried easily, had to be sent from the room. Eventually, the next morning, Suleiman, who had hardly stirred from his post at the bedhead, curtly told them to send for the Chief Physician.

Hafise ventured to expostulate. 'He can only hold her hand from behind a curtain, and ask her questions, and since she – ' she waved her hands towards the restless whispering girl. 'What can he do?' she finished helplessly.

Her son shook his head. 'I don't know, Mother, but we must try everything. And I suppose he can listen and try to under-stand. As I do,' he finished.

The Chief Physician had immense authority and his presence

comforted them, but beyond that he could not be of much help. He questioned the nurse and agreed that the pain arose from broken ribs.

'They are nothing, but very painful, of course,' he said. 'As to the delirium and fever, when I had the honour of serving under your illustrious father in the field I sometimes saw soldiers in this state — ' He hesitated and added, 'Of course, what the honourable young lady is saying is all gibberish — '

'Not all of it. But it is in Russian, of which I understand only a little,' said Suleiman shortly. He added urgently, 'Can you say nothing more?'

The man sighed. 'There is nothing more I can *do*. She has the best of care. When the fever passes and with it the delirium, then, if Allah wills, she will sleep normally. That is all I can say.'

Three days passed. The bruises began to fade and the scratches to heal. Khurrem seemed in less pain but still knew no one. She still talked, but not so compulsively. Suleiman sat holding her hand and listening. On the morning of the fourth day he rose and went to his mother who was resting on a mattress in the outer room. When she sat up and looked at him expectantly, he took her hand and said.

'Ever since I returned I have known there was something wrong. Now you must tell me the whole truth and leave out nothing.'

Hafise sighed and pushed back her hair. 'I shall be glad to,' she said simply, and began. When she had finished he condemned her with faint praise.

'You meant well,' he said, 'but it doesn't do to try to be clever. We are not characters in some stupid Arabian tale, but living people. Now that I understand her need, I will gladly marry her.'

'But — ' her hand outstretched towards the door of the inner room mutely indicated Khurrem's condition.

'She'll get better, she must,' he said, 'I need her.'

It happened that when the Chief Physician was proved right, and Khurrem, restored to her senses, and on the way to physical recovery as well, opened her eyes and looked around her, the only person beside her of all those who had tended her so lovingly through the past anxious days, was Meylisah, who, worn out, slept peacefully with her chin sunk on her chest. Khurrem looked at her, knew her, and croaked, 'Meylisah!'

Meylisah's eyes flew open. She took one hurried glance at her mistress and, predictably, burst into tears.

This brought Hulefa hurrying from the next room. Her reaction was equally predictable. Sinking on her knees beside the bed, she felt Khurrem's forehead, and said all in one breath, 'God be praised! Do you want a drink? Be quiet, you silly girl! She's better!'

The news spread like wildfire, and in no time at all Khurrem's friends were all round her bed, exclaiming, rejoicing and pressing unwanted and unneeded advice on Hulefa.

Khurrem shut her eyes. The noise made her head ache, but she was not unhappy. Passively, she lay at the heart of the hubbub and took stock of herself. She knew she was very weak. The sound of her voice had astonished her. She had thought she was shouting at Meylisah and all that had come out had been a whisper. Still, the dreadful pain had gone, almost all of it, and with it the racking worry. Presently she would remember what it had been about. In the meantime, these were her friends about her, and somebody slipped a comforting arm behind her shoulders. She was effortlessly raised, and Hulefa's voice, somewhere above her, said, 'Now sweetheart, try this milk and honey. I don't think,' she added, apparently speaking over her shoulder, 'that all this noise is good for her, I really don't —'

Neither do I, thought Khurrem, drowsily lapping up the milk, it's like being in the middle of a beehive. I love them, but the people I really want aren't here. I don't want to go to sleep again before they come — and where's my baby? She nodded off. It seemed to her only minutes, but was in reality several hours later when she came to herself with the last word echoing in her head.

'Baby!' she said, quite loudly, and tried to sit up. 'Where's my baby?' she repeated urgently.

'Quite safe in the outer room, and my mother is with him,' said another voice, the voice she had been waiting to hear all along. She opened her eyes again. Hulefa was nowhere to be seen, and the throng of chattering women had gone, too. A dark face, reassuringly familiar and dear, bent over her.

That he was there when she had said she wouldn't see him was wonderful, but a lot had happened since she'd said that. She'd been to see her mother — or was that just a dream? She honestly didn't know, and it didn't seem important. In the meantime, she had remembered her overriding anxiety. She tried to sit up and failed, but found she could talk a bit more fluently now.

'My mother didn't understand at all and Hafise said you wouldn't either — ' she began urgently.

He knew at once what she was talking about, and laid his hand warmly over hers.

'For once, Hafise was wrong,' he told her firmly. 'It is really very simple. I love you, therefore there is nothing you can tell me that I shan't understand.'

He surprised himself with this simple statement on the nature of love, but having made it, he could see nothing wrong with it. As for Khurrem, she had known instinctively how it should be all along. Furthermore, there is nothing in their subsequent history which can be quoted to disprove it.

'Besides,' added Suleiman, 'we can't rid ourselves of our earliest beliefs. I understand that now. We will be married as soon as you are well, and because you are happy, I shall be, too.'

Khurrem lay back. She was suddenly tired again, too tired to talk any more. But it really doesn't matter, she thought, before she drifted off on another great wave of sleep, I'm too happy to talk. She did, however, manage to give the hand that held hers the lightest of squeezes. Before she finally surrendered to sleep, a totally unrelated and not unworthy idea drifted through her mind: I shall enjoy being Sultana Hasseki.

The marriage of the Sultan Suleiman to a radiant Khurrem was celebrated at the Old Palace. The wedding itself was, according to custom, a simple ceremony conducted by a doctor of the law. It was followed, also according to custom, by two great feasts. At one, the groom entertained his male friends. At the other, the Sultana Valideh, in default of the bride's mother, was hostess to the friends of the bride. Of the two, this went with the greatest swing and was enjoyed with the greatest gusto. The harem felt collectively that they had earned it.

# Glossary of Turkish Words

| | |
|---|---|
| *Aga* | A general officer |
| *Akinji* | The irregular cavalry |
| *Azab* | The irregular infantry |
| *Bostanji* | A gardener |
| *Caliph* | The Muhammedan chief civil and religious ruler, as successor to Muhammad |
| *Caravanserai* | A kind of oriental inn where caravans put up |
| *Deli* | 'Crazy' or 'madcap'; appellation of a scout |
| *Dervish* | A Muslim friar who has taken vows of poverty and austere life |
| *Devshirme* | A gathering or collecting of tribute boys |
| *Divan* | The Ottoman council of state |
| *Emir* | A commander; a governor |
| *Fatih* | 'The Conqueror'. Title given to Mehmed II for his conquest of Constantinople |
| *Gösde* | 'In the eye', i.e. favourite |
| *Halva* | A sweet based on semolina and almonds |
| *Hanim* | Lady |
| *Harem* | That part of the Muslim house occupied by the women of the household |
| *Haseke* | Favourite |
| *Hoja* | A teacher; the Sultan's adviser |
| *Ikbal* | 'Fortunate'; the first rank for advancement in the harem |

| | |
|---|---|
| *Imam* | A leader of daily prayers |
| *Kadin* | A woman of the Palace who receives the Sultan's special favours |
| *Kapi Agasi* | The white eunuch in charge of the Topkapi Saray |
| *Koziasker* | One of the two chief judges of the Ottoman Empire |
| *Kebab* | Turkish meat dishes of which the essential feature is that the meat is cut into small pieces before cooking; shish kebab consists of cubes of meat, usually lamb, grilled on skewers |
| *Kiaya* | Steward; lieutenant; housekeeper |
| *Kilerji-bashi* | The chief of the Sultan's pantry |
| *Kiosk* | A light, open pavilion or summerhouse |
| *Kizlar Agasi* | Aga, or General of the Girls; the black eunuch in charge of the harem, i.e. the Old Palace |
| *Mameluke* | A member of the military body which seized the Egyptian throne in 1254 and remained the ruling class until 1811 |
| *Mufti* | A Muslim legal authority; Head of the Muslim Institution |
| *Mullah* | One learned in theology and the sacred law of Islam |
| *Sanjak Bey* | A high officer of feudal cavalry, and governor of a district |
| *Sarai Agasi* | The Assistant Director of the Pages School |
| *Selamlik* | The men's quarters in any house; lit. 'the place of greeting', i.e. the one place where visitors can be received, as opposed to the harem, which is sacred to the women |
| *Seraskier* | A commander-in-chief |
| *Shahzade* | 'Son of the Emperor'; title given to the Sultan's sons |
| *Sherbet* | A cooling drink made of fruit juice and sweetened water |
| *Shi-ite* | One belonging to the Shia, a Muslim sect |

|  |  |
|---|---|
|  | which regards Muhammad's cousin, Ali, the fourth caliph, as the Prophet's true successor |
| *Sikander Nameh* | A Turkish chronicle of the exploits of Alexander the Great |
| *Sipahi or Spahi* | A cavalry soldier; a member of either the standing or feudal cavalry |
| *Solak* | A janissary bowman of the Sultan's personal guard |
| *Sufi* | One of a sect of ascetic mystics |
| *Sultana Valideh* | Queen Mother |
| *Sunni* | The orthodox Muslims who accept the traditions as well as the Koran |
| *Ulema* | The whole body of Muslims learned in the sacred law |
| *Yavuz* | Grim; title given to Selim I |

# Select Bibliography

Alderson, A.D., *The Structure of the Ottoman Dynasty* (Oxford, 1956)

Aslanapa, Oktay, *Turkish Art and Architecture* (London, 1971)

Coles, Paul, *The Ottoman Impact on Europe* (London, 1968)

Cook, M.A. (ed.), *A History of the Ottoman Empire to 1730: chapters from 'The Cambridge History of Islam' and 'The New Cambridge Modern History'* [V.J. Parry and others] (Cambridge, 1976)

Cragg, Kenneth, *The Mind of the Qur'an* (London, 1973)

Creasy, E.S., *History of the Ottoman Turks* (London, 1878)

Downey, Fairfax, *The Grande Turke: Suleyman the Magnificent* (London, 1929)

Forster, C.T. and Daniell, F.H.B., *The Life and Letters of Ogier Ghiselin de Busbecq* . . . 2 vols. (London, 1881)

Goodwin, Godfrey, *A History of Ottoman Architecture* (London, 1971)

Great Britain: Admiralty, Naval Intelligence Division, *Turkey* 2 vols. (London, 1942 − 3)

Hasluck, F.W., *Christianity and Islam under the Sultans* 2 vols. (Oxford, 1929)

Inalcik, Halil, *The Ottoman Empire: the classical age, 1300 − 1600* (London, 1973)

Jenkins, Hester Donaldson, *Ibrahim Pasha*. Studies in history, econimics and public law (New York, 1911)

Lamb, Harold, *Suleiman the Magnificent* (London, 1952)

Levey, Michael, *The World of Ottoman Art* (London, 1978)

Lewis, Bernard, *Istanbul and the Civilization of the Ottoman Empire* (Norman, Oklahoma, 1963)

271

Lewis, Raphaela, *Everyday Life in Ottoman Turkey* (London, 1971)

Lybyer, Albert Howe, *The Government of the Ottoman Empire in the Time of Suleiman the Magnificent* (New York, 1966)

McNeill, William H., *Europe's Steppe Frontier, 1500 – 1800* (Chicago, 1964)

Merriman, Roger Bigelow, *Suleiman the Magnificent, 1520 – 1566* (New York, 1966)

Nasr, Seyyed Hossein, *Ideals and Realities of Islam* (London, 1966)

Pallis, Alexander, *In the days of the Janissaries: old Turkish life as depicted in the 'Travel-book' of Evliya Chelebi* (London, 1951)

Payne-Gallwey, *Sir* Ralph, Bt, *A Treatise on the Construction, Power and Management of Turkish and other Oriental Bows of Mediaeval and Later Times* (reprinted Wakefield, 1973)

Penzer, N.M., *The Harem* (London, 1930)

Stratton, Arthur, *Sinan* (London, 1972)

Sumner-Boyd, Hilary *and* John Freely, *Strolling through Istanbul* (Istanbul, 1972)

Wittman, William, *Travels in Turkey, Asia Minor, Syria . . .* (London, 1803)